# THE PROPHET

# SHOLEM ASCH

# THE
# PROPHET

*Translated by Arthur Saul Super*

*G. P. Putnam's Sons   New York*

87740 C.

Library of Congress Catalog Card
Number: 55-10089

MANUFACTURED IN THE UNITED STATES OF AMERICA

VAN REES PRESS • NEW YORK

*To*

MELVILLE MINTON

*in grateful memory*

# PART ONE

# CHAPTER ONE

THE Palace of the Hanging Gardens that Nebuchadnezzar built for himself in Babylon was part of a chain of edifices that stretched from the exit of the Avenue of the Processions to E-Sagila, the sanctuary and citadel of the god Bel Merodach. Nebuchadnezzar had invested his palace with the character of a range of mountains in order to recall to his wife the skyline of Medea, the hilly country of her birth. Massive, looming walls crowded one upon the other in a menacing ring. The shapes of leopards, lions, and other beasts were carved into this structure and covered with mosaic work in glazed enamel. The heavy mass loomed skyward towards the upper heavens. Stone images, wild bulls, lions, monsters with faces of men adorned with characteristic Assyrian beards, stood out in a grim, silent guardianship and threw their shadows upon the fortresslike, broad stone stairway that led up to the palace. Every detail of the structure was intentionally designed to create an aura of awe and terror; to crush the spirit with the impact of the overwhelming might and terrible majesty of Nebuchadnezzar and Babylon.

But in a moment, as the eye follows the brooding façade of the crowding walls, they seem to float into the air and the desolation of deep shadow looming over the broad stairway is gone. One is reminded of a traveler, painfully toiling along, footsore and weary, over burning rocky ways, whose tormented and swollen feet suddenly find themselves solaced by green pastures beside cool brooks, while the rustle of water, purling behind the sedge and the deep shade of branches, enchants his ears with a refreshing murmur. For beyond the walls, the hanging gardens are spread out over the rugged

3

planes of the palace of Nebuchadnezzar. On the broad lawns, dappled with pools of shadow cast by the trees, strut peacocks and ostriches. Doves flutter down and quench their thirst in the crystal ponds half hidden in the seclusion of bushes flowering with a riot of color. As veins thread a body, so was the city of gardens criss-crossed by a system of narrow channels, their beds paved with green tiles. For it was indeed a city that crowned the palace of Nebuchadnezzar and spread away in the distance: a prospect of groves in mass array, a profusion of bushes and rows of flowers from which the gentle lapping of the water could be heard as it sang its way downward to the rivulets below. Everything—the gardens, the pools—appeared to be hanging in the air, suspended on nothingness, as though the hills were quite far away and as though below, only at a distance, could the teeming buildings of the city be discerned spawning in every direction and shut in by the thick wall which embraced all Babylon.

A multitude of three- or four-story houses built of a compost of clay and twigs were huddled together within the shelter of the walls and from their midst rose the towers of the temples soaring arrogantly skyward. In the alleys between the houses the arteries of Babylon's life branched out: the innumerable canals and their tributaries which fed the city with water from the Euphrates. From the gardens, the city seemed very far away as though stretched out in a valley in a distant plain.

Babylon had no raw building materials of her own; so in order to construct the mighty edifices which adorned his capital, Nebuchadnezzar was compelled to import wood, stone, and other necessities from far-off lands. His own land possessed only the pitch which exuded from the sticky clayey sun-baked ground and palms and reeds from the thickets which spread out over her swamps. Wood was very scarce and thus was highly valued in Babylon. Everything that was used in the construction of these enormous buildings was brought from a distance. Every stone block that was laid in the walls was dragged there by slaves harnessed to it like beasts of burden. They hauled it across wildernesses right from the rocky hills from which it had been quarried in remote lands which had fallen to Nebuchadnezzar the conqueror. Every cedar beam in the great ceilings of Babylon's halls was borne from the forests of Lebanon to the capital on the shoulders of prisoners of war who came by way of the wilderness of Damascus to the Euphrates, where it was launched on the swift current which floated it to Babylon to the palace of Nebuchadnezzar which the river embraced in its broad arms.

The gigantic images of the gods, the wild bulls, and the lion monsters, enormous blocks of stone, pillars of marble, masses of porphyry, bars of gold and silver, all the treasured loveliness which Assyria had taken as spoil in her cruel wars with the peoples of the world, were brought to the adornment and beautification of Babylon. The great and mighty ones of Nineveh, who had delighted in the dignity of their long plaited beards, now dragged them in the dust of the deserts as they bent down double under the burden of this treasure and hauled it from the harbors of the Tigris across the sands to the Euphrates and thence to the capital. Nobles of Tyre and Sidon were harnessed by their colored girdles of dignity to the cedar trunks which had been uprooted from the forest of Lebanon and they too swept the desert sands with their beards as they stooped and moiled along under the weight of the timber that would vault the roofs of Nebuchadnezzar's palaces with splendor. Caravan upon caravan of Cypriots, manacled together in endless chain-gangs, hefted upon their shoulders sacks of copper ore with which to cast the sockets and bars for the gates of the buildings that Nebuchadnezzar built. Just as the Jews were forced to carry up to Babylon the holy vessels from the Temple which Nebuchadnezzar had destroyed, so were the chiefs of the other vanquished peoples made to take up to the conqueror's capital the gold and silver treasure of their sanctuaries and the flint idols of their gods as a servile tribute to the victorious ruler and as a sign of the humiliation of their deities who had fallen low in esteem before the gods of Babylon.

The empire of Nebuchadnezzar stretched from the Caspian Sea

5

beyond the mountains of Ararat to the isles of Greece. Everything which lived beneath the shadow of the sword of the ruler of Babylon was his undisputed possession: men, women and children and all that they owned. By his grace they lived, beneath his scepter were they admonished, and by the rod of his anger were they condemned to death. They were permitted to live for him alone; for him they had to labor and for him they were destined to die. Like a vast spider which takes hundreds of creatures in his web and sucks out their marrow until their bodies are desiccated and disintegrate in his net, so did the palace of Nebuchadnezzar swallow up myriads of slaves from all peoples and lands. All the pleasant streams, the swimming pools, the plants in the gardens overhanging the high walls of the palace, were nourished by the waters of the Euphrates which lapped against the foundations of the citadel. Below in the bowels of the palace were the slaves' quarters, the workshops, the pillories, and the prison cells, all enclosed within huge cages connected by narrow stairways and ladders reaching the length and height throughout the palaces.

From the lowest dungeons in the bowels of the earth to the highest point of the airy gardens far above, thousands of slaves whose eyes had been gouged out were harnessed to gigantic wheels which worked pumps which had been designed and installed by Assyrian engineers and which, day and night, drew water from the river to the canals, to storage reservoirs and cisterns raising it from story to story until it reached the pipes and channels in the hanging gardens. The drawers of water, whose eyes also had been blinded so that they should not know where they were, trod silently around day by day and night by night in a ceaseless procession of living death and life of Stygian darkness moving the mighty wheels until their limbs disintegrated as the fly in the web of the spider, until their bones fell apart and they were crushed to dust by the rotating wheels. No sooner did they fall than others were put in their places and the vast cogs began anew to churn another set of living bodies into the eternal blackness of dead dust.

In the main, this work claimed old slaves whose bodies had already been exhausted by rigorous toil. The labor beside the water pumps was the last stage on the pathway of life-long drudgery which every slave had to tread. The young and vigorous were employed in digging the canals that Nebuchadnezzar wove over the whole face of Babylon and her suburbs. When the slave's strength was exhausted by this toil, or by packing mud or dragging pitch and bricks to the building sites, he was transferred to the slave quarters at the palace. Only the unskilled who could not be used for any artifice or trade of any kind were drafted to the water pumps. For in the bowels of Nebuchadnezzar's palace there were also workshops in which delicate and artistic work was executed. Here every slave who possessed a skill was employed. The womb of the palace held prisoner a multitude of olive treaders, spice apothecaries, and perfumers. They supplied the wigmakers and Assyrian barbers with the oils they required for plaiting and anointing beards and attending to the hair of the Babylonian nobles who were privileged to stand in the presence of the king. There were makers of rough cloth, spinners and art weavers who were devoted to the production of the fine, many-colored woolens which had spread the fame of the Babylonian garments throughout all the royal courts. There were smiths and ironworkers who devised all kinds of beaten vessels, molten cups and dishes, metal bowls in gold and silver and copper. There were carvers in ivory and fashioners of colored stones, goldsmiths, and silversmiths; cordmakers, jewelers who devised ornaments for the concubines who dwelt in the great seraglio of Nebuchadnezzar. There were stone cutters from Assyria and masons from Greece who carved the tablets showing the victories of Nebuchadnezzar and his mighty deeds when he went forth to hunt. There were embroiderers of quick invention and artists who devised the clay pictures and the wondrous colored enamel tablets, the mosaics of the fearsome moving monsters and the friezes depicting scenes of the hunt. There were tanners and leatherworkers to make harness, saddlework, and

7

belts; sandalmakers, coppersmiths, and beaters of swords; an infinite and bewildering variety.

In addition, there was the vast concourse of cooks, bakers, butlers, waiters, and other domestics who worked in the upper regions in the vicinity of the dwelling rooms and pleasure halls of the palace. There were grooms and animal tamers who groomed the horses harnessed to the chariots of war and of the chase; who cared for the wild beasts which brooded in the spacious stables which were situated near the camps of the king's special personal guard.

The palace proper began in the region of the extensive hanging gardens. Balconies and three- or four-sided windowless, blind arched compartments were interwoven with one another, here ascending a story and there descending one to give the appearance of a range of hills. Here and there a giant lion carved in the rock, his jaws gaping open and his claws extended, suddenly and frighteningly interrupted the flow of line or abutted on a corner of a building. On the flanks of the wide beaten stairways were set monstrous carvings of the gods, the guardians that led the way upwards to the massive doors which were thrown wide open. These porticos were fashioned of cedarwood, covered with copper plates of scenes of the chase. Beyond the door, the plastered walls could be seen crowned by a roof borne aloft on cedar beams and pillars illuminated by oil lamps set on pediments of porphyry. The walls were far from bare. They were decorated by a wealth of tablets, exquisitely carved bas reliefs of stone extolling the victories of Nebuchadnezzar in the chase and on the battlefield. On one tablet his armies were seen in detailed battle array. The men, clothed in armor, were bending their bows against a besieged city. The warriors were battering at the walls of the invested fortress with bars of iron, climbing up on ladders, breaking the necks of the foe who crowded out from within the defenses in a sally against the battering rams which thrust against the gates.

These halls, whose walls told the praises of the great Nebuchadnezzar, were now thronged with an assembly of Babylonian nobles

8

and foreign princes, the rulers of subjugated provinces who, with their families, had become the vassals and hostages of the king.

The great feast, arranged by Belshazzar, the prince regent, was in its third day. Acting on behalf of his father Nabonidus, the present king, he had summoned it in honor of Gimil, the chief of the harlot votaries or women who devoted the passion of their bodies to the worship of the goddess Ishtar. None of the participants in the revel was permitted to leave the hall of his own free will. The great ones of Babylon and the chiefs of the conquered provinces were assembled there according to their rank and station in the empire. In the antechambers leading to the throne hall were the second rank of the court: the superintendents, the inspectors, the deputies appointed over the provinces, the adjutants to the army commanders, in fact all whose station was inferior to the nobility who could claim that royal blood coursed in their veins. Majestic lords of kingdoms conquered by Babylon were there. They had been pardoned by Nebuchadnezzar in his time, and succeeding rulers had upheld the amnesty, but they nevertheless remained vassals of the great king and were kept as hostages in his palace. Concubines from the harem who enjoyed a spell of royal favor were among the company, which included the upper level of the priesthood of Bel Merodach, castrate priests of the Temple of Ishtar, army generals upon whom the king's face shone; in fact everyone privileged to wear a seal ring inscribed with the formula "Friend of the Great King." These all enjoyed the feast in the throne room itself.

Belshazzar was half sitting, half reclining on the royal couch beneath a golden canopy. To the right and left of the couch stood two naked slaves, black as ebony. One held a chained lion and the other a leopard. Behind the couch two of the highest nobles of the land stood waving large fans over the royal head. They were the envied holders of this great dignity. At his foot Belshazzar's wife reclined, a golden goblet in her hand, ready and alert to quench the royal thirst. The cup-bearer, a fresh-faced beardless lad whose flowing locks tumbled down in graceful curls over his shoulders, stood naked to the waist. From time to time he poured out a generous measure of wine from a golden pitcher. He, too, was of royal blood and a vassal of the king of Babylon.

Two rows of Assyrian officers were ranged on guard along both sides of the canopy, upright and motionless as stone sculptures, rigid of muscle and unblinking of eyelash. Rooted there, their swords on their thighs, their hands holding short lances with copper bowl-like hilts in their hands, their hair and beards waved and plaited in the Assyrian fashion, they gave an illusion of being graven in stone, an integral part of one of the great tablets which adorned the wall beyond the royal canopy.

The revelers were weary unto death from the drinking, which was rigidly in conformity with the etiquette. It had gone on for three days without pause. Every nerve in their bodies was enlisted in the struggle against the overwhelming fatigue which bore them down. They beat with their fingers on their palms in time with the sweet throbbing melody strummed by the king's musicians. They strained every sense to keep awake; every vestige of their strength was devoted to their attempt to cast off the web of sleep being woven so heavily upon their eyes. Only their terror lest the grace of the king depart from them banished slumber from their eyelids and compelled them to rival each other in artificial demonstrations of enthusiasm at the spectacles, both sacred and profane, which were presented to them. They were forced to listen to recitations, to hymns extolling the mighty deeds of the heroic gods, to the warlike exploits of Bel Merodach against his monster mother Tiamat; the adventure of Gilgamesh who built him a ship in the age when the great flood covered the earth. The presentations followed each other without pause, robbing the days of rest and the nights of sleep.

Suddenly the heralds sounded a fanfare and made proclamation that by order of the king there would appear before the company Gimil-Ishtar, the chief harlot votary of the Temple of Ishtar, to enact the role of the goddess going down to Sheol, Hades, the abode of eternal darkness, there to give battle with the god of Sheol to make him render up unto her from among the dead Tammuz, her brother and her lord, so that with his resurrection from the bourne from which none returns spring would come again bringing new life to the earth.

The flourish of the fanfare aroused the guests from their stupor and banished their lethargy. Quivers of apprehension passed from couch to couch. The priests of Bel Merodach were disturbed and depressed while the castrate priests of Ishtar were smitten with astonishment. The king was profaning the worship of Ishtar by ordaining a performance of her ritual in his palace and not in her temple. A deep silence reigned as deathly terror turned the gathering to stone. Naked slaves darted suddenly in front of the royal throne flashing long knives. They were escorted by spear-bearing, armor-clad soldiers. The two ebony slaves, who held the lion and leopard chained, stepped back a pace but remained alerted by the throne, ready to execute Belshazzar's slightest command. The priests began the high ritual of the worship of the goddess Ishtar.

A vast curtain rolled aside revealing a flight of lofty steps descending into a sepulchral cave. The guests could discern the shape of Ishtar gliding sinuously down into the depths. A black veil covered her from head to foot and a transparent gauze flowed from her brow. Young girls and women of various ages, their hair loose, their bodies covered in dark gossamer veils, surrounded the goddess and gave vent to bitter lamentations. They beat their naked breasts with their clenched hands, then stretched their arms high above their heads, seeming to project themselves into the air as they looked upon the central figure descending from above. The wailing women went down, step by step, lamenting and weeping as they trod solemnly from stair to stair in time with the wailing threnody that proceeded from their lips. Lute-playing slaves accompanied the women to the stairs, plucking on their strings while the girls and women sobbed, and when the cry of the wailing women died into silence, the voice of Ishtar was heard, the voice of Gimil:

11

"Wailing shall I wail over the heroes who forsook their wives;
Wailing shall I wail over the maidens who lost their lovers;
Mourning shall I bitterly mourn for the only son
Whose day had not yet shone
When he was snatched away and was no more."

Thus did Gimil and the women raise up lamentation after lamentation, regretting the love that man has lost, weeping over life, over nature, until Ishtar came at length to a locked door which shut off the cave.

She spread her sensuous body in complete abandon and surrender over the portal, beating upon it with her outflung arms.

"O gateman, open thy gates unto me, open unto me thy gates,
Or I shall burst them asunder.
I shall arm the dead;
They shall devour the living;
For more mighty are the dead than the living."

The guardian of the gate of silence appeared in the guise of a destroying angel, a cone-shaped helmet of copper on his head. He cried to Ishtar:

"Gently, gently; break not down the gate. Behold, I go to herald thy coming to the queen of the dark regions."

He departed and in a moment returned to the waiting Ishtar.

"What ails thee that thou comest to the gates of silence?"

He was answered by the chorus of wailing women standing above Ishtar on the stair:

"Alas, alas for the men compelled to forsake their wives!
Alas, alas for the women torn from the arms of their husbands!
Alas, alas for the infant untimely reft away!"

A voice was heard from the depths of the cave.

"Open unto her the gate!" It was the voice of the queen of

Sheol. "Open unto her the gate and do unto her as the ancient laws of Sheol dictate."

The gateman threw the portal wide open before Ishtar.

"Come, O powerful queen! Blessed be thy coming into the abode of the shades."

And thus saying he drew near unto her and drew off the veil that flowed down from her brow.

"Why, O guardian, dost thou take off the veil from my head?"

"It is the law of the kingdom of Sheol beneath. The law of Sheol is thy law if it is thy desire to enter the gates of the shadow of death."

The gateman passed her beyond the door and a new portal sprang up before her. Again the guardian drew near. He removed the heavy black veil in which her body was swathed.

"Why, O guardian, dost thou remove the concealment from my flesh?"

"It is the law of the kingdom realm of Sheol below. The law of Sheol is thy law."

So she passed through door after door, and before each portal yielded her passage, she was stripped of one of her veils till at last, except for a narrow girdle round her loins, she stood naked before the final door.

There she was compelled to remove the last barrier to nakedness. She stood revealed, with the profuse coils of her red hair alone covering her flesh, as the guardian took her through the last gate which opened before her. Ishtar vanished. An astonished silence fell upon the assembly at the disappearance of the goddess. The girls and women who remained behind at the top of the stairway burst into bitter lamentations. Again the threnody throbbed forth, again their voices broke slowly, susurrating, whispering, into a hymn:

"Ishtar hath vanished, hath vanished;
    The bull no longer rears itself upon his mate,
    The ass no longer covers his female,

13

A man no longer lies upon his wife.
Alone upon his bed slumbers the man;
Solitary, solitary is the woman upon her couch."

And suddenly, through the wailing and lamenting, the voice of
Ishtar rang out from the depths of the cave; it was a joyful voice,
rising and exulting in a cry of victory:

"I have steeped mine eyes in kohl;
The scent of cedars goes up from my shoulders;
The brightness of the moon of Sin my father
Hath clothed my body in the purity of alabaster.
A chaplet have I woven on my brow,
The savor of my flesh is the sweet savor of cedar;
Rejoice in it and gladden thyself
Tammuz my child!
Tammuz my brother!
Tammuz my beloved!
Who wakes when every plant wakes,
From the womb of night, from the womb of death,
And comest back unto me from beyond,
From beyond the river!"

The wailing women writhed out of their black veils of mourning
and stood upon the stairway.

The castrate priests, compelled against their will and in spite of
their wrath to take part in the ceremony, divided into two rows
and made a way for Ishtar-Gimil as she emerged from the cave.
A coronet of gold flashing with brilliants crowned her head and
her flesh scintillated through her flowing tresses which shone like
fine gold as they glittered over her body. Her breasts were encased
in golden bowls; her narrow girdle, embroidered with gold thread
and studded with precious stones, covered her nakedness. Her
eyes were etched out in greenish paint and heavy ornaments hung
from the lobes of her ears. Wide bracelets glittered on her arms

14

and the anklets on her feet made a tinkling as she slowly ascended.

The castrate priests of the temple of Ishtar fell into formation behind her, forming a processional group which enthroned her on a chair of pure gold. Naked from their navels up, their genitals barely covered by triangular white aprons, their eyes etched out in green, the priests began to offer incense on a brazier set beside the throne. They prostrated themselves before her, raised their hands in prayer and moved their lips in a psalm:

"Arise, Ishtar, raise thyself!
Thou reignest above all the gods,
For there is no brightness like thy brightness.
A star art thou called, O Ishtar!
Thy brightness shone in the stronghold of Sin and Shamash.
Thy beam illumines the heart of heaven.
Ishtar, thou art called the goddess of heaven!
Let the people reverence and hallow thee,
Let them bathe in thy god-given light
So that thy splendor be bestowed upon them."

The priests ended their supplication and the great ones and mighty princes of Babylon arose and passed in a throng before the royal dais of Gimil-Ishtar.

First to descend from his throne in majestic dignity was Belshazzar, the royal robe upon his shoulders and the graven crown upon his head. He bowed down before her, took a pinch of spices in his fingers and threw it upon the censer of incense. Then the great dignitaries of Babylon followed, the fan bearers, the legates of the provinces, the commanders of the hosts, the princes in whose veins flowed the blood royal, the alien kings who brought up tribute to Babylon; all who had the right to comb their beards into three corners. Every one of them drew near in reverent obeisance, bowing the knee before Ishtar who sat naked on the throne of her divinity; before Ishtar whose flesh was revealed in shining rose-whiteness under the profusion of her red hair as though her body was in truth compounded of the rays of the moon and the sun. Indeed, her broad supple loins did seem to have been hewn out of alabaster, like the body of an idol, while the rose splendor of her skin, freely displayed by the loosely strewn scarlet tresses, emanated an enchantment and kindled a burning fever in the very veins and being of every male.

# CHAPTER TWO

G IMIL, the name of this woman, was on everyone's lips in the city. Her fame was helped not a little by her scarlet hair; for a red-headed woman was a rare sight in that metropolis. Men stared lasciviously after her and the great dignitaries desired her, longing to gather her as a concubine into their seraglios.

Gimil was the daughter of a commander-in-chief, a leading aristocrat in the imperial court of Nebuchadnezzar. But when the dynasty which succeeded had swept away all members of that royal house, her father fell from favor and was removed from office. His daughter, Gimil, could then no longer hope to rise to an honored place as the lawful wife of one of the new lords of the kingdom or of any other member of a new aristocracy that arose. Her pride in her high ancestry being too great to permit her to be one concubine among many in the house of one of the great, she fell into evil ways.

While still a girl, Gimil soon learned how magically her body was endowed and that it could become a satisfying substitute for the loss of her ancestry which was now despised. She was aware that her physical attractions held the key to mastery over men, and even in her extreme youth she longed to exploit the blessings abundant in her flesh and use them to glut her desires. An aura of panting lust, exuded from her ripe body like a heavy scent, was more intoxicating to men than even her lascivious ways. The savor of the rare balms she used and the subtle ointments she rubbed into her flesh spread her notoriety among the nobles of Babylon. They vied with each other to win her favors and the

17

price she exacted was a high one. In a short time she was so renowned throughout the whole of Babylon as one of the most sought-after courtesans that even the servants of Bel Merodach fixed their eyes upon her and the High Priest determined to garner her into his sanctuary in order that she might become a harlot votary.

The glance of Belshazzar, the prince regent, also flashed upon her. He was prepared to take her into his House of Women; but Gimil nourished a deep aversion to the new Babylonian dynasty which had forcibly supplanted the legal heirs of Nebuchadnezzar. She devised all sorts of schemes to escape the royal harem. In the meantime, the priests of the all-powerful sect of the Temple of Bel Merodach had spread their net to capture her for their Temple. This left her no alternative but to surrender to the prince. To prevent her falling into the hands of the priests of Bel Merodach, Belshazzar consigned her to the keeping of the castrate priests of Ishtar. To this sect, which was famous for the part the Temple votaries played in the worship, Gimil was a most precious asset. She was the lodestone which drew men who reverenced the goddess Ishtar and became a principal source of revenue to the sanctuary.

One of the hallowed fundamentals of the worship of Ishtar obliged every woman who believed in her and worshipped in her Temple, to give herself at least once in her life to a strange man. This obligation was universal without respect to age or rank. Every female worshipper had to sit in the sanctuary with veiled face and expose her nakedness to the lustful eyes of strange males. If a man halted in front of a woman and desired to have intercourse with her, he would, as a sign of his desire, place a piece of silver or some other article of value in her bosom. The woman was then compelled to surrender to his lust. This gift was taken by the priests as an offering to the goddess Ishtar.

Besides this compulsory whoredom, which was carried on by the priests of Ishtar, there were attached to the Temple permanent harlot votaries or kedeshot. During the spring festival, when Ishtar descended into Sheol to beg the shades to release Tammuz

18

from the bonds of deathly slumber and send him back to earth to renew its fruitfulness and fertility, the kedeshot participated in the wildest orgies in the Temple in honor of the returning newborn Tammuz.

While she served as chief votary, one of Gimil's functions was to inflame the enthusiasm of the women for the immoral worship when they came to bewail Tammuz. She had to arouse their excitement at the thought of the god who had come back to life and vigor. Gimil excelled in her personification of Ishtar and knew how to impart her flaming excitement to women as well as to men, as though she had indeed been possessed of the prurient, erotic spirit of the goddess. She completely captivated the senses. Her lush body writhed and struggled in every limb, her eyes stared wildly and raptly into distant space; suddenly she broke out into a hymn. Her burning song of the emotions of the goddess Ishtar, when, passionate with desire, she joins her body to that of her husband Tammuz raised again into life from beyond the grave, stirred the worshippers to their depths. They hastened pell-mell to the Temple to behold this wondrous miracle with their own eyes; a kedeshah impersonating Ishtar so that she seemed indeed flesh of their flesh and spirit of their spirit. The priests crowned her with extravagant praise and the rumor spread in Babylon that Ishtar had in truth selected the very body of Gimil for her own corporeal dwelling place. The priests encouraged the superstition, assiduously adding to it the announcement that Ishtar spoke through the human lips of Gimil, foretelling the future and resolving hidden mysteries. Through her, women could ask Ishtar the questions dear to their hearts: whether they would be fertile and bear a male child; what would be the fate of their domestic beasts; the yield of their fields; remedies for their ills. The answers emanated from the lips of Gimil-Ishtar in a moving musical monotone. The replies were formulated in an equivocal oracular manner capable of contradictory interpretations. It seemed that Ishtar had indeed entered Gimil's body, cleaving unto it as a familiar spirit. In this way the worship of Ishtar gained myriads of additional worshippers and new devotees among the Babylonians, drawing away the believers from the shrines of other gods; not excluding the sanctuary of Bel Merodach the mighty.

The jealousy of the priests of Bel Merodach against the eunuch servants of Ishtar burned like a flame. They never ceased to weave devious webs of plots to ensnare Gimil away from the Temple of Ishtar into their own sanctuary. So successful a kedeshah, upon whom the spirit of godhead so clearly rested, was obviously destined only for the service of Bel Merodach the mighty, and if she did not come to them of her free will they would not refrain from taking her by force. But though the law allowed them to devote to Bel Merodach any woman they pleased, the priests had been prevented from using extreme measures. It was the prince regent who determined that Gimil would remain in the sanctuary of the goddess Ishtar, for there he could have access to her. The privilege would be withdrawn from him had she been in the service of Bel Merodach in the Temple at E-Sagila. He was the all-powerful protector of the kedeshah, and his authority sufficed to inhibit the priests of Bel Merodach from attaining their end by force.

The chief dignitaries of Babylon, and her nobility, who had been invited to the feast in the palace, bowed the knee in reverence to the goddess Ishtar despite the fact that the ritual had taken place in the royal halls and in secular surroundings. While doing so there were some who did murmur a protest against the profanation of a religious rite, but most bowed with a right good will, even with enthusiasm, for their senses had been helplessly ensnared in the net of the kedeshah's seductions.

But there were still two groups among the feasters who refrained from bending the knee before the goddess Ishtar, refusing to prostrate themselves before the throne of her divinity and to offer incense to her nostrils. One section was quite numerous, consisting of the officiants of Bel Merodach headed by the High Priest, Sharezer Bel. They sat in an isolated company. Their long and

20

plaited beards, their conical helmets and their colored aprons, indeed their whole aspect exhaled an atmosphere of chilly and contemptuous disdain. They openly expressed their bitterness and wrath at this profanation of the worship of Ishtar which had been hallowed for so many generations.

The crafty Belshazzar knew quite well that it was not on account of the profanation of the ritual that the faces of the priests of Bel Merodach were so hostile, that their nostrils flamed and they refrained from participation in the worship. He was convinced that envy was eating them up over the widespread fame that the scarlet woman, Gimil, the kedeshah, was bringing the rival Temple of the priests of Ishtar. Nor was he unaware of the open demonstration of discontent that had been manifested by the mighty Sharezer Bel, High Priest of Bel Merodach, in the sight of all the guests. There he sat, bald of skull, fierce glances of fury burning out of his eyes which gaped from staring wide sockets, nude as they were of the slightest trace of lashes or eyebrows. He only of the whole priesthood was allowed to approach the presence of the idol of Bel Merodach. Therefore, not a single hair was permitted on his body lest by some fatal mischance a flea should crawl from him to the image of the god. The High Priest was consumed with rage that he had not managed to ensnare the beautiful Gimil and hold her close within the halls of the golden sanctuary of the god Bel Merodach at E-Sagila. He alone, the High Priest Sharezer Bel, would then have been allowed to enter the holy of holies where the god dwelt and receive from the lips of Gimil what the god spake unto her. He only would then have been with her, for he alone, as chief of the servants of the golden idol, was permitted to minister to Bel Merodach. Belshazzar was filled with satisfaction that he had managed to get his hands upon the ravishing Gimil before the priests of Bel Merodach had ensnared her. This was yet one more triumph over his rivals and enemies among the priesthood and the families of royal blood. Such hatred had long existed from the time that his father, Nabonidus, had begun to give honor to other gods, bringing them to Babylon in order to weaken the influence of Bel Merodach's priests over the Babylonian people.

The anger of the prince regent burned against yet another group which had shown their contempt at the holy ritual and whose faces indicated a perverse refusal to participate. But if he had to withhold himself from censuring the all-powerful priests of Bel Merodach he had no reason to restrain himself from giving his feelings full vent against this body and he determined to mete out condign punishment to them on the spot.

In a place of honor, in one of the corners of the throne chamber, the highest nobility of the exiles of Judea reclined upon couches. They were headed by members of the royal house of David. Since Evil Merodach, the son of Nebuchadnezzar, had freed Coniah, the king of Judea, from his cell and restored him to his royal rank, placing him higher in degree than the other vassal princes who sat in the royal court, his family were granted permission, and were even obliged, to attend every ceremonial palace function. They were quartered in the royal precincts, having been allocated one of the squares near the Avenue of the Processions adjacent to the Gate of Ishtar. Some of their needs were supplied by the royal purse. In Coniah's day, their section was known as the hall of the King of Judah. Later the Babylonians referred to it as the palace of the Judean Princes, while the exiled Jews called it the palace of the House of David. No one who had sat on the throne of his kingdom was now left alive and for this reason the rank of prince was conferred on his immediate descendants and all in Babylon who could claim relation to the House of David.

Far back in the days of Nebuchadnezzar, the Jews, in contrast to the other peoples carried captive to Babylon, had fought a bitter struggle for the right to adhere to the religion they had brought with them from their native land and not to worship the local gods. Many exiles endured martyrdom for their ancestral faith. Some were burned alive in furnaces, others were thrown into lions' dens, while slow death came to many by all manner of tortures. But the fury and determination of the oppressor failed to break the

22

spirit of those who survived. They remained steadfast until finally, in the days of Nebuchadnezzar himself, they secured certain rights. They could inhabit separate villages in the provinces, could gather together in special quarters in the cities, observe their festivals and holy days at their appointed times and in their due fashion and build synagogues. These were the first such to be instituted among Jews in exile. With them came an elaboration of the order of exilic prayer. In the latter, the exiles poured out their passionate attachment to the God of Jacob, their longing for Jerusalem and their hopes for a speedy redemption. Strangely enough, it was just here in exile that the chiefs of the people, hitherto careless of their faith, attached themselves with a burning zeal to the God of Zion, observed His law with a devotion only paralleled by their obliviousness and neglect in the land of their fathers.

That is why their hearts were so racked with grief and terror when Belshazzar, who acted as though he were indeed already king in Babylon, turned a gay festival to which they had been summoned into an act of pagan worship and glorification of the goddess Ishtar. Since the days of Evil Merodach, they had been exempt from participation in such worship and were not even obliged to be present at it. Therefore, the heads of the exile did not refrain from showing their distress in their faces, a fact not hidden from the eyes of the king and his dignitaries.

"I perceive that all gathered here, rulers of provinces and representatives of the many peoples in our great empire, give honor and glory to the mother of the gods, the queen of heaven, Ishtar the most holy," cried Belshazzar. "Only the princes of Judah refrain from doing as the law requires and others among the Jews here present follow their example."

The heads of the exiles and those who sat behind them paled with fear. Frozen in their places as though turned to stone, they sat there dry of throat, with compressed lips and hearts trembling in terror, not knowing what to reply.

Zerubabel, grandson of King Coniah, fixed his eyes on his

23

father Shaltiel, the elder of the House of David, his young face showing clearly the fire which flamed in his heart. Would the elder of the royal line lift up voice and, in the name of his ancestors David and Solomon, pronounce to Belshazzar the Word which would go burning down the corridor of generations yet to come? No! The elder of the House of David was silent. But the young Zerubabel stood up to speak in the name of his house and of the elders of Judah who sat, cowed of head and perverse of lip, like stone images listening obsequiously to the words of Belshazzar.

"O great king, live for ever! If it be pleasing in the sight of the king, let the youngest of the House of David speak a word in the name of my father and the elders of Judah. The great king, Evil Merodach, in his glory and his power, was pleased to remit to those who came to Babylon with the exile from Judah the duty to worship the local gods. He strengthened our hands so that we might worship our own great God."

"Two sins have you sinned, O princeling of Judah," Belshazzar answered him at once with suppressed anger. "You have dared to refer to Evil Merodach as the Great King and that in the presence of the heir of Nabonidus and his mighty ancestors. Moreover, you have presumed to call the God of Judah the Great God in the presence of the great goddess, mother of the gods, the queen of heaven, Ishtar, and in the presence of the priests of the great god of Babylon, Bel Merodach. Be seated in your place, O prince of Judah, and my will and my decree will be made known unto you.

"If the elders of Judea, her princes, and her nobles who are in Babylon and the provinces which appertain unto her refuse to pay tribute and homage to the goddess Ishtar, then their very God himself will do so and will do homage to the great goddess. Ho! Treasurer Mithradates!"

The Lord of the Treasury Mithradates rose up from among those nearest to the king, resplendent in his chain of office which gleamed behind his flowing curled beard. He prostrated himself and inquired:

"Let the will of the great king but be revealed for it is already performed."

"Go, take out from the treasury the vessels of gold and silver that my great ancestors brought when they first conquered the sanctuary in Jerusalem. Let them be brought here to the throne room so that the princes of Judah and her priests can offer incense upon them to the great goddess and so that they may drink to her honor from the vessels of their God."

A sound of thin, stifled wailing emanated from the corner where the chiefs of the exile were seated.

The soldiers entered in procession, the Lord of the Treasury at their head. Each man was laden with a vessel of gold or silver, censers, pitchers, and goblets. Like acolytes taking part in a holy ritual, they trod solemnly and reverently to the long table covered with precious fringes. Upon it they arranged the vessels before the enthroned queen of the harlot votaries, Gimil.

The glowing gold and silver, fashioned into strange exotic shapes, held every eye. None among the guests had hitherto been privileged to behold such vessels in any royal court or in any temple. Their curiosity proved too much for them and many presumed to rise from their couches and draw near the table upon which lay the vessels, filched from the mysterious temple of Jerusalem. They peered close to examine the vessels of the strange and famous God of Judah, whose image no man had ever seen but whose name had gone out among the nations.

The exiles lifted up the corners of their robes and covered their faces so as not to profane the sanctity of the vessels with their gaze, and once more the wailing stifled sobbing was heard from their corner of the chamber.

Belshazzar drew himself up proudly and magnificently, his conical crown lifted up like a tower on his head. He trod majestically towards the table. He stood beside it, contemplating his choice of the many goblets. At length he indicated one to the chief cup-bearer and stretched out his hand. The latter filled the cup to the

25

brim and handed it to the king who raised it towards Gimil, the harlot votary, and cried aloud:

"Unto thee do I lift up the goblet of the God of Judah so that thy glory may be exalted, O queen of heaven, mother of all the gods!"

Scarcely had he raised the wine to his lips when his ears caught a sudden whisper behind him—a rustle of excited stirrings and heavily suppressed murmuring. Terror and consternation grew in the hall, at first like the susurration of a faint breeze, then mounting suddenly to a raging whirlwind. Belshazzar turned towards the assembly and beheld a host of eyes staring and starting from their sockets and mouths gaping wide in terror. The focus of their amazement was a point on the wall just beneath a tablet depicting Nebuchadnezzar sitting in glory upon his throne while his executioners severed the heads of Jewish captives and laid them at his feet. There on the wall, beneath that very tablet, the fingers of a human hand were writing wondrous mystic symbols in an unknown script. Then the hand slowly vanished but the writing remained upon the wall.

Beneath his conical crown, the features of Belshazzar turned pale, his knees dissolved and knocked together, he shook and trembled and was near collapse. All the guests likewise, all the nobles and mighty ones of Babylon, were seized by a fearful horror. Their eyes, almost torn from their sockets, gazed gauntly into space. The goblet slipped from Belshazzar's hand and fell to the floor. He no longer saw the kedeshah, Gimil Ishtar. She had faded completely from his mind. The other revelers also forgot her very existence. Their horrified eyes clung to the esoteric inscription which stood out from the wall as clearly as though it had been graven there in relief with an adamantine stylus. Silently, insistently, the words seemed to demand an interpretation. What did they mean; what did they signify; what was hidden in these symbols?

"The magicians, the astrologers, the soothsayers; where are they?" Belshazzar gasped out at length.

26

They were at their stations as always; ready and prepared for the orders of the king. No festival or feast was ever held in the court, no order of worship or games or entertainment took place without the astrologers being consulted first to ascertain what fate the stars and planets held in store for the king of kings.

They stood in their multicolored robes and their characteristic conical high hats, some of which were furbished with horns, and looked at the writing. They took counsel of each other; they argued and disputed, weighing and examining the script, utterly unable to extract any meaning from the words. Among them stood the king Belshazzar and his myrmidons, breathless and tense, impatiently awaiting an interpretation. Finally the astrologers backed away from the wall, fell prostrate with their faces to the ground and cried:

"O great king, live forever! The interpretation of the words is hidden from us, O thou great king!"

"Bring the magicians; the magicians!" cried the king in a stifled voice.

The magicians, clad in cloaks studded with stars, came forward. With them they brought a platter of porphyry on which lay the liver of a newly slaughtered beast. They examined the writing, comparing it with the configuration of the veins and blood vessels in the liver. They too broke out into a fierce disputation; they too weighed, considered, debated. But like the astrologers, the soothsayers, and the necromancers, they were unable to venture an explanation. Finally, they drew nigh the king, fell prostrate with their faces to the earth and wailed:

"O great king, live forever! The interpretation is hidden from us. Thou art the great king!"

"Blot it out, erase it!" screamed the king. "Since the strange god does not desire us to know his secret, let it be wiped out and remain hidden. We have our own gods. They are stronger than he. Great ones of Babylon! Let us do reverence and sanctify the great goddess Ishtar, the queen of heaven."

Servants had already been summoned who were cunning in

plaster work. They attempted to erase the writing by scraping it with sharp rough stones. The writing defied all their efforts, so they plastered it over with fresh clay.

"Come let us return to the worship of our goddess," exclaimed the king.

But his voice was hollow as though it issued from an empty cask. Every eye was bent upon the wall. As quickly as the writing was covered over, so quickly did it reappear, penetrating the wet plaster layers and bubbling onto the new surface of the wall as clearly and as prominently as before. No matter how thickly the frantic plasterers laid on their trowel-loads of material, the writing burst through. It appeared to each of those present as though it was directed specifically to him and him alone, boring into his mind and into his eyes and demanding an interpretation. Every heart was turned sour with fear before the hidden and mysterious; every eye was glued in terror to the writing on the wall.

"There is no one—no one who can tell what the words mean! No one who can expound and decipher what is written." The king broke down in a cry of utter despair. "I must know. I must be told what the writing says. We must all know what the writing demands of us!" The king spread out his hands in supplication towards the great and wise men of the kingdom.

While he was still entreating and pressing them, an old woman, accompanied by her handmaidens, entered the halls from one of the inner chambers. She was very aged, dry and shrunken like a mummified corpse. She hardly had strength to move and leaned heavily for support upon the arms of her maidens. Fear and trembling seized upon the throne room as she came in. The mighty ones of Babylon, the captains of the host and even the priests, all rose from their couches and welcomed her with deep obeisance. This was the dowager queen, the widow of Evil Merodach, the last survivor of the stock of the ancient dynasty of Nebuchadnezzar the great. The new rulers had had compassion upon her when they seized power, respected her and allowed her to live.

The handmaidens conducted the aged queen to Belshazzar. She

stood before him, upheld by the arms of her attendants, and spoke in a clear voice.

"May the great king live forever! Let not thy thoughts distress you nor thy face be darkened. Send and summon Daniel and he will explain to you the meaning of the words."

"Who is this Daniel who has the power to explain what the astrologers and the soothsayers and all my wise men cannot understand?" asked Belshazzar in wonder.

"He is a man who resides in your kingdom and in whom dwells the spirit of the holy God. What the soothsayers, the magicians, the astrologers, the necromancers, sorcerers, and the Chaldeans cannot interpret, he can interpret. He it was who explained the dreams of my father, the great Nebuchadnezzar, king of Babylon."

Scarcely had the aged queen uttered the name of Daniel than the memory of the advanced in years among the guests pierced through the shrouds of forgetfulness and recalled legendary tales of a strange wise man who had been famed for wondrous deeds and mysterious sayings.

"Daniel! Was it not he who was cast into the fire and emerged without harm? Was it not he who, thrown into the pit of lions, but prayed to his God and the lions bowed down at his feet?"

"Daniel, that interpreted the dreams of the king!"

"Daniel? The wisest of men? Can he still be alive?"

"Daniel.... Daniel...." The name was on every lip.

"Where shall I find him?" asked Belshazzar.

"He is one of them...." said the old queen pointing with a trembling finger in the direction of the couches where the chiefs of the exile of Judah sat.

"Of them? He ... a Jew?"

"In very truth. They know where he is...."

"O princes of Judah! Do you know the place of this Daniel who is wise in finding out hidden things and who can interpret this wondrous writing?"

"He dwells among us, within the gate of the courtyard of the chiefs of the exile of Judah. Beside the great gate. There he dwells

29

with his disciples, the sons of the prophets. If it be pleasing to the king we shall send a deputation from among us and bring him into the throne chamber."

"I shall send my royal litter to fetch him in. I shall clothe him in purple. I shall place a gold chain upon his neck. He shall reign over a third of my kingdom if he will read and decipher this writing and interpret it for me," exclaimed the king.

Several of the king's chief nobles left the hall with the deputation of the heads of the exile to bring back Daniel in the royal litter to the king's court.

The assembly sank back in their seats, stunned and deeply perturbed by the mystery that lay hidden in the writing which stared at them from the wall. The kedeshah Gimil, who was Ishtar, was completely forgotten by everyone, nor did Belshazzar attempt to direct the attention of the guests to her. The castrate priests of Ishtar veiled her so that none of the others should see her.

The heads of the exile, together with the royal emissaries of Belshazzar, soon returned. With them they brought an aged man, clad all in white from the sole of his foot to the covering of his head. Although advanced in years, he towered head and shoulders above the young men who accompanied him. These were his pupils. They walked surrounding him, keeping close to him as though guarding him from the defiling touch of a strange hand. The eyes of the sage were almost completely enshrouded by the shadow of his white eyebrows. A white turban crowned his head, and the radiant snowiness of his beard shone against the incandescent purity of his white robe.

"Draw nigh unto me, O man of God in whom His divine spirit moves! Come hither. I have heard that nothing is hidden from thee. Read the writing on the wall and make known unto me its interpretation. In scarlet shall I clothe you, a chain of gold shall I hang upon your neck, and you shall rule over a third of my kingdom."

"Thy gifts shall remain with thee and thy honors devote to another," said the ancient, thrusting aside with his hand the gold

30

chain that the king proffered him. "But the writing shall I read for thee, O king! Its interpretation shall I make known unto thee."

They led the ancient Daniel to the wall. He stood and looked long and steadily at the letters, then turned towards Belshazzar, who waited transfixed, pale and troubled.

"Thou hast lifted thyself up against the Lord of Heaven; and they have brought the vessels of His house before thee, and thou and thy lords, thy wives and thy concubines have drunk wine in them, and the Lord in whose hand thy breath is thou hast not glorified. Now this is the writing upon the wall: MENE, MENE, TEKEL, UPHARSIN. And this is the interpretation thereof: MENE, God hath numbered thy kingdom and finished it; TEKEL, thou are weighed in the balance and found wanting; PERES, thy kingdom is divided and given to the Medes and Persians."

Belshazzar, frozen with horror, gazed dumbly on his nobles. The nobles, trembling, looked blankly back at him. Belshazzar had scarcely managed to gather his thoughts or say a word when a swift courier burst into the hall, fell at his feet and panted:

"O Lord the king! Cyrus has crossed the Tigris at Arbela and is advancing on Babylon."

Panic reigned in the chamber. The lords of Babylon sprang up in fear from their couches and milled about in confusion, their robes disheveled and their carefully nurtured beards all unkempt. "To arms! Bring chariots!" cried the generals in tumult and dismay, crowding around the bewildered king. "To the walls! To the defenses!" shouted others. Many guests dashed from the hall without asking permission of the throne. They hastened off in utter dismay to their cities to rescue their property and take care of their families. Order was lost, the awe of the king's majesty was dissipated. That discipline and rule enforced by the rulers of Babylon with a high hand and such relentless cruelty on their own citizens and subdued nations alike, broke down completely. The fear of death mastered everyone. Bereft of counsel, like one driven out of his senses, Belshazzar listened to the various wild orders of

31

his captains. "To arms! To the walls!" He could not summon up the power of decision. In the riot, rout, and confusion no one perceived the sudden struggle which broke out between the priests of Bel Merodach and the eunuch votaries of Ishtar, in which the former proved victorious. They were stronger and more numerous. They quickly vanquished the priests of Ishtar, forced them to yield up the kedeshah Gimil, and bore her away on their shoulders to the temple of Bel Merodach.

# CHAPTER THREE

ONE midnight, as bright moonlight flooded the labyrinthine fortress alleys beside the walls of the great city, two shadows appeared near the gate. They resolved themselves into two men, one tall and towering, the other dwarflike, crouching. The shadows glided along the length of the wall as the two paced slowly, silently and cautiously, talking in whispers:

"What do people say? Who is the prophet? Where does he come from? Where has he been until today? What has he been doing? Who could recognize him?"

The questions addressed to the dwarf by the towering black-cloaked figure betrayed an insistent and overpowering curiosity.

"No one knows who he is, O lord Zerubabel. No one knows where he comes from. No one knows him. He appeared suddenly among the children of the exile. He calls himself Isaiah after the prophet who lived in the time of King Hezekiah. He speaks with his tongue. Like his forerunner he also speaks in the name of Jehovah. The word of God is lifted up in his mouth even as it was with the great prophet."

"And what do people think? Who is this Isaiah?"

"Some say that he is indeed the prophet; that God raised him up from the dead to bring words of consolation and faith to the exiles of Babylon. Some say that the vision of Isaiah speaks from his lips and that the spirit of Isaiah beats in his heart. Everyone believes that he is sent by God as he says. One needs must have a stopped-up heart not to believe in him when he lifts up his word."

Zerubabel wrapped himself closer in his black cloak, was silent for a moment, and then said:

33

"And he sent you to me? To tell me that Seraiah, the messenger of the prophet Jeremiah, is still alive and still has the scroll of writing that Jeremiah sent by his hand to the exiles in Babylon?"

"That is so, O lord. The emissary of his son is waiting in a skiff at the canal gate. He will carry us to the aged Seraiah, who dwells with his son in a small clay hut on the bank of one of the tributary canals. He awaits us there."

"We certainly did not know that the messenger Seraiah, who brought the letter of Jeremiah to the Exile, is still alive. He was of those who stood before King Zedekiah and sat at the feet of the great prophet. He is living among us! How could this thing have been hidden from us?"

"They concealed him from the Babylonians lest informers betray him into the hand of the oppressor. Seraiah lives in his hovel at the harbor of the canal, waiting for the redemption, until the word of the prophet shall be fulfilled. You will hear it from his own lips, O lord!"

The two walked silently and swiftly until they came to the inner wall which divided the city from the River Euphrates. In addition to this rampart, there was a second great wall which enclosed the river harbor within the confines of the city. A network of tributary canals joined the river with the capital. Through vaulted apertures beneath this wall the waters entered the canals and spread throughout the whole metropolis through a complicated system of channels. In addition to these apertures, each street could be approached by water by way of a small postern which was guarded by the watchmen in charge of the water system.

Yeshu knocked on the gate with a wooden mallet.

"Who goes there?"

"Open the gate by order of the king."

The door swung open. A small boat was rocking on the surface of the water and knocking against the hollow in the wall where it was anchored. The moonlight which filtered into the vaulted chamber gradually revealed a dark shadow in the boat to be a man with a pointed black beard, a strong broad back and massive

34

shoulders. He rose up and assisted Zerubabel and Yeshu, the priestly son of Jehozedek, to take their places in the boat. In darkness and grim silence, he bent to his oars. He turned the vessel into one of the canals that branched off the main artery and, after covering a short distance, turned off again into a smaller channel, a kind of brook that meandered between the fields. At last the craft came to rest beside a clay hut built on the bank.

Neraiah, son of Seraiah, waited for them on the threshold. He bowed before Zerubabel and helped him to land.

"Neraiah, son of Seraiah?" asked Zerubabel.

"I am he. My father is waiting for you."

He led them into the hovel, where a crude clay oil lamp gave a feeble glow.

"My father is lying on his couch in the corner. He begs pardon, O prince of the house of the kings of Judah, that he cannot rise to greet you. It is not that he does not desire to do so. Because of his age his feet no longer support him, and he no longer goes forth upon them."

What looked like a heap of bones wrapped in a dried and wrinkled parchment lay stretched on a bench covered with lamb skins. The mummified figure tried to sit up and in the end only succeeded with the aid of his son. With great effort, he drew Zerubabel's hand to his lips and immediately began to speak. His words flowed clearly.

"O lord, scion of the kings of Judah! Give ear to my words. A cup of wormwood and gall has God given us to drink by the hand of his prophet; He has made us kiss the hand that afflicted us; He has forced us to walk in peace with the oppressor that despoiled the house of our God. He hath emptied out Jerusalem of the best of her sons, making it waste and desolate until it is like a den for jackals in the wilderness. After Nebuchadnezzar dealt so cruelly with your grandfather, King Coniah, who surrendered with all his family in good faith—to dwell in peace so that there might be peace in the city—and was imprisoned in a cage like a beast of the forest, he was not content with the gold and silver and beautiful

35

treasures which he took from our Temple, with the holy vessels of our Lord God, with the flower of our sons, with our daughters, with the young aristocrats and nobles, with our sages and elders. He squeezed out our blood like a ravening beast with taxes and imposts; nor was his thirst sated before he forced our King Coniah to bring him the last remnant of the holy anointing oil that was left over in the Temple. Then King Coniah, in his desire to appease this lust that knew no slaking, to satisfy the ravening hunger of this evil beast, gathered in the very last of the anointing oil, that precious fluid which Samuel had used to anoint your first ancestor David as king over Israel and which hallowed the brows of all his successors in the dynasty, and brought it to Babylon.

"I was the man placed over the levy at the head of the king's caravan that carried it by way of the desert as servile tribute to the king of Babylon. Before I set forth at that time, my brother, Baruch, son of Neraiah, came to me. He was the scribe who set down the visions of the prophet Jeremiah. He entrusted to my keeping a scroll of writing in the hand of the prophet that I might read it to King Coniah and thereafter in the hearing of all the great ones of the Exile when I reached Babylon. The command of the prophet was strong upon me that when I had read the scroll I was to tie it to a stone and cast it into the depths of the River Euphrates that it might sink without trace or remembrance; for just as it would sink so would Babylon go down and rise no more. Thus the prophet saw the future in his vision. But I did not do so. I did not cast the scroll into the river."

The ancient was silent for a moment. He breathed deeply and slowly. He looked palely into the far distance as one who summons visions from remote places. Then he began once again:

"Why did God not take the light of my eyes from me? It would have been better for me to have walked in darkness at noon than to see the stock of the House of David stretched prostrate on the ground tremblingly offering the cruse of oil of the holy Temple to Nebuchadnezzar who sat on the throne of his majesty...."

No. . . . No. . . . My heart has not broken from eternal hatred of Babylon but from sorrow and desolation. The zeal for Judah and the longing for her redemption with Israel broke the chambers of my heart. But my faith in the rock of Israel was balm to my heart and restored the breaches in its walls. So I said to myself: It is not the depths of the Euphrates which will bear witness to the promises God had given; I shall be a living witness of the redemption to come. So I did not throw the prophet Jeremiah's scroll of consolation into the river, as he commanded me. I hung it in a sack over my heart and from that day to this I carry it there as though it were the tablets of the covenant of testimony. I swore by God to preserve my breath in my nostrils and my soul in my body, to live and prolong my days; I would keep alive my soul within me until the day would dawn when the promise God had graven with a stylus of fire would be fulfilled and the vision of the prophet realized. I would be a living witness of the redemption even as I was of the destruction.

"Therefore, God added years unto me and allowed me to live a long life. He poured strength into my loins and the breath of life into my lungs. Thus my heart also fell not into fragments. God said unto me, 'Live!' . . . and I lived. God said unto me, 'See!' . . . and mine eyes have seen and I have drunk the cup of bitterness unto the very dregs."

Seraiah paused to gulp for air.

Zerubabel, who had listened entranced to the words of the old man, said impatiently:

"Tell me everything, O Seraiah. Tell me all for I must know all."

"Zerubabel, scion and stock of David the king! These eyes saw Zedekiah, king of Judah, who dared to revolt against Babylon, and his sons and the children of his household brought to Riblah to the judgment of Nebuchadnezzar.

"Nebuchadnezzar was seated on his throne of majesty and beside him stood the chief of the executioners. They brought the king and his sons before him, one after the other. The lackeys seized Zedekiah and bound him by his arms to the emperor's war

37

chariot in such a position that his eyes should see the executioner sever the heads of his sons. As the head of son after son fell, it was lifted up so the blood dripped on the throne of Nebuchadnezzar and was then laid down at the feet of the monarch. Thus they slaughtered the princes of Judah. One man cut off the head, another brought it to the throne and yet another counted the heads which were severed. And Zedekiah, the king of Judah, stood bound to the chariot of Nebuchadnezzar, and his eyes beheld it all. When all the sons had been put to death, the slaves of Nebuchadnezzar gouged out the eyes of Zedekiah so that he might take with him into eternal darkness the sight of the heads of his sons wallowing in their blood and humbled in the dust. Then King Zedekiah was bound in fetters of copper and dragged to Babylon together with the captive daughter of Judah who went into exile.

"I was a handsome young lad then. My strength glowed in my loins and my muscles were powerful. So they had pity upon me and gave me bread to eat that I might live to slave in Babylon. They cared for every healthy young man in this way so that he could serve them. The officers of Nebuchadnezzar appointed me over one of the camps of the exiles and my blind king was committed to my charge. I was enjoined to bring him to Babylon alive. I was foresworn to pay with my life should any accident befall him. My heart grieved. Nevertheless, I rejoiced that God had allowed it to fall to my lot to care for my stricken king of desolate Judah.

"It came to pass one night when we were on our way to Babylon and had pitched our tents in the wilderness that our guards left us. They often did so, to go to steep themselves in their abominations, in their orgies before their gods of stone and iron. But first they entrusted me with the safety of the camp. Then in the darkness of the night, I gathered together the elders of Judah who were with me in the camp and seated them around our blind king. Even while we were on the way I had loosened his fetters. He was seated with us. Then from the sack above my heart, I took the scroll of the prophet and I read his words in their ears."

The old man was silent. He slowly raised the upper half of his body. Life flamed into his wrinkled features and fire flashed in his eyes. The wasted and dried-up body seemed to take on new life as though some mysterious vitality coursed through it. He spread out his hand and his eyes appeared to look into another world. From memory, he began to recite the words of the scroll. His voice was clear, vital and strong:

"Nebuchadnezzar, king of Babylon, hath devoured me;
He hath crushed me, he hath made me an empty vessel;
He hath swallowed me up like a dragon;
He hath filled his belly with my treasures;
He hath cast me out.

"The violence done to me and my flesh be upon Babylon,
Shall the inhabitant of Zion say;
And my blood upon the inhabitants of Chaldea,
Shall Jerusalem say.

"Therefore saith Jehovah:
Behold I will plead thy cause and take vengeance for thee;
And I will dry up her sea and make her springs dry.

"Thus said Jehovah of Hosts:
The broad walls of Babylon shall be utterly broken,
And her high gates shall be burned with fire;
And the people shall labor in vain, and the folk in the fire,
And they shall be weary.

"And it came to pass that when I had finished reading the burden of Jeremiah from the scroll that bitter weeping broke forth from the princes and elders. Tears of blood flowed from the empty eye-sockets of the king. And they said one to the other: 'See, Jehovah has sent us a burden of consolation by the hand of the prophet, and of hope, for He will live with us in the Exile. Let us return to the God of Israel with all our hearts; with our tears in Babylon let us blot out the sins of Jerusalem so that God will turn back our captivity.' "

The old man was silent again. Zerubabel sat mute. A moment passed and the clear voice of the old man was heard once more.

"I knew then that I was bearing the message of good tidings of salvation to the Exile. I was carrying the word of hope and promise. I knew that it was my duty to guard that word well until the day came."

"And whence do you know, Seraiah, that the day has arrived? Who told you?" asked Zerubabel.

"The prophet. He it is who said so!" father and son burst forth together.

"Which prophet?"

"The prophet who came from there. He suddenly came to me like a whirlwind and said: 'Seraiah, son of Neraiah, the day has come. Take out the scroll which Jeremiah gave you to cast into the depths of the river Euphrates. Call unto Zerubabel, the grandson of Coniah the king, who sits in the midst of the Exile, and read the scroll before him.' "

"But in God's name! Who is this prophet that everyone hearkens to his word? Do you know him? Who knows who he is? What miracle has he performed? What signs has he brought to bear witness that God has sent him in truth? Heaven forbid! but the hand of evil may be in the matter to lead the people into despair by vain hopes; to bring utter ruin to the remnant of Judah, may heaven forfend. Jeremiah sent us a letter by the hand of Elasa ordering us to wait for the appointed time for seventy years. That time is not yet fulfilled. Only when seventy years have passed will God remember the Exile and return its captivity. Now comes a strange and queer man, whom no one had ever heard of yesterday, and raises up premature hopes in the hearts of the people. They are all ready to be dragged in his train, to listen to his words as though he were an angel from heaven. Take careful thought and heed of what you are doing."

"You also will long to be lifted up on the wings of his prophecy.

You also will hear his words as though they come from the mouth of an angel whom God had sent from heaven. Only look upon his face and hear him lift up his word," cried the old man.

"I certainly want to see him and hear his words," returned Zerubabel. "Where is he to be found?"

"He prefers that his dwelling place be hidden. He appears and disappears without warning. On Sabbath he preaches in the synagogues. Last Sabbath he spoke in the congregation of our brethren from Bethlehem. Next Sabbath, so a rumor has reached me, he will be among the children of Bethel not far from here, in the camp of the brickmakers beyond the wall."

"He is going to the sons of Bethel, the children of Samaria, who worship the golden calf? They were blotted out from the book of Israel. They no longer know their descent by their fathers' houses! They are no longer reckoned as of the House of Jacob."

The protest burst from the lips of Zerubabel.

"The prophet says that even to them, to the lost sheep of Israel, he has been sent by God to bring them back to the God of Jacob. Even them had God mercifully pardoned and wiped out their transgressions. 'For soon shall the eyes of the blind be opened and the ears of the deaf be unstopped,' the prophet says."

"I shall see him and hear what he has to say. I will be among the exiles of Samaria while the prophet speaks to them," said Zerubabel.

41

# CHAPTER FOUR

WHEN Nebuchadnezzar led Judah into exile, the Sabaeans forced the surviving nobles who went captive in the train of the blind king Zedekiah to carry sacks full of soil on their backs. In this way Nebuchadnezzar hoped to break their spirit by preventing them from walking upright. The weight would bend them down and they would become accustomed to the stoop of servility. The priests thereupon took the scrolls of the Holy Law which they wished to save from destruction and sewed their parchment sections into sacks. They filled the sacks with soil taken from Jerusalem and loaded them on the shoulders of the children of the royal house and the nobles who were about to go into exile. Thus, together with the temple vessels which Nebuchadnezzar had despoiled, the heads of Judah took with them into the Babylonian exile the scrolls of the Holy Law and the soil of Jerusalem.

When they came to their places of exile, the captives secretly erected a synagogue and covered its floor with Jerusalem earth. This was to serve as a meeting place and assembly. In it they placed the parchment sections of the Law which they had re-sewn into scrolls. There they installed the elders of Judah, priests, and Levites that they might search into the Law of God and disseminate it among the people dwelling in exile.

This synagogue, called "Be Kenishta" in the Aramaic dialect they spoke, was the first of many set up in their various communities by the exiles in the course of time as the yoke of the oppressor eased. There they met for prayer and solemn assembly. Its ceremonial wall was always on the side facing Jerusalem. Every building had one span of Jerusalem earth and a re-sewn scroll of the Law. In every synagogue a priest, a Levite, or one who had formerly sat at the feet of some prophet, had his seat. These men enjoyed the honorable title of elders among the exiles. They read the Law of Moses before the assembly on Sabbaths and Festivals and recited chapters of the psalms of David.

In the days of Nebuchadnezzar, the exiles eventually had been permitted to move freely about the country. They began building houses and planting gardens as Jeremiah the prophet had ordered them to do in the letter he had sent to Babylon. Abandoning hope of a speedy redemption, they began a new life for themselves on alien soil. Actively encouraged by the authorities, who were anxious to colonize uninhabited tracts which were suitable for agriculture, the new immigrants, most of whom were accustomed to that kind of work in Judah, founded agricultural settlements. The land was fertile, fruitful, and very much better watered than the hard, rocky soil of their homeland. They also found a much wider market for their produce and a fine transport system based on the use of canals and waterways. Conditions were altogether suitable for the flourishing development of the new settlements. The exiles named their new places after their former homes. One farmer's colony of this kind was near the famous ancient city of Nippur, which they called Nophar. It was not very far from Babylon, and by using the canal it was possible to travel directly to the royal capital by boat. Jewish settlements also sprang up in the great salt plains, especially at Tel Melach, the Hill of Salt. The fame of the Jews, who had been well trained to heavy work on the land by the hard unyielding soil of their homeland, spread rapidly throughout Babylon, and their produce was in great demand.

But the exiles' occupations were not confined to farming and cattle rearing. In time they were permitted to engage in almost all types of work. They were smiths, metal workers, copper founders, stone masons, brickmakers, and woodcutters. Their crafts were urgently required in a country which was in a continual ferment of building and development.

The growing power of Babylon, which had swallowed up half the world, afforded ample opportunity for commerce between the many countries within the empire. Under the Emperor's strong centralizing and controlling hand, trade flourished in Babylon more than in any other place. It was a mighty royal city, steeped in wealth and luxury. Babylon was a greedy beast, ravening and devouring and knowing no satiety. It needed supplies from the whole world: silks from Persia, copper ore from Cyprus, wood from Lebanon, oil and ivory from India. Many Jews took to commerce and rapidly became serious rivals to the Chaldeans, Tyrians, and Sidonians.

After Nebuchadnezzar's death, his son Evil Merodach released King Coniah from prison and endowed the Judeans with certain rights, among them that of practicing their religious customs. Accordingly, the elders of Judah began to institute certain forms of worship adapted to the new situation in which they lived, in an alien land among alien people, and without a Temple. The king of Judah, his sons, members of the court in Jerusalem, the chiefs of the priests and the Levites resided in a palace that Evil Merodach set aside for them near the gate of Ishtar. Coniah was supported from the royal purse, and the exiles too took good care that their king should want for nothing. Gradually the king and his sons after him became the center of the spiritual forces of the Exile. The palace circle, or those who had access to it, fashioned the spiritual nature of the Jews. In this manner of life the prophets naturally fulfilled an honored role. Ezekiel, in his time, occupied as central and influential a position in the fallen tabernacle of David as Moses did in his. Alone and solitary, this gigantic personality waged an unrelenting battle against the idolatry that threatened to rend the pitiful lamb of Israel torn between Judah and exile as by a savage beast. Daniel, too, with the aid of his disciples in the king's palace, exercised a strong influence over the exiles. The palace infused a breath of life among them. It was the highest spiritual authority and its decrees set the religious and communal standards. It directed the establishment of the various synagogues and their conversion into small sanctuaries. It also regularized and unified the forms of worship. The synagogues were not only consecrated to divine service but became places of meeting and the center of communal life. They were set up in the cities where the exiles dwelt and according to their father's houses.

The God of Israel, it was taught, was not confined to one place as Bel Merodach was tied to Babylon and Ashur to Nineveh. He was the God of the whole universe; the whole earth was full of His glory and "wherever I shall cause my name to be mentioned," He told the people through the lips of His prophets, "there shall I come and bless thee." Deprived of an altar and of sacrifices, the Jews found a closer approach to their God. Prayer took the place of sacrifice. They did not possess many forms of supplication hallowed through usage, beyond the psalms which the Levites remembered that they or their fathers had sung in the Temple service. Poets arose among the Babylonian Jews, who wrote new psalms which gave expression to the grief pent up in their hearts and their longing for Zion and Jerusalem.

These psalms and songs of praise spread quickly among the exiles, and most of the Jews sang them and included them in their synagogue service. The priests used to read the commandments of the Laws of Moses and the rituals for the festivals and solemn assemblies which were written in the Holy Law which Josiah had re-discovered in the Temple.

The exiles of the first and second generation clung closely together, encouraging each other to be one people. Their faith in the God of Israel was strong and abiding. His Temple in Jerusalem might be destroyed but the whole world was God's sanctuary and all of the heavens the abode of His glory.

The synagogue of the Bethelites was situated in the suburb of the brickmakers behind the great wall. The congregation of Bethel was a mixed one, comprising exiles from Judea and from the previous dispersion of the ten tribes of Israel whom Sennacherib, king of Assyria, had taken into captivity after the destruction of Samaria.

Nebuchadnezzar needed an infinite supply of muscles and sinews to erect the buildings, the plans of which teemed in his brain, to dig the canals that he required. No value was placed on the lives of the slaves used up in these labors. In beginning the building of the great wall that surrounded the city, his father before him had started to gather in every young and ablebodied person from all the subjugated kingdoms. He had brought them to Babylon and put them to work on the wall. His son, Nebuchadnezzar, continued his father's vast plans and even expanded them. He had in very truth completely denuded all the conquered territories of every fit young man, bringing them to dig canals, hew out pools of water, rear fortresses, cast up highways and ramparts and erect palaces and temples to the gods.

By means of the great canal, Nebuchadnezzar sought to make the fame of Babylon rival and surpass that of Egypt in its glory. But the Euphrates was not the Nile. Unlike the latter, it did not overflow its banks at frequent intervals, saturating the broad meadows. The soil of Babylon was, therefore, not enriched like that of Egypt by layer after layer of rich silt and manure when the river subsided and shrank back into its channel. Instead of this, Nebuchadnezzar conceived the idea of irrigating his low-lying level plains by a system of artificial canals. He decided to weave over the land a network of canals, channels, tributaries, sub-tributaries, and small local ditches and watercourses. Implementation of the plan called for every ounce of labor that could be squeezed out of the subjugated lands. To this end he did to Nineveh and Assyria what Tiglath Pileser had once done to Babylon. He razed Nineveh from its coping stones to its foundations and took all working hands captive to Babylon. Among this horde of captives were some of the Israelites whom Sennacherib had taken to Assyria after the conquest and destruction of Samaria.

During the generation that elapsed between the conquests of

Sennacherib and Nebuchadnezzar, the northern Israelite captives had assimilated with the Assyrians until it was difficult to differentiate between them. Their faith had not been as firmly rooted as it had been among the Judeans. They had no Temple as a central binding institution; no Isaiah had instilled into them the hope of a Messiah; no Jeremiah had uttered words of rebuke or consolation such as the Judeans took with them into exile, giving them lively hope of redemption. Because of this, the exiles of Samaria had mingled very quickly with the surrounding peoples among whom their captors had settled them, becoming indistinguishable in the general rout.

It was when they came as slaves to Babylon that they encountered the exiles from Judah for the first time. A chord of the rusting, forsaken harp of memory was touched and the old melody aroused a faint echo in their minds of ancient days, of times long forgotten. These recollections had been buried beneath mountains of embers left by flames of thought that had burned out long ago. Dim shapes revived of tales told by their parents' parents of a God whom their ancestors worshipped in a distant land of green fields and fertile valleys. The land had been theirs and theirs alone. There they had been free under their own great king Jeroboam, son of Joash. They remembered prophets sent to them by God; their descent from Abraham, Isaac, Jacob; the exodus from Egypt; a man named Moses and a conquering warrior, Joshua. A dormant instinct, like that which brings a wild animal safely back to its herd, was aroused in them. Many began to long for contact with their older brother, Judah, whose worship of God was still so vital and to whom Jerusalem and the Holy Temple were so alive. Thus the descendants of the exile of Assyria began to seek out the exiles of Judah, desiring, as the hart pants after the brook, to steep their thirsty souls in the living waters of the God of Jacob.

But the exiles of Judah were very jealous of their purity of descent and pride of ancestry. For many generations they had abandoned the custom of adding the words "of the tribe of Judah"

47

to their family name. Now the cherished and important thing was the house of their fathers. The rock from which they were hewn was more precious to them than their sight and they guarded their ancestry as one does the apple of one's eye. The names of their fathers' fathers they carefully guarded from generation to generation. Their dignity forbade association with anyone who could not show that he was of the pure seed of Jacob. The unhappy exiles of Samaria who had undergone a second transportation from Assyria to Babylon did not know their origin. Not being able to produce a scrap of genealogy they were suspect in the eyes of the Judeans. Perhaps they were not of the house of Jacob at all but a mere mixed multitude from whom one should refrain from any contact or conversation.

But the exiles of the ten tribes, longing and panting after their God, imitated the actions of the exiles of Judah. If the latter organized themselves into communities according to their homes in Judah and their fathers' houses, so did they. If the exiles of Judah saw fit to build themselves synagogues and gather in them on Sabbaths and holy days to recite the prayers and psalms like those the Levites sang in the Temple, then the exiles of Samaria did the same. The exiles of Judah had called their synagogues after the names of their home towns and villages in the homeland, like "the children of Bethlehem," "the children of Lud," "the children of Anathoth," of "Jericho." The Samarian exiles who labored in the clay pits and the brick kilns in the shadow of the great wall of Babylon similarly decided to call their synagogue and their congregation "Bethel." This was the name of the city that had been the center of their worship long, long ago. It had been so named by Jacob in ancient times.

Time wrought its changes. The prophet Ezekiel labored to bring the exiles of Judah and Samaria closer together. As year followed year, the exiles gradually began to enter into each other's congregations. In particular, the poor and oppressed, whom circumstances forced to live in the same quarters, came together. Some-

48

times they attended the nearest synagogue even if it were not of their own community. Many thousands of Judeans were uprooted from their new homes and brought far away to labor in the vast projects in Babylon. Being no longer able to maintain living contact with their communities, they turned to the nearest synagogue even though it belonged to the Israelites.

The exilic prophets and the synagogue preachers tried to draw the communities together and break down the fence that had separated them for hundreds of years. They equated Israel and Jerusalem and called all the exiles indiscriminately "Children of Israel" or "the people of Judah." Gradually but surely the exiles became accustomed to association and tended to regard themselves as one people, Israel. But the gentiles were accustomed to use the name "Jew" even when speaking of the Israel exiles who came from Assyria.

A Sabbath service was in progress in the synagogue of Bethel. The synagogue was in the center of the settlement and resembled a dwelling house of the neighborhood. It consisted of one long room. Its walls were made of reeds held together by loam and pitch. The roof was of palm branches and the door a woven embroidered curtain. The visitors to the meeting house would sit on the clay floor with their bare feet folded under them. Most of them wore shirts made of sackcloth and white kerchiefs covered their heads. The better class were dressed in coats and robes of several colors. Several were attired in black cloaks, had rings on their fingers and signet chains hanging down from their dyed girdles. Apart from this group of elders and chiefs whose long soft hair was carefully tended, the congregation presented a massed group of dark brown faces, baked dark by the sun. Their hair was short, brittle and unkempt, hanging down over half-crazed and burning eyes which peered out under beetling brows. Their fingers were thin and gnarled and they held their limbs rigid as stone as they gave their attention utterly to the figure who stood

49

before them. Their ears were alert to the words which went forth from his mouth, their very eyes seemed to listen, the tips of their fingers listened, every pore in their skin was sensitive to him, drinking in his words, warming to him and becoming enthralled.

The man who addressed them was young; he was full of health, strong, upright and solid as though hewn out of one cedar trunk, and dry as seasoned wood. His bones protruded from his taut brown skin so that it seemed there was not an ounce of fat in his whole body. He was all skin, bone, and sinew. His glowing, flashing eyes were set deep under a high brow and his face was adorned by a short, thick, black beard. He was speaking to those sitting at his feet, his hands outstretched towards them with bony fingers interlaced. His congregation were crowded together as though they had coalesced into one body. They hearkened with all their soul and being: heart, body and spirit yearning to hear. What was he saying to them? Was he talking at all?

He was not just speaking. He was like a raging hot wind that seizes upon four corners of a house, shakes it and makes it tremble. For his word was a furious, fiery whirlwind, a mighty cry of victory. It was as though all the angels of heaven were with him under one canopy and that the song of the celestial beings was heard in its mighty trumpeting. It was a roaring cry, a thunder that reverberates and breaks back again but still does not terrify as it crashes. It was the kind of thunder that rolls and brings good tidings, sounding a message of consolation and salvation.

"Comfort ye, comfort ye, my people.
A voice calleth out. In the wilderness make ye clear a way
   of Jehovah, make straight in the desert the highway for
   our God.
Every valley shall be exalted and every mountain and hill
   shall be made low, and the crooked shall be made
   straight.

O Zion, that bringest good tidings, get thee up into the high
    mountain.
O Jerusalem, that bringest good tidings, lift up thy voice
    with strength.
Lift it up, be not afraid.
Say unto the cities of Judah, 'Behold your God!' "

Whoever had spoken to them before in this strain? What
prophet had ever comforted them as this one did? His God is not
a God of vengeance. He does not stand over them with rod and
scourge in his right hand, ready to rain down blows on their
flesh for every sin, for every transgression, for every deed of per-
verseness. No, He is not like the taskmasters and overseers that
stand over them, who judge them and execute sentence upon them
and drive them. He is not of these. This God is a shepherd. He
will be a shepherd to them, He will pasture them and lead them in
pleasant ways, by the still waters. God is with them. He knows
the lot of every one of them and pleads his cause. He lifts up in his
own arms the lost and weary lambs who have stumbled from the
way. He holds them close in his bosom and the young ones among
them He leads gently along. Gently ... gently.

Tears flowed from their eyes and descended into the scars and
furrows of their scorched and toil-worn faces. They drained into
the tangles of their unkempt beards.

"What does he say?" A spirit wrapped them in its wings like
a heavenly cloud and transported them into the heights beyond
every rough place.

"I have chosen thee, and not cast thee away.
    Fear not ... for I am with thee. . . .
    Fear not, O thou worm Jacob, O men of Israel.
    I will help thee, saith the Lord and thy Redeemer, the holy
        one of Israel.
    When the poor and the needy seek water, and there is none,
    And their tongue faileth for thirst,

I, Jehovah, will hear them, I the God of Israel, will not
forsake them.
I will open rivers in the high places and fountains in the
midst of the valleys."

He hints to them that salvation is close at hand, that redemption is knocking at the door.

"I have raised up one from the North, and he shall come;
From the rising of the sun shall he call upon my name;
And he shall come upon the princes as upon mortar,
And as the potter treadeth clay."

They stare at one another and their eyes are confused. To whom does he refer? Can he be thinking of Cyrus, the king of the Medes and Persians who is coming up against Babylon?

But the prophet is silent. He stands like a stone pillar with his eyes staring into nothingness. His eyes see something far, far away. No. Not here. Far away. His eyes pierce through walls and barriers, they bore through into far universes. Distance is annihilated, the barriers of time are dissipated before him. Past . . . present . . . future . . . they are one . . . one from which he draws his vision.

Suddenly, the prophet sways upon his feet as though he would fall. His whole body trembles as touched by an unseen hand. His face turns white, ghastly as if all life had drained away from it. He shuts his eyes tightly as though fearing to see what he sees . . . then words escape from his mouth: thoughtful, suppressed as a spirit speaking from within him. His voice is soft and musical, melodious with grace like a child singing to itself:

"Behold my servant, whom I uphold;
Mine elect, in whom my soul delighteth;
I have put my spirit upon him;
He shall bring forth judgment to the gentiles.

52

He shall not cry, nor lift up, nor cause his voice to be heard
    in the street.
A bruised reed shall he not break,
And the smoking flax shall he not quench;
He shall bring forth judgment unto truth.
He shall not fail nor be discouraged, till he have set judg-
    ment in the earth;
And the isles shall wait for his law.
Thus saith Jehovah, he that created the heavens, and stretched
    them out;
He that spread forth the earth and that which cometh out of it;
He that giveth breath unto the people upon it;
And spirit to them that walk therein.
I, Jehovah, have called thee in righteousness,
And will hold thine hand, and will keep thee,
And give thee for a covenant to the people, for a light to
    the gentiles:
To open the blind eyes, to bring out the prisoners from
    the prison;
And them that sit in darkness out of the prison house.
I am Jehovah, that is my name; and my glory shall I not
    give to another,
Neither my praise to graven images.
Behold, the former things are come to pass,
And new things do I declare;
Before they spring forth I tell you of them."

The prophet is silent. He stands still and his eyes are as in
deep slumber.

A moaning, as of an angry sea, passes through the congregation.

"Who is this man of whom he speaks? Whose coming does he
announce? Can it be the coming of Cyrus? Shall the Lord take
hold of the hand of a stranger, a gentile?" "No, heaven forbid;
did not the prophet say, 'My glory I shall not give to another,
neither my praise to graven images?'"

53

"You heard what he said: 'A bruised reed shall he not break.' He will not be like the kings of Assyria and Babylon who fall upon the weak. He will stand on the right hand of the weak and the broken. He will proclaim freedom unto him."

"Will he bring all peoples to the Lord God?"

"To the covenant of the peoples, God will make his people Israel the light to the nations."

"Messiah!" "The anointed one!"

"The redemption is coming . . . the redemption!"

"All the isles await the Law of the God of Israel!"

Every man seized the hand of his neighbor and even thus, sitting upon the ground, embraced hand in hand, cleaving together and joined heart to heart, they began to sway as one mass . . . like one solid . . . like one . . . one vital thing with many bodies. They murmured and whispered together, singing sweetly and silently but fervently:

"By the waters of Babylon, there we sat down. . . ."

Someone arose from among the seated throng. He was cloaked in a black robe. The ephod which showed behind his robe was embroidered in silver and from this and the ring on his finger, the Bethel congregation recognized that he was of the royal seed of David. They made way for him. He approached the prophet who was still standing motionless.

"Stranger, who are you?"

The prophet opened his eyes and glanced piercingly at the man before him. He, too, perceived from the signs who it was that stood before him.

"I am the bearer of good tidings of the God of Israel to His people of Israel in Babylon," he answered.

"What sign have you that it is indeed God that has sent you?"

"The word which God has put in my mouth; that is the sign of my message," the prophet answered. "By my mouth God makes known what is to come before it comes to pass."

"Jeremiah gave us a sign. He fixed an appointed time. The seventy years are not yet fulfilled. You are hastening destiny and

54

leading people after you into delusions. Hear what I say. You are playing with fire. Your words are likely to prove a strangling halter around the neck of Israel rather than a message of consolation. They will bring them down to the abyss of destruction."

"Who can set a time for Him? He that created the seasons can change the seasons. The appointed time has come. This is the appointed time. The people of Israel shall be redeemed and will return to the place whence God sent them into exile."

# CHAPTER FIVE

A LAD of Judah grew up among the Judean hills, where the
rocky walls raise themselves up like arms or necks
stretched out in prayer. The remnant of the poor among
the people, like eagles fleeing to their refuge, had taken up their
abode in clefts in the mountains, in their crevices, even in caves.
They clung by their fingernails to the poor soil, which they re-
claimed from the craggy hills by the sweat of their brows. They
attached themselves to the patches of fenced-in ground which
descended into the bosom of the hills. They did not let go.

Samuel, the son of Solomon of the tribe of Judah, was born and
brought up on the hope of the redemption. The faithful and steadfast ones of Judah among the remnant were firm in their belief
that the promise that Jeremiah had made would surely be fulfilled, that at the end of seventy years the Babylonian Exile would
be brought back by God, and His peoples Israel and Judah would
unite and return to the land He had given to their forefathers.
Like every other child of Judah who grew up alone in the hidden
fastnesses of the mountains, Samuel also learned from his father
to pronounce the "Shema Yisrael," the "Hear, O Israel," as the
Holy Law of Moses prescribed. As soon as he had learned to read,
his interest was captivated by the scroll of the prophecies of
Isaiah, the son of Amoz, which he found in his father's household.

The hope for the redemption, for the coming of the Messiah of
the God of Israel who would redeem not only Judah but all the
peoples, who would bring all nations to the mountain of the Lord's
House and cause peace to dwell throughout the world for ever,
pulsed in the bloodstream of the lad almost from infancy as

56

though he had imbibed it with his mother's milk. The prophet Isaiah's vision of the exalted future were written upon individual parchments, and they taught the children to learn them by heart, as they did the "Shema Yisrael."

The child used to leap like a young buck over the hills of Judah. His heart, cherishing dreams of universal peace, almost burst with joy in his delight over the world which God had created. The dew-drenched shady valleys were the vale of vision of Isaiah, where the leopard and kid would lie down together and a little child would lead them from vale to vale and from meadow to meadow. He saw, on the high places at the tops of the cool and lofty hills, like the massing of silver-bordered clouds, multitudes, multitudes of men—peoples from far-off lands which dwelt at the ends of the earth, from beyond the mountains, from the shores of many oceans, from the far-flung islands of the sea. All the nations were floating on the wings of shade-heavy clouds which cast their purple shadows on the hillsides. Aery and ethereal they were, borne along within the blueness of the firmament, closer and closer to the mountain veiled with its thick mantle of cloud. He knew whence they were leading, what their purpose was. It was God's mountain to which they were drawn upon the wings of the clouds: the mountain which was shrouded from the sight of mortal eye—the mountain of Jehovah—the mountain of Jerusalem —the mountain in the vision of the prophet.

Once he was lying on the slope of a hill in the shadow of a bush, watching the flock of skimpy sheep which his father had entrusted to him to pasture, when he cast his eyes downward to the depths of the valley beneath. There he saw through the swirling mists a flowing brook which burst forth from the clefts of the rock and boiled down in a foam-covered torrent until it poured itself into a broad green meadow. Flocks whiter than snow were feeding on the green grass, which was lush and high. He saw day-old lambs with their mothers and all the flock sheltered beneath towering cypresses which lined the banks of the stream. He heard the mur-

57

mur of the river's happy song as it poured over the stones that lay in its path. The scene, in his eyes, was very much like the one he remembered from one of the psalms of David. The words were ready to his lips, and he saw them before his eyes: "The Lord is my shepherd, I shall not want; He causeth me to lie down in green pastures; He leadeth me beside the still waters."

Towards evening the lad came home to his father's hut with his flock. He said to his mother:

"Mother, I have beheld with mine own eyes God pasturing men in green meadows by still water."

"Where, my son, did you see men pasturing their flocks in green pastures beside still waters?"

"There. Down below. In the valley. By the still waters. Just as David our king said in the psalm. Through a break in the cloud, my own eyes saw it at the foot of the mountain."

"You are dreaming, my son. You dream like our ancestor Joseph, son of Jacob."

"I saw it with my own eyes. I saw God pasturing men in green meadows. I also saw other things. I saw clouds coming and bearing on their wings peoples from the many lands. They were descending to the mountain of the Lord when they came from beyond and when they flew over the mountain of Jerusalem. Exactly in every detail like the vision of Isaiah, son of Amoz. Just as it is written in the scroll. You can see many visions in the hills of Judah, mother."

"The time has not yet come, son. The House of Jacob is forsaken and abandoned. Aliens dwell on its inheritance. Does your ear never hear the voice of Rachel weeping in Ramah, weeping over her children while the hills echo her plaint? The prophet told us that Rachel refuses to be comforted for her children who are no more."

"Yes, mother, I often hear the lamentation of Rachel. From the scroll of Jeremiah my father taught me about her mourning. I learned it well and I also know that the voice of Jehovah is heard in Ramah restoring and comforting the mother. 'Thus saith Jehovah, hold back thy voice from weeping and thine eyes from tears, there shall be a reward for thy labors, saith Jehovah, and thy children shall return from the land of the enemy.'"

"So. You hear the voice of Jehovah? And you hear him comforting Rachel?"

"Yes, mother. And today I heard other voices too."

"What else did you hear?"

"Some that I understand and some that I do not. Some seemed to call me."

"Call you! By name?"

"Some called me by name 'Samuel, Samuel!' Like the voice that called Samuel in the house of Eli, when he walked about in the House of God at Shiloh."

"My dearest child, dare not mention these things! Such talk is forbidden." His mother, terrified, fell to her knees beside him.

"Why should I not speak about them? I hear the voices calling me."

"No, my son. These are dangerous dreams."

"Mother, I am not dreaming. When I woke up, there I was among the hills. I heard voices calling me, as though from a split in the rocky wall; there were others which seemed to call me from a stream in the valley. I have to tell you that I feel I am ordered by a mighty force to do as the voices bid me."

"To do what, my child?"

"They order me to go up to Jerusalem and enter the courtyard of the Temple ruins. There is a cave there in which the sons of the prophets dwell. The command of the voices is strong upon me. They call me from the hills to come to the cave and to live among the sons of the prophets."

"I am afraid, child. You must not think and talk like this."

"I have to say it, mother. The voices order me to go to Jerusalem and come unto the sons of the prophets."

"I will talk it over with your father, my son. Till then you

59

must guard your lips and say no word to anyone. You have always been a dreamer, my child."

Solomon of the House of Judah called his son Samuel and said:
"You dream empty dreams. You speak empty words. You are hearing misleading voices. You shall not go to Jerusalem."

"Why can't I go, father?"

"Because God has destroyed His House and handed His people over to enemies who seek its life. He has forsaken His city Jerusalem and left it wide open to the abominations of the heathens. Your father's father's foot and your father's foot have not trodden the ground of Jerusalem since its glory was profaned. The Temple of God is a heap of ruins, a haven for the jackal and the hyena—human jackals and hyenas and real ones. Evil spirits stalk about its ruins. God has left the place of His Holy Sanctuary to the destroyer. The Mount of Moriah is like the infernal Sheol. Abominations and filthy idols profane it with fornication, incest, adultery, and every wicked practice. Therefore thy father's foot and that of thy father's father have not trodden the ground of Jerusalem, and thy foot too shalt not step there. Here let us dwell, in the high mountains and the deep valleys, safe from the fury of the destroyer. We shall live like eagles on the craggy heights and hide ourselves like ravens in the valleys. Thus shall we remain until the great and terrible day of the Lord comes, until God pardons our father's sins and purifies Jerusalem His city from the filth of the nations and returns his people to its inheritance. So I have said and so you shall do."

"Father, father, listen to me! I hear the ringing in my ears of the voice which tells me, 'Rise and go up to Jerusalem. There is a cave in the Temple mount in which the sons of the prophets dwell. Come among them and be one of them.'"

"You see a deceitful vision, my son. You hear strange and imagined voices. You saw Samuel because you are called by his name and you yearn to be like him. Voices which arise from a person's longing are often lying and misleading. Do not follow them and go a-whoring after vain visions. Come, let us wait and see how things fall out! If God has anything for you and you are commanded to do something, He will let you know of it in His own good time. Till then, dwell with us as you have done till now. Now go to the cave where lives Aryeh, son of Zachariah, and hear the word of God from his lips, as He spoke it unto his prophets, as it is written in the writings which he has with him."

In a humble hut on a rib of the mountain dwelt the household of Solomon, son of Judah, and supported themselves on the produce of a farm and the few lean sheep that eked out a living on the rocky outcrop and the green of the valleys. Like the others who, after the Temple had been destroyed, fled from the city and went into hiding in the mountains southwest of Jerusalem, the family of Solomon, son of Judah, sustained themselves by the labor of their hands and the sweat of their brows. Like the others, they sundered themselves from all joys and forwent all pleasures. They were Mourners of Zion, lamenting every day and always the destruction of the Temple, with inexpressible longing for the redemption.

They used to meet secretly and perform an order of service of mourning in congregation. They were heedful not to utter any word of complaint against the God Jehovah. God was righteous and it was His people who were wicked. They accepted the justice of the fate which God had decreed upon Judah and were careful not to sin in the matter of their lips or in even a wrong thought about God. Therefore with broken hearts and contrite spirits they would recall the sins of Judah and her kings. They would repeat and recount the chastisements with which the prophets had admonished the people and in particular the words of Jeremiah and later those of Ezekiel. They counted over separately every sin and every transgression that the leaders of Israel and Judah—the highly born, the judges, the magnates, the purse proud, and the kings— had committed against God and the poor of the people.

Usually, as the sun was going down, in a kind of natural bowl

61

in the rock, the Mourners of Zion would gather together and sit around a bonfire. The lad Samuel, trying to forget the voices he had heard, listened with a wondering and trembling heart to the terrible deeds that were recounted. Between one admonition of one prophet to that of another, between lament and lament, he learned to know how bitter was the portion of Israel and how sharp were the chastisements of the prophet. From the lips of old Aryeh, son of Zachariah, who was head of the Mourners of Zion in their part of the mountains, he heard reminiscences of the times before the Destruction of the Temple. In particular his memory was impressed by the tale of King Zedekiah and the prophet Jeremiah, when the king gave orders to cast the prophet into a pit of loam so that he should drown therein. Aryeh also told the tale of the freeing of the slaves and their immediate re-subjection and described other unjust acts of which the kings of Judah had been guilty. After seducing the hearts of his princes and captains to seek friendship with Egypt and to stand up against Babylon, the king had hoped to win the approval of the people through a new covenant. He proclaimed freedom to the Hebrew slaves who had been tyrannized and subjected to imprisonment and confinement because of non-payment of the unjust taxes laid upon them. They had been taken with their wives and children, nor were they set free after six years as the Law of Moses required. The news of the covenant went out over all the land, and a great hope sprang up that a new era was dawning, that better days were at hand. The people cried to one another: "Now there are no rich and poor, no fine and mighty and poor and worthless, there is no slave and no corrupter, we are all free."

For a few days it seemed that justice would prevail; then the oppressors returned to their evil ways. Their officers went out into the streets once more, into the fields and vineyards. Their cruel grasp stretched out to the children of Judah, to the freemen who had yesterday been slaves. They took them, their wives, and children into custody and made them into slaves as though no word had been given.

Then Jeremiah saw the abominable thing that had been done and he arose and went to King Zedekiah and said to him that his latter end would be bitter indeed. He spoke to the king in the name of the God of Israel: "I made a covenant with your fathers at the time I brought them forth from the land of Egypt, from the house of bondage, saying, 'At the end of seven years shall you send forth each one his Hebrew brother who was sold to him, and he shall serve you six years and you shall send him free from you!' But ye turned and polluted my name, and caused every man his servant and every man his handmaid, whom he had set at liberty at their pleasure, to return, and brought them unto subjection, to be unto you for servants and for handmaids. Therefore, thus saith the Lord, Ye have not hearkened unto me, in proclaiming liberty, every one to his brother, and every man to his neighbor: Behold, I proclaim a liberty for you, saith the Lord, *to the sword, to pestilence, and to the famine;* and I will make you to be removed unto all the kingdoms of the earth. And I will give the men that have transgressed my covenant, the princes of Judah and the princes of Jerusalem, the eunuchs and the priests, and all the people of the land, which passed between the parts of the calf; and I will even give them into the hand of their enemies and into the hand of them that seek their life, and into the hand of the king of Babylon's army, which are gone up from you. . . ."

Aryeh, son of Zachariah, spoke much to the congregation of the sins of former and later generations for which Israel and Judah had gone into exile from their land and for which the Temple had been destroyed. "For they continued to do evil in the sight of the Lord and not only did they sin against the poorer sort among the people. They sinned with the abominations of the nations whom God had driven forth from before the children of Israel. They built altars to all the idols of the heathens and sacrificed to strange worship on the high places. King Hezekiah had destroyed the high places and smashed their altars and then King Manasseh had come and reigned in his stead. He built the high places up again, set up altars to Baal, erected Asherot, and built

63

altars to all the host of heaven in the courtyards of the House of Jehovah. He passed his son through the fire to Moloch—the most abominable of all the perversions—in the valley of the son of Hinnom, so that a child of the royal House of David met his end in the burning fire that flamed in the belly of the molten idol of dark metal. They did not repent of their evil way and continued to do evil. Every generation thus went astray even unto our own generation. Zedekiah did evil in God's eyes, his princes acted perversely, and the sword of Nebuchadnezzar, king of Babylon, was stretched out over their necks. They did not go back from their evil way, even when the decree was fixed against them. They did not turn to the God of Abraham to seek salvation; they turned to Moloch and cried to him to save them. Then Jeremiah saw that their way was corrupted, and the indignation of God burned within him and he reproved them. He said to them in the name of Jehovah, that because they had put their abomination in the House of God to pollute it, and because they had built high places for Baal in the valley of the son of Hinnom to pass their sons and daughters through the fire to Moloch, the city would be given into the hand of the king of Babylon with sword and famine and pestilence.

"Sin piled upon transgression. Manasseh sawed the prophet Isaiah in two because he reproved him for the image he set up in the sanctuary. Zedekiah cast Jeremiah into a dungeon of loam where he might drown or perish of hunger and thirst. So why should God have mercy upon us? Alas and alack! Woe is unto us!"

Thus lamented Aryeh, son of Zachariah, over Judah which had corrupted its way and over its children whose teeth had been set on edge by the sour grapes that their fathers had eaten.

"Are the heathen better than we are? Why should God take vengeance on us and seem not even to notice their evil deeds? God has exacted retribution, penalty, and punishment for every sin and transgression we did. Only His own people did He exile from their land. Why is our portion worse than theirs?"

Thus spoke Samuel, out of the darkness, hoping to find some plea for the righteousness of Judah, even the sin of Judah.

"Why is our lot worse?" roared Aryeh. " 'You only have I known out of all the nations of the earth. Therefore shall I visit upon you all your iniquities.' That is what the prophet said in the name of Jehovah." The voice of Aryeh re-echoed through the mountains. "That is why the city was given into the hands of the king of Babylon and its precious ones were slain by the sword, famine, and pestilence.

"But in spite of all these things, even though they corrupted their way, even though sword, famine, and pestilence have been decreed for the city of Jerusalem, in which the princes set up the abominations of the heathen in the House of God and passed their children through the fire, it shall still be saved. For thus said the prophet in the name of Jehovah: 'Thus saith Jehovah, the God of Israel, to this city of which ye say: it is given into the hand of Babylon's king, sword, famine, and pestilence; behold I shall gather them in from all the lands to which I scattered them with my anger, wrath, and great indignation, and I shall bring them back to this place and I shall make them dwell securely. And they shall be my people and I shall be their God.'

"Thus, even thus, He spoke. But he also said when this would be. When we turn again unto God with a perfect heart. Thus spoke the prophet and this you should surely remember: 'I have given them one heart and one way to fear me all their days so that it be good for them and their children after them. And I shall make an everlasting covenant with them, that I shall not turn away from behind them, to do good to them. I shall put the fear of me into their hearts so that they turn not way from me.'

"Let us now arise, all as one man, and return all of us with a perfect heart and with an upright spirit to our God. Let us lay our supplications and prayers before Him—forgive and pardon for the sins of our fathers. . . . Come, for Thou alone can save us. Thou, with Thine own Hand and not flesh and blood. Then we

65

shall be saved. Arise, let us pour out our prayers, let us confess our sins and the sins of our fathers before Jehovah our God."

The whole congregation of Mourners of Zion arose, men, women, and children, and fell on their faces to the ground. They lifted up their hands to heaven. A heavy weeping and a great cry pierced the night. "Forgive us for our sins... our fathers have eaten sour grapes and the teeth of the children are set on edge." The men beat their breasts with their fists. They scooped up dust in the palms of their hands and threw it on their heads.

A bitter lamentation went wailing through the stillness of the night, in the vast hollow strewn with stars which embraced the mountains of Judah. It was like the howl of the jackal and the hyena, who lay in the clefts of rocks, making the desolation of night fearful with their desperate wailing.

The lad continued to dwell among the Mourners of Zion in the forgotten valleys of the mountains of Judah and used often to visit the cave of Aryeh, son of Zachariah, to learn from his lips the words of the prophets who prophesied in Judah and Israel. Their words became fluent in his mouth.

Samuel drank deep from what fountains of consolation he could find. At twilight he would come among the great ones of the Mourners of Zion in the bowl of the mountains. But his heart was beginning to rebel against the heavy nature of the penalty that the children had to endure for the sins of the fathers. His thoughts were not prepared to accept the truth that the zeal of God was such that it punishes sevenfold for every transgression with sword, suffering, pestilence, and plague.

The real and constant teachers of his heart were the mountains of Judah. Severe though these heights were, with their grim crags and cruel peaks, he still drew from the sight of them a lesson of the lovingkindness that God lavished on all his creation. His kindness was on everything and in spite of everything. His mercy extended to the flock of sheep and lean cattle that were in his keeping.

The love of a ewe that licked her lamb that she had just borne, which rolled beneath her feet and nuzzled her face as it tottered on uncertain legs. The love of the eagle and the hawk who soared proudly on their pinions and brought their daily prey in their beaks; the worms and insects; the fledglings in their nests. God's grace was the tranquillity which spread over forest and thicket, on the slope of the mountain and the ascent of the valley. This grace was in the cumulus clouds which floated like new-washed sheep in the firmament of the broad clear sky and cast joyous shadows like curtains rustling in the wind on the peaks of the hills. His grace was over the green valleys that twinkled upward through the clefts in the hills. The great joy which all creation expressed in songs of praise and thanksgiving to its Creator filled the heart of Samuel with love and thankfulness to God. He could in no circumstances attribute to the Creator of such a living happy world those words of rebuke, those harsh threats of punishments and retribution such as the prophets spoke when they reproved the people, laying bare their iniquities and pillorying their evil deeds.

The God of Israel was the Creator of the world. The God of Israel is not a cruel God, a jealous God, a Lord of Vengeance. He is merciful; He is the Creator of all. His love extends over all His creation. Man is the chosen of His creatures, formed in His image. He desired to endow some of His attributes upon him—His attributes of mercy and love—and to bring him unto Himself that he might love all things and be gracious and merciful even as He was. Man was the chosen of His creatures.

Once, on a bright clear day, thick heavy clouds began to appear in a corner of the west. The lad was pasturing his flock on a gentle slope when he beheld the dark menace of the sky; the clouds appeared full of wrath and indignation, like a pack of hounds hungry for blood. He had scarcely noted them when they emptied out their load of wrath, like skin bottles that burst and pour forth their contents in boiling, scalding streams. A moment passed and the foggy gloom was dissipated and succeeded by raging winds.

Like beasts of the forest let loose upon their prey, they blustered through the forests on the mountain roof, shaking and bending the trees, claws tearing and rending treetop, branch, and root. Thunder crashed and rolled, and the wind raged on, breaking and desolating everything in its path.

Samuel saw the sheep trying to dig in their hoofs and keep their foothold in the face of the all-devouring wind. He saw that it was too strong for them and that its fury was likely to sweep them away. The lambs were the first to slip; they lost their footing, failed to right themselves, and, struggling, hurtled out of sight. In agonized fear Samuel's heart turned to stone. He ran forward and threw his body down at a point along the slope where he might keep some of the flock from the fearsome drop to the rocks below. In his mind's eye he saw their legs broken, their blood in crimson patches on the steep mountain wall. Then he peered over the edge and, unbelieving, saw the sheep safe and sound below, in a green meadow which God had spread beneath them, as a mother spreads her apron to gather in her child. The older sheep, which had managed to grasp the teeth of the rocks with their feet, gaped down at the lambs and young ones safe in the meadow. There was joy in their gaze and happiness at the sight of their young ones who had miraculously been saved. Samuel, and the sheep with him, breathed again and relaxed after the mortal terror that had come upon them so suddenly.

He surveyed the cleft into the valley below. Between the up-rooted trees, the whole width of the steep mountain wall was jagged with spurs of rock that stabbed upward like needles. Evidently the whirling wind had been so strong that it carried the sheep over the stony jaws unharmed, to fall smoothly on the green bosom of the valley. How could this happen!

His eye was open to see visions and his ear sharp to hear a heavenly voice. The sheep which had fallen and been tossed about by the raging wind changed and were transformed in his imagination to Israel.

He came home and went to his mother.

"Mother," he said, "my eyes saw the hand of God."

There was a certain place on one of the peaks of those mountains from which a view on the east opened up and in a corner of which Jerusalem could be seen like a young hart on the hills. From the day that God had forsaken His city and handed it over to the destroyer so that the Holy Place became a center of impurity, the Mourners of Zion had refrained from entering its precincts. They even withheld their feet from treading on this peak lest they see Jerusalem from afar. Samuel had been straitly enjoined by his father not to go there, lest by some careless glance his eyes behold the city.

Samuel tried his utmost to obey his father in this and had to drag his feet back by force lest they find themselves at this observation point. But the power of his meditations was too strong, and there came a day when his sense of obedience was overcome. His head proved too much for his feet, and his desire to catch a glimpse of the city seemed to force his steps automatically to the forbidden spot. As he looked, it seemed to him that the city had not been built by men's hands but had come down from heaven and rested on the mountain. He saw heaps of houses sown on the slopes and paths going down into the wadis. His eyes looked for Mount Moriah. He imagined he saw fallen walls and heaps of ruins. He seemed to see pillars of smoke going up from altars among the ruins. He thought that they resembled a destroying presence with its hand outstretched over the city.

He closed his eyes quickly, for he wished to see no more; but the sight of the city could not be banished from his thoughts. He thought his father and the rest of the Mourners of Zion were right in not wanting even to catch a glimpse of the city in whose holy places foul impurity had taken up its lodging.

He was torn between two forces, one which drove him from the spot and another which magically drew him thither. He had scarcely gone down from the peak when he felt a compulsion to

69

return and see Jerusalem once more. Every morning at sunrise, his feet seemed drawn there of their own volition. His sentient mind turned in another direction, but his imagination directed them to the peak and made his heart dwell upon the ruins on Mount Moriah.

One morning:

The dew was heavy on the ground. The whole mountainside was shrouded in a gray-white mist, a kind of steamy vapor. Torn clouds floated in the vault of heaven and veiled the pinnacles of the hills in their bosom. They brooded heavily over the slopes of the hills and swirled up from the deep wadis. Everything hovered and swam. The sun did not go out of its canopy but seemed to proceed from a river of blood which was spread out in the eastern heaven. It seemed to struggle to free itself from the red billows and to put on strength from moment to moment. Finally the sun strode forth in power, robed in glory and majesty. Thousands of rays thrust out points like sharp spears and penetrated the mists and the veils of shadow which brooded over the hills. The rays broadened into sunbeams, to pillars of light in the grayness about them; they came down in shafts of light from the sky and illumined the earth below.

Suddenly Samuel, son of Solomon, now grown into a sturdy youth, noticed that his feet had led him once again to the peak from which one beheld Jerusalem. His flock of sheep was with him. His bare feet were planted in mossy undergrowth. His head was bare and the long black locks which hung over his neck were moist with dew, which also saturated his torn shepherd's tunic. He stood and looked at the city through the patch of brightness in the foggy sky. It seemed lifted up on the mighty pinions of cherubim and illuminated by thousands of rays. Jerusalem was suspended in space and surrounded by dewy clouds, misty with the swirling vapors and delicately veiled with fluttering, pure, light, cerulean, radiant wisps of cloud.

A magnificent dome was exalted over the pillars of sun-shot fog and swirling mists. It was effulgent with a golden halo which

70

encircled it like a rainbow and shone with all its glory of the seven primary colors. Suddenly a paean of song burst through to Samuel. The voice of the prophet made him tremble: "Come, let us go up to the mountain of Jehovah, to the House of the God of Jacob."

The lad said in his heart: My eyes are beholding the sacrifice of purification whereby God is cleansing the world with a cloud of incense.

Samuel closed his eyes. Afraid to look at the clouds, he stood shaking and quaking with an awful terror. Deep silence reigned, and Samuel felt it spread out and fill the whole vault of the universe. It wrapped him round and fear encompassed him. His whole body trembled with the awe and glory that the whole world apprehended.

Suddenly a voice rent the silence:

"You are not a jackal howling in the night unto Me. You are a songbird singing in the dawn unto Me. With song bring My comfort unto My people."

Samuel, son of Solomon of the House of Judah, knew that the voice was speaking to him, that it was he to whom the order was given.

He shut his eyes and with a fearful voice, shivering with terror, with arms stretched out to Heaven, he spoke into the cloud:

"They will not believe me. I am called Samuel. They will say: 'Your imagination makes you believe you are like him.' They will say: 'The lad is a dreamer, just like Joseph.'"

"From this day your name is no longer Samuel. From this time onwards you will be called Isaiah. His spirit is upon you."

"I am an ignorant shepherd lad, completely without instruction. My speech is stammering. I have no knowledge."

"Arise and go up to My city, Jerusalem. Find the sons of the prophets there in the cave; dwell among them and become one of them. When the day will come, I shall put a learned tongue in your mouth. Every morning I shall open your ear to know what you have to say and what you have to do."

# CHAPTER SIX

SHORTLY after Nebuchadnezzar had destroyed the Temple and exiled all but the poorest of the people, Jeremiah, before he was forced to go down into Egypt, had gathered together the remnant of his pupils who still cleaved to him. He found a hiding place for them in one of the hidden caves of the Temple Mount, beneath the ruins of the Sanctuary. The Chaldeans who besieged the hill knew nothing of this refuge. Jeremiah handed the sons of the prophets the scrolls of his own prophecies and those of the prophets who had preceded him. These had been deposited with him for safekeeping. There was, also, a copy of the letter that he had sent to the exiles in Babylon. Jeremiah exhorted and impressed upon his disciples to guard the holy spirit of prophecy so that it be not quenched, to study and repeat the words of the great Isaiah, to mourn the destruction of the Temple, to look forward with expectation to the coming of the redemption and to fit themselves to be prophets of truth and holiness.

When the young prophet Isaiah descended from the mountains of Judah and came among the sons of the prophets, his spirit of the redemption, which was dormant in them, awakened and uplifted them, and with him they sang the song of everlasting Israel: "Fear not, my servant Jacob, and be not dismayed, O Israel, for behold I save thee from afar and your seed from the land of captivity and Jacob shall return and be at rest and flourish and none shall make him afraid. Therefore, do not fear, O my servant Jacob, saith Jehovah, for I am with thee, for I shall wreak destruction upon all the nations to which I have dispersed you but you shall I not utterly consume and I shall chastise you in judgment but shall by no means clear the guilty. You shall receive your punishment but I shall not utterly make an end."

Judah and Israel, they concluded, are essential for the redemption of mankind, for the peace of the whole universe, for the change that will take place in the character of man and beast, for the eternal good that shall reign at the end of days. Without them there can be no redemption; among them, in their midst is sown the seed of the Messiah; their loins will bring forth the child as the prophet saith: "Unto us a child is born, unto us a son is given and the government shall be upon his shoulder and his name shall be called Wonderful, Counsellor, the Mighty God, the everlasting Father, the Prince of Peace...." Mighty God, obviously the Divine rulership with which God endowed Moses over Pharaoh. "And it shall come to pass in that day that the root of Jesse shall stand as a sign for the nations, nations shall seek him... and it shall come to pass on that day that God will again put forth his hand to gather in the remnant of his people who shall remain in Assyria and Egypt and Pathros and Ethiopia and Shinnar and Hamath and the isles of the sea; and He shall lift up an ensign to the nations and shall gather in the dispersed of Israel and the scattered ones of Judah shall He gather from the ends of the earth."

"For this day," cried the disciples of Jeremiah, "wait patiently; for this day prepare yourselves."

Although the sons of the prophets were few and isolated and hidden away in the clefts of the rock; although they were continually meditating on the words of the prophets and bearing them at all times on their lips, they were aware and alert to everything that was happening in the world roundabout them. Since they saw the finger of God in every incident that befell, believing that without His providence no blade of grass grows nor moves in the breeze, they used to weigh and consider every event by the gauge of its relevance to the redemption of Judah and Israel, to the return of the seed of Jacob from exile to the land which had been given to him to enjoy until the coming of the longed-for days of the

73

Messiah. The hope of the redemption of Judah and Israel was the only balm their thirsty souls knew. When the spirit of God descended upon them they would indulge in prophecies about the future. Their mouths would utter words moulded in the style of the great prophets of old and foretelling the coming days of the Messiah. In secret and hidden fashion they maintained living contact with the exiles. They set emissaries to Babylon and Egypt, the two great Diasporas. They encouraged and restored the souls of the exiles, comforting them and raising their hopes. They reminded them of the promise that God made through his servants the prophets, that he would once again gather in the scattered ones of Judah and Israel into their land. Sometimes one of them, when the holy spirit moved him, would be lifted up to prophecy in his own name. Sometimes the spirit came into him and he spoke in the manner of the great prophets of yore. Each one of them loved his own particular prophet to whose spirit he cleaved and by which he lived, whose style he adapted to himself and whose manner of prophecy he used. Thus they kept the coals of the great prophets aglow, and the flames they fanned were made to warm the hearts of the exiles.

But in those days the redemption seemed far, far away.

The outlook was black both in Babylon and Egypt. Not even the faintest ray of hope was discernible in the darkened heavens of Judah. It seemed as though his coal was utterly quenched beneath the ashes of heathen worship and impurity. The poverty of the remnant left in Judah had dragged them down.

Deprived of the presence of the priests, the Levites, the members of the royal family, the nobles and well-born, all of whom Nebuchadnezzar had taken to Babylon, the remnant were abandoned to the vagaries of fate. They quickly came under the influence of the Canaanites among whom they dwelt, adopting their customs and devoting themselves to their abominations. They were between two arms of a pincers. The Philistines on the seashore to the west and Moab on the east, profiting from the state of lawlessness which succeeded the fall of Judah, tore pieces from the living flesh of the State.

They devoured the district of Jericho and Hebron, coming close to the city of Jerusalem itself. Despised and humiliated in the sight of the neighboring peoples because of the low condition to which God had brought them, the shattered remnant of Judah began to declare openly that their downfall was because Bel Merodach and Ishtar, the gods of Babylon, were stronger than their God, Jehovah. A generation did not pass before they were openly and unashamedly serving the idols and abominations, in particular Ishtar, whose worship was widespread and deep-seated among all peoples from the Caspian Sea to the isles of Greece and beyond, from the mountains of Ararat to Ethiopia. Ishtar was sometimes worshipped under different names. Shrines and caves dedicated to her were established throughout Judah and even invaded the Temple mount and the ruins of sanctuary beneath the altar of Jehovah. The women baked sacrificial cakes and offered dough, bewailing Tammuz, the husband and brother of Ishtar. This they did not only in the streets of Jerusalem but among the broken walls of the Temple itself. They also practiced the vile customs of the Sodomites and the perversions which desert-wandering Moab brought to Judah, the worship of Moloch in the manner of the Sidonians and the Philistines. High places for the service of all these abominations were set up in the ruined Temple of Jehovah. At first the Judean remnant worshipped them in secret, but as time passed they did so openly. "Jehovah has forgotten us," they said; and it seemed they were glad to break off the yoke of His commandments and mix with the nations round about them and do just as they did.

While Ezekiel, the greatest prophet of his generation, was alive, he journeyed to and from Judah, continually chastising and rebuking the remnant in Judah and in Babylon, reminding them of their past and rousing their hopes for a happy future. He thus managed to preserve the coal of Judah by his words and his consolations so that the flickering flame did not die out altogether. He it was who first enunciated the principle of the individual responsibility of every man for his own sins that he had sinned. God does not demand punishment for sins from the whole people but from the individual. Each shall be brought to judgment only for his own offenses. "Are not all souls mine, as the soul of the father so also the soul of the son is mine; the soul that sinneth it shall die. The son shall not bear the iniquity of the father nor shall the father bear the iniquity of the son; the righteousness of the righteous shall be upon him and the wickedness of the wicked upon him." The people were warned not to delude themselves and think that God would pardon them on account of the merit of their ancestors or just because they dwelt in Jerusalem. "Even if Daniel, Noah, and Job dwelt among them; as I live, said the God Jehovah, they would not save their son or daughter." They would have to save themselves by their own righteousness.

But the mouth that decreed death upon man, woman, and child also knew how to speak words of consolation and to strengthen the confidence in redemption of those who remained. "And I shall gather you from among the peoples . . . and I shall put you in the land of Israel . . . and I shall take out the heart of stone from their flesh and give them a heart of flesh . . . and they shall be my people and I shall be their God." Whether they want it so or not! "And I shall gather you from the lands to which you are dispersed, with a strong hand and an outstretched arm and with wrath poured out."

Ezekiel set before them the wondrous vision of the dry bones which "came nigh bone unto bone and sinew unto sinew and flesh went up upon them and skin covered them . . ." also the vision of Jerusalem rebuilt and the house of God renewed and the worship restored for the redeemed people of Israel.

Thus the prophet transported them like some heaven-sent giant, with one hand to Sheol below, to the Valley of Dry Bones, and with the other he gathered the bones he had scattered and dispersed and roused them up to new life, planting within them not a heart of stone but of flesh, and a spirit of humility and submission.

But the prophet Ezekiel had been dead a long time; his voice was still and the situation in Judah and the Diaspora deteriorated. In Judah they backslid into the worship of abominations and idols. Even in the Exile they were not free of the taint of heathen worship, in Egypt and Babylon alike.

This was especially so in Babylon, where the flame of Judah and Israel still burned and flickered, where it seemed that on alien soil there might yet be a future for the people of Israel, where the scattered ones of the lost ten tribes and the exiles of Judah might be born anew. But it was actually from Babylon that ugly rumors began to reach the sons of the prophets who awaited the redemption in Jerusalem. A new class had made its appearance and become prominent among the exiles: a stratum of merchants, traders, and contractors to whom Babylon was the promised land. But besides those who lived in luxury in Babylon, the common folk, the smallholders, share-farmers, and tenants who worked the fat soil by the river Chebar and made it yield its rich produce, looked upon the words of Jeremiah exhorting loyalty to Babylon as a promise that it would be their home forever. They compared this fertile land with the barren rocky plots in Judah which had to be tilled with so much toil, to be cleared of stones and ploughed deep in every span. There were, of course, exiles who longed for their homeland, but these belonged to an older and aging generation whose hearts still retained memories of the Sabbaths and festivals in the Temple, whose minds had not lost the last echoes of the consolations of Jeremiah and Ezekiel.

But the second generation, Babylonian born, was assimilating into its environment. Their eyes wandered increasingly astray after the gods of the Babylonians, who inspired such reverence in the peoples and who had brought so much happier a lot. They compared these gods with the God Jehovah whom they knew only by hearsay and who was recalled as a severe God, stringently visiting punishment on every transgression small or large. These younger people were enchanted and bewitched by the majesty of the processions that were arranged in honor of the gods within the framework of the birth of the Babylonian New Year. Bel Merodach, Sin, and Shamash gradually became the revered deities of the younger generation of the exiles. Ishtar's worship took possession of the hearts of many women and young girls.

Sad and bitter, too, was the situation in Egypt. There there was no prophetic tradition, no leavening of the elders of Judah and its royal house. So the Jews rapidly assimilated. They became indistinguishable from their neighbors. They served in Pharaoh's armies. So great, indeed, was their desire to blot out the memory of Jerusalem and be free from even the slightest nostalgia for it that they resolved to build themselves a temple in Elephantine and offer up sacrifice in rivalry with the temple in Jerusalem.

From ancient times the prophets foretold the destiny not only of Israel but of all nations. God watches over all people and judges them according to their deeds. In the annals of the sons of the prophets in Jerusalem were inscribed the deeds and punishment that befell the nations for their sins, as the prophets foretold. When the young Isaiah came among them, he learned of the destiny of Ashir, of their behavior and their abominations and their end. He was told of the wild customs of the Sodomites, of their perversions, their cruelty in war, of the destructiveness which was left after the trampling of their chariots. Ashir was like a dragon with many poisoned tongues which sucked the blood of nations which they overran and Ashir believed that they would forever dominate and make waste many lands. Even in the days of their mightiest reign God branded them with the sign of death, as in the words He put in the mouth of Nahum of Elkosh:

> "Beloved, I am against thee, saith the lord of hosts.
> And I will burn the chariots in the smoke,
> And the sword shall devour the young lions;
> And I will cut off thy prey from the earth."

78

No other but Babylon did God choose to destroy Nineveh to its "foundations" and to wipe out Ashir from the face of the earth. In the eyes of the prophet Babylon became the inheritor of Syria, and as God sent the bull of Babylon to trod with his hoofs the serpent of Ashir, so will he send a lion to break the bull's neck. What Ashir did to Israel the prophet had been told, but what Babylon did to Judea he saw with his own eyes.

Like a lost soul, the young Judean prophet wandered among the ruins of the Temple, the desolate streets of Jerusalem and the broad places and silent squares of the city.

The city of David was reduced to heaps of dust and ruins, its houses piles of rubble. Miserable wretches, clad in rags and emaciated with hunger, roamed barefoot over the ruins, broken stones and gravel. Living corpses, consumed by leprosy and other diseases, skeleton-like figures crazy with suffering, seemed cast away in every place like utterly useless broken potsherds. They, too, looked like part of the rubble and heaps of dust around them. The houses which were in a somewhat better condition, having withstood the battering of the iron rams and projectiles of the conqueror, had been seized by Moabites, Edomites, Ashkelonites, Tyrians, and Sidonians who had come up to Jerusalem with the armies of Nebuchadnezzar. Many of these were set up as officers over the subjugated people. Wherever the eye of the prophet turned, it beheld ruin and desolation. An alien dwelt in the palace King Solomon had built and in which generations of the House of David had reigned. The conqueror exacted the servile tribute and the forced labor, squeezing out the last sap from the dried-up bodies of the remnant of the people.

Starving, abandoned to their misery by the wise and wealthy of their people, the forsaken remnant relapsed into the ignorant superstitions and idol worship of their neighbors. Here in the center of any square, in any market place, the prophet might behold a hastily erected altar, a carved monstrous image of Moloch, with a swollen belly which concealed a furnace which could be kindled with olive or palm branches. There an unhappy Jewess crouched with her sick child beside an image of Ishtar set up in the middle of the street and tended by a priest and kedeshot. The image of Baal looked down upon the wide square. There he stood, her perpetual staff in his hand, symbolic of power and might, while the Ammonite who came to him with his wives prayed that they be granted only male children.

Everywhere that the prophet turned in the city of David and Solomon, he beheld desolation and ruin of soul and spirit as well as of wood and stone. God had made Himself strange to them and they had estranged themselves from their God. So the vast majority of the poorest remnant of the people sank down into the barbarous customs of their neighbors, who had streamed into Jerusalem like a river which bursts its banks.

But worst of all was the situation on the Temple mount. Here was complete desolation; not one stone was left standing upon another. The site which Solomon had hallowed as a House of Prayer for all peoples was now dedicated to abominations, foremost among them being that of Moloch. The inner sanctuary, the Oracle of the House, had been half built up again, probably on the very spot where the priests had beforetime offered up the daily sacrifice. In it there now stood the image of Moloch, the abomination of desolation, whose belly was a vast and fiery furnace. The skies above the sanctuary, which had once hearkened to the psalms of the Levites praising God with trumpets and loud sounding cymbals, which had heard the song of King David, were now torn asunder by the screams of children cast into the burning maw of the molten image. Those floors which had re-echoed the word of God of the prophet Isaiah, the stones which had thrown back the reverberation of his preaching of salvation and redemption to all people throughout the whole universe, now gathered in the yells and shrieks of the raving devotees, the priests of Moloch. They capered in drunken frenzy and mad lust before their idol, their nakedness bare and revealed, in a dance of triumph to

Moloch whose tumult almost drowned out the wailing of the children thrown alive into the flames as a sacrifice.

On the sacred steps that led up to the sanctuary and the holy chambers, on the floors where Jeremiah had poured out his heart in lamentation over the disaster that was destined to be, harlot votaries sprawled lasciviously, priestesses of the prurient worship of the goddess Ishtar.

But in spite of all this, it never entered the young prophet's mind even for a moment, even by way of parable, that Jehovah had forsaken his people forever and chosen another to bear the responsibility for His Law. No! God was not a man that he should change his mind. The Holy One of Israel does not deceive. He had bound up His glory with that of Israel, from the beginning of their days, from the time of the covenant with Abraham, and would not give of His glory to another. But how long? How much strength has a man, has a people, to wait? The people of Israel were close to annihilation, like a candle-end whose flame burns feebly, fluttering to extinction. Judah was like a tiny island upon which the breakers were crashing and the storm rolling in on all sides in such relentless fury that it seemed likely to be engulfed; that its very place would know it no more. In but a short time, Israel would be indistinguishable from the petty, savage tribes of the wilderness. Those maggots, Ammon and Moab, were slowly gnawing at her vitals from within, while from without the ravening beasts, Egypt and Babylon, were tearing living portions from her. Jerusalem would be reckoned as a desert, as one of the cities of Ammon or Moab or Edom that surrounded her and threatened to strangle her. If this indeed be the lot apportioned unto her, then what would happen to the promises made to the fathers? Would the labors of Moses, the work of David, be at last in vain? What would happen to the hope of every living man for redemption here upon earth? The cry of Isaiah and the lament of Jeremiah would have been but a voice crying in the wilderness. Yet a little while longer and there would be nothing left to save!

When his soul was too heavily burdened under the weight of

81

reflections such as these, the young prophet would go into solitude in one of the caves underneath the Temple mount. He would remain there withdrawn, and pray alone. As his body dried up as a result of his spiritual sufferings and continual fasting, his soul became more and more exalted. His yearning for redemption, his zeal for the God of Israel, his love for Jerusalem and his passion to see the redemption of Judah and Israel, ennobled and lifted up his spirit. He began to see visions. He heard a voice talking out of the midst of them. It was as though God had rent asunder for him the window of the future. At times he saw Jerusalem, her glory renewed, new radiance shining upon her, song and exultation bursting forth in melody from her ruins. Like the prophet whom he revered, Isaiah the great, he too saw the mountain of the Lord set up at the head of the mounts and lifted up above the valleys. He saw all people flowing unto it and awaiting the Law which would come out from Zion. He saw peoples living in the far-off islands raising up their eyes towards Jerusalem, longing for the light which would shine forth from her to light up the dark places. The House of Israel and Jerusalem were bound up with God in one bond of glory and the name of God was called upon them. So long as Jerusalem was still a ruin and the House of Israel dispersed, the honor of God was despised and made a byword among the nations. When Israel was redeemed and Jerusalem built up again upon its mound, then the glory of God would be lifted up on every lip. The House of Israel would never perish again and Jerusalem would never more be laid waste, for God had called His name upon them both, saying, "Mine art thou!"

The imagination of the sons of the prophets had created almost a living image of Zion. She was personified in the form of a widow who wandered among the ruins of the Temple and raised up her lamentation in the night watches, as our mother Rachel had done, whose voice the prophet of the destruction had heard in Ramah, a voice of weeping and bitter lamentation, as she bewailed her children and refused to be comforted.

In the meditations of the young prophet, who had but recently come among the sons of the prophets, the two matriarchs, mother Zion and mother Rachel, became fused into one entity—mother Israel.

His stark desire to see this mother of Israel with his own eyes bore fruit in his imagination as a visual image. He beheld her likeness as a kind of shadow of a woman, wandering among the ruins of the Temple as the sun went down, or sitting upon a stone with her arms outstretched to heaven and tears flowing from her eyes. Ah, how his soul was consumed with longing to see her with his own eyes! Ah, to comfort her with the blessing of hope and consolation! The bounteous abundance of that blessing filled his heart as juice fills a pomegranate! He felt the hope burst into life within him like a burgeoning fruit. Israel would not be consumed for ever, for God was with her, and would be though she suffer what she had to suffer. Had he not heard in his heart the voice of God speaking about Israel? "When thou passest through water, I am with thee, and through the rivers, they shall not sweep thee away; when thou goest through fire—thou shalt not be burned; flame shall not scorch thee, for I am Jehovah thy God, the Holy One of Israel, thy Saviour."

He went out at night and sought the shadow that brooded over the ruins of the Sanctuary. He sought her as a lover seeks the adored one of his heart, for his soul went out to her until he saw her.

She appeared to him by the light of the moon. Over the whole of Mount Moriah was woven a silver tapestry of pure moonlight and misty darkness. The jagged points of the broken walls were blurred and blended in the daze of the chiaroscuro. The stars looked down from the heaven in gentle radiance and their twinkling sparkle mingled with the effulgence of the moon in the hollow of night, forming a curtain now opaque, now transparent as a veil, which shrouded the ruins of the Temple, the whole mountain, and its slopes and deep valleys.

While he stood there with trembling and fearful heart he heard a voice: "Who out of all my lovers shall comfort me?"

He looked around and his eyes beheld her. There, wrapped in darkness, was standing the mother, mother Israel, with the radiance of the moon and stars falling upon her ebon veil and weaving a tapestry of brightness upon the black of her mourning.

Isaiah closed his eyes, so as not to behold her with his sensory vision. He fell on his knees before her: "Alas, O our mother!"

"I am the mother of the child Israel. All have left him to his groaning; all his friends have acted treacherously towards him. But I shall not forsake him even though he be thrust away from before God. I know of no wrong that he has done. I know only of the chastisements that he has suffered. My blood is in his veins, my blood feels the pain when he is in affliction even before he himself feels it. Who, who shall comfort me, for great is my trouble...?"

"O my mother, O my mother, behold and see, God has woven a precious garment for you; he has robed you in a cloak of his lovingkindness and mercy, the robe of your glory for the great day, the day of rejoicing when it shall come. Behold and see, God is cleansing your house, purifying it of all uncleanness. Straight and pure shall your House stand to welcome your children when they come in unto it. Pure shall they go forth from the furnace of affliction, purged by flames of fire. Like sheep going up from their washing, like a lamb after shearing, your children shall come back. Listen to the voice of your God who calls to you, in the days of starlight welcoming you:

"Thus saith Jehovah; thus he speaks to you:
For the Lord hath called thee as a woman forsaken and
    grieved in spirit,
And a wife of youth, when thou wast refused,
Saith thy God.
For a small moment have I forsaken thee,
But with great mercies will I gather thee."

"Since the days of Jeremiah no man has comforted me as you have done, O my son. Rise up, my son; go unto my children who are scattered and driven away in the Exile. Be the comforter of Israel as you have been to me. O my son! 'Comfort ye, comfort ye, O my people...'"

He opened his eyes. The woman was no longer there. Isaiah returned to the sons of the prophets with a new song in his heart, the song of comfort for the mother of Zion.

Thus God every morning opened Isaiah's ear to hear and his eye to see. He heard voices which none of his companions, the sons of the prophets, had heard and saw visions they had not seen. While the sons of the prophets were sunken in the darkness of mourning and beheld only ruins and destruction and desolation that the ravagers had wrought, the young Samuel, that is Isaiah, saw the hand of God preparing the way for the redeemed ones to pass over. He was a beam of light cast in the darkness and a path of green grass stretching out in a desert. "Prepare the way! Prepare the way!" The words sang themselves from some depth within him and burst out into a joyful shout of comfort.

"Do you not see that the redemption is hastening to come?"

The sons of the prophets did not understand him and great was their amazement at his words, for he claimed to see the redemption while all around was mortal darkness, destruction, and ruin. They said one to the other:

"A bridegroom has come among the mourners. He is setting up a wedding canopy in a graveyard. What voices are these that he hears, that come not to our ears? What visions does he see that are not vouchsafed unto us?"

He was called by the name Isaiah, after the great prophet. He spoke in the manner of his namesake and his spirit rested upon him. It seemed as though Isaiah had risen from the dead in the person of this newcomer, this mysterious youth whom no one knew; that the spirit of Isaiah really moved in him. The power of prophecy surged within him to a greater measure than any of the sons of the prophets in the caves. A supernatural inspiration rested upon him. It seemed that the Holy Spirit had truly endowed him and consumed him as a sacrificial calf is burned upon the altar. Then his mouth poured out such powerful words of hope, such mighty confidence in the redemption, that consternation fell upon the other sons of the prophets.

He broke forth into song and good tidings of the redemption that was on its way. He proclaimed that the iniquity of Jerusalem was appeased, that God had blotted out the transgressions of the house of Israel and would no longer remember its sins. There was no setting of a fixed time for God. When He felt so inclined, He would burst every dam which stayed his progress, even the rule laid down by His prophets. Throughout the city feelings of excitement, awe, and wonder were aroused by the utterances of the new prophet.

Sometimes he sang the Oneness and Uniqueness of the God of Israel, the First and the Last, uplifted over all things beside Whom there was no other, Whose righteousness was upon every man. Sometimes he would recount the lovingkindness and love of God for all His creation, bringing out of the hidden darkness of the cave new hope for all. He would stress the loyalty of the House of Jacob to their God and their high privilege that He had chosen them from all the nations. Sometimes God would bring him a vision of the coming of the Redeemer, of the feet of the harbinger of good tidings moving over the hills of Jerusalem. He would tell of the advent of the Messiah of Jacob, for whose coming the distant isles also waited. His words found a ready response in many of the sons of the prophets. The spark of prophecy was kindled in them too. They too saw visions of the coming of the redemption. Then everyone would begin in his own language and in his own style to recount the greatness of the Holy One of Israel, the hope of Israel which is that of the whole world; that of the redemption and the Redeemer.

One day, rumors spread among the remnant of Judah that Cyrus, king of Persia, had prevailed over the king of Babylon and was lopping off province after province from his empire. Without even having to bend his bow, he was subduing land after land. He had reached the isles of Greece; the island of Cyprus was his, and his armies were already encamped at the gates of Tyre and Sidon. Wherever he came he proclaimed freedom to the nations and liberated them from the Babylonian yoke. He drove away the Babylonian officers and the taskmasters who thirsted for their blood, and restored the rule to those who had held dominion before the Babylonian conquest. He proclaimed the slaves freemen and lightened taxes and exactions. Hope and expectations were aroused among the remnant of the people in Judah.

When the good tidings reached the sons of the prophets who were hidden in the caves beneath the Temple, the new Isaiah was hidden away in solitude in a cleft in the rock under the ruins of the Sanctuary. After several days of isolation and exaltation, his soul was uplifted. In a vision he heard a voice of troops, of hosts coming from afar. He heard the march, the tramping of feet of many legions borne on the wind like the noise of the breakers of the sea beating upon the coast with a great sound. Nothing could withstand the onsurge of their mighty power. Every way was made clear before them; all the rough places were smoothed out. Suddenly, a mighty hand seized him and lifted him up to the land of vision.

The prophet saw the redemption by the inner light of his senses. He saw Israel going out for the second time from the house of bondage: their literal exodus from Egypt. A highway split open in the sea. Great billows rolled backward and rose in two walls on both sides of the path and in their midst passed Israel. They gathered together and came from the four corners of the earth. Then he heard the beating of strong pinions descending, winging down over the high, bare places, bringing the dispersed ones of Judah and Israel from the four corners of the earth, from West and East and North and South. All who belonged to Jehovah, all who had God's name called upon them, all whom God had created for His glory, all came and gathered together. But this was a different house of Israel. The pierced eyes of the blind slave were opened and he could see. He beheld the Unique God in His Holiness ruling in lovingkindness over all his creatures.

The voice of God was heard in his heart; a new spirit breathed in him, like dew, like rain freely falling upon the parched places of the wilderness, like a howling desert that becomes fruitful and blossoming. Thus did Israel flourish and become refreshed with the new spirit. The soul of Israel was thirsty for God and He gave them to drink deep of the springs of His praise. Israel was purified and the House of Jacob was newly born, walking with a song in its heart along the road that leads to the homeland. The wilderness was a fruitful garden at its feet, a Divine garden green and fragrant, for it was watered with the dripping of dew by God Himself. Nor did Israel alone walk this way of the wilderness with God in their hearts and His praise on their lips. The beasts of the field, the serpents and scorpions went with them. They crawled out of the clefts of the rocks and the cisterns, creeping unto the brooks, to the pools of water that God had spread out in the howling wilderness for Israel's sake. They imbibed the pure waters with which God had moistened the desert and they were redeemed from the lot of the cursed creeping things. Their eyes, too, were opened to the knowledge of God. A mighty song rose exultant in the wilderness from the throats of man and beast; a paean of praise to the One and Unique God Jehovah of Israel. For when God purified the House of Israel from all their sins, He purified the whole earth and wiped away all evil from His creation.

Then the prophet heard a voice calling in his heart: "Arise and go to Babylon and bring my people the word of consolation. . . . Comfort ye, comfort ye, my people!"

# CHAPTER SEVEN

H E lodged in the hovel of Neraiah, son of Seraiah, who
worked as a day laborer on the ferry boats of the wealthy
Malchiah Gavra, who possessed a fleet of such vessels
which plied on all the canals of Babylon. They carried passengers
from shore to shore and from street to street, for Babylon had no
bridges. Malchiah had obtained the concession for the ferries from
Balshazzar, who was his sleeping partner in the venture.

Neraiah lived in this hovel with his aged father. Ama-Bar, his
wife, cared for them. When the prophet came to Babylon, the
family took him in. Neraiah built a hut of reeds roofed with palm
branches beside his miserable hovel and placed it at Isaiah's disposal. Its sole furnishings were a pallet, a table and a crude bench.
On the table lay a supply of parchment, some scrolls including
works of the prophets who had spoken in Judah and Israel, especially those of the former Isaiah and Jeremiah. There were also
writing materials, quill pens, styluses, and clay tablets. The prophet
would pronounce his prophecies as the spirit of God rushed upon
him in synagogues on the Sabbath and in the market places during
the week. Then in the quiet of his hut he would write them down
on the clay tablets just as they poured from his heart. Neraiah
would dry them in the sun. Sometimes he wrote them in a kind
of dye upon plates of clay, especially the psalms of praise which
took shape in his mind in moments of grace.

The generous Ama-Bar took care of his modest wants. She prepared his simple meal of barley bread, olives, grits, and vegetables, saw that his robe and headdress were clean, and changed
the straw of his pallet. She believed that a man of God dwelt in

the shadow of her roof and revered him as such. Her husband, Neraiah, had devoted himself utterly to the prophet from the moment his foot had first crossed his threshold. The hut of reeds and thatch appeared to the couple as a holy tabernacle since it was there the prophet prayed. There he sought solitude and shut himself in with the Holy Spirit in the times when grace descended on him. In all Babylon, only this family knew the prophet.

The prophet wished to know everything that went on in the strange city. He often accompanied Neraiah, who worked on the ferry which connected a great marketplace with the Avenue of the Processions as it debouched near the gate and sanctuary of Ishtar. The exit to this thoroughfare was dominated by the E-Sagila, the sanctuary of Bel Merodach. This was a very ancient tower soaring up to the sky from a ziggurat, a building formed terrace upon terrace like the plinth of a vast monument. The tower began to rear its height heavenward only from the seventh layer. Narrow staircases leading from terrace to terrace and from tower to tower covered the surface of the outer walls. Along the whole length of the Avenue of the Processions, which was closed in by massive high walls, merchants sold their wares to the devout who came to worship; small idols, teraphim for the household and images of the gods fashioned from wood, clay, or copper. The sick, diseased, halt, blind, and lame were brought by relatives on litters, crossing the canal by ferry to the temples.

"Where are they taking the sick, to the gates of the temples?" asked the prophet.

"Yes. They come here to buy amulets and charms, to purchase enchantments from their priests, or to ask advice of others smitten with the same disease."

"Neraiah! I want to go to the gates of the temples, to behold these heathens in their impurity and blindness."

"Thou, O prophet blessed of God, to go to the gates of the idolatrous worship!"

"Let us draw near and see these heathen in their abomination, so that I might know how exalted and chosen are Israel."

Thus the prophet, who had been enjoined not to defile his body with any manner of contact with the strange people or their strange worship, stepped off the ferry and joined the stream of idol worshippers.

Behind the Temple of Ishtar was a vast tract completely bare of buildings. This space was kept clear of houses or obstructions for use in an emergency. Should the city be besieged or should famine break out, then these fields could be ploughed and made to yield a harvest to feed the citizens. In normal times, the space served as a market place especially for craftsmen who made, and merchants who sold, all manner of idols; carved, molten, chiseled, and hewn. It was thronged with a multitude of worshippers who covered the plain like a troubled sea of moving heads. Men, women, and children of every people and tongue crowded up against the stalls of the peddlers and the tables of the craftsmen. Persians, Medeans, distinctive in their black robes and their woven beards, pushed through the crowds mountainous under their bales of sheepskin furs from the land of Elam. Syrians and Assyrians jostled shepherds and bedouin from the deserts of Kedar. All haggled over the images of Ishtar, Bel Merodach, Sin, and Shamash as quickly as their makers finished them.

The prophet drew near a woodcarver's stall and saw an artist forming a wooden figurine of Ishtar holding two doves to her breast. As the shavings fell the craftsman swept them under a small stove on which stood a pot in which his gruel was cooking. A Babylonian woman holding a sick child in her arms was already dealing with him over the price of the idol before he had completed it. She was imploring him not to be sparing of the red dye for its face. The craftsman finished the figure off, smeared its navel with honey and put it, with deep reverence and religious awe, to the lips of the sick child. In exchange, he took what the conversation had revealed to be the very last kid of the poor widow's flock.

Nearby a rich Babylonian was bargaining with a seller of idols. The negotiation concerned a mighty stone statue of Bel Merodach.

It was embellished with a crown of false precious stones and a carved serpent twined around its feet. This was an important transaction, and the parties were surrounded by a large and gaping crowd. All were enthralled with the idol. They freely expressed their views on its size, workmanship, and value, encouraging the purchaser and telling tales of how it had wrought wonders; how it had the power to perform miracles on behalf of whoever was fortunate enough to set it up in his house.

"Six years were my wives barren and I had no heir. Then I got a small figure of Ishtar and installed it in the chamber of my favorite wife. She merely looked at it, offered a pinch of incense and immediately became pregnant." So, glancing longingly at the idol, declared a gross and corpulent Babylonian, whose fleshy and thick neck supported a fat eunuch-like visage.

These praises captivated the heart of the purchaser. A scribe was called to draw up the contract of sale. The terms were cut into a clay tablet. The seller impressed his seal, which hung from his girdle, upon the writing. The bargain concluded, huge Ethiopian slaves hefted down four large sacks of barley flour from a wagon harnessed to two oxen which was standing nearby. They deposited them at the feet of the merchant, heaved the idol on to the wagon, laying it down reverently on the chaff-strewn floor and covering it with a large beautifully colored cloth. The wagon creaked into motion and drew away from the square accompanied by receding cries of admiration for the idol from the crowd which gradually dispersed.

The rich, who panted after the great idol, did not claim the attention of the prophet as much as the poor and miserable who brought their sick with them. They scraped in the bottom of their sacks and satchels to buy something with the last of their possessions. The few eggs, small pieces of handwoven cloth, balls of wool, which they produced were grudgingly accepted by the traders. In exchange, they received small and poorly executed figures of Ishtar which they coveted in the belief that they would cure a sick child, open a barren womb, make a cow fertile or increase its milk yield. In this place, Ishtar prevailed over all the gods. Her name was on everyone's lips. There was a perpetual wild scramble to buy images of her made of all kinds of materials in all sorts of shapes. Pushing eagerly through the crowd, a feeble father, a poor mother, a brother, a solicitous sister, made their way to the litter of the sick person and held the newly bought idol to his lips. The patient gathered up the last remnants of his strength and took the idol in his eager hands confident of its virtue to heal. Feeble moving lips were pressed to its navel; trembling hands caught it to the heart while the patient with tight-shut eyes murmured a fervent prayer. The image was his last hope.

The Temple of Ishtar so overflowed with the hordes of worshippers that the priests were forced to arrange services in the open air, offering up incense on tripods set up around the temple to serve as altars. The open space in front of Ishtar's sanctuary was lively with the fluttering shadows of flights of doves circling above it. A multitude of women, young and old, congregated about the steps and threshold, feeding the doves with crumbs of wafers and all kinds of holy bread which they had prepared as a sign of reverence for Ishtar. The square resounded with the whirr of wings, the cooing of the doves, the stir, movement, and chatter of the devotees. But this innocent sport of feeding doves was not the only way in which the women served Ishtar. They also offered the most precious gifts they could devote: their virginity, chastity, and sense of modesty and shame.... The pathways and steps of the temple were infested with women of all ages.

The Babylonians were not the only people to be sunk in this degrading sin. The whole world, all peoples, races, and lands, polluted themselves with it. From the Caspian Sea to the Isles of Greece; from the mountains of Ararat to the deserts of Yemen and beyond. Every knee bowed to the goddess, every hand was stretched out to her imploringly; her name was on every lip.

That night the prophet lay wakeful upon his pallet in the hut adjoining Neraiah's hovel. The stars looked down on him through the openings between the palm branches. Isaiah lay gazing at the deep blue of the star-strewn heaven as though seeking to penetrate the film which veiled off the upper worlds and come into contact with the supernal beings; with the chariot that Ezekiel had seen, bearing the cry of his heart directly to Heaven. His heart was one consuming flame—a fire of jealousy for the God of Israel.

"Are their eyes plastered over so that they see not ... their brains paralyzed that they know not; that they serve the work of their hands? For their gods are wood and stone, ivory and iron! Is there no understanding among them to perceive that they are groping like the blind in total darkness? And we? Shame and isolation have overtaken the House of God in Jerusalem. The House of Jacob is dispersed among the nations; the whole world is bathed in pollution. They have erected temples for evil and abomination. They have established sanctuaries towering up to high heaven. Their priests are eunuchs and harlot votaries, their holy places are brothels.... And the God of hosts fortifies himself within His Heaven of heavens!

"How long, O God of Hosts; how long will You wait and hold Your peace?" the prophet roared like a lion in his bitterness of heart. "You yourself said that You are the First and the Last and beside You there is none else."

He buried his face in his hands. His heart, rather than his eyes, wept within him; he thought:

"Alas! Maker and father of all creatures, why have you thus smitten with blindness the beings you have set upon earth? Why have You spread a disease of dark nights over their eyes? You have made their hearts hard as flint and their intelligence and comprehension have You turned into ignorance and stupidity. They neither know nor understand, neither see nor feel. Their eyes are not opened nor do their brains reason that they should say: 'One part of the tree trunk I burned in fire. I even baked bread upon its coals. I roasted meat and ate it; then from the rest I made me an idol? Am I then worshipping a block of wood?' O Father of all creatures, have mercy upon Your creation! Open

94

up one crack in the mortal darkness of their lives so that they should see that You alone are the First and the Last; there is no God beside You. O God of all the Universe! fill the whole world that You created with Your glory. Open the hearts and eyes of all beings that are sealed so they see not straight. Let every knee bow before You and every mouth call unto You; for You alone are God over Your creation!"

While he was lying thus immersed in the intensity of his prayer, he heard a voice calling in his heart. It pierced through his mind saying: "Cyrus shall do this."

"Cyrus," he thought, "is God's servant who sent him not just to free Israel, but to release the bonds everywhere and set the prisoners free. It is God who opens all the ways before Cyrus, throws open every gate and breaks down every wall. Cyrus will drag down all the abominations from their pedestals, will destroy all the idols, will bring all the peoples to the God of hosts, to the God who holds him by his right hand and leads him along. Then the eyes of the people will perforce be opened; they will see that their gods have no power to save them from Cyrus. Moloch is not wise enough to deliver Tyre and Sidon from him. Assyria's gods are useless to her. Bel Merodach stands like a senseless block unable to rescue Babylon from the legions of Cyrus. The wisdom of Nebu is of no avail to save the great city. In vain do they pray to Sin and Shamash; in vain they supplicate Ishtar, goddess of fornications. All of them, to the very last of them, are as broken potsherds, whose only fate is the dung heap. They have no purpose and no manner of mission to fulfill. The gold and silver idol of Bel Merodach will be melted down and vessels for the use of men be fashioned from it, goblets and pitchers. The images of Ishtar will feed the bonfires. They will light a fire to warm men's bodies and heat the ovens to bake their bread. The stone image of Nebu will be a doorstep or a lintel and the iron statue of Sin shall become a ploughshare or a sledge. Dust and sand will they become as they were in the beginning. But the God of Israel, the God of

95

Hosts, will once more rule alone over earth and heaven and all His creatures.

> "Thus saith Jehovah, King of Israel
> And his Redeemer;
> I am the First and the Last
> And besides me there is no god else."

A longing burned within him to see the fulfillment of his namesake's and predecessor's prophecy that "the mountain of Jehovah's House shall be established in the top of the mountains, and shall be exalted above the hills and nations shall flow unto it." This desire so penetrated his bloodstream that it determined his whole prophetic outlook and gave him clarity of vision to foresee future events. His prophetic spirit raised him up and carried him to distant lands; but so realistic was his vision that he seemed to see what he imagined with corporeal eyes. Ships sailing the seas, caravans of camels and asses crossing the desert, throngs of men ascending the hills, going down into the valleys and toiling up the heights, all pressing on to one goal: the mountain of Jehovah, the House of the God of Jacob. He beheld them, all the peoples of the world, in their distinctive national dress, each with the mark of his nationhood upon him, holding their children by the hand and bearing gifts for the God of Israel; saying one to the other: "Come ye, and let us go up the mountain of Jehovah, to the House of the God of Jacob; and He will teach us of His ways and we shall walk in His paths; for out of Zion shall go forth the Law and the word of Jehovah from Jerusalem."

Israel was but a vessel in the hand of God, Who had created her only that from her midst should the Redeemer go forth who would bring good tidings of God to all people that dwell on earth. For this reason the salvation of Israel could well come from an emissary whom God would choose from among the gentiles. For were not all nations and all kings His messengers formed to do His will? Cyrus, going up with his hosts against Babylon, was

His agent, charged to proclaim freedom to Israel and bring redemption to the whole world.

Did he not hear the earth trembling under the tramp of the feet of the mighty hosts? Their warriors are innumerable, they cover the eye of the earth. As all rivers flow to the sea so they all come, all the nations of the world. All nations whose necks were bowed under the yoke of Babylon come unto Cyrus, who releases them. They join the ranks of his armies and they all march together forward against Babylon. He hears their tread, the stamping of the hoofs of their horses. Their arrows are sharp and all their bows bent. Their wheels are like a whirlwind, quiet at first, but increasing in tumult and terror, coming nearer and nearer with fear in its wings.

The prophet sees them approach. They come. They come. He sees Cyrus and his hosts nearer and yet nearer. With his very eyes he beholds him. His heart is stirred and his hands and feet are a-tremble. The Spirit of God goes with Cyrus. Powerful is the Spirit, like that of a whirlwind, breaking a way for him in the wilderness. It is a terrifying spirit, rolling like a pillar of fire before the hosts of Cyrus, sweeping every obstacle from his path, crushing every wall, throwing open every gate, drying up rivers, grinding every army that withstands him exceedingly small. This can only be because Jehovah has taken Cyrus by his right hand and is leading him to Babylon to loosen every bond and fetter. He will lead him into the innermost dark places, into the most remote chambers where deathly darkness reigns and will make him illuminate them. For the darkness is Babylon and the light is the radiance of the God of Israel, Who opens all eyes and implants wisdom in all hearts. This is the knowledge of the God of Israel, the One God beside Whom there is none else, Who breathed life into the nostrils of man, creating all living things and keeping dominion over them.

Word passed swiftly from mouth to mouth among the exiles that the strange prophet was a man of vision bearing good tidings.

He was indeed to proclaim the word of God concerning the immediate future in the synagogue of the exiles of Bethlehem which was situated in the Street of the Saddlers. On the coming Sabbath, he would announce his good tidings.

Clothed in his white cloak he stood a little above the mass of worshippers who crowded and overflowed the house of assembly. They saw a man incandescent with the fire which flamed from his heart. He lifted them up over wildernesses as an angel from Heaven who soars in his mission beyond the empyrean heights. First he painted a picture of his experiences in the broad place before the temple of Ishtar, amid the makers of abominations. He cried out against the blindness of the heathens immersed in idolatry, their lack of understanding and feeling. He reminded Israel of her duty, from which there was no escape, to cleave to the One God, since for this alone had Jacob been created. God created His people to be His servant. Even though they sin, He still retained them in that office. "I have blotted out your transgressions like a cloud; return unto Me for I have redeemed you."

"All my bones say who is like unto Thee...." In very truth every limb of the prophet expressed his burden of utterance. Now he sang the song of deliverance, now he seemed to dance in the joy of redemption.

The body of the prophet swayed almost sensuously in a dance rhythm as his mouth sang:

"Sing, O ye heavens!
Shout aloud, O earth below.
Burst out in song, O ye hills! the forest and every tree therein;
For God hath redeemed Jacob
And glorified himself in Israel.
Thus saith Jehovah, thy Redeemer,
And He that formed you from the womb,
I am the Jehovah that maketh all things....
That confirmeth the word of His servant,
And performeth the counsel of His messengers;

98

That saith to Jerusalem, Thou shalt be inhabited;
And to the cities of Judah, Ye shall be built,
And I will raise up the decayed places thereof:
That saith to the deep, Be dry,
And I will dry up the rivers.
That saith of Cyrus, He is my shepherd,
And shall perform all my pleasure;
Even saying to Jerusalem: Thou shalt be built;
And to the Temple: Thy foundation shall be laid."

A wave of emotion passed through the congregation, a rustle of men disturbed, amazed, and bewildered. Half suppressed cries of mingled exultation and rage broke out on every side. This was the first time the name that rang in every brain had been mentioned openly and aloud. It had been whispered from lip to lip but none had dared to proclaim openly: "CYRUS!" What did the prophet mean by the words: "Cyrus, he is my shepherd"?

But the prophet took up his parable again and spoke words about which there could be no misunderstanding:

"Thus saith the Lord to his anointed, to Cyrus,
        Whose right hand I have holden
To subdue Nations before him;
        And I will loose the loins of kings.
To open before him the two-leaved gates
        And the portals shall not be shut.
I will go before thee
        And make the crooked places straight.
I will break in pieces the gates of brass
        And cut in sunder the bars of iron.
And I will give thee the treasures of darkness
        And the hidden riches of secret places;
That thou mayest know that I, Jehovah, which call thee
                by name,
        Am the God of Israel."

99

"A message from God! Good tidings from Heaven!..."

"Cyrus will burst apart the walls of Babylon? Will he break down the gates of brass?"

"What! He, conquer Babylon?"

Such were the cries that arose from every side. People shouted in frenzy: "The redemption is at hand!" But some among the congregation also cried aloud:

"Cyrus! A gentile? You call a gentile the anointed of God?"

"What have you to do with Cyrus, an idol worshipper! A man who knows not God. Is that the Messiah of Jehovah?"

But the prophet did not allow the congregation to interrupt him. His voice soared far above their heads, beating down the cries of dissent:

"For my servant Jacob's sake, and Israel mine elect,
I have even called thee by thy name;
I have surnamed thee, though thou hast not known me.
I girded thee, though thou hast not known me.
That they might know from the rising of the sun and from
    the West
That there is none beside Me."

"He speaks in riddles and parables," cried an elder. "Tell me what he means when he talks of 'the treasures of darkness and the riches of secret places' that Jehovah will give Cyrus!"

"He refers to the heathen nations who dwell in darkness, in whose hearts night dwells; they will be handed over by God to Cyrus," explained another.

"What! To Cyrus and not to a Messiah from the House of David! Cyrus will be the King Messiah? He is out of his mind!"

The shouts of dissent did not cease. They increased. Threatening hands were uplifted, clenched fists were raised towards the prophet.

"He called a benighted heathen and idol worshipper the Messiah! He surnames the Messiah one of the devotees of the blind abomination! Now this prophet shows how useless and

100

barren he is! Where does he come from? Who sent him? The spirit of darkness?"

The prophet ignored the shouts. He answered his interrupters in the name of God:

"I am Jehovah and there is none beside Me.
I form the light and create darkness;
I make peace, and create evil;
I, Jehovah, do all these things."

"The God of Israel is not like those of other nations," one of the elders of the congregation explained to those about him. "The heathens have gods of light and of evil, of darkness and of good. But our God is One, there is none beside Him."

"Do you mean to say," asked another, "that both good and evil are the work of God and if He chooses to make use of evil to achieve His ends, it is in His power to do so?"

"Yes. Just as He used Babylon as the staff of His anger to smite Assyria, He now uses Cyrus to smite Babylon."

"In other words, Cyrus is not the Messiah but merely a tool in the hand of God," argued a third elder.

The prophet paid no heed to the disputants. He was in such an ecstasy of melody and dancing, praising the redemption, that he appeared transported out of his body and removed from the physical presence of the worshippers. He seemed lifted far off on high, contemplating the heavens splitting asunder and redemption dropping gently down:

"Drop down, ye heavens, from above,
    And let the skies pour down righteousness;
Let the earth open and let them bring forth salvation
    And let righteousness spring up together;
I, Jehovah, have created it."

# CHAPTER EIGHT

THE House of Murashu, an ancient Judean family, had been long established as bankers and merchants. Best known as the House of Murashu of Nippur, the firm had its origin in Jerusalem where, while Judah was independent, it had carried on an extensive commerce with Tyre and Sidon. They exported wine and choice oils and imported wood, colored cloth and dyed woven fabrics ranging from fine Milesian wool to cheap shoddy. They belonged to the "backbone of the country" and were among the first rank of those exiled by Nebuchadnezzar to Babylon, with King Coniah. When the second transport of captives took place after the destructive of the Temple they had already been resident for a long time in Babylon. They enjoyed Nebuchadnezzar's active encouragement since he wished to make Babylon the metropolis of the whole world. The House of Murashu prospered and expanded, dispatching goods to all the countries with the Babylonian suzerainty. Their caravans carried beautiful choice woolens, wine, dates, and palm oil to the market places of distant kingdoms. They brought back iron, tin, copper, and other metals from Cyprus, slaves from Sidon, and wood from the Lebanon. The net of branches of the House that spread throughout Babylon employed a host of factors, agents, inspectors, and supervisors. Their caravans crossed the length and breadth of the deserts, and their fleet, flying the flag and emblem of the House of Murashu at the peak, plied the Tigris and Euphrates. The firm's wide reputation for fair dealing and good faith largely assisted its expansion in Babylon.

The House had its center in Nippur, the ancient city near the mouth of the Chebar, from which a network of canals and water-ways branched out all over the fruitful district of the Euphrates. This district also included the flourishing settlement of Tel Aviv, which had been populated with Judean exiles. Although the Euphrates never overflowed its bank in the same way as the Nile, it did from time to time burst from its channel and flood cities and villages. To deal with this situation, Nebuchadnezzar had set up a system of canals throughout the land which he joined up with the Euphrates, enabling the merchants' vessels to convey produce between all parts of the Babylonian plain and bring their rich harvests to Babylon. Thus Nebuchadnezzar showered prosperity on the Jewish settlement of Tel Aviv.

Produce ripened there twice a year when the fields were covered from horizon to horizon with rich golden barley stalks, principal food of Babylon. The colonists at Tel Aviv sowed the barley, and the harvest they reaped went into the granaries of the House of Murashu of Nippur, which contracted for the whole output. The grain was poured into sacks, sealed with the stamp of Murashu, and then conveyed by merchant fleet or caravans of asses to the local and distant market places throughout the empire. Since there was no fixed currency of constant weight and most of the trade of the empire proceeded by barter, these sacks of barley bearing the seal of the House of Murashu served as an accepted stable medium of exchange convertible into goods of all sorts.

Nippur, however, was only the center of the House's trade. The notables of the family lived in the capital in palaces surrounded by extensive pleasure gardens. They were the first flower of the aristocracy of the exiles and were received with great respect at the court. The king and his son, the prince regent, were in fact secret partners of the firm in most of its transactions. This ensured the grant of profitable concessions and privileges to the family. Not surprisingly, therefore, the members of the Davidic house who moved in court circles looked upon them as almost their equals in rank. Their children were educated together and became bound by family ties. The House of Murashu were the largest and main contributors to the support of the Davidic house and of the high priestly families and other nobles and keepers of the gates, who had no means of livelihood in Babylon. Let the House but utter a word and it was immediately accepted, without question, among the keepers and hereditary palace guards known as "Children of the Servants of Solomon," since their very sustenance depended upon the generosity of Murashu. Nothing was ever projected or determined in the communal life of the Exile unless it had first been approved and made known to the House. Every decision of importance affecting the Exile was mainly theirs.

During the period of the prophet's stay in Babylon, the heads of the House were the brothers Nebo-Gad and Mordechai-Gad. Nebo-Gad, the elder, was the head of the firm and his was the decisive voice. His brother was the courtier. He frequented the royal palace and maintained relations with the rulers of the Empire. His main concern was the affairs of the prince regent.

Mordechai-Gad was born in Babylon and had become almost completely identified with it. Like most of the cream of the Judean aristocracy he was educated in the academy of the nobility of the highest degree. He had a deep love for Babylonian culture, adopting its history as his own. He considered her legislation the most enlightened and thought Babylon not only the mightiest empire on earth but also the most civilized, her history the most sublime and her laws the very pattern of justice. He looked upon her deities as the symbolization of the yearnings of man for order, justice, and beauty. Bel Merodach was the god of order, of justice, the eternal antagonist of chaos and sin. Ishtar was not just the goddess of fertility and abundance, but also the bestower of the happiness of sensual ecstasy. His own personal deity was Nebo, the god of writing, commerce, logic, wisdom, and culture. His image took a more human form than those of other gods. He was represented as wearing a short modest beard and shorn locks, his head crowned by a wide low turban. The idol which Mordechai-Gad had set up in a special chamber in his luxurious palace showed the god standing sunk in thought, his hands clasped together.

Every morning Mordechai-Gad would place fresh flowers on his altar and offer prayers to him, asking for the grace of wisdom and understanding in the day's affairs.

Because of his intimate relations with the rulers of the kingdom, Mordechai-Gad often invited them to his palace to partake of feasts of truly royal splendor. The prince regent often condescended to be present; for not only was Mordechai-Gad host to the elite of the court but he also ensured the attendance of the most desirable courtesans of the empire. By their seductive wiles the latter were able to influence the mighty in the interest of the House of Murashu and its multifarious enterprises. In return the finest Jewish gold- and silversmiths and jewelers were constantly employed by the House in creating rich gifts for the adornment of the courtesans: chains, earrings, bracelets, jewelry set with the rarest gems.

One day the report reached this Croesus that a strange prophet had appeared among the exiles and had dared to name Cyrus, the arch-enemy of Babylon, as the Messiah of God. Worse than that, he had said that Jehovah was raising Cyrus up over Babylon in order to free His people Israel. This prophet could be none other than one of the spies whom Cyrus regularly dispatched in advance of his armies to spy out Babylon and rouse the subject peoples and alien elements to facilitate his conquest. Mordechai-Gad looked upon the prophet as a source of great potential danger to the security of Babylonian Jewry. He lost no time in seeing that an urgent assembly was summoned in the palace of the House of David so that the matter could be considered at once by the rulers of the Davidic house.

The buildings which Evil Merodach had apportioned to King Coniah after he had freed him from prison did not differ from the other palaces of the earlier Babylonian dynasty. They were all situated in the Avenue of the Processions near the gate of Ishtar. The palace was an ancient edifice dating back to the age of Hammurabi before Babylon had fallen under Assyrian domination. It contained innumerable halls and chambers, hidden stairways which led to a labyrinth of colonnades, offices, and cells where slaves and servants worked and dwelt.

The toleration extended to the Jews had brought them a great measure of prosperity. The youth of the royal house and the well-born were educated along with the young Babylonian nobility to fill important offices of state. They served as officers in the army and engaged in commerce. Even while King Coniah was in prison, his wives and family had accompanied him, and though his movements were restricted, he still received the respect due to a king. When he was finally freed, Evil Merodach restored him to his title and honors, which included the privilege of holding a court. His guards, the "Sons of the Servants of Solomon," dwelt in his palace, walked before him, and had jurisdiction over all his court affairs.

Indeed the palace was a small self-contained state. Its chief ministers and officials were the priests, the family of the chief priest Jehozedek and his son Yeshu. Also at court dwelt the sons of Barzillai, and notables of the families settled at Tel Aviv, Tel Melach, and Bnei Jericho. There were also, of course, the chiefs of the Levites, who stemmed from the singers in the Temple, among them the sons of Asaph, and the gatekeepers, the sons of Shallum.

The latter, traditional guards in the palace at Jerusalem since ancient times, now stood on guard in the hall where the assembly of chiefs of the Exile was to take place. The meeting was of such prime importance that its convocation had been kept very secret and only the most notable and loyal of local Jewry were invited: those who occupied important offices at Court, the most renowned of the merchants, and specially selected delegates of the priests and Levites of the larger settlements. The subject to be dealt with was the situation in Babylon in the light of Cyrus's conquests and his crossing of the Tigris. A decision would have to be taken by the exiles on the manifesto issued by Cyrus and conveyed by trusted secret emissaries. It proclaimed freedom and repatriation to the Judean exiles if they would assist Cyrus in subduing Babylon.

The situation had been made unduly critical for the exiles by the public declarations of the prophet. He had announced that Cyrus was the Messiah of the God Jehovah and would certainly conquer Babylon and return Judah and Israel to their land as a united people.

Mordechai-Gad, abetted by his brother Nebo-Gad, Malchaya Gavra, and other leading merchants, demanded that the guardians of the gate immediately bring the prophet before the assembly. He was summoned and brought by force.

At the head of the conference sat Shaltiel and his son Zerubabel, clothed in silver-embroidered robes. Near them were Jehozedek the elder, son of the last High Priest to officiate in the Temple at Jerusalem, his son Yeshu, and the heads of the Levites. Behind them sat delegates from the various centers, the heads of the proudest families, and the leading merchants. All were clad in rich cloaks of woven blue and purple. Their girdles were of silver thread, their necks were adorned with golden chains from which depended brooches overlaid with precious stones. Two guards, spear in hand, stood watch at the door of the great cedar-beamed hall which, like all such in Babylonian palaces, was not lit by daylight but illuminated by oil censers made of copper and set upon pedestals of marble.

Clad in a loose white robe which lay open and revealed his lean and sunburned chest, the prophet stood before them. With him was his faithful friend and protector Neraiah the son of Seraiah.

Because of his standing at court and his great influence among the exiles, the chief of the inquisitors was Mordechai-Gad. He was a powerfully built, broad-boned man in the prime of life. Of lofty stature, he wore a short well-groomed beard, and his long hair was well-tended and carefully dressed. His robe was of finest Sidonian stuff, and his delicately shaped sandals scarcely seemed to belong to a member of the Exile. He might have been a high-ranking judge in one of Babylon's supreme courts. He did in fact occupy such a position, thanks to his great erudition. He was also much consulted by the great Jewish merchants whenever they had any business in which questions of law and equity were involved. They all went somewhat in awe of him. Their chief spokesman was Mordechai-Gad and his view prevailed.

Mordechai-Gad demanded of the prophet that he should explain why the God of Judah should choose an alien of a strange religion as the Redeemer of His people. He found the whole concept most difficult to understand. Did he not value tradition? Did his thoughts not march with the accepted faith of the exiles and with the prophecies of the seers who had flourished in Judah in the past and who had asserted that the Redeemer of Israel would be of the House of David? Furthermore, how could a gentile who believed in other gods, who did not recognize the God of Judah and betrayed complete ignorance of Him, be the redeemer? In such a case, why could not Nabonidus or his son Belshazzar, who had bestowed such a rich store of favor on the Jews, be the redeemer and the Messiah?

The prophet answered him simply:

"Who can know the ways of God? Who can tell Him whom He shall choose as His emissary and whom He shall thrust aside? There is no stranger as there is no companion before God. All are the work of His hands. Just as the potter chooses an instrument for his needs, so Jehovah chooses emissaries and peoples to do His will. He took and made Assyria the rod of His anger to bring retribution upon His people Israel. Then he summoned Babylon that it might in its turn bring retribution upon Assyria. There was a time when Babylon was the vessel of God's wrath to bring His punishment and perform His will, to be the object in the potter's hand. Now He has rejected Babylon just as the potter casts away a clay bowl that he made upon his wheel when it no longer holds water. God has now chosen a more righteous and better people to serve His ends."

The prophet raised his voice. "Can the vessel say to the potter, what doest thou? Woe to him who says to the father, what begettest thou?"

"In what is Persia to be preferred to Babylon? In what way

should this vessel called Persia be better than that called Babylon to perform God's will? On what grounds should He prefer Persia?"

"God weighs in a just scale. Those who more nearly keep His laws are closer to Him. Persia is not sunken in idol-worship to the same extent as Babylon. She does not offer incense so readily to blocks of wood and stone. She is not filthied in harlotry and impurity. She does not torture the aged nor does she sell her women in whoredom and devote her babies to abominations of desolation. The Persian keeps far from deceit and teaches truth and uprightness. Righteousness was the staff of his instruction from the time he was a small child. He is virgin soil. For this reason he is an acceptable instrument and a good staff to perform God's will, for Israel and for all the nations of the world."

"And what is that will?"

"To bring all nations to the God of Israel, to the House of the God of Jacob so that every knee might bend before Him and every tongue swear by His name."

"Why should all peoples worship the One Jehovah? Why should not every one have its own God? Bel Merodach is famous among all peoples; his works are hallowed everywhere. Assyria and Babylon bow down before him. So do Tyre and Sidon and the inhabitants of the distant isles who come to him with rich gifts, sacrificing upon his altars and pouring out their supplications in his ear. Ishtar too is thus renowned as the mother of all gods and of man. But despite all this Babylon does not enforce the worship of her God. Babylon does not prevent the Jews from building their synagogues and entering therein to pray to Jehovah. Why are we so favored, we Jews; small and despised as we are among the nations of the world; persecuted and oppressed because of our God, the God of Judah, more than any other people? For the Babylonians have made an exception and specially excused us from worshipping their gods, granting us a privilege no other nation enjoys at their hands. Has our own God been so good to us? Has He been so victorious over our enemies? After all, it is we who are sunk in exile in Babylon, not the Babylonians who have been taken out to Judah. Babylon is still not subdued. Nor will anyone conquer her. She is invincible."

"Why," burst forth the prophet. "Why?" His voice changed and seemed to take on a musical singing quality. His eyes closed and the words poured from his lips; his body throbbed and trembled greatly as though it were not the man who was speaking but a spirit which had possessed him and was using him as a passive instrument with his senses entranced.

"For thus saith Jehovah that created the heavens;
God himself that formed the earth and made it;
He hath established it,
He created it not in vain,
He formed it to be inhabited.
I am Jehovah, there is none else."

"Babylon! Is not Babylon inhabited! Is Babylon a vain thing?" shouted Mordechai-Gad. "Did not our king weave a network of canals over her territory which brought abundance and prosperity to all her inhabitants? Does not her commerce extend over half the world? Look at her cities tumultuous with swelling populations. What other land can compare with this? She is covered with cities and villages and all her courtyards are full of people. Babylon made into a wasteland! What other country in the world has a system of law so fair and equitable and of such venerable antiquity as Babylon's, going back as it does to the mighty Hammurabi? Is it for nothing that people come from the distant isles of Greece and far-off lands to learn judgment and law? Babylon a wasteland!"

"Babylon is a stagnant and ugly pool breeding insects and scorpions. Her cities are filthy sewers causing a foul stench. May God grant that one day she become bare and clean as the desert; that her land may be consumed with longing to be sown with the word of God. Babylon shall surely be purged of her impurity before she can be fit to receive that word."

An excited ferment swept the assembly.

"Close all the doors. Bar the gates. The man is saying terrifying things."

"He will bring down calamity upon our heads!"

"Get him out of here! Close his mouth! Silence him! Disaster will come upon us!"

"Let him finish. We must hear what he has to say!" A weak and timid voice was heard.

"He has a vision." Another tried to defend him in trembling accents.

But Mordechai-Gad was not the sort of man to allow anyone to withstand him. Looking out fiercely from his dark and threatening brows, he bent fiery and angry glances on every side and silence fell. He wanted to impress upon the gathering the grave danger inherent in the utterance of the prophet, whose strong words did not shake him out of his calm. He tried to continue the inquiry in the quiet and judicious manner characteristic of him.

"The Babylonians do not interfere with our worship and why should we interfere with them? They do not come to our synagogues to mock at us because we bow before a God whom no man has yet seen to this very day. Why should we go round the market places and scoff at their purchasing gods made of wood and stone as this prophet is wont to do? Why should we thus endanger the very existence of our Jewish community here?"

"Why?" exclaimed the prophet. "Hear the word of Jehovah of Hosts. Thus saith the God of Jacob:

"I have sworn by Myself,
    The word is gone out of my mouth in righteousness and shall
        not return.
    That unto Me every knee shall bow,
    Every tongue shall swear.
    Surely, shall one say, in Jehovah
    Have I righteousness and strength."

"Are we to learn from this that all peoples will be compelled to change their status and become Jews?" asked Mordechai-Gad.

"In Jehovah shall all the seed of Israel be justified and glory," answered the prophet.

"Implying that all nations shall be forced to acknowledge that we were right in serving the One God and cleaving to Him." One of the priests essayed to interpret his words.

"The prophet speaks as though the word of God were in his mouth. Let him be. Let us hear!" some voices were heard saying.

"Thus saith Jehovah," the voice of the prophet was again raised:

"The labor of Egypt,
The merchandise of Ethiopia and the Sabaeans,
Men of stature shall come over unto thee and they shall be thine.
They shall come after thee; in chains shall they come over,
And they shall fall down unto thee and make supplication unto thee
Saying, Surely God is in thee; and there is no god else."

"The labor of Egypt and the merchandise of Ethiopia! Wherefore? It is obvious that the man is crazed." One of the merchants interrupted him with a clap of the hands.

"Are we to allow a madman with his demented visions to endanger all that we have achieved in two generations? We should be lying and deceitful, hypocritical foxes in the eyes of the emperor and would be regarded as belonging to the enemy camp. An enemy whose nature we do not know. . . . And this at time of general peril! When our soldiers are being drawn up to do battle against him in the field. Who can forecast what the fate of the battle will be? Take good heed what you are doing and intend to do," Mordechai-Gad warned the assembly in serious and deliberate tones. Then turning to the prophet he inquired:

"What harm have the kings of Babylon done to us? Why should

we turn coat and cease to be faithful subjects? Have they not been merciful rulers over us from the very first day?"

"Merciful rulers! To whom?" asked the prophet in indignation. "Merciful rulers to you. To you who helped them place the yoke of slave labor on the necks of the old? Or merciful to the poor of my people? Go out and look at the canals and gates, the towers and sanctuaries that Babylon has erected. With whose toil were they raised? The mortar was kneaded with the sweat of the peoples and the bricks baked in furnaces kindled with the fire of dried human blood. Like a huge spider Babylon has ensnared nations in her web and sucked out their vital force in return for a crust of dry bread. And thus it has been from the very first day. She swooped down in our sky like a hawk. Babylon is a fitting sister to Assyria whose legacy she inherited. Their common mother was iniquity and both had learned from her to squander human life without mercy."

The prophet turned to Shaltiel and Zerubabel. "When your father surrendered to Nebuchadnezzar in good faith, with full confidence in his justice, what did he do? He took Judah captive, emptied the land of its fairest and best and left it naked and bare, a prey to the fowl of the heaven, the vultures and her ravening neighbors. Three and thirty years Nebuchadnezzar kept your father in prison. He decreed eternal darkness upon him just as he did upon your uncle. He robbed him of old and young. He extracted the finest flower of Judah and left over the poorest of the poor. Then when he needed slaves to erect his magnificent buildings he dragged them off into exile. Surely you speak right when you say he allowed them to live. But for whom if not for himself? To dig his canals, to plow his fields, to build his houses, to erect sanctuaries for his abominations. They tilled the fields of Babylon, folded her sheep, and excavated her canals. But their own fields were left uncared for, a prey to plunder and robbery. The Tower of Babylon pierces the heavens while the House of God is a heap of ruins, shamed and confounded, abandoned to all sorts of idolatries, an altar for every strange god. By the taskmaster's lash

113

Babylon has sought to whip out of the hearts of the exiles here every longing for redemption and liberation. If she gave any concession to alleviate their bitter lot, it was but the bone a master throws to a hungry dog barely sufficient for one tooth to gnaw on. And so their sons completely forgot their land. And now they no longer even think of freedom. Even a tear shed in memory of Zion is looked upon by you as treachery and rebellion against the oppressor. Yet these things you call lovingkindness! You label the exploiters and oppressors men of lovingkindness. Judah has forgotten the rock from which it was hewn and the remembrance of Jerusalem has been extinguished from the hearts of her sons. No! This thing shall not be. Judah was not created for debasement or slavery. God planted in her the seed of eternal salvation. This seed shall bud and give forth fruit only in the land promised to the patriarchs, in the soil on which the House of God has been lifted up. Israel was not created to be a bondman nor to go bowed down and stooping in alien furrows. She will return to her land again. And as for Babylon; she shall share the fate of Assyria, for she is of the same mother."

Powerful indeed was the impression the prophet made on the assembly as the stillness which fell upon the hall and the tears which welled up in every eye indicated. King Coniah, the father of the Exile, who pined away his best years in prison, was held in reverence by the exiles. The mention by the prophet of the unhappy king touched a trembling and forgotten tender chord. Here and there a muted note of lamentation was heard expressing the sorrow which dwelt in every heart. "By the waters of Babylon. . . ."

Appreciating this, Mordechai-Gad gathered together all his mental forces.

"Who claims that we wish to return to Judah and dwell once again in Jerusalem?" he asked in his deep and somber voice. He stood up, powerful, tall, and dominating. He towered to his full height and his masterful glance shot forth from his beetling brows and raked Shaltiel and Zerubabel who sat before him.

"Who and what were we in Judah? What have we to hope from

114

there? To what could we look forward? Our fathers were ground down between the nether millstone of the Philistines, who gnawed away at us from the west, and of Tyre, Sidon, Assyria, and Damascus from our other borders. What was left us? A few rocky patches and barren plots in bare and windswept hills? With tears and sweat and tooth and nail our miserable ancestors had to toil and moil to wrest a bare living out of every small pocket of soil. And when the eagerly awaited early rain came each year it washed away the topsoil. Our people hungered for bread and thirsted for water. We were too weak to defend ourselves and were a pawn in the plots and intrigues of every large kingdom who felt like crushing us or imposing heavy burdens of exactions upon us. They used to take our flocks and herds away to their lands and haul our children off into slavery. What profited us the Holy Temple in Jerusalem? The very Sanctuary itself sucked our blood like the horse leech. Sacrifices and tithes and imposts without measure. But protection? None. Now against all this weigh up the situation of our people here, in the Babylonian exile. Our brethren dwell on the most fruitful tracts of the country and eat off the fat of the land. Our children may gain knowledge and wisdom at the same schools as the nobility of the Empire. Our daughters are accepted and respected in the best circles. Our commercial net is spread over the whole Empire and its tributary states. And this man claims that we should wish to return to Judah! If God indeed loves us and wishes us well He will leave us here where we are. Great indeed was the lovingkindness He showed us when He sent Nebuchadnezzar to save us from the trap that Judah had become, from the sore strait called Israel to which Moses had led us to be oppressed and miserable."

Mordechai-Gad's words caused general unrest. Voices were heard supporting him, though loud cries of dissent were not altogether absent. But the man who arose to speak was the head of the House of Murashu. His beard was plaited in three as a symbol of his very exalted rank and connotation as a "Friend of the Great King."

"I am a merchant and I intend speaking to you as a merchant would speak." Thus Nebo-Gad began in quiet and reserved tones, like one who is always reasonable and ready to listen to argument. "We of Israel are prosperous in Babylon. We have lived here only one generation and we already command the lion's share of the Empire's commerce in barley, wool, and produce. Our settlements market their produce not only in Babylon but far beyond Mesopotamia and have penetrated the markets of Tyre, Laodicea, and even Egypt. We are strong commercial rivals of Tyre and Sidon today. We challenge them in the wine trade and have already captured the Cyprus copper trade. We see no practical obstacle to prevent our pushing Tyre and Sidon right out of the trade with the Grecian islands and the harbors to the far west of the Great Sea. As soon as we have defeated Cyrus the harbors of the Great Sea will be fully open once again to our commerce. We shall even establish new harbors far to the west as Sidon and Greece did years ago. Those who try to force us back to Judah are like people who try to push one back into his mother's womb."

"What do we need it for? Why should we trouble ourselves about the Temple in Jerusalem? Let them build a Temple here in Babylon such as our brethren built for themselves in Egypt." So spoke Malchaya Gavra, the pious, interjecting his suggestion with a sanctimonious glance at the assembly. "Let us build a Temple to Jehovah like that at E-Sagila. The tower need be only a mite lower than Bel Merodach's. We have the means to furnish it with gold and silver and marble so that the splendor of our fame will be the envy and glory of Babylon. Our princes will be recognized as of the highest degree, and it is from Babylon that the fame and glory of Jehovah and the House of David shall go forth. Why should we return to impoverished Judah?"

During the whole of these merchants' discourses the prophet stood as one stricken dumb with amazement. An expression of grief passed over his paling features. Suddenly he seemed to grow immensely tall as he spoke slowly and solemnly in a low voice.

"From thy mother's womb have I chosen thee of Israel to be My servant. And as a man deals with his servant so shall God deal with thee. If you refuse to return to Judah willingly, then He will drive you back thither with the whip and goad like cattle which stray rebelliously from the herd or like a lazy slave who has to be flogged to his work. For thus saith God by the mouth of His servant the prophet: 'You have I known out of all the nations of the earth, therefore shall I visit all your iniquities upon you.' "

"He insults us. He dares call us slaves!" Angry fists were raised towards the pale prophet.

"But Jeremiah the prophet bade us seek the peace of the city to which God exiled us. He ordered us to build houses, plant orchards, and take wives in this land, saying that in the city's peace would we find peace. That is just what he said."

"This fellow that stands up in front of us and whom nobody knows anything about, puts our whole existence here into jeopardy. He arouses false hopes in the people. He is one of the false prophets against whom Jeremiah warned us. He wasn't sent by God. It's Cyrus who sent him here. Cyrus sent him to confuse the people, to stir them up and lead us into an abyss. As soon as the Babylonians hear what sort of speeches he has been making they will hold us all responsible and we shall all suffer for the sin of one individual. This man is a menace, a danger to all of us."

So explained Mordechai-Gad in tones of solemn conviction. "Take heed. I give you fair warning."

"A peril. A danger to all of us. His words are like a knife at our throat."

"We must prevent him from spreading his words."

"Seal his lips!"

"Serpents and scorpions swarm from his lips!"

The prophet stood up tall, pale, and gaunt. His eyes were shut tight but his face was vibrant with life. He was very much aware of what was happening. He spread his arms wide towards the assembly and explained in a voice charged full with confidence:

"Thus saith Jehovah:
  Declaring the end from the beginning,
  And from ancient times the things that are not yet done,
      saying,
  My counsel shall stand, and I will do my pleasure.
  Calling a ravenous bird from the east,
  The man that executeth my counsel from a far country;
  Yes, I have spoken it, I will also bring it to pass;
  I have purposed it and I will do it."

"Only listen to what he is saying. He will call a ravenous bird from the east. He has the temerity to utter the name of Cyrus, our arch enemy here."

"Traitor. Hand him over to the king!"

"That's what to do with him. Hand him over to the king! Hand him over!"

Several of the guardians of the gate hastened towards the prophet prepared to lay hands on him at a mere nod from Mordechai-Gad.

"Touch not the prophet!" came a cry from young Zerubabel. "Remember Jeremiah!"

The aged Shaltiel, who had remained completely silent, was heard to say decisively:

"I would like to hear the opinion of the Chief of the Priests, before we lay hands on him."

As aged Jehozedek rose, every one stood up. The old priest was one of the last of the exiles who had seen the Temple in Jerusalem still standing in all its glory. He arose clothed in dignity in his white robe and turban and said:

"Members of the royal house and chiefs of the Exile: the words of the prophet are strange and hidden from us. But so were the words of the prophets in our fathers' day also mysterious and too deep for us. They too did not heed them in their generation. Therefore be ye guided by my counsel. Lay not hands upon the prophet so that we do not fall into the sin of our fathers. But let him be forbidden to speak until God gives us a sign."

118

So it was decided.

The prophet was forbidden to preach in the synagogues. They warned him that should he transgress the ban he would be handed over to the king of Babylon.

# CHAPTER NINE

IT was only yesterday that Cyrus was little more than a petty king, ruler of Ansan and vassal of the king of Medea.

King Nabonidus of Babylon was a lover of antiquities. Once, having conceived the notion of restoring the broken-down sanctuaries of various gods, he decided to go to Haran and renew the worship of Sin, the moon god. He asked counsel of the god Bel Merodach.

"Let Nabonidus, king of Babylon, bring bricks with his horses and chariots and let him build up anew the temple of Sin which is in Haran." But there was a stumbling block which prevented the fulfillment of his desires. Haran was in the hands of the Medeans and they were in open revolt against Babylon at the time. So Nabonidus asked Bel Merodach again: "O Merodach, Merodach; behold the temple of Sin is besieged by Medeans. Do you desire that Cyrus, king of Ansan, should assist me?"

This was the answer delivered by Bel Merodach:

"The Medeans of whom you speak, his land and his ally shall no longer be."

Accordingly Nabonidus armed Cyrus of Ansan with war chariots enabling him to rebel against Medea, vanquish her king, and subdue the land.

Meanwhile, Cyrus set himself the task of winning the hearts of the Medeans. He represented himself to them as a liberator rather than as a conqueror. He gave them just laws, freed them from heavy taxes that the king of Medea had imposed upon them, cemented the kingdoms of Persia and Medea together, and became lord of a united and powerful Persian empire.

He then began a policy of piecemeal reduction of province after province of Babylon. Nabonidus was occupied in the desert somewhere near the borders of Egypt. His son, Belshazzar, in opposition to the priests of Bel Merodach, was immersed in the constant celebrations of festival after festival in honor of this or that kedeshah all the time that Cyrus was expanding and fortifying his empire. His swift squadrons of horsemen, clad in light armor and armed with short swords, bows, and large quivers of arrows, were mounted upon fiery Persian steeds. Riding at their head, Cyrus won victory after victory eastward of the Tigris. When he conquered the important empire of Lydia, he took possession of all the Greek cities along the Aegean coast of Asia Minor which had belonged to King Croesus. When he reached the shores of the Black Sea, the other provinces fell into his hands. As he entered every capital at the head of his armies, he announced himself as a liberator. He proclaimed the freedom of every state from the yoke of Babylon, made a covenant with the armies of the conquered provinces, and entered into treaties of peace with their rulers and priests.

With the armies of his new conquests incorporated into his own host, Cyrus felt ready at last to cross the Tigris. Having drawn Assyria to his banner, he passed over the river and pitched his tents for the first time on the very soil of Babylon. The capital had been brought into imminent danger of war.

But it was still a great distance to Babylon from Arbela, the city situated at the point of Cyrus's crossing. The path he would have to take from the Tigris to the Euphrates was well guarded by fortified cities, the most important being Babylon itself; Babylon the unconquered, the invincible, the impregnable citadel whose walls were so thick that four war chariots and their horses could pass abreast upon them. It was protected by wide, deep, swift canals which flowed along the whole length of the walls. The inner defenses were the labyrinthine spawn of courtyards and buildings packed close together, crowding up against the walls and connected by narrow passages which were a death trap to an invader. Even should a besieger storm these outer defenses he would stand bewildered before the inner fortress. The network of courtyards, streets, and alleys, shut in by high buildings, would prove the burial place of his soldiers, exposed as they would be to the casting down of stones and a hail of arrows and spears from the defenders lying in ambush on the heights of the walls and the fortified buildings. No one to whom the secret of the maze of alleys was unknown could hope to find his way out of them into the heart of the city.

The first confusion that had seized the rulers of Babylon upon receipt of the news of the crossing of the Tigris and the incursion of the Medean and Persian forces upon their soil subsided gradually. Belshazzar and his counselors grew calmer. His strategists and warriors advised him to wait until Cyrus and his hosts had penetrated deep into the country and arrived in the vicinity of the capital. Meanwhile there would be time for Nabonidus to bring up his armies from the Egyptian deserts and fall upon him from the rear. This would be the cue for Belshazzar and his forces to issue forth to meet him face-to-face in a pitched battle. Cyrus would have to contend with enemies on two fronts, and if they failed to annihilate him in the giant pincers, they could at least hold his armies in its tightly closed jaws until he perished through hunger and thirst. Meanwhile the army had to be equipped, the city granaries had to be filled with supplies from the rural districts, new canals had to be dug as traps around the walls and protected on top by a layer of weak bricks so that the enemies might fall into them. Stocks of stones for the catapults had to be piled up on the ramparts and everything made ready for a long siege.

Belshazzar relied upon the good advice of his counselors and gave orders for the reinforcement of the walls of Babylon.

*Was it for nothing that the great gods Bel Merodach and Ishtar dwelt in Babylon? Was it not a well-established truth that they would shield the city and its inhabitants against those who scoffed at their divine power?*

*   *   *

Extensive clay fields spread out beneath the shadow of the walls which completely encompassed Babylon. They formed the center of the local brickmaking industry, and the noise and bustle of the slaves employed there never ceased. Groups of workers dug out large lumps of clay with spades and mattocks and cast them into pits in which others trod them with their bare feet, kneading them with water until the clay took on the consistency of dough. A choking smoke rolled up from hundreds of kilns whose greedy jaws were continually fed with newly fashioned bricks by rows of porters, busy and industrious as ants. They drew near in an endless chain, every man laden with a shovelful which he fed into the yawning mouths. The furnaces greeted them with a belch of smoke and flame which drew out their vital sap in profuse sweat and scorched their skin with the monstrous licking of its fiery tongue.

Gangs of slaves chained together like prisoners were yoked to enormous blocks of stone which they dragged to the plain. Here sculptors, shaded by huts made of palm branches, were busily at work carving the unhewn rock into shapes of monsters with human faces. The finished product was destined to be set in the wall to terrify the enemy should he try to approach. Endless chains of laborers toiled at the gigantic water wheels which pumped a steady stream of water from the canals through pipes into the pits where the clay was trodden.

The ground surrounding the brickworks was soaked and saturated with the fearsome sweating which poured from the copper tanned bodies of the myriads of slaves who groaned beneath the oppression of forced labor. The thick towering wall at whose feet the canal ran shadowed off the light of the sky. The slaves' horizon was cut off. They seemed to have come to the end of the world. Hard, dead, and cold though the wall was, yet it seemed alive and watchful, for it was carved into the likeness of hundreds of lions, leopards, and wild oxen, of serpents whose heads and fangs projected from its surface.

Along the bank of the broad canal a long line of ships, barges, and rafts lay at anchor. Slaves were busy loading them with newly baked bricks, clay, pitch, loam, and unhewn stone. Swarms of them, in machine-like precision, passed backwards and forwards in endless lines, weaving to and from the shore burdened with hods laden with bricks, with wooden buckets containing pitch and clay while the chain gangs hauled at the blocks of stone.

On the opposite shore which adjoined the city wall lay an equally long line of ships busily unloading their cargo. High ladders extended from the decks to scaffolding set in the walls, and hosts of slaves unloaded the bricks, clay, loam and pitch and stone from the holds of the vessels to the first scaffolding. There they were seized by grappling irons and raised by huge wheels to a second scaffolding and thence to a third until they reached the top of the wall.

The number of ant-like humans who crawled and swarmed about the plain by the wall was legion. They covered the boats, ladders, and scaffolding. They were a moving dark blotch against the dun-colored surface of the plain. They moved back and forth; they climbed ceaselessly up and down. The relentless sun burned down upon their copper-colored bodies, drawing out the pouring sweat which glistened and shone until they resembled a milliard of fire-flies or a plague of locusts infesting the plain and covering the fortifications of Babylon.

The activity was an expression of the desire of Belshazzar to fortify the defenses and strengthen points of possible weakness. Workmen were tearing out embrasures, erecting watchtowers, furnishing sally ports, establishing positions of ambush and providing emplacements for the catapults and the nests of spear throwers.

Nabonidus and Belshazzar joined forces near the shore of the Tigris beside the city of Opis. Because the Tigris frequently inundated its banks, the land between this city and Sippar was largely marsh. Nebuchadnezzar had partly drained it and joined it to Babylon by means of a canal whose banks were marked by a chain of fortresses. However, the ground in general retained its swampy character.

Babylon had been at ease for many years, resting upon the laurels of the conquests of Nebuchadnezzar but relying even more upon its mighty walls and the inflexible tyranny of the administrative machine. The kings who succeeded Evil Merodach, however, had neglected the personal management of state affairs in favor of other pursuits. Thus Nabonidus was devoted to the beautification and restoration of historical buildings and sanctuaries.

The essential factor in the tactics of Nebuchadnezzar and his successors was to implant fear and terror in the enemy. This was achieved by the walls of Babylon, made monstrous as they were by the shapes of horrifying animals built into their structure. In the field the effect was achieved by the massing of a veritable flood of chariots which advanced with an overwhelming tumult. These tactics had been learned from the Assyrians. Numbers of trained lions, leopards, and other wild beasts were also enlisted and loosed at the strategic moment against the enemy. The whole concept of Babylonian life was founded upon this notion of terror in times of peace as well as in war. Since the stranger might well be an enemy, he had to be intimidated and overwhelmed. This method was employed at every opportunity.

The iron chariots that Belshazzar brought up against Cyrus belonged to an old type inherited from the Egyptians, the design of which dated from the time of Rameses II. Since they were originally made to serve the ambition of the individual warrior seeking to excel in acts of single-handed prowess they were ranged in the field of battle as though they were taking part in a ceremonial parade. The warhorses were plumed with ostrich feathers, their harness was gilded, and they were altogether splendid with a profusion of streaming ribbons and bands. Each chariot carried three and sometimes four riders. There was the noble who bent the bow, a man of massive strength of arm; the armorbearer, who held his quiver ready to hand; and a second armorbearer, who also served as a fan-bearer, shielding the head of his master from the sun.

If the charioteer was of very high rank he might carry two fan-bearers, who stood on a plank near the wheels behind him sheltering him with their broad fans from the blazing sun. These charioteers, always of the flower of the aristocracy, wore armored breastplates, curled wigs, and beautifully plaited and scented beards. The infantry, who comprised the bulk of the array, were similarly protected and adorned. The whole purpose was to give the enemy an impression of discipline and an almost legendary appearance of heroic valor.

Against this glorious panoply, drawn up as though for a military display or review, Cyrus opposed a living wall of infantry. They stretched back in ranks without number until it appeared that he had brought to the field of slaughter all the nations of the world. These mighty masses of foot soldiery were not protected with steel cuirasses nor primped out with flash wigs and beards. Their hair was cropped short, their beards pointed or stubby. Where they favored long hair it was secured in a tight queue. They wore short leather jerkins in place of coats of mail. Their weapon was a bow with a sheaf of arrows carried in a shoulder quiver. One hand held a long spear, and their protection was a metal disc-shaped shield. Cyrus's men were highly mobile and could maneuver rapidly. Belshazzar's chariots, with their prancing horses, crashed against the front ranks of Cyrus and burst through the living wall. But they immediately found themselves enmeshed and absorbed by the second rank, who at once cast their lances against the terrified and confused horses. For the first time Cyrus had brought camels into battle, and the sight of them served further to frighten the horses of Belshazzar's host. The Assyrian-Babylonian chariots, hitherto invincible, stopped in their tracks. The horses refused to advance.

In Cyrus's army only the captains rode in chariots. The cavalry were mounted on small, agile ponies. They were half naked, wore light helmets, carried long lances, and blended perfectly with their steeds to form a perfectly flexible and highly mobile engine of attack. They were unhampered by a heavy chariot whose wheels prevented swift maneuverability. As Belshazzar's chariots came to a halt before the solid mass of flesh that the Persian infantry presented, this light cavalry stormed at them from the flanks. Led by Cyrus's son, they effectively shut off their retreat and over the whole front only one weak point remained by which a breakthrough was eventually effected to the canal joining Sippar with Babylon.

The proud and valiant chariots of Babylon sank down in the swamps which stretched along the Tigris from Opis to the Sippar canal. Thus that fortress city, the first link in the chain guarding the approaches to the capital itself, fell into the hands of Cyrus.

Belshazzar and his staff hastened to extricate themselves from the Opis-Sippar line and withdrew in confusion to Babylon, losing contact with Nabonidus en route.

There was now nothing left for them to do but rely on the fortified walls of the capital.

When the priests of Bel Merodach heard that Nabonidus and his son had suffered a crushing defeat, they said that the great god had avenged himself upon them both for their unfaithfulness to the deity and their defection to the god Sin at Ur of the Chaldees.

As a mighty river roars irresistibly into an empty watercourse, the power of Cyrus rushed on from Sippar to Babylon. They marched along the length of the canal, carrying their arms and equipment on horses and wagons. They floated down the current on barges and ships. They spread out over the fields, treading down orchards and vineyards and trudging through the clayey fields. No obstacle seemed to stay their onset. Every stumbling block seemed to melt away until the words of the prophet apparently found literal fulfillment. "Every valley shall be exalted and every hill and mountain brought low, and the crooked shall be made into a plain." It seemed that all the nations of the world had broken the yoke of servitude from their necks, that soldiers of every climate and tongue, in a bewildering array of costumes and colors, were coming up against Babylon in the ranks of Cyrus's armies.

There were Kedarim from the sandy deserts, in whose ears the wail of the jackal had not yet faded and whose eyelids were still bleary with sand. They rode on swift camels and dromedaries, leading pack-asses and mules bearing their equipment, provisions, and sacks laden with spoil taken from the slain of Belshazzar's armies; bridles, images of the gods in stone and metal, tents of Assyrian and Persian make, horses' cloths, saddles. . . . Hosts from the isles of Greece rolled along, tall Spartans, Achaeans, and Dorians who were Cyrus's mercenaries, Cappadocians and Cilicians, highlanders from the mountains of Ararat, shipwrights from Tyre and Tarshish, levies from Persia, Medea, and every land between Egypt and Babylon. They streamed in from every clime, they came by every road and by-way, their eyes yellow and savage with rage, their clenched fists trembling with blazing anger. The flame of hatred and lust for vengeance had goaded and driven them to Cyrus's standard. The years of bitter Babylonian oppression and slavery had piled up a massive account which boiled in their blood and carried the passion for retribution to every vein and sinew of their being. They were elated, uplifted, and borne along on the wings of their wrath to slake their thirst for revenge for the long generations of subjection and tyranny to Babylon and Assyria. Their drive and onrush towards Babylon resembled the progress of some vast, black protean monster that moved along, breathing heavily, getting remorselessly nearer. They came onward to pour out the flood-gates of their indignation upon Babylon, to shatter the gates of the city and trample down its walls as one stamps a repulsive insect underfoot.

# CHAPTER TEN

BABYLON, in her turn, was not waiting helplessly. After the defeat on the Opis-Sippar line, the city woke into activity like a hive of bees which buzzes into busy life when danger threatens from without. Vast crowds assembled outside the royal palace, the sanctuaries, and near the walls. The heterogeneous population, representing almost all the races of the world, rose in one united effort to strengthen the walls and prepare for siege.

Great caravans arrived from neighboring cities which had not yet fallen to Cyrus. Supplies of food and idols and images were being hastened into the city by ox-carts and convoys of pack-asses. There the gods would be safe from the advancing enemy.

Reinforced watches were set along those parts of the banks of the Euphrates which had been enclosed within the walls of the city, and extra vigilance was imposed upon the one bridge which joined this outer section with the main metropolis. All fields, vineyards, and orchards in the outer suburbs were laid completely waste and all fountains and wells in the adjoining fields were stopped up. The military experts fabricated all sorts of devices for the destruction of the enemy, planting traps and snares and increasing the complexity of the labyrinthine system of narrow alleys and courtyards. Pitfalls of all kinds were dug, and false bridges over the river were constructed that were designed to collapse as soon as a column of men had reached the middle. Ambushes were laid near them from which a rain of missiles could be poured down upon the hapless floundering army.

During this time the prophet was walking in the Avenue of the Processions. As he approached the gate of Ishtar he saw passing through the portals a procession of camels and asses that were laden with images of different gods and goddesses. There were graven and molten images, sculptured idols of clay and stone, all heaped in confusion on the backs of the pack animals as though loaded in great haste. Behind the camels and the asses came a long procession of wagons, each yoked to two oxen. These too were packed in a disorderly manner with a jumble of monsters. Some represented beasts with human heads and some humans with the heads of beasts. They were hewn and carved from stone, camphor wood, and ebony, some in a state of decay and falling apart, some of beaten copper now bent and twisted and split, heaped up like scrap. Naked shapes of women with the heads of birds, clad in multicolored veils and bedecked with jewels, crammed the carts or hung down in disorder from the backs and sides of the beasts of burden.

The Babylonians were anxious to bring all their pantheon within the safety of the fortified walls. There was Nebo, the god of wisdom, Sin, the moon god of Ur, and all the other golden deities of the Chaldees. It was felt that these must not be taken by Cyrus and borne off in triumph as the spoils of war. Even worse, Cyrus might bring all manner of enchantments to these idols and so change their disposition that they might transfer their favor and their power to his side. The caravan of wagons and pack animals drew on towards the tower of Babylon in the sanctuary of E-Sagila. There they would find repose and a safe refuge from the hand of Cyrus.

On the Sabbath of that week, the prophet, completely ignoring the ban which had been put upon him by the notables of the Exile, described Babylon in its sore straits and pictured the gods in their headlong flight.

"Bel boweth down, Nebo stoopeth,
    Their idols were upon the beasts, and upon the cattle;
    Your carriages are heavy laden; they are a burden to the
        weary beast,

130

They stoop, they bow down together;
They could not deliver the burden,
But are themselves gone into captivity."

The utterance of the prophet reached the ears of the leaders of the Exile ensconced in the palace of the House of David. Mordechai-Gad knew that he had ridiculed the gods of Babylon in all the court-yards of the people, and deliberately disobeyed the ruling of Shaltiel, the aged prince of the exiles, not to preach in any synagogue and assembly whatsoever. Consternation fell upon the rulers of Baby-lonian Jewry. What would befall if the matter got to the ears of the king? All the Jews of Babylon quaked with terror and shuddered for their skins. A secret assembly of notables and merchants was held under the presidency of Mordechai-Gad and it was decided to hand the prophet over to Belshazzar as a rebel and traitor. In this way the danger threatening the community might be forestalled.

That same day, before the gates of the city were shut, Zerubabel and his companion Jeshu the priest hurried to the prophet in his hut beside the hovel of Neraiah.

"It is clear to us," they said, "that the word of God was in your mouth and that Babylon will be destroyed by Cyrus. We believe in you and have come to warn you. Your life is in danger. Do not venture to come within the walls of the city again. Lie low in one of the suburbs until Cyrus arrives with his armies. Do not enter the synagogues, and you will be well advised to refrain from preaching on the Sabbath, since the House of Murashu wish to hand you over to the authorities. Their agents have already gone out to search for you. You are in the gravest and most immediate danger."

The prophet made answer: "God does not allow His word to remain in darkness or be hidden in secret places. What is happen-ing today is part of His design and it is His finger which is the stylus that has graven it upon the record. How then can I justify myself if I seek to hide His word? You cannot hide the sun in a barrel of butter nor can you conceal the voice of thunder. If I suppress His word it will still emanate with the roar of a young lion."

"Listen, O prophet! I have warned you. You are uttering words against the king and his chief officers. No one will dare cross the threshold of any synagogue that you enter. The House of Murashu has warned our brethren that they should keep away from houses you frequent, that they should not listen to you, since your words are as the venom of adders likely to bring them great grief."

"God has many means of bringing His word to those whom He wishes to hear it. If I remain silent and fail to utter His message, then the wings of the wind will lift it up and bear it along. If ears are stopped up, then it will enter directly into the heart, for nothing can prevent the word of Jehovah from being fulfilled."

Neraiah took his aged father Seraiah, his wife Ama-Bar, and the prophet and removed them to his townsfolk in the court of the Bethlehemites in the Street of the Leatherworkers within the city.

When the sons of the servants of Solomon came, by order of Mordechai-Gad, to arrest the prophet in the hut of Neraiah, they found no one there. The hovel was deserted.

A change had come over the exiles since the prophet came among them. His word was a life-giving dew which put new sap into their dried-up bones.

The Sabbaths, festivals, and new moons on which he preached to them became holy days in real earnest, days of God. He brought them the precious gift of the Sabbath as it was rightly to be observed. Before the advent of the prophet, their synagogues did not capture the extra soul which emanates from the true hallowing of the Sabbath as God's day. He purified and purged them by his words of comfort and tidings of redemption. He enriched their consciousness, inspiring their souls by the chapters of psalms which he taught them to sing on Sabbaths. He did everything possible to revive in them recognition that they were a dedicated people.

Among the tasks which the sons of the prophets set themselves was the collation of the psalms which were current among the people from the time they still dwelt in Judah and Israel. Recited while the Temple still stood, they had become deeply embedded in the folk memory. There were psalms for Sabbaths and for festivals of the new moon, of the harvest, and the ingathering. All the perplexity of man in the face of the mysterious works of God were poured into them. Songs of war, of gladness, and bitter lamentation; the cry of the broken heart; the shout of triumph, and praises and eulogies of God who grants rich gifts of salvation to His people. Many chapters had been handed down from generation to generation from the earliest times, from the days of the Egyptian exodus and the wanderings in the desert. Many psalms were composed in the heyday of the state when David and Solomon had themselves enriched this literature. When the Temple was laid waste and the cream of the people had gone into exile, the psalms gradually faded from active use and memory. Therefore the sons of the prophet set themselves the task of gathering in these pearls, writing them down on clay tablets and trying to give them currency once more among the exiles.

When the prophet arrived in Babylon, it was mainly the aged and the elders, the second generation of the Exile, who still recited them. Particularly popular were the Songs of Degrees which the Levites used to sing in the Temple and which were also recited in formal order by the priests and Levites in the courtyard of the royal palace of David. But the young people of the second generation of the Exile were much inclined towards assimilation. Because in the main they spoke Aramaic, the use of this foreign tongue in daily intercourse meant that the psalms and the rest of the holy books which were familiar to the lips of their parents were forgotten by them. The prophet brought many chapters of psalms with him. He sang them, intermingling them with his prophecies, on the Sabbaths and festivals in the synagogues. He gradually popularized them among the younger generation. He gathered the little children and youths around him and made them learn by heart the chapters which so elevated the soul.

This work performed wonders. The psalms aroused almost forgotten memories and stirred national longings which had apparently passed into complete oblivion. The prophet used them to cause a new well of emotion to break out among the exiles. He put prayer in their hearts and turned their dumb lips into expressive instruments.

In times of grace when the Holy Spirit rested upon him, the prophet composed new songs. These expressed his deepest feelings about daily events and as such struck a responsive chord in the heart of the people who were similarly troubled. The people did not just pray for themselves as they sang the psalms. They also poured out praise and exaltation to God. While thus recounting His strength and praise they felt themselves lifted up on the wings of vision which broods over the very existence and essence of the Jew. They found an anchorage in their earliest history, in the time when they were a people, thus gradually losing their feeling that God had forsaken them and beginning to think honorably of themselves. They gained self-confidence and learned to cast their lot upon God. There were those among them to whom this faith in their God and in themselves as a people was such that it could never again be taken from them.

Despite all the threats and warnings issued by the great merchants, the mass of the people would not forsake their allegiance to the prophet and knew where he could be preaching each Sabbath or festival. The knowledge was kept a deep secret, being conveyed by word of mouth only to the utterly reliable. These were informed that on such and such a date and in such and such a place the prophet would preach.

In those days, when the predictions of the prophet had in great measure been fulfilled and when Babylon had suffered a crushing defeat in battle, the stock of the prophet rose not only among the masses of the exiles who dwelt in the city courtyards and the more distant settlements but also with the chiefs, priests, elders, and Levites who frequented the precincts of the palace of the House of David. If before many of them had belittled him and ridiculed him, they were now filled with a kind of awe. The masses, particularly the Bethlehemites in whose courtyard the prophet had taken refuge, protected him from his persecutors and watched over him. When Sabbath came the crowds, despite dangers and threats, streamed to the synagogue from the streets and alleys to listen to his words.

That same Sabbath the prophet went once again to the synagogue of the Bethlehemites and lifted up his burden against Babylon with even greater force and venom.

"Come down and sit in the dust, O virgin daughter of Babylon. Sit on the ground; there is no throne, O daughter of the Chaldeans; for thou shalt no more be called tender and delicate. Take the millstones and grind meal; uncover thy locks, make bare the leg, uncover the thigh, pass over the rivers. . . ."

Thus the prophet continually announced the downfall of Babylon and also enumerated all her sins:

"I was wroth with my people; I have polluted mine inheritance and given them into thine hand: thou didst show them no mercy; upon the ancient hast thou heavily laid thy yoke. And thou saidst, I shall be a lady for ever; so thou didst not lay these things to thy heart, neither didst thou remember the latter end of it."

After the prophet had indicted Babylon's arrogance and her vainglorious assumption that she was the greatest power and there was none beside her, that she not sit as a widow nor know the loss of children, and after he had depicted the terrible fate that awaited her, he glowed with a fiery excitement and burst into the psalm of the freedom that was drawing very close, singing the radiant vision that his spirit saw:

"When the Lord turned again the captivity of Zion,
    We were like those that dream.
    Then was our mouth filled with laughter
    And our tongue with singing.
    Then said they among the heathen,
    The Lord hath done great things for them.
    The Lord hath done great things for us, therefore are we glad.

"Turn again our captivity, O Lord, as the streams in the south,
They that sow in tears shall reap in joy.
He that goeth forth and weeping bearing precious seed,
Shall doubtless come again rejoicing
Bearing his sheaves with him."

The dreams of the exiles gathered in the synagogue, of the nation, and of the prophet coalesced into the dream of the redemption and the return to Zion. With one heart and with one united spirit they joined in with the prophet in his new psalm. The building seemed to move and throb as the hearts of every one of them exulted movingly together.

"When the Lord turned again the captivity of Zion
We were like those that dream."

# CHAPTER ELEVEN

DESPITE everything, the gates of Babylon remained shut before Cyrus. He could neither break them down nor take them by storm. All the cities between Sippar and Babylon were in his hands. Some had been reduced by the sword; some had surrendered; some fell to him like ripe plums. Those which put up a stiff opposition were scorched with burning pitch. But the walls of Babylon apparently put an end to the victorious advance of his armies. The world seemed to melt away before them and all that was left was the mighty wall rising heavenward in its terrifying aspect. Nothing seemed real any longer, only the wall, built of great blocks burned into the hardness of stone, sprouting with a forest of turrets from which observation slits multiplied, projected, and interlocked one with another. Hundreds of fierce yellow lions, gigantic in size, with glaring eyes, gaping jaws, and claws outstretched, looked down terrifyingly from the wall ready to seize and rend. The armies surrounding the city knew well that these lions were but images unable to utter a sound, move their jaws, put forth their talons, or close their eyes. They knew quite well that they were frozen, immobile stone, dumb images, but awe of them still disconcerted the legions of Cyrus. Most of the soldiers were too ignorant to know better. There were highlanders from Phrygia, Cilicia, Cappadocia, savage levies from the mountains of Medea to the mountains of Ararat. There were Kedarites from the deserts of the south towards the Yemen, Assyrians, Cypriots, Bedouin from the wilderness and the Arabah. Each people and tribe brought their idols and abominations with them, their witchcrafts, their sorceries and sorcerers. Just as a wild horse when first put under bridle and rein recoils and bucks at every obstacle it meets, so the multitude of Cyrus's warriors recoiled and kicked at the frightening prospect of the wall crouching like a gigantic monster behind the broad stream of the wide canal which ran around it and shut off every approach.

But even greater than the terror of the savage and superstitious soldiers was the confusion of the captains of the hosts, except for Cyrus and his heir Cambyses. It was not the beasts set in the wall that disturbed them but the fortifications themselves. They had heard many reports about them, how they could not be approached or breached; now they saw with their own eyes. This wall was too strong to be taken by assault. There was no question of storming the jagged rocks projecting one above the other and encompassed by the canal. Moreover, veritable death, not the mere fear of it and chance of combat, lay in ambush in ten thousand sure forms from myriads of arrows, lances, and sling stones which would hail down from the observation towers and hidden traps with which it was abundantly bestrewn.

Gubaru, the governor appointed over the satraps of Babylon, had gone over to Cyrus at the very beginning of the war. He stemmed from a noble family which had always been loyal to Nebuchadnezzar and his dynasty. He nursed a poisonous hatred for Nabonidus and his prince regent Belshazzar and indeed for all the dignitaries who had only yesterday been adorned with the plumes of nobility by the usurping house. He was already advanced in years, somewhat between seventy and eighty, but nevertheless he took his life in his hand and organized a network of espionage for Cyrus which covered the whole of Babylon. No one would have dreamed of suspecting that an aged noble who for years had been devoted to a life of asceticism would have contact or intercourse with the enemy. He was a Chaldean of purest stock and ancestry, a living symbol of all that was best in Babylon, from the noble blood which coursed through his veins and from his appearance, conduct, and way of life. He possessed the right to plait his beard into three and was a fan-bearer of the king. He was thus very well equipped to spread such a spy net over all Babylon and it included many and varied elements of the population.

Cyrus called a Council of War. He, his son Cambyses, and the staff officers were trying to elaborate a strategy to besiege and storm the city. Gubaru gave the Council a review of the situation within the walls.

"O king of kings, redeemer of all peoples, I am compelled to warn you and your war council that according to information put at my disposal by my agents and from the conclusions I draw from it the city can by no means be taken by storm. As you and your honored Council know well, the defenses of fortress Babylon are dependent on three walls which surround the city in three parallel rings joined by a road built above them. Around the outside of this wall, which is built of bricks baked in pitch, runs a canal, while the waters of the Euphrates encircle it from within. Even if fate should smile upon us and we should, by some stroke of fortune, breach the outer wall and cross the Euphrates, we should only encounter the second wall, which is very thick indeed. There is only one feasible approach, by way of the gates of Ishtar, where the only stone bridge across the Euphrates is situated. This gate of Ishtar is not fortified. It is made of cedar beams covered with plates of copper. Day and night bowmen and slingers mount watch in its towers. One has to take into account the possibility of opening the dams across the river and flooding the bridge with water. But even if one were to break through here, he would find complete annihilation awaiting him. The gate of Ishtar is a deadly trap. If the assailant should pass through, he would walk into a closed sack, the Avenue of the Processions, at whose entrance the gate of Ishtar stands. This street, in which the palace of Nebuchadnezzar and the sanctuaries of Ishtar and Bel Merodach are built, is shut off from the inner city by fortified walls which cannot be circumvented. They have embrasures and ambuscades without number. Whoever enters the Avenue of the Processions puts his head inside the jaws of a beast of prey. There is no exit to this street. True, innumerable alleys branch off from it as do the vaults to the canals, but these are likewise a snare. They are narrow and tortuous; they weave like threads coiled one into the other; and whoever enters them falls into an intricate maze. It is not enough that he wanders about seeking an exit but he is laid wide open to the bowmen, slingers, and stone throwers on the high buildings which overlook it. All this leads me to the conclusion that there is no way into the fortress from outside. Whoever dares an assault would be wiped out without catching sight of a single Babylonian."

"What is the food and supply situation in the city?" asked Cambyses, son of Cyrus.

"Ever since the time of Nebuchadnezzar," answered Gubaru, "the Babylonians have hoarded up in the granaries and warehouses of the city vast stores of all kinds of food and provisions for a state of emergency. For this purpose, a definite proportion has been regularly deducted from every harvest and all produce. In addition to this the Governor appointed over the city itself has at his disposal large tracts around the sanctuaries and in various districts of the city. These are open ground and can be cultivated during a siege. This war finds them especially well prepared, for no sooner did the news reach Babylon that you had crossed the Tigris than they began to bring into the city from outlying points enormous quantities of provisions of all kinds. These they stored in vast warehouses, in the cellars of the palace of Nebuchadnezzar, in the sanctuary of Bel Merodach and various towers. Reports indicate that the city's supply position is assured for a long period."

"Has the fact that I have come to rescue them from exile and return them to their own lands been brought to the knowledge of the alien inhabitants of Babylon?" asked Cyrus.

"O king great in lovingkindness! the people who dwell in Babylon no longer wish to return to their countries of origin. Babylon no longer has an alien population. Those who were brought there either by compulsion or of their own free will have assimilated and have forgotten their former homes. The Assyrians who dwell there are more Babylonian than the Babylonians. They claim Bel Merodach as their god, the god of gods. Since he conquered their deity Asshur, he became their god and the place where his glory dwells became their homeland. So also with the other strangers who came to the city. Believing that the gods of Babylon are mightier than their own, they have all transferred their allegiance to Bel Merodach and Ishtar. These they now worship with a faithful zeal greater than that evinced by the true Babylonians. The Assyrians and the highland tribes are the most powerful element in the Babylonian armies. The only people who remember their homeland and cleave to their God are the Judeans who went into exile out of Judah. They worship their own God, Jehovah; they no longer possess a sanctuary or offer sacrifices. Lately a great enthusiasm has been kindled among them and strong longings for their native land have been stirred by the report that you, O king great in lovingkindness, have promised to free them from the yoke of Babylon and return them to Judah, sending with them the sacred vessels taken by Nebuchadnezzar from their holy temple. They believe that you will give them permission to rebuild their Temple to Jehovah. So great a pitch has their enthusiasm reached that a prophet who latterly appeared among them has declared that he brings them good tidings from the lips of their God, to the following effect: Jehovah told him that He had chosen you, O king great in lovingkindness, to be His servant and was sending you to perform His mission. What is His mission? To destroy Babylon and free all the subjugated peoples. The chosen servant of Jehovah he calls you. He says that Jehovah holds you by your right hand; that He will smash the walls of Babylon before you and break down her gates, and you will proclaim freedom to the multitude of the peoples. He so reverences you that he has conferred upon you the name that they have treasured for ages for their great redeemer, who is supposed to be born only from among them. Messiah is the name. This man, who has the temerity to confer this title upon you, has aroused great wrath among the princes of his people, who cherish a savage enmity for him."

Cyrus exclaimed with great curiosity, his eyes open wide in

141

wonder, "God holds my right hand? Does this mean that He will crown me king of Babylon?"

"More than that! This prophet hints that you will free not only the Judeans but all other enslaved peoples; that you will recognize Jehovah as the One and Unique God of all creatures, even as they believe. Even more than this: they believe that you will bring to all nations upon whom freedom shall be proclaimed by your agency, an understanding to destroy their own gods, whom he calls abominations and shameful things. They will thus acknowledge as you will acknowledge and be convinced as you will be convinced, that their God is the One Unique God. Even more: Jerusalem their capital, the crown of their kingdom, will become the focal point and center of the earth, the most exalted meeting place of all the nations and all peoples. They will come to serve Jehovah, the One, Only and Unique God, in His Temple, which he calls the House of God."

A shrill laughter broke out among the generals and the satraps, but Cyrus was silent. It was clear that the prophet and his utterances interested him.

He asked, "When did he bring his good tidings to the Jews? Before or after the battle at Sippar?"

"Before."

Cyrus was deep in thought.

"What is the name of this prophet?"

"They call him Isaiah. This is really the name of an ancient prophet whose name is hallowed among them. This seer lived in the time of the Assyrian king Sennacherib. He had prophesied beforehand that Sennacherib would not subdue Jerusalem to which he was then laying siege and even as he foretold so it came to pass."

"Has this prophet many followers?"

"The poorer of the people give him great honor; those who are wealthy and mix in court circles show him much enmity. They wish to hand him over to Belshazzar on the pretext that he is a spy and a danger to the dynasty by his incitement of the people. It is only the poor, the craftsmen and the smiths, the ordinary folk and the paupers, and those of their sages who retain the recollection of their homeland and their divine worship in their Temple who give an ear willingly to the prophet and believe in him. But this will not contribute much to our cause. Even were all the wealthy and powerful among them devoted to us there would not be much of an accretion of strength for us."

"Why?"

"They are too few and their status is of little account. Our task is to get hold of the allegiance of those who hold the reins of leadership among the Babylonians themselves. I have to make it clear to you, O king full of lovingkindness, that the main thing is not that the gates of Babylon should be secretly opened to us—and this in any case the Jews could certainly not do—for it is Babylonians and Assyrians who keep the watch there. Our principal task is to find in Babylon faithful allies who can influence the captains of the host who command the guardians of the gates. In other words, quite simply, we have to find a means of winning the guardians of the gates over to our side. I have already explained that the sole entrance to the city is by way of the gate of Ishtar; but the opening of the gate will not help us. We must be assured of passage through the Avenue of the Processions and the maze of alleys coiling out of it. Obviously, this must of necessity take quite a time. It will take a long time before an adequate number of our armies, particularly our spearmen, penetrate the complex of narrow streets and reach the inner city. We must win over those who command the guards of the gates and even more some of the most influential of the leaders of Babylon at the court itself. These will have to lull the Babylonians, even Belshazzar himself, into a deep slumber, so that they become completely unaware of the danger that lies in wait for them from the walls. For this task the Jews are of no use at all. There is only one man who can help us in the whole of Babylon."

"Who is that?"

"The High Priest of Bel Merodach."

"By what means?"

143

"The High Priest will convey the word of Bel Merodach to the watch of the gates and even to those near the king of Babylon, saying: 'I, Bel Merodach, the god of Babylon, have sent Cyrus to you, to Babylon.'"

"How do you expect to achieve this?"

"We have good reason to believe that Sharezer Bel, the High Priest of Bel Merodach, is not deeply enamored of Nabonidus or Belshazzar or the rest of the great ones of their dynasty. The plan has not yet matured to the point of a concrete suggestion. Give me leave, O great king, to maintain a reserve about the details."

"You have our permission, Gubaru, and our thanks also for the important information you have brought. I have only one more question to ask. How long was Nebuchadnezzar employed in building the wall around Babylon?"

"On the tablet recording his acts he states that it took him but fifteen days. But we think that this is a boastful exaggeration on the part of the great king. Perhaps fifteen days passed before they were able to lay the foundations. We have a tradition from our ancestors that he employed hundreds of thousands of slaves and captives in the work and that it nevertheless took him fifteen years, not days, to raise the wall. There is no doubt that to build the wall and citadel took a very long time indeed. The work has been expanded and fortified by every succeeding dynasty."

Cyrus paid no further heed to the speaker. With a clap of his hands and a voice of great impatience he signed him to be silent.

"If Nebuchadnezzar needed no more than fifteen days to raise the wall by means of slaves, why should not we be able to pull it down in the same time by the hands of free men?"

All eyes centered on Cyrus. On every lip hung the question: How?

"The lifeline of Babylon is the Euphrates. If we can only divert the river from the city, all the canals upon which it depends will dry up automatically. They all flow into Babylon through vaulted openings in the foundations of the walls. Our soldiers will enter

144

by means of the dry channels and penetrate to the heart of the city."

The Council sat overwhelmed and amazed. No one dared open his mouth. They looked at one another and held their peace.

Finally, Cambyses, Cyrus's heir, plucked up courage and asked: "How, O great king, shall we divert the waters of the Euphrates from Babylon?"

"Very simply. Hundreds of thousands of our soldiers comprise our hosts. They are spread over the whole area from here to the Tigris. They are sprawling about in idleness with nothing to do but wait for a miracle or some good news that might or might not come from the priests of Bel Merodach. Idleness is dangerous for the morale of an army. Soldiers should be kept busily employed. Each man must be made to feel that victory depends on his own special effort. He must have something to do every day. So we shall harness hundreds and thousands of our men to the task of diverting the flow of the Euphrates from the point where it enters the city. We shall turn it aside into the lake near Babylon. Since this reservoir is lower in level than the river we shall thus dry up the canal beds and open a way for our armies to enter the city dry-shod."

Still no one dared utter a word. The stupendous daring of the plan which the king put before them literally took away their breath. Cyrus had not felt the same degree of fear as had his satraps and the rulers set over the local governors when they finally faced the wall of Babylon and came face to face with the insuperable tactical problem that it presented. Their spirits had fallen to a very low ebb. Fear took possession of them, the terror that Babylon had been so successful in implanting in every nation from time immemorial. It was the same fear indeed which was beginning to move the people in the country roundabout so that the supply of provisions to the armies of Cyrus was beginning to fall off.

Cyrus withdrew part of his forces from the walls, thus throwing dust in the eyes of the Babylonians, who thought he was abandoning the attempt to take the city. He withdrew to the lake in the center of the country between the two rivers, to take counsel with his engineers and technicians about his scheme to divert the waters of the Euphrates. Only part of his force was left in front of Babylon under the command of Cambyses. They, however, continued to hold the city in a ring of iron.

# CHAPTER TWELVE

BABYLON took fresh heart and breathed more freely. The situation had eased and life slowly returned to normal. The city was like one who stands upright when a heavy iron collar has been removed from his neck. "See what I told you," ran the word. "Did I not say so before? Cyrus cannot conquer Babylon. He can't even get near it. Babylon never has been and never will be conquered." People retailed all sorts of fantastic stories about the camp of Cyrus in which the wish determined the picture of reality. Everyone tried to show how loyal and faithful he was to the king and the Empire. "The gangs of Cyrus took one glimpse of our walls and the lions with their glaring eyes and gaping jaws and fled terrified in all directions."

In the Street of the Taverners stood an Assyrian in a torn cloak through which his naked flesh could be discerned. Water dripped from his hair and beard and streamed down his bare chest. He had just swum the Euphrates, he reported. They had not allowed him to enter the city by way of the gate of Ishtar. When he showed his seal to the watchmen indicating that he was a king's man they had seized him nevertheless and intended hauling him before the authorities. A definite rebellion had broken out among the troops of Cyrus, claimed the Assyrian.

They dragged the damp and dripping Assyrian from tavern to tavern. They soaked and filled him with liquor, with cheap date wine so that he should tell all he knew and disclose everything he had seen beyond the wall. The mob yelled at this news of sudden victory. They were frenzied with joy and jug after jug of cheap spirit passed from hand to hand.

In the Street of the Donkey Drivers they pointed out a carter who had escaped by a real miracle from outside just after the gates had been shut. He related that from the walls of Sippar to the Tigris the whole way was swarming with the armies of Cyrus. A fierce panic had befallen them when they reached the mighty fortified walls of Babylon and now they were going back, in full retreat.

The news spread through the whole city from the observation posts on the wall. The main force of Cyrus had withdrawn and turned inland towards Mesopotamia. There all trace of them had been lost. It was certainly a fact that the forces of Cyrus investing the city had been definitely reduced in number.

Once more the clay oil lanterns shone with gay but murky flames before the doors of the wine cellars and taverns. Once more the canals were merry with a vast concourse of people crowding the pleasure boats that cruised up and down, their prows lively with torches, their hulls overloaded with the travelers in festive array almost hysterical with joy and merriment.

The officers appointed over the storehouses opened their doors wide in their great confidence that the siege would shortly be lifted completely. Bread could now be bought freely and the food markets throbbed with life. Smoke and fumes and stenches emanated from the fires underneath the tripods in the Square of the Slaughterhouses next to the main market area. Cooks roasted beef and mutton on spits that was snatched eagerly from their hands as soon as it was brown. The market, brightly illuminated by a plethora of torches and clay lamps, swarmed with humanity. People bought everything: multicolored kerchiefs, woolen cloaks, gewgaws, leather belts, oils and perfumes for their wives and courtesans, all preparing to celebrate the victory over the enemy. They showed their enthusiasm in the triumph which had not yet been consummated by abandoning themselves publicly to lust and bestiality. Acrobats, mimes, and rope dancers represented the terror that had fallen upon the enemy at the sight of the lions carved in the walls. Astrologers pointed with their fingers to the stars and planets and proved by signs and symbols from their movements in their orbits that a strange end awaited Cyrus and his host. Babylon was deceived by the thick clouds of illusion that she herself had stirred about in her own head.

The Temple of Ishtar was crowded with harlot votaries. Saturated with lust its devotees overflowed into the streets and the squares roundabout. They announced to the seething multitudes congregated there the glad tidings that the goddess Ishtar had announced in distinct terms that the lot of the enemy had been decided and that he was doomed. Cyrus had fled; his armies, beset with the terror of death, were wandering aimlessly in the wilderness.

The news reached the Jewish quarter that Cyrus had turned away from Babylon, that his host had been scattered to the four winds, and that the siege would be lifted any day. A fearful panic seized many who had paid attention to the word of the prophet and had been deceived and disillusioned by his lying and empty words that Cyrus would bring redemption. They now hastened to deny to all and sundry that the prophet ever meant anything to them and that they had ever really listened to him.

Now the storm in its full fury burst against the prophet in the palace of the nobles of Judah. Mordechai-Gad arose in the highest conclave of the Exile and spoke quietly but incisively.

"I predicted from the very beginning that it would end like this. I wanted to warn you but you were really disinclined to believe me. A strange man, a man of dubious origin, preaches in public, proclaiming that the inveterate enemy of our Empire is he whom God has chosen to redeem His people. Nor does this suffice him. He hands over, as it were, the kingly crown of the Messiah, promised by God through His servants the true prophets to a scion of the House of David, to an utter stranger. Moreover, to add to the disgrace and wrath that is piling up for us, one of our own number, among the highest in rank and station, has entered into the closest ties with this agitator of Cyrus. He went to him and entreated him to beware of the emissaries we sent to restrain him so as to prevent calamity befalling our community. I shall not labor the treachery that was perpetrated by this highborn member of our council against the Babylonian sovereign although it was a betrayal sufficient to warrant the penalty of execution. I shall not even elaborate on the danger he brings upon all of his people because of this. But I cannot refrain from touching upon the evil he brings to his own ancestral house. If a scion of the House of David is prepared to abrogate his title of 'King Messiah' which will appertain to one born of his seed, then we have reason to question whether we have any longer a share and inheritance in the royal house and in Judah itself. We have no land of our own. None of us who came to Babylon wishes to return to Judea. We have nothing to hope for there. There was only one link which bound us to that land and that was our loyalty to the royal House of David. But if the sons of the house themselves are prepared to hand over their heritage to one of the uncircumcised—and to whom? To the bitter and deadly foe of our country—then what have we in common with the House of David? Let us proclaim the king of Babylon as our Messiah and our redeemer and not Cyrus or one of his lick-spittles."

"Who dared to do this? Whom do you mean?" asked Shaltiel, rising pale and trembling in his place at the words of Mordechai-Gad.

"It was I, O lord and father!" affirmed the young Zerubabel, standing up proud and erect. "And not because I am either ready or willing to hand over the crown and dignity of the Messiah or his mission to a stranger or to anyone else who does not stem from our House of David. I did it to save the innocent blood of the prophet from those who were planning to shed it unwarrantedly. If I have your permission, O revered father, and yours, O chiefs of the Exile, and yours, O priests, I will make clear my feelings on the matter. The ways of God are hidden from us. We do not know His thoughts. What seems to us today to be perverted and tortuous He may on the morrow show to be straight and direct. He makes

150

known His will to us by means of His chosen ones the prophets. But we do not know exactly what constitutes a prophet. He shares the divine mystery that is hidden from our eyes. Nor do we know just how the divine spirit comes down upon the prophet and takes control of him so that he is able to announce the shape of future events before they are yet formed. It may be very difficult indeed for us to accept the fact that what he foretells will indeed come to pass, since it may fly in the face of all reason that things should fall out as he predicts; nevertheless they do so come about. Whoever was prepared to believe what happened in the time of my grandsire, that Babylon would conquer Egypt as the prophet Jeremiah foretold? Had our forefathers listened to Jeremiah we would still be dwelling in our own land. The prophets see things we cannot see; they know the paths of God. So long as we listen to them we are saved and when we fail to heed them retribution comes upon us. It was such a retribution that I sought at all costs to prevent."

Zerubabel lifted up his voice and spoke with great passion.

"I wished to prevent the shedding of innocent blood. There will be no innocent blood shed here such as was brutally spilt in the days of King Manasseh in Jerusalem and for which the city was in consequence destroyed. I wanted to stay those hands which would have dealt with the prophet as our fathers dealt with Jeremiah when he minted words out of his heart's blood hoping to save them from ruin, and they rewarded him by casting him into a pit. That was what I wished to do and that is what I did."

The words of Zerubabel made a profound impression upon the gathering. Tears started into the corners of the eyes of the elders among them.

But Mordechai-Gad was not abashed.

"To save one life, you were prepared to bring calamity upon a whole community?"

"What do you mean?"

"You can see for yourself. The spirit of Cyrus could not stand up against the very sight of the walls of Babylon. His forces have fled in panic and he is plodding along the path of retreat. It is well known in the court of Belshazzar who supported Cyrus and who was his enemy. The prophet did not speak in darkness. He did not preach in secret. He came out into the open so that everyone could hear."

"There was no need to kill him. Heaven forbid that we should shed the blood of the innocent," interrupted the aged Shaltiel. "We could, however, have sealed his lips."

"Did I not warn him? Did I not entreat him to cease his preaching?" said Zerubabel. "He answered that the word of God forces itself out of his mouth and that no man on earth can close that which God opens."

"Still we do not know for sure whether the words the prophet utters come from God or from Cyrus."

"Nevertheless he foretold rightly what would happen at the battle of Sippar."

"We are now dealing with the incident at the walls of Babylon and not with Sippar. Just consider the words of the prophet in the light of present realities. Will they be fulfilled or not?"

"My good friend, will you not consider what I am telling you," said the aged prince. "We can remove the sting from this prophet without shedding his blood. Come here to me, O chief of my guards, chief of the sons of the servants of Solomon, and you too, O heads of the House of Shallum."

Sotai and Shallum, the lords of the presence, arose from among the assembly and drew near the seat of Shaltiel. He studied their faces for a moment, then said:

"Go at my command, find this prophet, and bring him here to me. We have more than enough hiding places here where we can keep him shut away and solitary until the will of God shall more clearly reveal what we should do with him. It is forbidden for the prophet to preach and assemble the congregation lest he bring disaster upon us as Mordechai-Gad has made quite clear with his rare breadth of understanding."

As soon as the session was concluded, Zerubabel hastened to

the Market Place of the Teraphim, found the shipman Neraiah working his ferry between the square and the Temple of Ishtar, and extracted from him the secret of the prophet's place of concealment.

Meanwhile the prophet, completely innocent of the storm which raged about him, or perhaps deliberately ignoring it, stood before the Bethlehemites and preached to them in the streets, in their places of work, in their courtyards.

"O men of Bethlehem, do ye not see the green hills that cluster around your city as little girls cluster round their nurse? Do you not see the flocks that graze and pasture in your vineyards? Do not your ears hear the voice of your mother calling to you in the stillness of the night—'Come back, O children, to your inheritance.'?

"The wind is lifted up over the face of the wilderness and brings a moaning with it. As the ancient prophet spake: 'Rachel is weeping over her children.' How can you reconcile yourselves to sit at ease and unperturbed on alien soil while your own land is shooting up thorns and thistles and the high places carry the abominations and filthy practices of the heathen? In vain do the stars in your clear heavens sing their song to the earth below. No ear listens and no heart comprehends their burden."

Again and again the prophet kept opening their hearts so that they should understand why Israel had a duty to return to her native soil. He spoke to everyone who would give ear: "Is there no understanding in your hearts? Do you not know that Israel is destined to leave Babylon and return to her land? Jacob will not be like all the heathen. He will not degenerate into uncleanness and idolatry. Jacob will surely observe the Law of Jehovah just as a bound servant; he will keep its statutes and commandments. Jacob will surely tend the holy fire that was kindled on Mount Sinai. Not for himself alone will he do so but in order to bring this light and fire to all the peoples of the world. For there is no God save the God of Israel and no strength save His; no dominion save in

153

His dominion. God is Omnipotent, there is none beside Him. All perform His will; all observe His commandment. His purpose lies at the end of all things and He will bring all the nations unto Himself."

He went to the bazaars and market places where he could find an ear to listen: "God did not create the world to be an empty vessel without use, nor did He create a small, lone people to live apart in isolation, in righteousness and justice, while the other peoples ran about in utter savagery like the beasts of the forest. The whole world is Mine, saith the God Jehovah. Man is Mine and every knee shall bow before Me. Therefore it is laid upon the people of Israel that it must leave this land of impurity, this cursed land of Babylon to which Jehovah exiled it because of its sins, return to Judah and rebuild Jerusalem and the Holy Temple. Israel must be a people peculiarly set aside, and for this reason God has chosen her. She must be a gateway through which the nations of the world will find their way into the House of God. Because of this, God sent Cyrus, the work of His hand, the vessel He selected to break the ring of walls about Babylon, to free Israel and restore her to her land. Cyrus will take Israel only a small distance along the road to redemption; he will but bring it a little nearer to the Messiah, the redeemer whom He will bring when all nations will come to the mountain of Jehovah.

"Just as Assyria and Babylon were the staffs of His wrath and the rod of chastisement for Israel and Judah, so is Cyrus the vessel in which God keeps the oil of His grace by which He will heal the wounds of His people. In this measure will Cyrus be Jehovah's anointed, the emissary bringing God's healing to his folk. Because of this shall Cyrus enjoy victory and see all obstacles turned aside from the path of his triumphal march."

Thus spake the prophet to the men of Israel in Babylon, using simple common speech to them in their courtyards in the evenings and in their synagogues on the Sabbath, despite the ban and the danger that threatened him.

"Has not God opened our eyes and shown us the way the

154

children of Israel will go when they return from Babylon? Have I not seen the wilderness turning itself into a Paradise? Have I not seen the many streams of water pouring over the sand dunes of the desert, coming with reviving power to quench their thirst? God in His glory would lead them through the wilderness and if He chooses to go forth with His people what power can withstand Him? Have I not heard the whirr of wheels, the beat of horses' hoofs, the clash of armor, the tramp of marching armies as they come, crowding in from all directions and coming up against Babylon? And did I not hear the voice of Jehovah crying in my heart, 'And thou, O Israel, my servant, Jacob whom I have chosen...I, Jehovah thy God, hold you by your right hand. ...Fear not, O worm Jacob, O men of Israel.'"

Such thoughts pressed on the mind of the prophet at that time when he looked down upon the streets of Babylon and heard the tumult and exultation of the inhabitants prematurely celebrating the victory over Cyrus. His eyes wandered over the faces of the wildly jubilant throngs, drunken with wine and fornications in the broad places of Babylon.

"They dance at their own funeral," thought the prophet. "They guzzle wine and wax drunken over their own graves."

But the grief which pierced the vitals of his heart was not on their account. He lamented over the mad festivity which broke out among his own people as they rejoiced over the calamity that had apparently befallen Cyrus. These people had been resigned to exile, but nevertheless only a few weeks previously they had thronged the synagogues to overflowing when Cyrus had won his victory over Babylon at Sippar. They had come in order to hear his words of comfort and learn of the hope of the swift deliverance of Judah as though emanating from the mouth of God. Now, these willing exiles who had only recently been exalted by his words and his vision and had lifted up their hands towards Jerusalem and had sworn, "If I forget thee, O Jerusalem, let my right hand forget its cunning," were completely at one with the peoples who dwelt in Babylon. They were like the Babylonians, the Assyrians,

155

the Sidonians, the Kedarites, and the other rabble. They, too, like Canaanite slaves, suppressed every feeling and instinct of freedom; like them, they shouted aloud, "We love the bonds that bind us; we kiss the rod that scourges us." When he came to their synagogues on the Sabbath they yelled: "Get out, unclean one! Get you gone, man of impurity! You have brought us nothing but trouble!" In their courtyards, in front of their stalls and stores and workshops, whenever he tried to draw near and speak to them, they screamed, "Get away from here, man possessed of demons! The Babylonians may see you here and suspicion will fall on us!" They had even smitten him, had spat in his face, had driven him from the synagogues and every place where the exiles were to be found. They had threatened to bind him with chains and hand him over to the Babylonians or the agents of Mordechai-Gad who were seeking him. They would indeed have done so had not Neraiah protected and saved him.

The exiles in general lived in small congregations based either on their city of origin or their ramified family groups. They inhabited brick houses of two or three stories with narrow stone stairways leading from one level to another. The dwellings were impoverished and cramped, the inside courtyards little more than gloomy narrow cells illumined by a feeble light which found its way through slits cut in the walls. The inhabitants of over-crowded Babylon spent practically their whole time out of doors, only returning to their hovels at night to sleep. Work and family life went on in the courtyards or narrow alleys.

The Bethlehemites, who were but a small group, occupied one pent-in and neglected close which differed in no respect from hundreds of others in the city. It consisted of brick houses with a fenced yard in front of each. The Bethlehemites were known throughout the city as spinners, weavers, and dyers of wool, crafts they had brought with them from Judah. They also included sandal makers and tailors. Their workshops were situated either in the courtyard or beside the stalls in the alley where they sold their goods straight from the bench.

Like all the other exiles, the Bethlehemites had their own synagogue. On weekdays it served as a storehouse for their goods and tools but was converted into a place of worship on Sabbath and festivals. Since their native town was so near Jerusalem they were closely bound with ties of love to the Holy City and its worship, and the passion for redemption was cherished deep within their hearts. They still retained vivid memories of Jerusalem, recalling how their fathers used to go up on the Festivals, how they brought the first fruits of their harvest and their toil, their weaves of delicate wool which they spun with their own hands from the fleece of their own sheep pastured in their own fields. The second generation still treasured the tale of the glory of Jerusalem at festival time and handed it down to their children as a precious heritage. They told them of the sacred service and so inspired them with the longing for the lost days of splendor and the desire for redemption.

It was in the synagogue of the Bethlehemites that the prophet had often uttered his words of comfort, promises of return to Zion, and psalms of deliverance. In general the small building could not contain all the worshippers who gathered from all parts of Babylon. In such a case when the crowd filled the whole yard, the prophet would go forth and speak to them in the open. As time went by even this expedient did not suffice. He thereupon began to preach during weekdays also, in the evening when the labor of the day was done. He would stand among them, by the light of the moon or the gleam of oil lamps, and utter words of comfort which would arouse in them a passion for the redemption.

Even in these later days, when the prophet was closely persecuted and driven forth from every synagogue, the Bethlehemites still gathered together and gave ear to his words as before. He himself showed no sign of fear of the threats which went forth against him but continued to visit the small synagogue and pour out the hot passion of his heart before God.

The days were gloomy; all hope seemed to have vanished. The pregnant woman had come to the bearing stool but could not bring forth her child. Never for a moment did Isaiah's constant belief falter that God would fulfill His promise. Not for the blinking of an eye did he entertain a particle of doubt as to the validity of his experience of the Holiest of the Holiest. He had not seen the mystic chariot that Ezekiel had visioned nor the vision in the heavens that his predecessor and namesake had observed. He had not attained the highest sphere in which a vision of God was vouchsafed to him and speech granted him face to face. He heard it only as a voice speaking within his own heart and believed with perfect conviction that what he thus apprehended was true and right.

Nevertheless he longed to be given a sign not for his own sake but for others: the lost sheep of Israel caught between the arms of the pincers of Belshazzar and Cyrus. Cyrus stood before the gate of Babylon and it was shut in his face. But the gates were not just barred to Cyrus and his legions; they were closed fast before the redemption, before Israel and Judah. And the worm Jacob was terrified and confused. Israel was in the sorest straits and the heart of the prophet melted with apprehension. He wanted a sign for the sake of the worm Jacob. No, it was not a sign he wanted but a word! God must kindle a glow of consolation in his heart so that he, Isaiah, might bring it to the terrified and lost sheep of Israel.

He lay stretched on the floor of the synagogue, his face pressed into the ground. He immersed his whole body in fearful reverence and prayed:

"God of Israel, my help and my Saviour, who sent me with the word of Thy comfort on my lips. Thy sheep are standing as if lost and know not which way to turn. Have mercy upon them, O my God, for their hearts are melted with terror. Put into my mouth a word of comfort for thy servant Jacob who is nigh to perishing."

When he opened his eyes he thought he saw King David standing before him, King David himself in the prime of his youth. He was dancing in a white linen ephod before the Ark of the Covenant. It was in fact Zerubabel who stood before him. He remembered him from their meeting a few days previously, but he was completely transformed. His tall form was robed in a white ephod such as David had worn and his ruddy joyful face was radiant with the light of holy longing and passion for God. His prophetic eyes pierced through to the inner being of the man who stood before him and he saw him as the builder of the Temple that was to be—a scion of the House of David. It seemed as though an invisible crown floated above the swarthy locks.

"Dance before me, O son of David," cried the prophet.

"Dance?" asked Zerubabel in wonder. "I came to warn you against dangerous hands who wish to shut the mouth that God has opened. Your life is in danger."

"Dance before me, O son of David, as your father danced before the Ark of the Covenant."

"Why should I dance?" Zerubabel repeated in amazement. "Is there cause for rejoicing?"

"Dance for joy. Dance to express your thanks for the salvation that God is bringing to His people Israel."

As he spoke the prophet raised himself from the floor and began to sway slowly and gracefully. His youthful body moved rhythmically backwards and forwards in a dance and his song poured from him:

> "Go ye forth from Babylon,
> Flee ye from the Chaldeans,
> With a voice of singing declare ye,
> Tell this,
> Utter it even to the ends of the earth,
> Say ye:
> Jehovah hath redeemed his servant Jacob."

Zerubabel stood and stared at the prophet with startled and expectant eyes as the ringing voice mounted to a feverish excitement. His eyes, tightly shut, began to look like two dark pits in his ghostlike pale face; his body was writhing and contorting as though a great fever racked him, as though vast storms were spending themselves in him and transporting him to other worlds. He repeated his words over and over in changing rhythms, sinking at last to the softness of a lullaby in which there was the faint echo of a distant storm. Finally the prophet aroused himself from the entranced dance, drew near to the stunned Zerubabel, and looked at him with glazed and wandering eyes as one blinded by a vision and said:

"Thus saith the Lord; thou, Zerubabel, shalt raise up Mine House which I destroyed and shalt return My people to its inheritance."

"I!" The word burst from the lips of Zerubabel in tones full of dread and astonishment. He was pale and terrorstricken, and he went away bewildered, unable to fulfill his father's command.

Swiftly the rumor passed from lip to lip that the prophet had seen a vision and would, on the following Sabbath, bring new good tidings of the God of Israel to the congregation in the synagogue of the Bethlehemites. The danger to anyone who associated with the prophet was now very great, since the House of Murashu, with the consent of the princes of Judah, had sent messengers to seize him on a charge of rebellion against the Empire. In spite of this, crowds of worshippers flowed to the conventicle from all parts of the city. One could never tell beforehand what the prophet might say, what tidings he might bring. There were not a few among the exiles who differed from the prophet, claiming his prophecies were false and a danger to the Jewish community of Babylon. When the little synagogue was full and the courtyard outside packed with congregants, the prophet went out to the concourse which filled the open space. Watchmen were stationed on the walls to look out for the officers of the royal court. They were not afraid of the sons of the servants of Solomon who had been sent from the palace of the House of David to keep the prophet under surveillance but did not dare arrest him. Neraiah had stationed a bodyguard of powerful young men of the Bethlehemites around him.

They were all devoted followers of the prophet pledged to protect him. They did not stir from his side. But when the prophet stepped out into the courtyard and prepared to speak, he was assailed from all sides with a hail of insults, curses, and imprecations.

"Just look. Here comes the windmill that grinds straw, the thresher that threshes chaff, the empty skin bottle full of east wind."

"He has not come to bring us a blessing but a curse, trouble and mourning. He will not lead us into pleasant pastures but to Sheol below."

"A serpent is hidden in his mouth which spits out poison and adder's venom. It is not the word of God that issues from his mouth but that which the enemy puts into it. It is the smooth tongue of Cyrus."

These shouts were instigated by men of the following of Mordechai-Gad.

"This uprooter of Israel has chosen an alien to be the Messiah," cried a double hunchback who leaned on another's shoulders. "He is a spy of Cyrus, not an emissary of Jehovah. Where is the sign that the true prophet would bring from God? You can see with your own eyes what has happened to Cyrus."

"Judeans, if you value your lives, keep away from him! Don't go near! It is dangerous to stand where he stands."

"Let us not seek to close a mouth that God has opened," one of the Bethlehemites was heard to shout.

Amid the rain of objurgations which were showered upon his head, the prophet, wrapped in his long white cloak, stood upright and aloof. His blazing eyes gazed silently upon the storming crowd; a faint tolerant smile of sorrow and understanding played about his lips, like a glance a father bends upon a willful child. He waited until the congregation was completely still and began only when absolute quiet reigned in the yard. He started to speak quietly. His soft voice rose and swelled. He was like a tamer of wild beasts who enters a cage of lions and dominates them by his steadfast eye and the whip he raises aloft over their heads. But the lash he raised over this stormy crowd was the rod of moral chastisement. Even if momentarily they were moved with an impulse to break the rod he held in his hand his silent reproof soon turned them to stone. And for the first time, the prophet was constrained to express not just the comfort and consolation of God but also His burning anger:

"For I knew that thou wouldst deal very treacherously
And wast called a transgressor from the womb.
For my name's sake will I defer mine anger
And my praise will I refrain from thee,
That I cut thee not off.
Behold I have refined thee, but not with silver;
I have chosen thee in the furnace of affliction.
For mine own sake, even for mine own sake will I do it;
For how should my name be polluted?
And I will not give my glory to another."

Then the prophet once again affirmed that what he had promised would be fulfilled, as the things he had previously spoken of had been:

"All ye assemble yourselves and hear;
Which among you hath declared these things?
Jehovah hath loved him;
He will do his pleasure on Babylon,
And his arm shall be on the Chaldeans.
I, even I, have spoke;
Yea, I have called him;
I have brought him and he shall make his way prosperous."

Confusion broke out among the listeners. Faces blanched with fear. Fists were raised towards him as people pushed and forced their way through the assembly trying to break through to the prophet.

"Close his mouth. Don't let him speak!"

"It is dangerous merely to stand and listen."

"Hand him over to the authorities. To the royal power."

The sons of the servants of Solomon thrust hard to get at the prophet.

Neraiah and his men proved a sure shield around him.

"Let him speak. Let him say what he has to say! We must know what was Jehovah's word to him!"

"If the word is from God, who can possibly close his mouth?"

"Let us hear, let him finish."

"And now Jehovah the God and his spirit hath sent me.
Thus saith the Lord thy Redeemer, the Holy One of Israel."

"Silence, quiet! Let us hear what the prophet has to tell us!"

"I am the Jehovah, thy God...."

The name of God pronounced aloud struck awe into the assembly and petrified the blasphemers. Once again quiet reigned and the people listened with bated breath to the burden of the prophet.

"I am the Lord thy God which teacheth thee to profit,
Which leadeth thee by the way thou shouldst go.
O, that thou hadst hearkened to my commandments!
Then had thy peace been as a river,
And thy righteousness as the waves of the sea;
Thy seed also had been as the sand,
And the offspring of thy bowels like the gravel thereof;
His name should not have been destroyed or cut off from
before me."

The crowd stood silent, every head bowed in grief and remorse.

The prophet too stood dumb and silent. Caught in the spell of his own prophecy, he began to turn around in an ecstatic dance symbolic of the approaching redemption. In a singing voice, joined to the rhythm of his dance, he murmured, speaking half to himself, the melody of the dance:

'Go ye forth from Babylon,
Flee ye from the Chaldeans,
With a voice of singing declare ye
Tell this.
Utter it even to the ends of the earth;
Say ye:
Jehovah hath redeemed his servant Jacob.
And they thirsted not when he led them through the deserts;
He caused the water to flow out from the rock for them;
He clave the rock also and the waters gushed out."

At first the congregation stood stunned. But the words of the song, the melodious voice, and most of all the movement of the prophet in the dance was like the touch of a sorcerer's rod upon them. Here and there people began to sway as though the magic of the redemption had entered into them. Instead of seizing the prophet and handing him over to the royal power, they all broke out into song and loud shouts acclaiming the redemption:

"Go ye forth from Babylon,
Flee ye from the Chaldeans...."

# CHAPTER THIRTEEN

THE Temple of Bel Merodach stood upon seven towers of solid masonry built one on top of the other, with the sharp pinnacle of its highest story piercing the sky. A narrow flight of steep steps mounted the sides of the outer walls from story to story until it reached the tip of the ziggurat which appeared to blend and dissolve into the clouds. Like Nebuchadnezzar's palaces, the seven levels of the sanctuary contained halls, chambers, and vaulted rooms which served as stores or living accommodation. Here, for instance, dwelt the permanent priests of E-Sagila and the multitude of slaves who served the needs of the temple. On the festival of the New Year, which fell on the first day of the month Nissan, the hosts of pilgrims who came up to Babylon from all parts of the Empire were lodged in its precincts. The temple was fabulously wealthy, being possessed of countless treasures and broad estates which were cultivated by thousands of slaves. These were termed "the Tillers of the Soil of Bel Merodach." Surrounding the sanctuary were barns, stores, folds, stables, and pens. Here food was stored up and the livestock required for the estates were corralled. Vast chambers held a treasure of idols and images of all sorts and of all materials: of hewn stone and molded clay, votive gifts in profusion, weaves and precious stones, rare oils and unguents, precious perfumes and medicinal plants for healing and witchcraft.

The Temple of E-Sagila was a dominion within the state possessing independence and sovereignty and owing nothing to the royal court. At times its strength waxed greater than that of the kings of Babylon.

The interior of the tower was a vast and lofty chamber, the dwelling place of Bel Merodach. The gigantic idol, which weighed one thousand and seventy talents, was stretched out on a couch of proportionate dimensions. Beside it, in a golden basin, surrounded by a latticed railing, was a gigantic two-horned serpent. The priests of Bel Merodach were indefatigable in their search for grotesquely shaped snakes of the desert, survivals of beasts which had long become extinct. They were a symbol of Rahab, whom Bel Merodach had conquered, and were therefore sacred to Babylon. Adjoining the vast hall was a chamber of more human proportions. Here dwelt the woman who bore the title of the wife of the god. Her duty was to do his will, to render him gratification and delight, to relate the words of vision, and to answer oracles which proceeded from his mouth in reply to questions put to him by the king through the high priest. These related to the affairs of the realm, to war, and to more personal matters. This room was furnished with a wide couch capable of receiving the god when he manifested himself. But it was much smaller than the enormous litter in the great chamber, being of almost normal proportions. Thus, when it entered the mind of the god to honor his mortal wife with a visit, he shrank to human size and took his carnal pleasure of her in a human manner. There was also a banqueting couch and a table of gold set with sumptuous viands and liquids constantly prepared for the refreshment of the god when he chose to assume human form. The woman was brought into a state of trance-like ecstasy and delirium in order to satisfy the god on the exalted occasion of his visit. She had to be completely and utterly devoted in soul and strength and flesh to act as his oracle, to become the vessel through which future events might be foretold before they had even shaped themselves.

After the priests of Bel Merodach, led by the High Priest Sharezer Bel, had violently captured Gimil, the chief harlot votary of the sanctuary Ishtar, from Belshazzar's palace and brought her to their own sanctuary, they handed her over to the temple handmaidens to be prepared for her exalted function. She

166

was shut away for many long weeks and groomed and made ready for the divine service. The votaries offered incense and burned herbs and spices of all kinds before her, doing everything prescribed to drive away any evil spirits which may have found lodging in her when she served as chief kedeshah of Ishtar. They steeped her flesh in ointments and unguents, massaging her with heavy embrocations and steeping her well in ritual baths. To prepare her spiritually to be the wife of Bel Merodach, they made her imbibe many drugs compounded of mystical formulae and secret preparations. These were designed to invade her imagination with such delirium that she actually believed she saw the god Bel Merodach just as he was depicted in the praises, exaltations, songs, and legends of Gilgamesh. She learned to declaim and sing the songs herself and to transport herself into a religious frenzy at the vision of the young god going forth in his fiery chariot, robed in the seven winds of the smoke-racked thunderstorm, to wage war on his mother Tiamat and the hosts of Rahab. When her delirium reached its zenith, she sank to the ground, foam flecked her lips, and she sang songs of praise about the mighty god and his wondrous deeds. She was his betrothed, sanctified to him as his wife, prophetess, and votary. He, in his turn, did indeed appear to her as the young deity clothed in the seven winds, the thunderstone in his hand, resplendent in power and might, going out alone against the fearful Tiamat, whose tongue was seven miles long and steeped in deadly poison and whose vast mouth gaped open to swallow him. All the gods were terrified of her and had deputed the young deity to go and war against her on their account. She mentally exalted Bel Merodach to be not just her god and husband but also her lover, the desired one of her soul, the hero of her dreams, her omnipotent lord. It was an incomparable privilege that had fallen to her to serve him, to submit to his will, to be his prophetess and act as his oracle.

With impatient longing and trembling desire, with a mounting excitement of unrestrained passion, she awaited the moment when she would be found pure and holy enough to receive the god, her hero and her husband. The priests strictly warned her lest she dare approach him before he gave the sign that he was ready to take his pleasure with her. The slightest forward move, the smallest untimely step in his direction might well cost her her life, lest he lay his body upon her when it was all flaming fiery radiance which would utterly consume her.

When the harlot votaries had completed all their preparations for the meeting between Gimil and Bel Merodach they brought her to the bed-chamber in which were the couch and the golden table set with royal delicacies.

All that night through she awaited the coming of the god in trembling eagerness and fear. Her ears caught the faint sound of the plucking of lutes and the muted singing of young men's voices from the adjoining hall. These were psalms of praise to the young god. The night faded and the god did not appear. Time and again she was sure she heard a heavy tread approaching her door, but time and time again her hopes fell dead.

Thus passed the second night, and the third. The god hesitated to come to her. At last the High Priest Sharezer Bel told her that she should be ready that night to receive her divine lover. When he entered the holy of holies to lave the limbs of the god, the High Priest had received an intimation that Bel Merodach intended to visit his bride. Sharezer Bel ordered her to ask the god what fate lay in store for Babylon and whether he would aid Nabonidus the monarch and Belshazzar the prince regent and grant them victory in the war against Cyrus.

Special rites were celebrated in anticipation of the night. The votaries taught her special psalms with which to welcome the god and instructed her in the forms of praise and panegyric with which she should address him. They made her expert in every movement she must make from the time the god appeared unto her until the moment that he retired from her bed into his own chamber.

Night descended. In honor of the god, the chamber was made fragrant with all manner of pleasant incense until the whole house was filled with rings and curling vapors and became befogged in the swirling shadows. The sound of muted lute strings was heard gently recounting glories of the god, Bel Merodach, as he comes into his house.

Steps were heard drawing near the door, then a heavy tread, coming closer and closer. The sound of each pace echoed in the vast lofty hall. The door opened and the god crossed the threshold. His appearance and his stature were that of a man. He was robed in a cloak of gold interwoven with precious stones and adorned with mystic symbols. The cloak swathed his whole figure from the neck to the feet. He wore a high conical hat upon his head and a beard gleaming like pitch adorned his countenance. A gigantic living snake writhed and glided along behind him and when the figure lay down on the couch the snake coiled and reclined at his feet.

Ecstatic and delirious from the potions with which she had been saturated and the prolonged expectation of the god's coming, a frenzy of passion overwhelmed Gimil. She threw herself back at full length upon the floor, hid her face in her hands and burst forth into a song which recounted the praise of the god:

> "Ah, consume me not with thy fire,
> Ah, gather me beneath thy wings,
> For I am thy chosen handmaiden."

Her whole body thrilled with terror and desire. She raised herself slowly with a languorous shudder and began the sacred dance in honor of the god that the votaries had taught her. Her firm breasts, the muscles of her stomach, the arching of her back and her strong loins rippled and flowed in the smooth movement of the dance expressing her complete surrender and passionate desire to abandon her body completely to the masterful use of her god, so that he too should desire her for herself. Her wiles succeeded. The god motioned her to approach. She came near and put the fragrant flowers she had prepared for him under his nostrils. She poured him a goblet of wine and he drank. He ate fruit and other deli-

169

cacies which she proffered him. The fact that Bel Merodach consented to eat from her hand inflamed Gimil with the joyous expectancy of consummation and she stretched herself out at his feet and burst into songs of praise lauding his heroic deeds of valor when he defeated Tiamat. The deity was appeased; he showed his satisfaction with a benignant smile of approval which, as he gazed on her, suddenly turned to fire as his eyes blazed on her rosy flesh. ....

Gimil reminded herself of the question she had been instructed by the priests to ask concerning the fate of Babylon in the war against Cyrus.

"O Merodach, mighty and omnipotent god, lord of gods and of men! Thy people are perplexed and devoid of counsel. The city of Babylon is besieged. A cruel foe has come up even unto our gates. Wilt thou come to the aid of thy children and servants Nabonidus and Belshazzar so that they prevail over the enemy?"

Thus she posed her query in the formal style she had been taught.

As soon as Merodach heard mention of the names of Nabonidus and Belshazzar his countenance darkened; a cloud formed on his brow as though a black veil had covered it; his eyes flashed fire and his beard quivered. He lifted himself up from the couch. The serpent coiled at his feet reared its two-horned head ready to strike.

"Go to my people and say unto them: 'I have rejected Nabonidus; Belshazzar is an abomination unto me.' "

Treading heavily the god turned and left the chamber.

This was the day after the news had reached Babylon of the defeat of Nabonidus near Sippar.

Sharezer Bel assembled the chiefs of his priests, and Gimil related the curt decision of the god. As she spoke, she panted with a hot fever of love and devotion to her husband and divine hero. Inflamed by the constant glow of enmity that burned in her heart towards the dynasty of Nabonidus, her whole body writhed and twisted with the venom of her description as she vividly depicted the depth of loathing that the countenance of the god had expressed when he uttered the hated names of Nabonidus and Belshazzar.

The priests were stunned and astonished. Terror took possession of them. Bel Merodach might abandon Babylon entirely and go over to the enemy. But Sharezer Bel soothed them. They began to plan how to meet the situation, considering in particular how to bring the decree of Bel Merodach to the notice of the generals and especially Gaala-Ba, the head of the Guardians of the Gate in whose special keeping was the citadel of Babylon and the keys to all its portals. It was decided to do nothing until Bel Merodach had made his will quite clear and announced whom he wished to reign in Babylon in place of the dynasty of Nabonidus.

Gubaru was well acquainted with what went on among the priests of Bel Merodach. He had his agents among them as in every other stratum of the population. He knew well the depth of the enmity which existed between the priests and rulers of Babylon. They hated Nabonidus for his straying after the worship of other gods, in particular for his preference for Sin, the Moon god. Belshazzar was condemned by them because he exalted the worship of Ishtar over that of Bel Merodach.

Gubaru had long sought a way of bringing the priests of Bel Merodach over to his side, but this was a delicate matter. He knew how they suspected and loathed every influence that did not come from Babylon. It would be very difficult for them to accept the thought of Cyrus, an alien, becoming ruler of the city. His victory was quite likely to harm the worship of Bel Merodach by suggesting that the power of the god was waning; indeed Cyrus might well bring a god or gods of his own to Babylon. Gubaru's prospects seemed a little brighter after the priests of Merodach had taken Gimil away from Ishtar and transferred her to their sanctuary. Her deep aversion to the dynasty would be a great help to him and he knew that her hatred was nourished on the same soil as his.

Following the latest oracle Gubaru sought a meeting with the High Priest himself. His agents busily employed themselves in the matter and arranged an interview. And so the two sat down together—Sharezer Bel, High Priest of Bel Merodach, and Gubaru, lord of the metropolitan province. Within a secret room they met and talked over the situation of Babylon.

"The Persians as yet have no settled and crystallized religious belief," explained Gubaru to the High Priest. "They do not worship many gods. Their devotion to Ormazd, the god of light, is but superficial and they are far from zealous about it. They do not celebrate many festivals, and Zarathustra, the prophet of their god, is not too renowned nor much thought of as yet. But they have certain principles. They reverence purity of body, abhor deceit, and seek to act justly. They are virgin soil which has yet to be ploughed. They are a powerful people and still seek a god of their own.

"Now I beg of you to consider for a while what the effect would be were Cyrus to become a devotee of the god Bel Merodach of Babylon and proclaim that it was he who brought him triumphant to the city, that the god of Babylon walked at his right hand, fought at his side and opened the gates to him, that the god of Babylon had adopted him, Cyrus, as his son and servant in order that he should rule there in place of the dynasty of Nabonidus whom he has come to hate.

"Think for a moment," urged Gubaru, "of the effect throughout the world of such an announcement. Cyrus would not only bring his own people, the Medes and Persians, to the worship of Bel Merodach; he would draw in his train all the nations he had conquered and all the states who, freed by him from the yoke of Nabonidus, have flocked to his banner. From beyond the Grecian isles and Cyprus to the shores of the Persian sea, all the mountain folk and the shepherds of the vast steppes; the farmers of the deep valleys and the fishermen who reap the harvests of the seas and rivers; all these have as yet no settled belief and no hallowed gods. When they hear that Bel Merodach helped Cyrus to triumph over his enemies they will at once bow their knee in your sanctuary. The name of Bel Merodach will be lauded and praised in every tongue and his fear will spread over the wide world. Cyrus would not be known only as the king of the Medes and Persians. He would be styled the Emperor of Babylon, which would then stand at the peak of the universe and be reckoned as the pivot upon which the whole world turns, especially since the temple of Bel Merodach is found within her. Wherever Bel Merodach was found, there Babylon would be. She would once more reign as queen of empires as she did in the time of our great monarch Nebuchadnezzar."

"I feel constrained to agree with you," answered Sharezer Bel, "but how can you be sure that Cyrus will pass over to Bel Merodach and announce that he is indeed the god who helped him to subdue Nabonidus? And how can we be assured that his victory will be accepted only as a defeat for the Nabonidean dynasty and not as the crushing of Babylon? How can we be sure that Cyrus will not maintain that it was his own gods who gave him victory?"

Sharezer posed these questions with deep anxiety.

"The outcome of the matter depends entirely and only upon you, the priests of Bel Merodach," answered Gubaru, hiding a thin smile in his thick beard.

"How so?"

"With you in your temple dwells the wife, consort, and oracle of Bel Merodach. Send her to the camp of Cyrus. Let her tell him personally of the words of the god, bring him the tidings that he holds him by his right hand and leads him to Babylon just as the prophet of the Judeans has openly proclaimed of Jehovah that indeed he it is who so conducts Cyrus."

"Who!" asked Sharezer Bel in tones of mingled rage and contempt. "The Judeans! Exiles!... whose king was freed from his dungeon and granted privileges by that vile degenerate Evil Merodach! These dare assert that their God Jehovah, whom no man has ever seen, whose nature no man knows, helped Cyrus to conquer Babylon?"

173

"More than this," answered Gubaru. "Their prophet claims that Cyrus will bring all peoples of the world to the sanctuary in Jerusalem where every knee shall bend before their God."

"Impertinent arrogance! How can such lying, treachery, and corruption be permitted in Babylon? Whoever heard of this Jehovah? Bel Merodach vanquished him by the hand of Nebuchadnezzar and he no longer exists. How can He speak through the mouth of one of His prophets when He does not even possess a sanctuary?"

"Nevertheless his words have made a perceptible impression upon Cyrus. The Judeans may possess no sanctuary but they have prophets who bring them the word of their God. I myself related to Cyrus the actual words that Jehovah revealed to the Jews by the mouth of His prophet. He was much impressed. So much so that he promised to send them back to their land and help them rebuild their Temple. He showed great interest in this prophet who brought them the word of Jehovah."

"But this Jehovah, their so-called god, no longer exists! His sanctuary is torn down. He has no place in which to dwell and no city in which He can be found," cried Sharezer Bel.

"Cyrus can bring him back to life. The Jews say their God dwells in heaven and is also found everywhere on earth. The whole universe is His, say their prophets; all creatures upon it belong to Him. For this reason He is in no need of a special sanctuary or city. Cyrus inclines an ear to these tales. He seems to be seeking a god who will have dominion over all the earth, since he wishes to extend his own kingdom universally. It is therefore advantageous to him that his peoples everywhere should serve one god. If the priests of Bel Merodach do not bring him knowledge of Bel Merodach and persuade him to choose him as their god, then he will go over to Jehovah of the Judeans or even Apollo of the Greeks."

"Apollo! The god of those barbarian Greeks who had to come to us to learn the paths of the stars in the sky; who have to learn mathematics from us; who borrow our building methods and seek to find out the secrets of our medical skill. These are ignorant people!"

The High Priest almost spat out these words in his contempt.

"O revered priest, do not underrate them. Latterly they have made immense strides. Their Solon has given them just laws."

"They are all plagiarized from the work of our great lawgiver Hammurabi."

"Whether that be so or not, Cyrus is meditating and considering whether to go over to the worship of Apollo. He granted special privileges to his priests in the sacred groves at the city of Magnesia because they brought him a favorable oracle from their god. I wish to leave no room for misunderstanding. I am not attempting in the slightest to make any comparison between these godlings and Bel Merodach the mighty. But many say that Apollo is revered among the Greeks for many qualities and magic characteristics similar to those for which Bel Merodach commands our devotion. Like him Apollo rides upon a chariot of flame to which fiery steeds are harnessed. He is their god of health and peace. He causes tranquillity and content to dwell in the hearts of men and order in all creation; so the Greeks say."

In this and many other ways the old conspirator tried cunningly to kindle envy in the High Priest's heart.

"There is no god but our Bel Merodach. He is the god of gods!" shouted Sharezer Bel, rising tempestuously to his feet with a violent gust of emotion.

"Of a certainty. Of a certainty," soothingly murmured Gubaru. "The thing is beyond all doubt. Only the stupid, ignorant, and benighted who are so blinded in their minds that they cannot see straight would claim otherwise. But for my part, my only purpose is to try to explain to you that Cyrus is more than ready to embrace the worship of a powerful god who could aspire to dominion over the whole world. If we lose this opportunity and do not bring Cyrus to our own god Bel Merodach, the priests of other cults are likely to anticipate us. This is the sole purpose of my words. I am a loyal Babylonian," concluded Gubaru with a quiet smile of hidden self-satisfaction.

The smooth conspirator and the prelate were silent. The bald head of the High Priest shone and perspired while the deep wrinkles on his brow showed how profound was his meditation. Finally he said:

"We must ask counsel on this matter from Bel Merodach himself. Tonight the wife of the god will inquire of her husband. What he tells us to do we shall perform. My venerable Gubaru, tomorrow you shall have my answer."

That selfsame night Bel Merodach was gracious enough to honor his mortal wife Gimil with another visit. She inquired of him as Sharezer Bel had commanded of her:

"O god of gods, have mercy upon Babylon thy city and come to the aid of thy sons! Tell, I pray thee, whom hast thou elected to reign in Babylon in the stead of Nabonidus?"

The answer she received resembled that which Jehovah put into the mouth of his prophet.

"I will take hold of the right hand of Cyrus. I go by his side bringing him to Babylon."

The oracle of Bel Merodach was sacred to the Babylonians. Nothing was done in the city without first consulting it. Once the word had gone forth there was no appeal. Whatever the god ordered had to be carried out to the letter. One had to sacrifice everything, soul and possessions, to fulfill what had been commanded.

The High Priest and the great ones of Babylon, headed by Gaala Ba, the chief of the Guardians of the Gate, heard the oracle and sat stunned in abject superstitious terror as the wild cries communicating Bel Merodach's will emanated from the lips of Gimil. When the astonishment had subsided somewhat, all eyes seemed to turn naturally to Gaala Ba, who was entrusted with the keys of the city. He sat there, a figure of grave dignity, his great beard descending in plaited fringes, his wig beautifully waved. He remained stonelike and immobile.

Assyrian blood flowed in Gaala Ba's veins. His ancestors had passed over to Nebuchadnezzar's camp after the conquest of Nineveh and they had served him faithfully and well. He was already considered as a Babylonian born but he too nevertheless felt no immoderate love for the Nabonidean dynasty. In his heart of hearts he retained the ancestral loyalty to Nebuchadnezzar in whose days his family had risen to greatness in Babylon. He was a disciplined warrior but still would not hesitate, as a pious Babylonian, to carry out as a sacred duty every command, to do or not to do, laid upon him by Bel Merodach. He was the first to break the spell of silence.

"Kings come and kings go, but Bel Merodach is eternal. Dynasties come and go but Babylon endures as the place where Bel Merodach is found. It is not the king who rules in Babylon that counts. What is important is the command of the god Bel Merodach."

"The only rightful king of Babylon is he whom Bel Merodach holds by his right hand," cried Sharezer Bel, thus indicating that he was of one mind with Gaala Ba. He solemnly proclaimed; "Great is Bel Merodach!"

"Bel Merodach is the god of gods!"

"Where Bel is, there is Babylon," shouted those present at the conclave.

After Gubaru had communicated his suggestion that the gates of Babylon be left open for Cyrus and that he be vested with the imperial crown on condition that he should in his turn publicly announce that Bel Merodach was his supporter and shield, it was decided to send a deputation of priests secretly to Cyrus. The group would be headed by Gimil and the High Priest and would be empowered to negotiate terms for transferring the rule over Babylon to the new dynasty of the kings of Persia and Medea.

\* \* \*

Cyrus had scarcely dug the first mattock in the earth in fulfillment of his plan to divert the waters of the Euphrates from Babylon, when his son Cambyses hurried to bring him quickly back to the camp of the armies left in front of Babylon. He brought him news that a deputation of priests of Bel Merodach was waiting in front of the wall.

The serious position of his forces, the dwindling supplies coming from his satraps, and the wise considerations urged by Gubaru had already made Cyrus determined to take advantage of any honorable means of extricating himself from his dangerous straits. Now in the proposal of the priests of Bel Merodach, he was being offered a chance to deliver himself and at the same time fulfill all the desires and ambitions he secretly treasured in his heart. He had already mentally ripened a plan for an attack upon Egypt. In order to materialize his design to join the land of the Nile as far as the mountains of Ethiopia to his dominions, he needed allies and friends among all the peoples who dwelt within the shadow of his power. The suggestion of the priests of Bel Merodach could be woven very neatly into the web he was spinning. No alien king it would be that would enter Babylon, but a monarch after the people's own heart, whom their own god had chosen for them in his power and might.

Now Cyrus was not just skilled and wise in the arts of war. He was also a past master in the arts of government and a consummate student of human nature. He had first to try out the opinions of his satraps and generals on the idea of his accepting the suzerainty of a strange god's worship. He had to bear in mind too his own people and the others over whom he had latterly come to rule. What would his decision mean to them? He was well aware that the worship of no particular god was deeply ingrained in them and that they were always ready to succumb to the temptation to exchange their gods for others who had proven stronger, mightier, and more successful in war than their own. Who among the gods was as renowned as Bel Merodach? But he still did not wish to take a hasty decision. He would wait and see how the matter would fall out and what degree of readiness his own people and his allies showed to transfer their allegiance to the god of Babylon. Because of this he took a private decision not to be crowned personally as king of Babylon just yet. He would await the event and be content in the meantime with his present title of "King of the Medes and Persians." He would set his first-born son Cambyses upon the throne of Babylon. It would thus be his son and not he who would take upon himself the yoke of the religion of Bel Merodach and the other Babylonian deities. Only when his own people and other vassal kingdoms had become accustomed to the new state of affairs would he be able confidently to take the reins of empire of Babylon into his own hands, proclaim himself as king and acknowledge Bel Merodach as his god. The other matters fell out just as Gubaru and the priests of Bel Merodach had planned.

By orders of Gaala Ba the watchmen of the city had all taken up positions well within the walls where there was nothing to guard but the posterns of the inner wall which led to the river crossings. These were not needed by Cyrus at all, for if he had made use of them his army would have had to swim the waters of the Euphrates; and this could not be done without drawing the attention of the whole defending host. The only possible way to enter the city without being observed was by way of the bridge near the gate of Ishtar now that the guards there had been withdrawn. In fact the portals were thrown wide open and, at the command of Gaala Ba, guards were detached to act as guides to the hosts of Cyrus and lead them safely through the deadly "sack" of the Avenue of the Processions. They were to show them the way through the maze of alleys and courtyards into the heart of the city.

The armies of Cyrus quickly penetrated to the center and captured wide stretches of it while Belshazzar, who knew nothing of what was going on, indulged himself in drunken unconcern at a great feast he was giving in his palace in honor of the new chief temple votary who had succeeded Gimil at the temple of Ishtar.

It was at this feast that the captains of Cyrus's army took Belshazzar's life while he sat upon his royal throne against the background of the tablets which celebrated the victories of the great Nebuchadnezzar.

A few days later the head of Nabonidus was removed from his shoulders when he emerged from his hiding place to go to the city to beg the protection of Cyrus.

Cyrus went forth from Babylon, having entrusted the city to his son Cambyses, who for the time being reigned upon the throne of the imperial city.

# CHAPTER FOURTEEN

CAMBYSES, the new king of Babylon, deigned to receive the heads of the Exile in audience. He promised them that his father Cyrus, ruler of all the earth, would, at an appropriate hour, proclaim freedom to the Judeans at present in exile in Babylon. He would grant them permission to return to their own land, restore the Holy Temple vessels of which Nebuchadnezzar had despoiled them, and assist them to rebuild their Sanctuary. No one would be compelled to return to Judah, but those who wished to go could do so.

Cambyses asked the chiefs of the Exile about the prophet who had foretold the victory of Cyrus over Nabonidus in the name of the God of Jerusalem. Just as Nebuchadnezzar had long ago inclined in grace toward Jeremiah, so did Cambyses, in his father's name, offer the prophet Isaiah the privilege of eating at his table and having all his wants supplied out of the royal bounty. But despite the pressure brought to bear upon him by the heads of the Exile, the prophet refused to see the king and certainly did not fall in with his suggestion. He continued to dwell among the Bethlehemites in whose courtyard he had hidden during the siege. The renown of the prophet was considerable at that time even among the higher aristocracy and chiefs of the exiles. The princes of the House of David invited him to come and dwell in their palace as Daniel had done. Daniel was now very advanced in years and spoke in deep parables whose meaning no one seemed able to penetrate. The new popularity of the prophet even extended to the ranks of the great merchants and entrepreneurs who but yesterday had felt a venomous hatred towards him. They were now only too anxious to make peace with him. He became honored and respected by the whole Exile, enjoying the greatest esteem among every class of the community.

Gubaru was appointed satrap over Babylon. Immediately on assuming office he summoned a convention of the great Judean and Babylonian merchants and assured them that nothing had changed radically in Babylon except the dynasty. They would continue to enjoy the rank and privileges they had been granted in the era of Nabonidus. In fact, stated Gubaru, the new regime offered them extensive new opportunities. With the incorporation of Babylon into the network of kingdoms which were gathered under the suzerainty of Cyrus, wide horizons opened out for the merchants and contractors. They would be able to develop their commercial contacts with the many new lands. The markets of Persia and Medea would become available to them and their trade could penetrate to the Caspian Sea and even pass beyond the northern Alps since Cyrus had already obtained a foothold there. In glowing colors Gubaru painted the bright prospect which lay ahead of the merchants and promised the protection and assistance of the government in all their transactions. One thing they had to know : Cyrus had not come to the city as a conqueror tyrannically bent on razing Babylon and the state. On the contrary, he had come as a liberator at the request of the Babylonian gods, to restore the pristine glory and dignity of the city, and even to raise it to a level greater than any it had enjoyed since the halcyon days of Nebuchadnezzar had been clouded over by the dynasty of Nabonidus. To this end he needed the cooperation of the merchants and contractors.

The sons of the House of Murashu and the other merchants were greatly encouraged. They looked upon the new reign as a new redemption. Cyrus, they felt, had brought salvation to Babylon, not to Jerusalem. Surely then he was the redeemer as the prophet had foretold. It must be indeed Jehovah who had sent him and Isaiah's prophecy must have borne the stamp of truth.

"When Jehovah turned again the captivity of Zion we were

like them that dream. . . ." Intoxicated by his dreams, as one overcome by wine, the prophet walked about the streets and market
places singing his visions aloud in words of radiant poetry.

Cyrus was no longer Jehovah's servant. Israel was now His
servant. Cyrus had fulfilled the appointed mission set for him by
God. The staff of God had smitten that which He despised, had
opened the gates of Babylon wide before him in order to free
Israel from the yoke and send her back to her homeland. Now
Israel was taking over the divine task and would carry its fulfillment a stage further. Henceforth, Israel would be the light to the
gentiles so that God's deliverance should spread over the whole
earth. The prophet looked upon the concourse of peoples from all
lands crowding into Babylon as part of the armies of Cyrus, as
creatures God had entrusted to him to help them attain to the
mountain of Jehovah in Jerusalem. Here were bands of savages
from the desert clad in their black mantles, Phrygian highlanders
in sheepskin, darkly sunburnt, their bodies like molten copper,
their hair and beards long and wild. Their hands clutched hunks
of roast meat which they had snatched straight from the cauldrons
which sizzled in the streets and market places and from which they
bit and swallowed with bestial appetites. Simple Cilicians, their
green eyes gazing in naïve wonder and perplexity at the size of
the buildings and the tumult of the streets. Cappadocians, robed
in cloaks of many-colored wool, walking with stately mien; Greeks
from the islands of the sea in their bright tunics, mentally recording with curious eyes the strange ways and institutions of the
Babylonians. Of all these varied hordes, many, drunken with cheap
wine, danced in the open squares with unrestrained merriment to
the music of lutes and soaring flutes. The prophet saw dark-skinned
Lybians, tall light-hued hillmen from the far north; a flood of
peoples and races whom Cyrus had brought up to Babylon.

His prophetic eye visioned all these nations, from the most
savage to the quietly cultured, reverencing at some future date the
God of Zion. They would all learn the Law of Israel and walk in
the ways of Jehovah. Like a tiller of the soil who comes to un-

broken virgin ground fat and fertile with manure, or a fisherman who finds himself in an unfrequented bay whose waters swarm with schools of fish, so the prophet felt as he visualized this mass of unformed people as future believers in the God of Israel destined to ascend the mountain of Jehovah and learn the Divine Law which would go out of Zion even as God's word would go out of Jerusalem.

Despite his mystical imaginings of one united world which would be utterly devoted to the God of Israel, despite his burning faith in the omnipotent power of God to change the order of creation and how much more so the nature of man, the prophet, like his great predecessors, had a strongly developed sense of reality. God would not make his purposes succeed among men by miraculous acts emanating from Heaven, but by tangible deeds. He would arrange them through the instrumentality of men, His chosen messengers. He would leave it to them to do His will though they might be quite unaware that they were serving His purposes. They might often do so even against their will and despite themselves. "God makes use of the good and also the evil," he reflected, "both of those who know Him and believe in Him and those who do not. For all creation is His and all works, whether performed by members of the covenant or by aliens. No, there are no aliens before God; nothing is outside His jurisdiction, for wittingly or unwittingly all creatures are directed to one end: to bring Israel back to his land. Not just Cyrus, but all peoples, are enlisted in bringing this purpose to fruition." A magnificent vision passed before the prophet's eyes:

"Behold I will lift up mine hand unto the gentiles,
 And set up my standard to the people;
 And they shall bring my sons in their arms,
 And thy daughters shall be carried on their shoulders."

Israel was the channel through which the waters of salvation would flow, not to her alone but for all the peoples. The redemption of the gentiles depended upon the redemption of Israel.

Winged words brought the report to all the settlements of the Exile that the prophet had seen a new vision and that the song of redemption was in his mouth. Now the message of Jehovah was no longer communicated in secret but in the full blaze of day before a representative gathering of the whole people in the palace of the House of David. It was spoken in the presence of the heads of the Exile, before its chiefs and rulers and carters and ass-drivers alike. It was there in the palace that the prophet was now lifting up the word of the God Jehovah, the song of redemption that welled up so melodiously within him. The sons of the House of David on their exalted thrones, the elders and heads of houses, the priests and Levites, the stewards and all who occupied themselves with communal affairs—the whole of Israel was assembled together as in the legendary assembly at Mount Sinai when the Law was first proclaimed.

All the harps and lutes of King David of old burst into music together while the Levites sang Hallelujah, not a Hallelujah to God only but also to Israel. Israel had been exalted and raised up to the heights. She was not just a servant of God but also the vessel He had chosen to bring redemption to the whole of creation.

The prophet opened with a call to the distant isles and far-off peoples. He and Israel coalesced. They became one entity. He spoke of himself while meaning Israel and referred to Israel but meant himself.

"Jehovah hath called me from the womb; from the bowels of my mother hath He made mention of my name. And He hath made my mouth like a sharp sword; in the shadow of His hand hath He hid me, and made me a polished shaft; in his quiver hath He hid me. And He said unto me, thou art my servant, O Israel, in whom I will be glorified. And I said, I have labored in vain, I have spent my strength for naught, and in vain, yet surely my judgment is with Jehovah and my work with my God."

Then, firm and strong, with a clarity and power which he had never before revealed, he announced the mission of Israel; why God had called him from the womb of his mother; why he had chosen him from all peoples to be His peculiar people, to be altogether His own. Not for his own sake had He done so and so chosen him but for the whole world and all men who dwell therein:

"And now, saith Jehovah,
That formed me from the womb to be His servant;
To bring Jacob again unto him.
Though Israel be not gathered,
Yet I shall be glorious in the eyes of Jehovah,
And my God shall be my strength.
And he said:
Is it a light thing that thou shouldst be my servant,
To raise up the tribes of Jacob
And restore the preserved of Israel;
I will also give thee for a light unto the gentiles,
That thou mayest be my salvation unto the ends of the earth.

"But who was to be this light to the Gentiles through whose agency the salvation would reach the ends of the earth?

"Thus saith Jehovah, the Redeemer of Israel and his Holy One,
To him whom man despiseth,
To him whom the nation abhorreth,
To be the servant of rulers.

"You shall surely see. The day will come when the nations will recognize and know that you, the despised, the abhorred, the subjugated, are the bearer of the mission of Jehovah. You have accepted the yoke and you suffer, yea, you suffer for their sake. But when that time come before the despised, abhorred and rejected:

"Kings shall see and arise,
Princes also shall worship,
Because of Jehovah that is faithful,
And the Holy One of Israel and He shall choose thee.

"He shall choose you to be His vessel to bring redemption to the whole world."

Then the prophet began to describe the radiant vision which he had seen of the return to the homeland. He saw them like sheep pasturing in green meadows. He pictured the way from the desert places to Zion. "They shall feed in the ways and their pastures shall be in all the high places. They shall not hunger nor thirst; neither shall heat nor sun smite them, for He that hath mercy shall lead them, even by the springs of water shall He guide them." He saw them coming from all the ends of the earth, from the north and the west and those from the land of Sinim.

The prophet raised his voice and as in a great symphony his voice blended with the lutes, harps, and choir of the Levites in the Palace of David. He sang and moved and swayed in the Davidic tradition even with the rhythm with which David had danced before the Ark of the Covenant:

> "Sing, O ye heavens, and be joyful, O earth,
> And break forth into singing, O mountains;
> For Jehovah hath comforted His people
> And will have mercy on His afflicted."

When the prophet's song had come to an end Zerubabel approached him:

"O prophet! Daniel has sent me to summon you. He needs speech with you and desires to see you."

"Daniel!" exclaimed the prophet in wonderment. "Is he still alive? Why did I not know of it?"

"Daniel is very aged and no man understands his speech. We keep him hidden in the palace away from all men lest his prophecies come unto the public ear, for they are indeed terrifying."

"Take me to him, O son of David. I wish to greet him and show him reverence."

Zerubabel led the prophet to the inner chambers of the palace. They went alone.

Daniel had been brought to Babylon in his childhood and lived there throughout the years. But nevertheless his life was shrouded in deep mystery, so much so that even though still alive he had taken on a legendary character. A ravening wild beast had once been shut up with him in a pit and had not dared go near him. He had been cast into a fiery furnace and the flames had not harmed him; he had contended with kings and princes and they had not vanquished him. Daniel was very old and yet not old at all, for advanced years had not cast even the faintest shadow on the clearness of his spirit. His body was reduced to skin and bone. It appeared transparent as though he were not made of earthly flesh but of some ethereal substance. He ate so sparingly that a normal person would not have managed to subsist on such a diet. It was as though the nourishment he took turned immediately to the sustenance of his spirit rather than of his spiritual frame. His spirit inhabited unseen worlds. He spoke in mysteries, parables, and riddles which none could interpret; he gave forth concepts utterly strange to the world around him.

In the room set aside for him he was tended by his disciple Zachariah. A mere bundle of bones wrapped in a cloak, he lay upon his bed or sat half-reclined upon it. His silver hair and his long beard covered the upper half of his body. But his glance seemed to pierce through every mortal barrier and contemplate worlds with which mortal man and mortal life had nothing in common whatsoever.

As Daniel lay in his room he saw clearly into the future as a man looks on prospects which are familiar to him. What the eye saw in its journeys of vision the lips formed into strange parables of beasts and stormy spirits soaring into hidden ways and the impenetrable time yet to be: ways which God nevertheless revealed to His chosen ones.

Zerubabel and the prophet found Daniel resting half-reclined upon his couch. He was waiting for them. The young prophet made obeisance and cried:

"Peace be unto thee, my father and teacher, the eye of Israel."

Daniel raised his white eyebrows and gazed at Isaiah for a moment. Then he extended a white hand.

"Peace be unto thee, my son!" He spoke in a thin clear voice. "I sent for you to enjoin you to pray to God lest your thoughts become darkened at the time your eyes and ears are opened."

The prophet was terrified and astounded. He went white and answered in a trembling voice:

"Father of Israel! Have mine eyes deceived me in what I saw; have mine ears misled me in what I heard?"

"God in heaven forbid! Your eyes have seen straight and your ears have heard aright. But your heart is too hasty and your soul too thirsty for the redemption. You repose more confidence than is seemly in flesh and blood, which is here today and gone on the morrow, vanished and without remembrance. You have seen a branch and taken it for the whole tree."

The aged Daniel closed his eyes. His face seemed to take on a new translucency and a pure light spread over his countenance. A faint sound issued from his lips:

"I saw in the night visions,
And behold one like the son of man
Came with the clouds of heaven.
And came to the ancient of days,
And they brought him near before him.
And there was given him dominion, and glory and a kingdom,
That all peoples and languages should serve him;
His dominion was an everlasting dominion
Which shall not pass away,
And his kingdom,
That which shall not be destroyed."

Daniel was silent. It was apparent that his spirit was exhausted. He seemed to sleep.

Silent and troubled the prophet went from the room.

"I told you that Daniel was exceedingly old and no longer knows what he is saying," said Zerubabel.

"Daniel knows well what he is saying," whispered the prophet as though speaking to himself. "He sees very far—to the very end of days."

# PART TWO

# CHAPTER ONE

AS a river swells when streams of water from the hills flood into it, so Babylon surged as the multitudes of people came pouring into her gates. Never since she first became a city had she been invaded by so mighty a concourse, as though the whole world had burst its dikes, hurling a cascade of humanity into the metropolis. Flood upon flood they came: people of every hue and tongue in a bewildering riot of colorful costume. They thronged within her walls, crowded her streets, massed in her squares and markets, and filled the broad avenues beside the canals; an inexorable flood inundating everything.

The Street of the Hairdressers and Wigmakers was gay with curtains festooned with hangings and adorned with palm branches. It was besieged by row upon row of women and children. They had come to the fair to sell their boys' or girls' hair, which would be made into wigs and beards. Among them moved the tradesmen and their clients making their choice. Hardly had they made a bargain on the number of sacks of barley or groats or the weight of silver to be paid for a wig or beard, than the wig-maker appeared, gleaming instruments in hand, pounced upon the child and in a twinkling left its head as bare as the back of a lamb after shearing.

A loud medley of voices and raucous cries rose from the crowd. "In honor of Bel Merodach the mighty!"—"A new beard to adorn your features!"—"Make haste; hurry. Look how natural and glossy is this hair. How profuse these locks. Fifty shekels on the scale!"—"A beard like that of Gilgamesh; as like as two drops of water! I'll make it for you from this head of hair." The merchant ruffles the lovely locks of a comely child with eager fingers. "Sell me the little lioness as well as her mane," leers a prospective buyer, bloated of stomach and swollen of chin. From his girdle a rich chain depended, and closely attendant on him was a slave carrying a large bag of silver.

"How much for the girl and her hair?" he asked again.

"I can sell you only the hair," the merchant answered. "The whelp belongs to her father. He is standing over there by the dais of the goldsmiths. I'll tell you the truth. I think he's quite ready to sell the girl. He'll part with her for enough to get him a multi-colored robe. He wants one to wear in honor of the feast of Bel Merodach the mighty."

On the block in the adjacent slave market shrinks a luscious young Negress smooth of limb and fluid of body. Beside her stands her owner, a merchant of Kedar, his nakedness covered by a single white cloth which helps by contrast to emphasize the girl's nudity and blackness. He cups her breast in his palm and cries feverishly:

"A concubine for sale. Buy her in honor of Bel Merodach the all-powerful. A concubine for your pleasure. For every kind of use. Just look at this breast. No weak suckling's milk here. Milk for a warrior, for a man. A concubine to honor the year's renewal; in honor of Bel Merodach the omnipotent."

In every alley and passage, wherever the foot could find a cubit to tread; everywhere in the dark maze of mews and courtyards of the vast market area, merchants were poised before their stores and counters crying their wares. "In honor of the New Year!" "For the glory of Bel Merodach, god of gods who delivered Babylon from ruin."

"Fragrant spice sticks for incense; buy!" "Myrrh and frankincense from dark Araby, buy." "A perfume offering for Merodach the glorious; buy, oh, buy!" "This way, this way. Come and buy!" "Choice oil squeezed from Indian herbs. Anoint your body in honor of the great festival of Bel Merodach the Magnificent. Sweeten the sap of your skin with saffron honey and ginger!" "Let the fragrance of your body rise up as a sweet savor into the nostrils of the god and his beloved consort, the goddess Gimil who saved Babylon from certain doom."

In the weavers' shops the merchants offer cloth for cloaks; fine silks of Persia; linen of Sidon; wool weaves burning with many colors—all in honor of Bel Merodach. Silver- and goldsmiths make lavish display of women's belts embossed with silver, nose-rings, bangles, necklaces, pendants, and rings in honor of the festival of the awesome god. Sandals are piled up in the Street of the Sandal-makers. Potters shout of their kitchen utensils. The smell of broiling lamb from the shambles . . . Taverners mixing wine and strong drink in their hostelries . . . Greengrocers swamped with the produce of market garden and orchard . . . Makers of barley cakes in the Street of the Bakers . . . Every one with goods to sell and everyone with goods to exchange and money to spend seeking each other in the vastness of the scattered market. Anything at all; from a male slave or a concubine to a humble shoelace. Shouting, vending, cajoling, persuading, selling, entreating, chaffering, bargaining, dealing; all in the name of the mighty deity, the exalted god, lifted up over the pantheon and exalted far above mankind; god of heaven and earth, Bel Merodach the omnipotent. His name haunts every lip. His mention rises from every mews and alley, from every square and street. Babylon is making ready for festival. The year is in renewal. The first of Nissan draws near.

From the thoroughfare where the prayer writers, psalmists, and liturgists practice their mystic calling, the tribute to the gods rises in an overwhelming volume of sound. Sitting on stools or crouched upon the earth, their legs gathered up tight beneath their swaying trunks, squat the poets of prayer, along the whole length of the street. Some are engraving their petitions and hymns on tablets and cylinders of clay. Famous in the metropolis and acceptable to the priests of Bel Merodach are their works, composed new in honor of the festive day, may it dawn with blessing.

Spread out on mats at their feet are new-written clay tablets, steeped in oil and drying in the sun. Others are finished and await purchasers. These are the costly wares, kiln-baked, firm and solid.

The prayer-writing scribes, slaves most of them, indite supplications to the order of their masters just as their counterparts in other trades fulfill their owners' behests.

Here stands the owner of some such slaves. He is a Babylonian, dignified of mien, magnificent in a rich, black cloak. He towers beside his store, his hands folded upon his chest like the image of Nebo the god of wisdom which is ensconced in a shrine at the opening of the emporium. His intonation is pious as he proclaims his wares; his eyes are raised sanctimoniously heavenwards.

"Here is a prayer fit to be bought by the holy priests of the great god Bel Merodach for recital on the New Year . . . A song of praise for the great miracle vouchsafed us when he delivered Babylon from destruction. Buy this prayer. Great is the good fortune it will yield!"

A god-fearing citizen, evidently a man of learning by token of a stylus and tablets contained in a small satchel hanging by a chain from his necklace, comes forth from the milling crowd about the store. He stands and contemplates the bargaining and haggling. He approaches the seller of hymns, picks up a tablet from the ground, and reads it with utter devotion; first silently, then piously fashioning the words with lips hushed almost dumb while his figure sways rhythmically backward and forward:

"Great is thy name, O Bel the god
In heaven raised high; on earth enthroned.
Lord of the sky above and the earth below.
Who is like unto thee among thy brother gods?
To thee, to thee alone are praises due.
Thou alone art to be lauded with thanksgiving
For the great miracle thou hast wrought on our behalf.

"Ha-a-a-h," he sighed deeply. "Really wonderful, a crown of glory." The devotee smacked his dry lips and in ineffable satisfaction smoothed out the corners of his long flowing beard.

"My Assyrian slave, Agaa-ma, composed that hymn," said the merchant. "The priests of E-Sagila have accepted it into the ritual."

The publisher gestured towards a slave, a wizened and dried-up old creature squatting on the ground near-by, engrossed in cutting characters on a clay tablet.

"No less a person than the most honorable high priest himself has affixed his seal to it and agreed that the prayer be used on the New Year. The priests of Ishtar wished to buy it from me. They desire this slave to write hymns and supplications for their goddess. But I have dedicated it to the priests of Bel Merodach."

"Splendid, perfect," agreed the connoisseur. "Name your price."

"Only five kah of barley or three eggs. A quarter of a shekel in silver and copper. I am giving it away."

The citizen extracted a piece of silver from his girdle, paid for the tablet, took it and with trembling excess of reverence stowed it safely within the bosom of his ample cloak. . . .

"Please, sir, kind sir. Have you among your wares a petition for a life free from trouble and sickness?"

The quavering voice comes trembling forth from an old woman who has just approached the merchant. Her withered face is ploughed deep with wrinkles.

"How my bones ache!" she whines. "The pain makes my whole life ugly. I have been to the priests of the queen of heaven, Ishtar. I wished to sit among the kedeshot, to offer my body to her worshippers in her temple. 'Your years are too many,' said the priests. 'What man would look at you to take you in the name of the goddess?' So I seek a prayer, kind sir . . . just a little prayer."

"A prayer won't help you, my good old woman. You can't even read. Better that you buy an amulet from me. I have one here tested and certain to bring you a good year. What have you to offer in exchange? A kid perhaps; a fat young duckling?"

"Alas, good sir, who owns a kid in these troubled times . . . or a duckling? I have a small bundle of pure wool which I sheared from my two lambs. Enough to make a fine shirt front."

"I can't part with this piece for the wool of two lambs. It cost me more than that," the merchant said. "But I will give you a charm that will guard you against the evil eye."

He put back the amulet which he had got ready for sale and in its place drew forth a camel's tooth which he proffered to the woman.

"This amulet was enchanted by a priest of the wise god Nebo himself; may he be honored and revered. It is good against the evil eye and toothache. Surely you suffer from toothache."

"What need have I for a charm against toothache? My teeth have abandoned me long since."

The hag mumbled these words through a shrunken mouth, the lack of molars making it difficult to understand the flood of words which issued from the cracked lips. "Everyone is praying to Bel Merodach today. I must have something, too. A prayer . . . a charm . . . In honor of the festival . . . To protect me in my old age."

"A prayer to Bel Merodach in exchange for the wool of two lambs! Never, old woman. Impossible. Prayers to Bel Merodach are being snatched from my hands today. Everyone adorns himself with jewels and amulets in honor of Bel Merodach . . . But, here; here's a prayer for you . . . May it help you . . . This prayer is for a ripe old age."

The merchant produced a shard out of a pot and thrust it on the old woman. "Here is a remedy for all your ills."

"This is a prayer to Bel Merodach?" she beseeched.

"Of course, of course. To him and him alone. The priests at the sanctuary of E-Sagila wrote it in his name. Leave me. Go your way in peace."

That year Babylon was to celebrate a double festival. There was New Year's Day, which fell on the first day of the month Nissan and was observed for four or five days. Moreover, it was a celebration to mark the fact that Bel Merodach had deigned to recognize the new ruler of Babylon. . . . For until the most high god Bel Merodach so signified his approval no monarch could be said to rule in Babylon with legal validity.

It was only after the king had acknowledged the lordship and sovereignty of the supreme godhead, committed himself to its protection, and sought its grace that such consent was given. Even Cyrus, the conqueror, had been compelled to submit and subject himself to these ceremonies, but he had held back from personal experience of the ritual and had empowered his son, Cambyses, to take his place.

During the war, the gods had been snatched from their temples throughout the land and concealed in Babylon. The climax of the celebrations was to be their formal return to their sanctuaries. The granting of permission for this was taken as a symbol that Cyrus identified himself with the religion of Babylon and was ready to serve her gods. For this reason, the ritual of sending back the divine images out of Babylon was to be carried out with the greatest pomp and circumstance.

Spring in Babylon was the most beautiful of the seasons, despite the fact that the city knew no real winter and several harvests were taken from the fields in the course of the year. The plains, well-watered by the canals, were a wide-spreading carpet of infinite colors stretching from horizon to horizon, a tapestry of white and blue and rose and purple. The spring barley was shooting out its tender spear points through the red earth. Gardens in city and suburb were in full flower. The almond trees were dazzling with their white veils of soft blossom, like a dewy bride entering the bridal chamber. Apricots and cherries were in flower. The ripening spice bushes were bursting with fragrance, with saffron and balm and intoxicating odors pouring forth from the groves. The market gardens which encompassed Babylon were like a great green girdle around a mantle spread along the length of the canals and their tributaries verdant with irrigated fields beside them.

The roads and by-ways were covered with garlic plants and onions, those vegetables so beloved of the Babylonians. Indeed every beard in the metropolis exhaled their odor; every cloak and garment exuded the heavy smell just as every mouth gave forth the scent of kohlrabi and wild cabbage. Babylon was altogether in

199

festive array. A city of palm and pomegranate, clothed in the virgin freshness of spring. Even the old olive trees, a vivid contrast in their deep-rooted and heavy branched sedateness, were nevertheless covered with young green leaves.

Adorned with garlands and wreaths of flowers the inhabitants of rural towns, hamlets, and villages had begun streaming into the city days before the festival was officially to begin. Permission was granted for anyone who entered the gates of the city to pitch his tent in any spot where he could find space. The visitors assailed the air with the noise of bustle and confusion typical of a festival eve. The whole city vibrated with shouts of laughter mingled with the song and melody of dance. Streets and squares were packed with masses of humanity. The pilgrims and their families crowded around bonfires kindled and stoked with dried dung, crude oil, and palm branches. Lambs, goats, ducks, chickens, and kids roasted whole upon the flames. Provisions spewed from earthenware pots and baskets. The stench of roasting meat invaded every quarter; dried meat, smoked meat, fried and spiced and pickled and garnished with onions and with garlic; heavy with sauces of saffron and ginger and sweet-smelling leaves and condiments. Reddish flames bloodied the faces of the people, smoke clouds from the frying grease blackened them. The sharp smell of onions and garlic blending with the acrid stink of cheap liquor tore at the nostrils and grated on the throat.

As day declined, the flame of myriads of torches lit up the riotously colored multitudes weaving ceaselessly in the haze with which smoke had wreathed the city. The beat of drums and timbrels sounded a monotonous background of repetitious sound. The crowds fumed and simmered together in a shameless dance as though possessed by demons, as though evil spirits had come up from the netherworld and taken over the city.

On the broad waters of the canal glided boats profusely garlanded in flowers. They were illuminated by flaming torches which cast blood-like patches on the surface of the stream, while the mirrored light made all the canals of Babylon take on the appearance of one large crimson conflagration of burning oil... Strains of sweet melody emanated from the various craft, hymns and songs to the gods. The singing was accompanied by the steady beat of drums. It announced the coming of the deputations sent to Babylon from near and distant shrines to return the gods to their temples, to redeem them from their enforced exile in the city fanes of Babylon during the days of Cyrus's invasion. Each deputation sailed under its own flag; on each vessel's prow was unfurled the banner of the sanctuary of the god who was to be escorted home. Each deputation announced its arrival with hymns specially composed in honor of its own particular deity and sung by priests clad in the vestments of their office. Here was a company of priests from the city of Sippar come to take home their god Shamash. Here a congregation of notables from Borsippa intent on delivering the god Nebo from exile. From the far land of Aram came envoys to bring back Hadad, the god of storm and thunder. From every town and city they came and the inhabitants of Babylon welcomed them with acclamations, weaved around them, and shouted paeans of joy.

The Avenue of the Processions was afire with red roses and verdant with palms. Every building in the long street from the towering temple of Bel Merodach to the gate of Ishtar was ornamented and decorated with a multitude of garlands and a wealth of flowers and branches. The square fortress turrets over the gates of Ishtar were carpeted with red roses from beneath which peeped glimpses of the blue and white and purple of the beasts inlaid in the enameled mosaic that covered the walls. The lofty walls of Nebuchadnezzar's citadel were engulfed completely in a sea of flowers that flowed down in a living waterfall from the lofty hanging gardens above it.

In the avenue itself, cubic pillars had been set up. Their sides were made out of trees complete with roots and blossoming branches. Among them were the willowed and ancient sycamore and every other species from the acacia to the almond. The street was carpeted along its full length by a layer of sawdust ground from cedars of Lebanon. These huge trunks were hauled to Babylon especially in honor of the festival, for the aroma of the cedar of Lebanon is pleasant in the nostrils of the gods. The priests were skilled in the art of distilling a perfume from the stock of the tree and they saturated the paving stones with it in honor of the festival, drenching the blue glazed tiles over which the procession would pass.

All that night deputations continued to arrive from every city and hamlet: civil officials and captains of the host, envoys, plenipotentiaries, and chamberlains of the provinces. Only the most honorable of the notables were permitted to pass by way of the gate of Ishtar into the Avenue of the Processions. But as soon as they entered, even they were pushed to one side and jammed close against the walls on both sides of the street while rows of helmeted soldiers armed with javelins kept order and saw to it that the main thoroughfare was kept clear for the carts to which priests were harnessed. These dragged the wagons laden with the gods through the gate of Ishtar to the river Euphrates where they were loaded on the ornamented boats which then set sail for their various cities.

The mass of the people had to be satisfied with observation posts beyond the walls which shut in the street. Priests of the second rank, kedeshot, lower officials, and subordinate army officers swarmed in masses upon the roofs of the turrets of the gate of Ishtar, on the heights of the walls, and many perched themselves in the hanging gardens of the citadel of Nebuchadnezzar.

The Babylonians, long accustomed to processions of the gods, conducted according to a ritual from which not even a deviation by a hair's breadth was permitted, waited breathlessly for the instant the planet Venus would appear. The moment came, and, before the dawn star had attained a fixed point in the heavens, the High Priest, at a sign given him by the astrologers, entered the holy of holies in which dwelt the mighty golden image of Bel

Merodach. He announced the tidings of the New Year to the god and prepared him for the worship. He washed him and clothed him and uttered the due prayers in his name. Meanwhile, at the moment exactly determined by the ritual requirements, Cambyses appeared as ruler of Babylon. He was robed in the traditional garments of kingship; his beard was woven into three plaits; a crown of majesty was on his head, the ring of royalty on his finger and the scepter of power in his hand. He came before the High Priest, Sharezer Bel, who, arrayed in his priestly garments, stood awaiting him before the citadel of Babylon.

Sharezer drew Cambyses into the holy of holies. He approached Bel Merodach's gigantic golden image set with precious stones, his crown on his head and the sea-monster crouching at his feet, bowed down before him, and began to utter prayers and supplications:

"Merciful Bel, king, lord of the earth,
   King of kings, light of man, determiner of destinies,
   Have mercy, we pray thee, on Babylon thy city.
   Turn towards E-Sagila, thy holy seat;
   Proclaim freedom to the children of Babylon;
   Protect them from the wrath of the oppressor,
   Break the chains of servitude,
   Let the light shine on thy children in Babylon."

Cambyses, the deputy of the glorious conqueror, made submission before the golden image, took the royal crown from his head and the ring from his finger, lifted up his scepter and handed them, crown, ring, and scepter, to the High Priest of Bel Merodach. He in turn laid the symbols of Babylonian kingship before the idol, then taking Cambyses by the hand led him before the god, tapped him with his hand on the back and plucked his ear, a sign that he accepted the suzerainty of Bel Merodach. The designate king of Babylon prostrated himself and recited the statutory prayer:

"I have not sinned, O lord of all the earth;
I have not offended thy godhead.
I have not laid waste Babylon,
I have not driven out her inhabitants;
I guard Babylon.
I have not stormed her walls,
I did not make war against thy holy habitation.
Have mercy upon me.
Pour out thy grace upon me, O mighty god!"

He concluded his prayer and remained bent before the idol.
The High Priest inclined towards him:

"Fear not. Bel hath heard thy prayer.
He will prosper thy reign;
He will ennoble thy kingship;
He hath made his Babylon happy;
He hath delighted E-Sagila, his sanctuary.
He, whose children are the children of Babylon,
Will eternally bless thee.
He will shatter thy rivals
And lead many nations in subjection to thee."

The High Priest concluded his benediction and once again invested Cambyses with the symbols of royalty.

Outside the drums beat, the trumpets blared from all four corners of Babylon, proclaiming to the whole world that the lord of gods, the master of the world, Bel Merodach, had taken hold of Cambyses by his right hand as he came to Babylon in the name and right of his father, Cyrus; had enthroned him and approved him as the rightful monarch of the empire and all its vassal states.

Now Cambyses, as the duly enthroned king of Babylon, had the religious duty of leading the New Year festival procession and treading in state at the head of the ceremonial parade in which the gods and images would be returned to their seats from their exile in Babylon.

The Babylonians almost went beyond the bounds of sanity in their extravagant enthusiasm as they looked upon Cambyses, the conqueror of their city, marching at the head of his generals, satraps, and notables, clad in the traditional regal robes, the Babylonian crown upon his head and the scepter of kingship in his hand, leading the cavalcade of the gods. The whole city already knew that the new monarch had utterly accepted the faith of Bel Merodach and submitted to him as the lord of lords in Babylon. He, himself, in his own right and also as the representative of his father, had paid him the homage of leading the ceremonial parade in which they returned to their proper habitations. There was no greater symbol than this to indicate that it was no strange god of a strange people that had conquered Babylon's deities.

Not loaded upon asses nor dragged along in ox-carts, as they had entered Babylon in flight before the advancing foe, did the gods return to their sanctuaries. In many-colored robes, wreathed in garlands, with chaplets on their brows, to the loud triumphant trumpeting, the sound of flute and harp, and the joyous shouts of the populace, they now went forth on wagons carpeted with flowers drawn by long rows of priests.

First in line, in a vehicle covered with beaten plates of shining gold, came the great Shamash. The idol, represented in his human form, sat on an ivory throne which was mounted upon the float. His face was adorned with a beard of noble proportions, for Shamash, the right eye of Bel Merodach, the father of the goddess Ishtar, was revered and worshipped as the sun god in many lands. The Babylonians wrote many prayers in his honor and sang innumerable hymns and songs to him. The notables of Sippar, where his main sanctuary was situated, who had come to fetch him home, had placed a crown of gold upon his head and decorated his body with a wealth of bracelets, rings and pendants so that he might throw back resplendently the rays of the sun. When the myriad multitudes saw him in the procession, the high dignitaries in their litters, the priests and harlot votaries on their sacred couches, a shout of joy, which split the heavens, broke from the throats of the thousands who manned the walls, roofs, and cornices of the houses:

"O Shamash, when thou appearest in the corner of heaven,
The gates of the sky bless you."

After Shamash came the entourage of Sin, the moon god, the left eye of Bel Merodach. Though she was the wife of Shamash the sun god, she was nevertheless represented in a male form or as a female from whose cheeks a beard grew. The wagon which bore the hermaphroditic deity under a canopy was also drawn along by lines of priests. But only when they had passed did the train of the greatest, paramount deities begin to appear.

In a cart upholstered in Persian silk, to which eunuch priests were harnessed, Ishtar appeared, surrounded by harlot votaries. The image of the goddess of love was grotesquely conceived. It was carved out of ebony and was so old that a fine dust crumbled from it. This Ishtar took the form of a tall thin woman, so elongated in fact that she appeared like a thin pole. Her face was sinister and grim. From one of her long ears dangled a round earring. She held two doves in her hand, clasping them to her thin breast. This particular idol had been hallowed for centuries and had been brought from afar from a city on the shore of the Tigris. It was revered and sacred to the inhabitants of Babylon also. When the train of eunuchs drawing the float appeared and the image surrounded by the votaries was seen standing supported by priests, the crowd broke into earsplitting acclamations and many, mostly women, prostrated themselves to the earth and cried:

"Aha, queen of heaven! Aha, goddess of eventide! Aha, goddess of the dawn! Lusty Ishtar, glory of heaven! Lusty Ishtar, queen of heaven!"

The votaries released flights of doves who circled the image with a whirring of wings. The womenfolk in veneration of Ishtar brought forth from their bosoms wafers which they had baked especially in honor of the festival, crumbled them and threw them with great excitement to the doves.

With the passing of Ishtar's cart the world seemed suddenly to become silent. Stillness descended from heaven as though in a mystic cloud and quieted the rivers of humanity who flooded the Avenue of the Processions; it kneaded them and molded them together into one solid mass, mute and motionless as though petrified. The silence grew and prevailed taking captive every ear. It permeated everything like a lake of death, like a heavy yoke oppressing every one of the festive mob. All eyes were fixed upon the walls of the tower of Babylon which reared its lofty and precipitous sides to the heavens. On the straight flights of steep steps which wound down from terrace to terrace, a long procession of white clad priests was descending bearing on their shoulders a shining image from the gilded surface of which the rays of the sun burst forth in splendor. A long hour passed before the image and its attendant cavalcade reached the foot of the stairway, but during the long weary wait the people were still as if turned to stone. Gradually the silence was dissipated by a soft and slowly chanted prayer which gradually swelled into a fearful moaning, a sinister sobbing from hundreds of mouths, a hymn and song in a subdued mode. The bronze gates of E-Sagila were flung open wide and in the opening the first ranks of the priests appeared. The people still stood transfixed in their places. Erect and stiff, row after row of priests issued forth, singing a hymn of praise to the slow beat of a hidden drum. As the procession with the figure of the god grew nearer and nearer to the people, they in turn gradually roused themselves from their stillness and, released from the spell of stunned immobility, fell like one solid wall of humans, prostrate, face to the ground, and lay there outstretched, silent, motionless, a world of stone.

Through the silent lanes of worshippers, the priests carried the image of Bel Merodach standing upright in gigantic stature, a crown of gold upon his head, his woven robe interwoven with precious stones and ingrained in mystical and wondrous symbolic patterns. As they went along they moaned praises and exaltations of the great god in faint and low-pitched voices. The multitude stretched along the ground were afraid to move a limb or lift their heads to look upon Bel Merodach. So they remained still, immobile, frozen until the priests with the idol reached the platform. This was a replica, on a smaller scale, of the temple of E-Sagila on its square terraces elevated one above the other, tripod altar on each story. They lifted the idol and set it upon its platform. Then came Sharezer Bel, the High Priest, shaven of crown and face, a red, fire-adorned apron on his naked body. He took a handful of spice sticks from a golden basin which stood before the altar, threw them upon the coals of the altar and began to pray for the peace of Babylon, the city and her inhabitants.

Only when he finished the prayer did the multitude dare to lift its face from the ground, spread out its arms to the golden image of Bel Merodach and utter, bowed in reverence, the New Year supplication:

"Merodach, lord of lords, by thy exalted command
Let me be healthy, let me be whole!
So that I may praise thy godhead
Make known to me thy will and it shall be performed."

This was the moment for the appearance, beside the gate of Ishtar, of Cambyses the son of Cyrus, the newly crowned king of Babylon, attended by Gubaru, the aged overlord of Babylon, satraps and generals and his whole retinue. The king went forth from his court leaving his attendants standing a little to the rear.

Then all Babylon saw Cambyses fall face to the ground before Bel Merodach and the gods of Babylon, thereby evincing his submission and reverence to the city's deities.

The people of Babylon were drunken with joy, and a mighty acclamation echoed and re-echoed from one end of Babylon to the other:

"Great is Bel Merodach, Lord of heaven and earth,
The shield of everyone born of man."

Bel Merodach was installed in the Avenue of the Processions surrounded by the gods of Babylon: Shamash, Nebo, Sin and the whole pantheon. And as he was the god of all gods in heaven so he was the king of all kings upon earth. The whole world was prostrate at his feet; the tower of Babylon lifted up with its ziggurat to the skies, the hanging gardens of the citadel of Nebuchadnezzar, were but the backdrop to his glory. Before him, in a vast review, spread out Babylon and her suburbs, all her towers and pinnacles, her fortresses, her canals, her houses—the queen city of the universe. And there, in front of him, face to the ground, lay outstretched, Cambyses, the mortal king of all the earth, the new sovereign of Babylon, whom Bel had led by his right hand and sate upon the throne of majesty, to determine destinies and decide the fate of the world and its peoples. The king's generals and his vassal rulers had all come in reverence before the god, and had bowed down to him, one after the other, falling utterly submissive with their faces to the ground.

A red cloud floated up from the city, from the Avenue of the Processions, and spread over the countenance of the evening sky. It emanated from the sea of torches and bonfires that were kindled according to the custom prevalent on the great festivals. The gilded head of Bel Merodach with its golden crown and his aureate robe, richly embroidered with precious stones, shone in the crimson glow. At this climactic moment, Gimil appeared in the Avenue of the Processions. She was seated in a golden throne borne up upon the necks of rows of castrate priests, naked to the navel, and surrounded by harlot votaries. She seemed to be floating upon air. She was exalted by all the degrees to which only the familiar companion of Bel Merodach could be raised. Her designation now was the "Woman of Babylon." The High Priest of Bel Merodach had proclaimed that she was a goddess, protectress of the children of Babylon. Just as the golden brightness of Bel

Merodach was illuminated by the red cloud of the fires of celebration, so the rosy lushness of the naked lusty flesh of Gimil reflected the fiery glow which incarnadined the Avenue of the Processions. As she thus glided by with naked breasts, high above the populace, upon the backs of her priests, ringed about her by her harlot votaries, the sound of flutes and the throb of drums accompanied her going and she seemed to be an idol in which some breath of life was nevertheless mysteriously stirring.

When the Babylonians saw her pink body shimmering against the red glow of the sky, they became frenzied indeed and their senses almost swooned from passionate ecstasy. They lost themselves completely. All the other gods were forgotten; even Bel Merodach dropped out of their consciousness. Their eyes beheld nothing but the "Woman of Babylon," symbol of everything for which the city stood.

When Gimil descended from her throne to dance the sacred dance before the god Bel Merodach and when the Babylonians saw the erotic tremble of her breasts, the sinuous contortions of her body, the rhythmic movements of her shoulders and neck in their shining sensuality, they accorded her the greatest tribute it was in their power to utter. They screamed and shouted:

"In thy breasts wells up milk for the god as for a man,
 Wife of Merodach, Woman of Babylon."

# CHAPTER TWO

YESTERDAY every eye had been turned towards the prophet and everyone had hung eagerly on the words of his mouth, cherishing every syllable that he uttered as the distilled essence of God's truth, sent through him to His people. And today?

After it had become known among the Judean exiles that Bel Merodach had "taken Cambyses by the hand" and that the son of Cyrus in his turn had submitted himself to Bel Merodach and proclaimed him as god of gods, lord of Babylon and all the kingdoms he had subdued, but had not recognized the God of Israel as the prophet had foretold, a great fear fell upon them. Isaiah had deluded and made fools of them. They had become an object of scorn and derision, rejected by the gods as though they were lepers. All the peoples were living and prospering in the shadow of Bel Merodach's protection, enjoying their heritage and benefiting from the grace of their rulers. Only Judea was still exiled from her land, wandering and straying like a lost lamb, stagnating, naked and bare in an alien land without the protection or grace of any king or of God.

"As long as we could nourish him with blood, with oxen and lambs, with cattle and sheep, so long as the Temple stood and we offered up sacrifices on His altar, Jehovah remembered us and from time to time even took our part. What benefit does He derive from us here and now? Pleasant phrases, psalms of praise? The gods are thirsty; the gods want blood, not the breath of words."

So complained Zachariah of the House of Zattu, obese maker of girdles, who sold his wares in the main market place.

"We simpletons listened to the empty mutterings of the prophet, to that swollen belly full of east wind."

"What are you talking about? Think you the Babylonians do not pour out pious phrases to their gods? Have you never heard their prayers and hymns, the sort of thing they sing to Shamash? You can pray to their gods also. Do you know what Nathan of Tel Melach said to me? You certainly must know the man. He supplies me with wool. His cow gave no milk for three months and his sheep became infertile. He prayed to Jehovah—no answer —not a thing. Then one of his neighbors gave some sound advice. He said: 'Get yourself a clay household godling—an image of Bel Merodach. You can buy them in the market place.' Nathan brought home a figurine of Bel Merodach and burned some incense before it. His cow immediately began to give milk and his sheep at once conceived. The gods want blood, and not the empty nothingness of lips. You were right, Zachariah."

"One hundred wild oxen, one hundred yearling calves, and five hundred female calves and a thousand kids only just weaned were offered by Gubaru as a sacrifice to Bel Merodach on the eve of the New Year. The whole body of the priesthood of Bel Merodach and Shamash were busy with the holocaust. Only the grease and the lungs were burned upon the altar, the remaining mounds of flesh were divided among the pilgrims and the soldiers of Cyrus. Gubaru ordered all the innkeepers to distribute strong drink and fermented wine, the whole stock to be found in Babylon, free to the populace, so that they might rejoice without restraint. The House of Murashu opened up their storehouses and handed out sacks of barley, baskets of olives, jugs of oil, and barrels of date wine without payment; everyone who wished could come and take away what he wanted.

"All that night the women baked cakes, the cooks roasted meat and in the temple of Ishtar the harlot votaries, and indeed every woman, completely devoted themselves to slaking the lust of any and every man who came along. Thus the Babylonians rioted throughout three days in drunkenness, gluttony, and fornication.

212

This is what you call real worship. Something you can feel and join in. Not as our prophets would have us do, telling us we have to pray and fast, fast and pray! It's no wonder Bel Merodach helps his devotees and our God forgets us. What do we remind Him with?"

So Zachariah expounded not without a trace of envy in his voice, licking at the dribble that trickled down from the corners of his sensuous mouth.

"Brothers, what is the matter with you? Didn't our ancestors sin against God enough, that we must add transgressions to their offenses?" Thus Rahum of the House of Zakkai tried to reprove them.

"Jehovah existed once. He is no more. He once lived in Judea but we are now in Babylon. There is only one in Babylon who is able to help us. That is the god to whom the Babylonians now bow and indeed all other peoples, too—that is Bel Merodach."

But most disappointed of all were many of the wives of the exiles, who now turned openly to the worship of Ishtar. Shamelessly and flagrantly they became habituees of her temple and participated in her rites. They baked votive cakes for the doves who fluttered about the sanctuary. Like the Babylonian women, they sat upon the steps as willing and ready to lend themselves to harlotry as any votaries. Large numbers of the women brought clay or stone figurines of the goddess home to their houses.

The prophet saw and heard all these things that went on about him as though with a thousand eyes and ears. God sharpened and developed all his senses. The very pores of his skin seemed to soak in all the agony and trouble which had come upon his people. The prophet became a bearer of sorrow and distress. His body gathered in all the poisonous glances which were shot like arrows against his God. He did not blame Israel for all this nor did he judge them as rebellious and forward. The extent to which he felt all their distress and sorrow was the measure of the degree to which he loved and yearned for them with every nerve and sinew. What guilt was theirs? Children rejected and cast off, forsaken by father and mother. They were the target for all the scorn and contempt that God sent against them. They were stripped of every-thing; that is why they were so embittered. The covenant their fathers had made with the God of gods still stirred them, although the promises it contained had not been fulfilled. It was the anxiety and disappointment over the unfulfilled promises which now broke from their hearts and burst from their throats.

But, nevertheless, God gave him occasion to see and hear in a thousand forms that the covenant was still firm and existent. He perceived that since the very foundation of the world until that day there was no compact made between the forefathers and God so strong, so unbreakable, as that which existed at that time. Day by day without cessation, God sharpened his senses so that he might be able to discern the God that abode in Israel. From day to day, He revealed to him by His deeds and works that His eye was open and watchful for Israel, that He had not forsaken His people, that He was their Shield and Shelter; that He was like a father who takes care of His child.

And was not God indeed the primal source, the father and mother as it were of all existent things? Did He not pour out His unique lovingkindness on all His creation? And was it not from the source of Divine love that every created thing obtained the feeling of mother love? This love is the first and primal condition of the existence of every living thing. And do we not see every day the uniqueness of motherhood revealed in every creature? How do the birds know how to refrain from quenching their hunger or thirst in order to bring the berry or the worm they find upon the ground to the nest built for their young? How often, standing on the banks of the Euphrates, had he not seen the eagle bearing a locust for the open beaks of its young eaglets who trustingly stretched out their necks, not yet covered with down, in order to take their food.

"Look . . ." the prophet began, with the expression which he was accustomed to use when speaking to Neraiah. He pointed to the young eaglets stretching their tender necks out of their nest in the rocks. "Do your eyes see these fledglings? They are Israel. Just as these depend for their existence on the food in their mother's mouth, so are Israel dependent on the salvation of God. Would He who poured out mother love on His creation withhold His love from His children? But Israel says that God has forsaken her."

One day, walking in the slave market, the prophet saw a Canaanite woman and her daughter standing upon the auction block. An eager buyer had already decided upon her as a suitable concubine. A second purchaser wanted to buy the little girl. The slave dealer, an Assyrian, tried to take the child from her mother. Like a tigress, she sprang upon the dealer, snatched her daughter from his hands, and hid the child beneath her knees. Shielding her with her whole body, she fought off the dealer. On no account would she allow the fruit of her womb to be taken from her.

This tragic spectacle was not unique. Almost every day similar scenes were enacted in the sight of the prophet in Babylon's slave market. And over and over again he asked: "Who endowed living things with the maternal instinct? Who can say that the Creator of all things, who lives eternally, the God of Israel, could ever reject His people?"

He went out among them to the open places of the city and the markets, to the dark alleys of the smiths and artisans, to the courtyards where the various groups of exiles sat occupied in their particular trades. He came near the stalls of artisans and saw how cast down and lacking in confidence and sense of their own worth they were, how bent were their backs, how broken their spirits and deep their despair. He spoke to them and tried to bring them comfort:

"But Zion said, the Lord hath forsaken me
And my Lord hath forgotten me.
Can a woman forget her suckling child?
That she should not have compassion on the son of her womb?
Yea, they may forget,
But I shall not forget thee.
Behold, I have graven thee upon the palms of my hands;
Thy walls are continually before me."

"Pretty phrases, for the bleary-eyed in the taverns."

"This chatterer rolled about the streets and boasted in the ways: 'Bel boweth down, Nebo stoopeth.' "

" 'Bel boweth down' ha, ha, ha; that's a good one. He must be a bit queer. Cambyses bows down—to Bel. He falls at his feet. And this fellow claims to be a prophet."

"Stone him out of here! What's he doing in Babylon altogether? Let him go back where he came from!"

But the prophet appeared to be quite oblivious that he was the target of this abuse, so deeply immersed was he in the visions that crowded before his eyes. Before those who muttered against him and threatened and reviled him, he spread out the vast horizons of the return to Zion. Against the background of despair and the loss of all hope, he painted a picture which had no relation to reality at all for the simple market people. Nevertheless, the number of those who were taken captive by his words grew greater. They were enchanted by his sympathetic voice, now persuasive and now singing with strong confidence:

"Lift up thine eyes roundabout and behold;
All these gather themselves together and come unto thee.
As I live, saith Jehovah, thou shalt surely clothe thee with
them all as with an ornament,
And bind them on thee as a bride doeth.
The children thou shalt have after thou hast lost the other
Shall say again in thine ears
This place is too strait for me,
Give me place that I may dwell.
Then shalt thou say in thine heart
Who hath begotten me these?
Seeing that I have lost my children and am desolate,
A captive and moving to and fro?
And who hath brought up these?"

"Bel Merodach begot them," a mocking shout was heard. But it was a solitary voice. All the rest stood around the prophet in silence. They listened to him. Once again he had taken their hearts captive. Even if he had fabricated the visions out of his own mind, even if they were the errors of a self-deluded seer, his enthusiasm and feeling communicated themselves to them. It was sweet to listen to such words of consolation in their bitter despair, for who had there been before who even knew how to bring comfort—as he had done.

Because of this, cries were heard among the assembly: "Let him be!" "Let him speak!" "Let us hear what he has to tell us today!"

Two old men standing beside him and listening open-mouthed were inclining their faces and beards towards him as though they could hear better that way and tears were streaming from their dim eyes.

The fierce love of the prophet for Israel knew no bounds and it was not diverted by the decisive events that had latterly taken place in Babylon. Cambyses, the son of Cyrus, may well have proclaimed that Bel Merodach, the abomination, was his god; but in spite of all that had happened, the prophet's ears still heard only the announcement of the God of Israel to the peoples of the world, ordering them to come and help Israel to return to her land:

"Thus saith the God Jehovah:
Behold, I will lift up my hand to the gentiles
And set up my standard to the peoples
And they shall bring thy sons in their arms
And thy daughters shall be carried upon their shoulders."

But this was too much for the people. Such exaggerated confidence after all the predictions had been proven false by events! Had nothing happened in the Avenue of the Processions on the New Year? Laughter and hissing were heard among the congregation.

"He is a false prophet, speaking more and more wildly. His mouth foams with soap bubbles."

217

"Spreader of delusions!"

There came a medley of insulting cries: "Cheat!" "Twister!" "Dribbler!" "Patterer!"

"He is a conjuror. He draws words out of his mouth like ribbons."

The prophet was not daunted. He stood unmoved amidst all the confusion and simply raised his voice above the rain of curses and imprecations and went on with his depiction of the greatness of Israel in the time to come:

> "And kings shall be thy nursing fathers,
> And queens thy nursing mothers.
> They shall bow down to thee with their faces towards the
>       earth
> And lick up the dust of thy feet."

"Ha, ha, ha! He is crazy. He has lost his senses!"

Many of his listeners became angry with him. Some showed this by laughter, other by shaking their heads. The outcries completely drowned the prophet's voice. Only those devoted followers who never had despaired of him even in the most recent times and who even now were enchanted and entranced by his magic, heard him out until the end.

Henceforth, the prophet was shamed wherever he showed his face in the synagogues, markets, and courtyards where the exiles congregated. Even the Bethlehemites, who up till now had followed him faithfully and shielded him from all evil, seemed to forsake him. Neraiah, the son of Seraiah, took him by force and returned him to his father's hovel by the canal tributary where his father had once more taken up his residence following the lifting of the siege of Babylon. He brought him back to his reed hut where the prophet sat awaiting the word of God.

Indeed, the word of God came to him once again in the visions which he saw in the clear nights which fell upon Babylon with a pale glow. Those nights were like a long twilight, neither day nor night but a sort of darkened limbo as though God had poured some light upon Babylon from his hidden store as a sign and portent for Israel that they should rejoice and put their trust in Him. Thus the visions which haunted the prophet on these clear Babylonian nights were in utter contrast to the distress and despair that tore the hearts of the exiles at that particular time. In his thoughts the prophet began to make his concept of God's mother-love for Israel more concrete. He clothed it in the likeness of a symbolic mother of the Jewish people: a transcendental mother, a heavenly Rachel, somewhat as she appeared to him when he was among the sons of the prophet in the Temple court in Jerusalem, but comforted now, since God had wiped her tears away and crowned her with the name of the "hopeful one." Her tears were still upon her cheeks but through them shone the glow of the grace that the new-found mercy had brought to her. The measure of the mother-love that God had vouchsafed His creatures was enshrined in the wrinkles and furrows graven in her features. Her eyes glistened with tears, but they were also lit up by the rays of confidence, strength, and consolation that were poured out upon her by the promise of God.

The mother was exalted and uplifted. She was no longer the heavenly transcendental mother of Israel alone; she was also a symbol of eternal universal motherhood, for in the new concept of the prophet the love of God as symbolized by a mother's mercy now embraced the whole of creation. The God of Israel was the sole and only Creator, there was none beside him, none but He. He could not tolerate the existence of other gods and establish relations with them such as those that existed between Bel Merodach and Nebo. He was the One Unique and Existing God and there was no other. Creation could not attain the perfection that God had destined for it until it came to Him and Him alone; until it drew upon Him His lovingkindness and received His grace. This was what God had designed from the beginning of time. To bring this idea of God into the scheme of created things was the

·purpose of all that existed and this was the way that led to the redemption.

The coming of Cyrus appeared to him very clearly as yet one more step on the way to the redemption in spite of the crooked twisting and diversion from the direct path. The process of redemption had begun; there was no power that could hold it back.

One day, shortly after Cambyses had been crowned as king of Babylon and adopted the religion of Bel Merodach, Zerubabel and Jeshu came secretly to visit Isaiah in the hovel of Neraiah to warn him of the storm that had broken out against him among the exiles and to advise him to leave Babylon and forget about the dream that he had dreamed.

Zerubabel asked the prophet if it was known to him that Cambyses, the heir of Cyrus and his deputy in the kingship, had prostrated himself on the New Year at the feet of Bel Merodach, proclaiming in his own name and that of his father that Bel Merodach had taken him by his right hand and brought him to Babylon. With great sorrow which darkened his features, Zerubabel added:

"You had said that Cyrus was God's Messiah and that He held him by the right hand and subdued nations beneath his feet."

"Who is this Cyrus that God should be mindful about him? A blind donkey whom God harnessed to draw the wagon until he was relieved. He was no different from Assyria and Babylon, who were also blind asses, also harnessed to the millstones of God even before Cyrus appeared upon the scene! 'I shall bind thee though thou knowest not me,' the Almighty told me in a vision concerning Cyrus. He girded him to do His task. Even before the world emerged from its primal chaos the God of Israel had marked the way to redemption. For this He sends His emissaries to fulfill His desire step by step, from stage to stage. For His deeds He employs both good and evil since both are the work of His hands. He created light and darkness also; for the emissary of every stage He created and determined His tool from the beginning. He appointed one agent to act as the staff of His indignation to chastise

Israel and set up another to heal her wounds. Just as He used Sennacherib and Nebuchadnezzar as a rod of chastisement, so Cyrus was chosen to execute this immediate stage of His plans: to return Israel to her land and inheritance. When Cyrus has fulfilled His will, his fate will be decided, as was that of Assyria and Babylon. Then another emissary will come to perform the next stage. This emissary, like Sennacherib, Nebuchadnezzar, and Cyrus before him, will be confident that he is the center of events, that all purposes are fulfilled in him, just as a worm crawling on a cabbage leaf thinks that the green expanse around him is the whole universe. But everything has a time and a place; all appertain to but one purpose, and that is the redemption."

"But it does not seem proper to me," said Zerubabel sadly, "that you should have come to a people shamed, saddened, and desperate, and proclaimed to them that salvation and deliverance were very close, if your words were not to be fulfilled. Look at Israel's present state. All the nations around her are joyful, singing songs and hymns of praise to the image of Bel Merodach; the very paeans that Israel had looked forward to hearing burst from all lips in honor of Jehovah, the God of Israel, as you had indeed proclaimed to them. Kings are falling down and prostrating themselves not to God but to Bel Merodach. Nothing fell out as you predicted. Do you wonder then, my prophet, that Israel is turning her back now upon her God? They say: 'God has forgotten us. Let us take steps to go over to Bel Merodach and mingle our prayers with those of all the nations in his worship.' "

"No! No! The nations do not reverence Bel Merodach; it is the God of Israel that they revere," the prophet interrupted in a loud voice. "Before they even know Him, God has planted in their hearts a passion for Him. The thirst for the God of Israel burns in their bones like fire and this thirst kindles the need for the prayers and psalms that they utter to man-made idols. They are seeking and fumbling for Him in thick darkness and since they cannot find Him they embrace idols of wood and stone, calling them the one living and existing god. Just as a mother whose

221

little girl has been taken from her cuddles and embraces the lifeless doll she left behind, so do these peoples embrace and hold close
to their hearts their idols. God is what they desire and long for
and it is this, a desire for redemption, that bursts from their
throats in songs of praise to their idols. Because of this Israel must
return to her land. Not for our own sakes but to act as an instrument to prepare the nations of the world for the true redemption."

"But does not Israel enjoy a purpose in life of her own? Must
she always live for others?"

"Israel is God's vessel, His holy servant; from His mother's
womb was she designated to be a light to the nations. This is
the will of God and His thought from the beginning. Just as the
arrow shot from the bow of a skilled archer flies straight towards
its target and does not turn aside without having smitten it, so
the will of God surely fulfills itself. It is to this will that God has
bound and harnessed the nations of the world; the purpose is to
bring Israel back to her land—whether they wish it or not. Cyrus,
too, will have to do the will of God. He may prostrate himself flat
on the ground before Bel Merodach as much as he will, he may
embrace Nebo, he can call Shamash his father and Sin his mother,
but when it comes to doing, it is the will of God that he will be
forced to do as God commands His servant. God has opened up my
ear and I have heard." The prophet raised his voice. "He put
understanding in my ear and I was compelled to know. I have
drunk His words as a strong draught and His word has come
into my bones. God has engraved it on the tablets of my heart
and who shall erase it? This is the word of the God Jehovah, who
says to Cyrus, 'My shepherd, who shall fulfill all that I require,'
and says to Jerusalem, 'You shall be built,' and to the Temple,
'You shall be founded.' Not Cyrus's son, and no other deputy, can
act for Cyrus; he alone was selected by God to fulfill His will."

The announcement of the prophet struck Zerubabel and Jeshu
dumb with astonishment. As they sat before him, they were
further profoundly impressed with the fervor of his faith. For it
was not just strong and firm words that he spoke. His eyes,

sunken in their sockets, flashed unquenchable and unmistakable sincerity and belief.

Finally Zerubabel said:

"Listen, O prophet. Pray to God that His will may be done quickly, for time passes and the people dwelling in exile are full to overflowing with bitterness and think that God has deceived and deluded them. Your enemies are increasing rapidly and growing in strength. They are not just Mordechai-Gad, Malchaya Gavra, and their ilk, but even the elders of Judah who sit in the high places in the synagogues, the priests and the Levites are also speaking against you. So indeed do the sons of the prophets. They all call you deceiver and seducer because you led the people into disillusion with vain hopes. I believe in you; I believe that your words will be fulfilled; so does the priest Jeshu here. But among the people you are dubbed a false prophet. This involves a danger to your life. Neraiah, keep a good watch over him. Do not let him go to the synagogues or walk about the streets, for the agents of Mordechai-Gad are looking for him and so are my father's guards. The matter affects his life."

"God forbid that I should do this," said Neraiah humbly. He had been quietly and self-effacingly standing at one side. "How can I dare try to prevent the prophet bringing the word of God to the exiles? Could my blood relation, Baruch, stop Jeremiah? Could it be possible, heaven forbid, that the prophet should shrink from his task?"

# CHAPTER THREE

A GREAT storm was brewing over the prophet. To his original enemies, the House of Murashu and its followers, who had from the very first stood out against his preaching in the synagogues and the market places, were now added the pious leaders of the various congregations, the elders and the priests. The eyes of many of the exiles were opened to the serious danger that could flow from the words and actions of the prophet. The impending calamity was not just to the people in the Exile—for the prophet had foretold Cyrus's readiness to return them to their own land. They seemed to be faced with a mass expulsion to Judea, without their being liberated or finding redemption. They saw a loss of faith in God as a consequence of the failure of the prophet's predictions and promises. Thus those who opposed the prophet for selfish reasons were allied to those who sought to suppress him for reasons of faith. It was because of this that the House of Murashu was joined by priests, Levites, and elders, particularly those who sat in the great synagogue in the palace of the House of David that had been granted to King Coniah by Evil Merodach. Now all the heads of the Exile were drawn up against Isaiah in a determination to bring his harmful influence to an end.

In vain did Zerubabel and other well-wishers of the prophet try to dissuade him from entering the synagogues until the danger had passed over. All their warnings and entreaties were of no avail. As soon as Sabbath came, the prophet took his way, not to the synagogue of the Bethlehemites, where he still had some sympathizers and followers who believed implicitly in him, but to the courtyard of the Traders of the Bazaar. Most of these

224

people were sandalmakers, tailors, and goldsmiths, living like all the exiles in small mews near the main market, where they had their workshops and emporiums. Among them, too, lodged farmers and herdsmen from Tel Aviv who came to Babylon to buy or sell and were forced to stay over for a few days. There were potters and other craftsmen from Bethel who also lodged until they had disposed of their stock of pottery and clay vessels.

The prophet had come among them and by the fierceness of his spirit fanned the spark of hope for redemption that was still alight beneath the heap of the ashes of despair, into a real glow. The hope the prophet had aroused in them was not just for personal redemption from Babylon. It looked forward to that of all the nations, including the Babylonians, hoping that at the same time they would come to recognize the One, Unique, Existent and Living God, the God of Israel. In their simple faith they took all the burning, poetical phrases in which the prophet had depicted the shining future as literal truth. They were simply and sincerely convinced in their innocence that Cyrus, the conqueror of Babylon, would not only recognize the God of Israel but would restore the Jewish people as one body to the land of their fathers; that the words of the prophet would be fulfilled; that kings would be their nursing fathers and their queens the nursing mothers for their children. They had boasted and gloried before their gentile neighbors about the prophecies and promises of the prophet. Then came the events of the New Year festival and immediately the Babylonians began to mock and revile them with taunting shouts, making fools of them and insulting them.

"Well, well! And when do you expect to set off for Judea? So kings will be your nursing fathers and their queens your children's nursing mothers, heh?"

To add to these last gleanings of despair and bitter disappointment and disillusion, the brothers of the House of Murashu sent their agents among them to incite them against the prophet.

"He will bring a fearful tragedy upon our heads. He will try to get the rulers of Babylon to expel us from the city. He wants to bring the worst possible kind of evil decree upon the remnant of Judah."

The prophet desired to bring once again words of comfort and salvation to these poor people who all in a moment had fallen from the splendid heights of hope into the abysmal depths of despair. He wanted to disperse the blackness of their mood with his thoughts of the motherlike love of God, revealed in mother Zion.

These were the dumb sheep whom he reckoned to be like virgin soil in which God had implanted the hope of Israel. These were the bearers of the promise given to the Patriarchs; these were the people in whom, by the grace of God, the eternal light would be forever enshrined. Just now they were depressed and confounded; the gentiles made mock of them, saying that He had abandoned them. They stood like dumb driven sheep who had been led to the top of a craggy mountain by their shepherd and left alone with only their moaning for company. The heart of the prophet was rent for his people. But greater than his love for them or his pity for them, stronger, deeper and holier than these, was the great task with which Israel had been entrusted. God would not break the tool He had fashioned and destined for the performance of His purpose.

As soon as the prophet entered the courtyard, his faithful follower Neraiah discerned the heavy, pent-up, and silent resentment that filled every breast. A moment before, the place had hummed and seethed with life and movement, but as soon as the prophet made his appearance, silence reigned: a black and brooding stillness which increased in gloom as a still murmur ran through the throng. But the prophet perceived nothing amiss. He saw nothing. His heart was so full of love and pity for the congregation; his eyes were so enfolded in the vision he was bringing them, for the commandment of God was strong upon him to afford them comfort and hope.

He opened with the high note of authority that marked all his prophecies. Not he was speaking, but as always:

"Thus saith Jehovah..."

"It is not Jehovah that speaks, it is you! Do not pronounce God's name in vain!" A bitter cry was heard from the congregation.

The face of the prophet went as white as the cloth upon his head. A sad smile formed about his eyes as though begging him to utter what he had to say. A tremble took possession of one of his outstretched hands. He repeated:

"Thus saith Jehovah..."

"It is not Jehovah that speaks, it is you." The same voice was heard once again. This time one could see that it issued from the mouth of a man who stood head and shoulders above those in the courtyard. His features were hard and the eye he bent on the prophet was full of a bitter hatred.

"Let him preach! Let us hear what Jehovah is telling him this time," another voice cried; but this one, too, was sharp and harsh. It emanated from a man with a trim black beard who was obviously a priest or a high official of some sort.

The prophet once again raised up his arms to the assembly and spoke in a voice rich with mingled agony and love:

> "Where is the bill of your mother's divorcement
> Whom I have put away?
> Or which of my creditors is it
> To whom I have sold you?"

"Enough of your parables. Tell us, what did Jehovah say to you?"

> "Behold for your iniquities have ye sold yourselves,
> And for your transgressions is your mother put away."

"Not for our sins but for those of liars like you, inventing falsehoods and uttering them as coming from the mouth of Jehovah!" came a shout which overbore every other sound.

227

"By reason of the transgression of a false prophet who perverted the faith of the people," cried yet another.

The prophet was silent but his eyes were full of tears of compassion for them.

"Sin not against the prophet," a wailing voice was heard. "You will bring great disaster upon us."

"Let the prophet speak. Let us hear what he has to say."

The prophet stood in silence; his sorrowful look pierced straight into the faces of those confronting him, and his wry lips once more began to utter words of pain and compassion. His voice was full of sadness and supplication as he continued:

> "Wherefore, when I came was there no man?
> When I called was there none to answer?"

"What, *we* never came?" the same echoing voice burst forth above everyone's head. "Your God, in whose name you speak, did not come. Where is the redemption you promised us in his name?"

The prophet was not dismayed or daunted by the angry shouts. Could the power of God to redeem His people be subject to any doubt? Could the power He had to save His people be called into question? The prophet girded himself with the strength with which the word of God in his mouth invested him; visions passed before his eyes, the manifestation of the omnipotence of God. He proclaimed in His name:

> "Is my hand shortened at all, that it cannot redeem?
> Or have I no power to deliver?
> Behold, at my rebuke I dry up the sea,
> I make the rivers a wilderness;
> Their fish stinketh, because there is no water,
> And dieth for thirst.
> I clothe the heavens with blackness,
> And I make sackcloth their covering."

This was all the prophet was able to utter of his vision of God's power. The song of His greatness was rudely interrupted. A brutal hand was smashed down heavily over his mouth and shut his lips.

"Enough of your imaginings. We know your sort well enough and you are the worst of them. It would be better if you told us in whose pay you are. Who has hired you to mislead this people with vain promises? Who is bribing you to keep up these incitements of the people to leave Babylon?"

So shouted the tall, bearded man, and leaping to the raised place on which the prophet stood, he swung his huge fist in a savage arc and brought his heavy knotted knuckles down hard on the prophet's face.

"Don't sin against the prophet ... you will bring down terrible disaster upon us." The voice of lamentation was heard once again from the midst of the assembly.

"Let us make him dance his dance before us; 'Go forth from Babylon, flee from Chaldea.' "

"That's what he had desired!"

"Ask him when the nations of the world will bear our children in their bosoms and our daughters on their shoulders."

"No, better ask him when they intend to prostrate themselves before us and lick the dust at our feet as he promised us."

"Didn't you see with your own eyes to whom they bow down and the dust of whose feet they lick?"

"Bel Merodach! Bel Merodach!" came a chorus of bitter voices.

The prophet was held fast in the arms of the giant like a baby in the talons of a bear. He was silent and stiff like a lifeless block of flesh.

In vain did Neraiah, who was held fast by other hands, struggle to come to the prophet's aid. He could only look upon him from a distance—his prophet, the prophet of comfort and hope, crushed against the man-mountain with violence.

"Quiet," roared the giant and raked the congregation fiercely

229

with his eyes. "I will show you who hired him to deceive the people, who pays him to take all that trouble."

He took his hand off the face of the prophet and seized the hair of his beard in his fingers and began to pluck it out together with patches of skin.

"So the Chaldeans pay you to seduce our folk with vain promises to go out of Babylon, heh?" he screamed and filling his mouth with spittle, he spat it full in the prophet's face.

"Make way! Make way!" shouted the assailants of the prophet, pushing with their shoulders against the crowd who were pressing up against him.

"Unclean! Unclean! Unclean!"

One after the other they passed by and spat in Isaiah's face.

He stood upright, tall and silent. The blood from his cheeks torn by the violent hand streamed steadily down upon his white robe and stained it scarlet. He made no move to defend himself. He did not turn his face aside from those who spat upon him nor did he flinch or try to evade the savage hands of one brute after another who sprang at him and sought to tear out the hairs of his beard with eager lust. He looked straight into the faces of his smiters with no sign of anger or contempt. He retained his glance of tenderness, running over with compassion and love. He summoned up all his strength to stand upright upon his feet although from time to time he swayed as though he would fall.

And all this time, amid the babel of voices, the yells of the milling people, a still voice was heard wailing through the ferment like a cry of a child:

"Disaster; disaster . . . you are bringing disaster upon our heads . . . you are sinning against the prophet . . ."

A long time passed before the passion of the mob cooled down and the rain of spittle ceased. Only then, the man with the plaited beard who had the appearance of a high officer came close to the pulpit. The chain of office which hung from his neck was now clearly apparent. With him, also, drew near several guards from the palace of the House of David. The officer placed his hand on the prophet's shoulder and said in a voice of authority:

"In the name of the prince Shaltiel and the Chief Priest, I am ordered to arrest you and bring you before the court of the elders of the synagogue for a strait investigation and inquiry into your acts. Come with me!"

The guards seized the prophet by his arms and escorted him from the courtyard. Released from the arms which held him fast, Neraiah quickly followed them.

The wailing lamentation, as of a beaten child, accompanied the prophet from the courtyard.

"Woe unto us! Woe! We have sinned against the prophet... we sinned against Jeremiah and now against this prophet... Alas! Alas!"

Dank and dark was the dungeon. There was not even a slit to allow the thinnest ray of light to penetrate. Silent shades enveloped the prophet. He had been thrown down into Stygian darkness and lay, a heap of aching bones, upon the clay floor covered only by his robe stained with blood. He lifted up his eyes and gazed into the darkness. His burning glance clave the thick gloom that shrouded him and seeing what he saw he cried:

"O my God! O my God! God of Israel! Hearken to my voice! I sold Thee to them. I gave Thee to them in pledge. In Thy name I brought them the good tidings and the promises. Now they demand Thee of me. Thou has opened my ear and I listened; Thou puttest Thy word in my mouth and I spoke it aloud. I gave them Thy hope and brought them Thy consolation. I lifted them up to exalted heights so that they might fall into the most abysmal depths. Israel is crushed like a worm beneath the heel of the nations. They have made the hope of Thee a laughing stock and Thy promise a matter of contempt. They demand the justification of Thine honor at my hands and avenge themselves on Thee in me. Thou hast proclaimed Thy name upon them and through Israel Thy name has become a by-word. Thou hast sent Thy servant to proclaim Thy message. Like a camel abandoned by his driver, so Thy servant drags his feet heavy with weariness over the face of a desolate wilderness. Thorns and briars pierce his bloody feet; scorpions and adders crawl under his belly; wild beasts lie in wait for him in their lairs. Thy servant hears their consolation. The jackals and hyenas who prey upon the corpses of the dead wail roundabout him hungrily, awaiting the summons of the ravening wild beasts to the feast. But despite all these things, Thy servant still goes forward, dragging the heavy burden Thou hast placed upon his shoulders. O my God! O my God! Send Thy consolation to Thy people Israel, for they are very weary and heavy laden. Light their way with Thy blessed promise; remove the mould from their eyes that they may see the strong light that goes before them. But if this Thou wilt not do, then shut up my ears so that I no longer hear the song of the redemption, smite me with blindness that I see not the path Thou hast cast up for them. My heart is crushed with compassion for them. Smite me with blindness, afflict me with deafness, blast me so that I be like them. Let me be consumed and pass away as the target for the arrows that they send against me."

As he lay there, drained of strength, weary and praying to God, his eyes suddenly seemed to see the likeness of a woman stalking along a long, long corridor of endless darkness. The figure was bathed completely in the surrounding gloom; only the shadow of her likeness was sharply defined. The reflection of her foot was shining bright, with a delicate and radiant pallor that shed a glow around it, illuminating the path she trod so that as she moved along, the small area of light accompanied her. Her step was so light, she seemed to hover. She came near and stopped beside him. She extended a hand from her dark veil and with her finger tenderly touched his feverish face. Her finger had the soft tenderness of a woman's breast. She exhaled a dewy coolness, and her hand on his countenance infused him with a holy, pure delight and turned his pain to heavenly sweetness. He recognized in her again the mother Zion. A hallowed slumber came down upon his eyelids. He was like an afflicted child who finds surcease at last in the warm enfolding arms of his mother.

In his sleep, he was visited once again by the man whom he had seen several times before in his visions of the wilderness. Once again he was in the desert on the way from Babylon to Judea. Once again the wilderness flourished like a garden of God as he had so often seen it. He heard again the babble and burble of the streams of cool water flowing like veins throughout the sandy wastes, welling amid the thickets of fragrant green plants and flowers, streaming along the length of the highway that God had built : a road of verdant lawn in the howling waste along which the redeemed could walk to Zion. He saw foxes, jackals, and hyenas creeping out of their lairs from the holes and clefts in the rocks under the sands of the desert, looking here and there, listening to the strange sound of the water, fearfully desiring the green coverts and longing for the living waters, greedily to quench in them the burning fires of thirst that the hot parched desert had kindled in their very vitals. Harts and antelopes he saw, straying about the green meadows, and birds on the wing, making fluttering shadows on the sand like small boats sailing a yellow sea. They were all agog and a-tremble, coming on wing and on foot with a great wonder in their eyes at the scene of fruitfulness and water that spread before them. The beat of wings and the strange cries of the wild beasts of the desert seemed to contain a note of joy. He heard a psalm and a song, a ringing paean of praise to the Creator that ascended from the dumb and wordless throats of the fowl and beasts of the wilderness.

The green highway through the desert broke off from the low-level plain and began to ascend higher and higher, leading into empty space. A city appeared before the eye of the prophet, floating ethereally on clouds of smoke. He recognized it. It was the transcendental Jerusalem! the Jerusalem that exists in the heights, floating upon rivers of amber. A mountain protruded from this heavenly Jerusalem and it too was suspended in the sky. It was

233

Mount Moriah, the Temple mountain, and in the thickest swirl of the smoke appeared a vast single altar.

Towards this heavenly Jerusalem, to this Mount Moriah in the firmament and to its altar, the prophet saw the children of Israel streaming out of Babylon. He heard them shouting and singing in the valley. He saw them flowing on in families, in "father's houses," the exiles of every city of Judah and Israel under their own banner: they and their wives and their little ones and their cattle. They were going out of the city of Babylon, which was spread out below the horizon. He saw them going forth and appearing on the rim of the wilderness. Slowly, slowly, the face of the desert lost its barrenness as they entered the highway that led through the Divine garden. See! They had already come into the garden and were walking beside the pools and singing streams, along paths ablaze with glorious flowers. Their singing came closer and closer. He could already pick out the priests and Levites among them, the heads of the Exile. He heard the steady beat of drums, the chant of the Levites, and the joyous exhalations of the people's gladness who went after them.

"When Jehovah turned again the captivity of Zion,
We were like them that dream;
Then was our mouth filled with laughter
And our tongue with singing."

They marched along, climbing ever upward, ever mounting; they were already gliding among the pillars of cloud that God had spread beneath their feet. The exiles were on the way from Babylon to Zion.

Suddenly Isaiah saw the likeness of a man hewn out of the cloud of smoke. The image was as yet obscured by the clouds that surrounded it but it gradually began to get clearer. It was an old man, very tall and white: a translucent whiteness. Beside him, as he seemed to float along, was a lad clothed in a shift and laden with a bundle of faggots. The old man held him by the hand. They walked silently in step, together, in the floating cloud of mist.

"God is showing me the origins of Israel, the lovingkindness of Abraham, and the merit of Isaac. We have all gone forth from the womb of our mother Sarah. The whole of Israel is Isaac, who went forth to be bound upon the altar. Just as the pillar of fire went before us in the wilderness, so the merit of Isaac and the lovingkindness of Abraham now go before us."

Overwhelming joy descended upon the prophet. It was as though the cup of consolation that God had given him to drink had made him drunken with happiness. God had shown him the merits that stand at the disposal of Israel, and who could stand against them? He was yet vouchsafed another vision. A hand seemed to come down and lift up the seer amid the swirling smoke as a mighty storm rends a great oak; it lifted him to the top of the mountain upon which the Temple stood.

The light was not that of common day nor night. It was a twilight of heavenly radiance. A great multitude, old men and young, were milling around him, all emitting white translucent light. The cloaks and turbans they wore were spun of no mortal fabric but woven out of the burning brightness of heaven. The hair of the man and son alike was snowy but the face was young and fresh. This old man was young. One hand pointed heavenward and his forefinger was very long, reaching unto heaven. He proclaimed in a loud voice:

"And it shall come to pass in the last days,
 That the mountain of the Jehovah's house shall be established
   in the top of the mountains
 And shall be exalted above the hills;
 And all nations shall flow unto it.
 And many people shall go up to the mountain of the Lord,
 To the house of the God of Jacob,
 And he will teach us of his ways,
 And we will walk in his paths.

For out of Zion shall go forth the law
And Jehovah's word from Jerusalem.
And he shall judge among the nations,
And shall rebuke many peoples;
And they shall beat their swords into ploughshares,
And their spears into pruning hooks.
Nation shall not lift up sword against nation,
Neither shall they learn war any more."

He heard a song at that moment, a song that was joy incarnate, a melody pronouncing good tidings to the world of peace for eternity, a voice proclaiming the great triumph of good over evil. The good news of the great salvation was lifted up from the mountains over the valleys with a noise of great rushing like that of mighty waters. The voice of the harbingers was soft and clear like the gentle falling of water. It flowed down from the mountain to the valley and, welling back to the mountain, proclaimed to Zion:

"Thy King reigneth."

Then all at once the clouds of smoke and mist were dissolved; they were rent asunder like a veil of silk; they parted like the sweeping aside of great curtains and his eyes saw vast horizons without end, the whole of the universe spread out in a panorama of cities and plains. Lands dwelling on broad green meadows and cities whose mountains were covered with snow. And from all lands and all cities came streaming crowds of men without number, men, women and children, fathers carrying their young ones on their shoulders, mothers with their babes in arms. All were hurrying eagerly to ascend the mountain of Zion to the place where the Temple stands. And as they pressed on, they proclaimed to Zion:

"Thy King reigneth."

The prophet shouted as one with the people of the whole universe:

"Say to Zion, 'Thy King reigneth.'"

He shouted aloud. The vision was reft away. The prophet

awoke and saw where he was. Neraiah and Zerubabel were standing over him.

"O prophet! I told you that you had many enemies and they were too strong for you. They intend bringing you to judgment before the tribunal of the elders. The peoples are deceived in their hopes; they murmur and cast a heavy burden of blame upon you."

"Jehovah will justify me. So who can contend against me?" asked the prophet.

"Take him, Neraiah, home to your house," said Zerubabel.

"What have they done to you, O my prophet?"

As a father whose bowels are moved with compassion over an afflicted son, so tenderly yet strongly did Neraiah lift up the prophet in his arms. His eyes were hot with the tears that poured down and laved the swollen and bloodstained face of the prophet.

# CHAPTER FOUR

NO mother bird on a dark and ominous night guarded her
precious brood more tenderly or with more devotion than
did Neraiah and his wife Ama-Bar tend the prophet in the
shelter of their poor hovel. With healing ointments and balms,
they soothed his torn skin. But the prophet was more troubled by
the weakness of their faith than by the physical harm done to him
by the cruel hands of men. He had utterly believed that his
prophecy was to be realized in the immediate present and now all
had abandoned him. No man believed in the truth of his predictions. A faint doubt had eaten its way even into the heart of
Zerubabel about the truth of his words, and hesitations gnawed at
the mind of Jeshu ben Jehozedek. It had never, heaven forbid,
entered the mind of either of them even to imagine that the prophet
was a false seer. Some of what he had foretold had indeed been
fulfilled. But they thought the prophet had been deceived and fallen
a victim to his own imagination, his zeal for the God of hosts was
so fierce and his passion to see every knee bowed before Him and
every tongue sing His praise was so overpowering. His love for
Israel, his desire to see her at the head of all the peoples, an
ensign for the nations, his longings for the redemption, may have
brought visions before his eyes which were purely subjective and
had not come from God at all.

The prophet lay outstretched on his straw pallet in his own hut.
His wide-open eyes looked up at the sky at which he gazed in a
manner no other man could emulate. His gaze roved the heavens
and sought and searched as though by its intensity he hoped to
draw down an answer to the question that was boring into his

mind. God had sent him to announce to His afflicted people the good tidings of redemption for which they were waiting with great impatience. God had pierced his ear day after day and he had heard voices. God had given him signs, had shown him manifestations. He saw the redemption coming nearer, but why did it delay? Why were its birth pangs so bitterly severe, so full of agony and affliction? Why were its symptoms so deceiving and disappointing? His impatience for the answer was not so that he should obtain peace of mind for himself. He wanted to know for the longing people's sake, for that of the exiles cast out of the radiance of hope into the outer darkness of despair. Their power to wait and endure was almost at an end and would soon be no more. What were God's intentions in so doing? Why the suffering? Why the cursed trembling that descended like impure dewdrops upon the ripening grapes of the redemption?

Over and over again he deeply reconsidered the vision of the redemption which God had so often revealed to him. He probed his own recollection of the prophecy of the return to Zion and the way of the redeemed from Babylon by way of the desert. A highway was cloven out of the wilderness so that they could pass by. Had not God split asunder the Red Sea to make a pathway for His people centuries ago when they went forth from Egypt? Could He not therefore just as easily turn the waste place into a garden of God before the exodus from Babylon?

While he was still wondering and agitating his mind about the meaning of the vision of the binding of Isaac, sleep fell upon him, a deep and perfect slumber. He dreamed that he wandered alone in thick darkness, oppressed with fears and bathed in cold sweat. The darkness was heavy but not with the quality of a moonless night in which the gloom is not even perceptible. This was darkness which could be felt. One could hear it and indeed see it. He made out the shapes of trees, that seemed petrified and had strange creatures bound to them. They were trying to struggle free from the trees with convulsive movements of their shoulders, attempting to break away from them. All their joints strained in the effort but the trees held them fast in a grip like iron tongs. Around the trees beasts were crawling. He heard them breathing heavily; he heard the pad of the soles of their feet; he heard the cracking of their sinews as they struggled; their movements reached his ear even before he saw them. Then he beheld them clearly as they emerged from their lairs. They were as black as the night about them, a limb of the body of the night: big-boned, sleek lions, gigantic wild oxen, leopards thirsty for blood. Most of these beasts had human faces adorned with beards. Others had the bodies of men, or long and squirmy necks with the heads of men. He recognized them; he knew them. They were Assyria and Babylon in the guise of giant monsters, man and beast in one. The man was dissolved in the beast just as the creatures blended into the petrified trees. The beasts were moving, moving. He heard the fall of their feet, the champ and grinding of their jaws as though they were sharpening their muzzles after smelling the scent and odor of blood flowing in the veins of living men. Their hot breath was already burning his body like a terrifying wind. They were coming continually nearer, angry, lusting for blood; gigantic and monstrous beings with the faces of men.

They were surrounding him; there was no escape. It was not he who was menaced but Israel. Israel was encompassed by a ring of ravening monstrous beasts. A great cry filled his mouth, a shriek of terror.

"God of Hosts, shield of Israel, the monsters of Babylon and Assyria have surrounded me. Come quickly to my aid, save me in my sore straits!"

He was in the midst of his supplication when a man appeared before him. His face was not visible; only his white cloak could be seen. It shone like the sun. No sooner did the monsters behold the shining light, illuminating the darkness, than the fear of God fell upon them. With a shuddering fearful roar that cleaved the bowels of the earth they fled away to their dark caves, their lairs of Stygian night, and Israel went out freely from its trouble. The prophet fell at the feet of the white-cloaked man and said:

"Tell me, I pray thee, O my master, where am I?"

He heard a voice answering:

"In the kingdom of night, in the heart of all darkness."

"And who are the beasts that I saw?"

"The inhabitants of the darkness of the shadow of death, the evil beasts with human faces who rule over the night."

"And the mortals who struggle to be free of the petrified trees?"

"These are the generations that long for my coming; they are straining to be free of the night."

"And who art thou, O my lord?"

"I am the light of Israel and the hope of the world. I am the Law and its preserver; for Teaching goeth forth from me and my judgment as a light for the peoples. I bring tranquillity. My righteousness is nigh, my salvation has gone forth, and my arms judge the nations. The isles expect me and wait for my arm."

The prophet fell down prostrate with his face to the ground at the feet of the man in white and asked:

"When, O my lord?"

"I am the fruit; Israel is the tree. The tree will be planted once again in its own field so that its fruit can ripen."

The dazzling shape dissolved. The prophet awoke.

Reinforced by this vision, the prophet faced the judgment of the elders. The trial was not held in the palace of the House of David but in Be Knishta, the great synagogue where the sons of the prophets sat, the elders who searched in the sacred texts. For the judgment was not being conducted along secular lines but on matters appertaining to faith. Most of the elders were disciples of the prophet Ezekiel, charged by him with carrying on his holy work amongst the exiles. They were tireless and indefatigable in their efforts to keep in the minds of the people at all times the law of Moses and the covenant made between the exiles of Judah and Israel and their God. They still burned with the fiery enthusiasm of their master. This synagogue still religiously preserved the ancient scrolls brought from Judea to Babylon. To the number of these elders, the disciples of the prophet Ezekiel in the great synagogue, had been added of recent time Haggai and Zachariah, two disciples of the prophet Daniel.

The prosecutor this time was not Mordechai-Gad, who did not intervene personally in the matter at all. The task fell to Manasseh of the House of Shallum, a highly placed levitical family of which he was one of the most important members. He was well versed in all that appertained to the rules of the Guardians of the Gate. He was completely aware of all that went on among the people and knew the direction of all their trends, movements, and tendencies. He was a familiar of the House of Murashu and worked completely hand-in-hand with them. The aggressive stand he took against the very idea of a return to Zion was, therefore, in no way surprising.

The manifesto that Cyrus or his son, Cambyses, was about to issue on the return of the Jews to Judea was not regarded by them as the gracious action of a monarch conferring a favor on a people but as a bitter and oppressive decree. Who was likely to bring about such a disaster? This false prophet who was prone to such misleading and seductive visions. Thus the judgment of the elders reiterated but one theme and one only: the prophet's words were not merely false prophecy, they were pregnant with a serious and immediate danger for the whole Jewish community of Babylon, from a spiritual as well as a material point of view. They could well bring the exiles to the point of destruction.

"Go out with me among the settlements of our brethren; come to Tel Aviv, draw near to Tel Melach; walk about the streets and markets and hear what the people are saying," cried Manasseh.

He was short in stature and his manner of speech was curt. Because of the thick layers of fat around his neck, he found it hard to breathe and his voice emerged harsh and croaking.

"Since this man appeared among us he has led the people astray and confused them with his false prophecies about King Cyrus ... Cyrus with the crown of David on his head and the mantle of the Messiah on his shoulder. Cyrus as the servant of

Jehovah. Not only will he soon redeem Israel, but he intends bringing the nations of the world to the God of Israel. But Cyrus through his heir has said that Bel Merodach is their god and that he it was who gave them victory. Thus he has placed our faith in danger.

"Just go about the streets and you will see the synagogues desolate. Our fellow Jews are not ashamed to worship to Bel Merodach openly and with bare heads. Our women expose themselves in their multitudes upon the steps of the temple of Ishtar whom they now revere.

" 'Judah will return to her land,' is what he tells us," continued Manasseh and pointed beyond the prophet who was standing before him. "She will return to the poverty-stricken land from which our fathers fled. And for what? For their good? No! They go to be a light to the gentiles, to bring them all to the worship of the true God; so he claims.

"He roused up soul-stirring hopes among the people, but they were not fulfilled. 'Kings shall be thy nursing fathers and their queens shall nurse thy young,' he said. What has come of his words? The people today are full of shame and confusion. He deceived and misled them; they are despised and a laughing stock among the Babylonians. 'Well, well, well! And when do you intend leaving us at last? What, are you still here?' God never told him anything and none of us ever had it in mind to return to Judea. It is his doing, not God's.

"Silence the seducer and deceiver! Shut the mouth that brings death and destruction upon us. Drive out the false prophet from among us! Let the people be told in clear and unmistakable terms that their God is to be found among them here in Babylon, too. They may well serve Him here and pray to Him here. He will hearken to their voice when they call upon Him. Let us have an end to tortuous lying and deceit!"

Manasseh of the House of Shallum did not stand alone or unsupported at the meeting. He brought with him a considerable company of false prophets, smooth-tongued, mellifluous of speech,

243

and of excitable temperament, who were called false prophets and who produced utterances according to the desire of whoever paid them. He also brought women who followed in blind fascination after the male attraction of the false prophets and whose devotion to them changed their whole character. These were all hirelings of the House of Murashu and the party who nursed a bitter enmity for the conception of the return to Zion. It was in this spirit that they pretended to prophecy. They incited the exiles and agitated against the new prophet, proclaiming him to be false. Now that despair and a deadness of the senses had overtaken the exiles, all those who had good reasons for not wanting to leave Babylon were encouraged and dared come out openly against anyone who suggested the return to Zion. They knew that the House of Murashu, some of the great families, and the wealthy merchants were solidly behind them. First and chiefest of these false prophets was Eliezer, son of Gamala, of the Sons of the Servants of Solomon. He was a tall and lowering fellow, owner of a thick black beard, burning dark eyes and a face that held an outward appearance of dignity. He exploited his impressive mien in order to gain the ascendancy over the men and women in his circle. They panted after him and were known as his disciples and followers. He seemed to exercise a kind of fascination over the women, who swooned over him in a kind of drunken sensual enthusiasm.

After the prosecutor, Manasseh, had concluded his charges, Eliezer, son of Gamala, arose to his full manly and dignified stature. He cast an imperious glance all around the room and began in a melodious voice:

"Hear my words, O ye sons of the prophets, and ye, also, O elders of the people of Judah, and ye, the heads of your fathers' houses! The prophet indeed saw no deceitful visions nor did he act as one bereft of his senses. God has also appeared to me in a vision and I beheld: Cyrus, king of Persia, leading the sons of Judah like a shepherd. And God likewise spake unto me, 'I have set up Cyrus over my flock.' The vision that the prophet saw was true but the interpretation he put upon it was a lying one. For the shepherd was not to bring his flock either to Judea or to Jerusalem. God set Cyrus over his flock to pasture them here in Babylon, on the land given them here as an inheritance to dwell thereon in tranquillity where none would revile or mock them. The God of Judah is not like the gods of the nations. Jehovah is not the God of one country or bound to one place. God is not a tree which has its roots in one spot only. He forsook Jerusalem because it became polluted by the iniquities of our ancestors. He abandoned it for all eternity. The heaven is His dwelling place and the earth is His footstool. Wherever His name is lifted up there He comes and brings blessing. Thus said God through His servants the prophets: 'Let my people pasture in the fields of Babylon. Let Cyrus be their shepherd.' So spake God to this prophet and so spake He unto me."

The band of women crowded fawning about Eliezer and shouted his words in chorus:

"Let my people pasture in the fields of Babylon; let Cyrus be their shepherd."

"He turns the word of God to falsehood! He involves us in disaster. Let a curse fall upon his head!"

"Stone him! Yea, stone him!" cried Eliezer's followers.

But others cried: "You ought to be stoned, not him. False prophets, sycophants of the House of Murashu!"

Eventually, Eliakim, son of Nahum, the last of the disciples of Ezekiel, who presided over the enquiry, managed to calm the rioting assembly and even the screeching claque that had accompanied Manasseh of the House of Shallum. Eliakim was a sere old man, literally dried up like a parched fig through fasting and asceticism and burned to a cinder by the flame of his devotion. He spoke in an almost inaudible whisper. His tone was wailing and mournful and his speech seemed to express a piety so deep that his heart was shattered by it. The subdued voice, with the note of authority that was in it, cut the tumult like a knife and stilled the screaming voices. When all was still, Eliakim spoke, or rather keened:

"Woe to the ears that have heard such words that have been uttered in this house, whose floor and walls are made of the earth from Judea and Jerusalem which the scions of David bore upon their shoulders. Day by day our hearts go out to Jerusalem in prayer, and you, Manasseh, you of the tribe of Levi, do you not know that when Nebuchadnezzar took your fathers into exile and their captives tried to force them to sing their holy songs of Zion upon their harps, they cut the fingers of their hands so as not to sing for aliens the songs that belonged to the Holy Temple? And you, a son of the Levites, have so slightingly and casually rejected Zion and Jerusalem? Vain and empty and wicked words have you cast upon our ears concerning the prophet from Jerusalem. Now we would hear what answer the prophet has to make to your charges."

All the time that the walls of the synagogue rang with the accusing words of Manasseh and the objurgations cast in his face by Eliezer, son of Gamala, the prophet from Jerusalem, for that is how they referred to him in the Be Knishta, stood pale and calm. His swollen face flared with the raw red marks of his wounds and showed dark blue shadows of bruises. He looked straight ahead of him, not even deigning to waste a glance on his accusers and revilers, for he was afraid they might find in his face some unconscious trace of anger or contempt. Only his upper lip was contorted in a smile which expressed great sorrow. He began to talk in a quiet and soothing voice, but as he went on it gathered strength. It gradually gained in majesty and power, like waters heard from a distance with a soft and murmuring lap which suddenly fall down with a roar from the crags and burst into the forest and thickets with the swell and tumult of an irresistible flood.

"The God Jehovah opened mine ear.
And I was not rebellious
Neither turned away back.
I gave my back to the smiters
And my cheek to them that plucked off the hair.
I hid not my face from shame and spitting.
For the God Jehovah will help me,
Therefore shall I not be confounded.

Therefore have I set my face like a flint;
And I know that I shall not be ashamed.
He is near that justifieth me,
Who will contend with me?
Let us stand together.
Who is my adversary?
Let him come near unto me.
Behold the God Jehovah will help me,
Who is he that shall condemn me?
Lo, they all shall wax old as a garment,
The moth shall eat them up."

From this language of rebuke, the prophet passed to a quiet and persuasive mood. He turned to the sons of the prophets:

"Who among you that feareth Jehovah,
That obeyeth the voice of his servant
And walketh in darkness and hath no light?
Let him trust in the name of Jehovah
And stay upon his God.

"Ho, all of you," cried the prophet, raising a challenging finger at his accusers at last, "that kindle a fire and compass yourself about with the sparks:

"Walk in the light of your fire
And in the sparks that you have kindled.
This shall ye have of mine hand,
Ye shall lie down in sorrow."

"O my brethren the prophets, you have now heard it from his own mouth!" exclaimed Eliezer, son of Gamala, with a cry of triumph. "He walked in darkness; he had no light. Since when has a prophet of Israel wandered in darkness? He walked in darkness and he remained in darkness and he wants to drag the whole people of Israel after him into the blackness. This man has dared rebuke the sons of God! Stone him. Stoning is his just desert. That is the penalty of a seducer and a blasphemer. So Moses commanded us."

"Stone him! Stoning is his desert! Fitting for a seducer and a blasphemer. So Moses commanded us!" fervently echoed his claque after him.

Without taking the slightest notice of them, the prophet resumed his discourse in a still and soothing voice. He swayed like grass in the wind to the rhythm of his own words.

"So be it. I walked in darkness and I had no light; but I put my trust in God. I lived with beasts of prey. Fear and terror surrounded me, but I put my trust in God and He opened my eyes and made a great light shine for me in the darkest places. Hear ye me, all of you that seek after righteousness, that search diligently for God." He turned to the elders:

> "Look unto the rock whence ye are hewn,
> And to the hole of the pit whence ye are digged.
> Look unto Abraham, your father,
> And unto Sarah that bore you;
> For I called him alone
> And blessed him and increased him."

The prophet raised his voice and sang in gladness and soaring exultation:

> "For Jehovah shall comfort Zion,
> He will comfort all her waste places;
> He will make her wilderness like the garden of Eden,
> And her desert like the garden of the Lord."

The prophet, all at once, lifted up his head to the sky. His hollow eyes stared into the highest heights and he seemed once again like a man transported to other distant worlds. He saw again the vision of hope which he had seen in the darkness of night.

"Hearken unto me, O my people,
And give ear unto me, O my nation;
For a law shall proceed from me
And I will make my judgment to rest for a light of the
    people.
My righteousness is near;
My salvation is gone forth;
And mine arm shall judge the people.
The isles shall wait on me,
And on mine arm shall they trust."

The prophet was silent.

"Whom does he mean? About whom is he hinting?" Whispering and anxious speculation were heard among the sons of the prophets.

"To a stock from the seed of Jesse, to the end of days, to the fulfillment of the prophecies that Isaiah foretold to us. To eternal peace." So spoke the circle of sons of the prophets who held fast to the words of Isaiah, the son of Amoz.

"He is referring to that which Jeremiah told us, to what our teacher and master Ezekiel told us," cried the disciples of the prophet Ezekiel.

"The prophet has said what previous prophets before him have spoken. We see not the slightest scintilla of falsehood or lying in his words; we see no iniquity on his hands. Why did they smite the prophet who was conducting himself uprightly?" Protesting voices were heard among the sons of the prophets.

"Disciples of Jeremiah, the prophet and pupils of Ezekiel, hearken to my words."

Zerubabel rose up from the secluded corner where he had been sitting quietly throughout the hearing.

"I am not a prophet nor the son of a prophet. I dwell amongst my people and as one with all of them await the redemption, the day when we shall return to the land which was given to our fathers as our prophets promised us in their day. Blacker than

249

darkness has been our night; no ray of light has shone to illumine it and put some hope in our hearts. Then, behold, this prophet came among us. He brought us the comfort of God at a time when we no longer dared to hope.

"He brought us three prophecies which we never believed would be fulfilled. None of us believed that Cyrus would triumph over Babylon as the prophet had foretold from the very beginning, yet the thing fell out exactly as he said. None of us believed that the gates of Babylon would be thrown wide open before Cyrus as this prophet foresaw long before. Yet the matter indeed came to pass in just that fashion. The prophet also told us that Cyrus would free our people and return us to Judea. And now just when all the signs seem to point to the fulfillment of this prophecy also, we are thrusting the prophet aside and doing to him what our fathers did to Jeremiah. Therefore, I say unto you: Sin not as our fathers sinned lest by thrusting aside the prophet we also thrust aside the redemption."

"That's just it," the grating voice of Manasseh was heard to shout. "Who says that to go out of Babylon will be the redemption? I have, it seems, to repeat my words. It would be a most terribly harsh decree if by the power of the prophet's lying teachings and visions it should come about that we were forced to leave Babylon and so fulfill all the wishes of our enemies. The exiles will never return to Judea. I say it to you and I repeat it. The exiles will never return to Judea. What did Judea give us? Poverty! Bread only after hard toil and water by measure. Wars and collisions with our neighbors who hate us. I know my people. I also know the Israelites of the ten tribes. They will never be a light to the gentiles. The gentiles have their own gods and we have ours. They don't disturb us in the worship of our God, so let us not turn up our noses at their beliefs. Every people to its own god! Do we want to be like all the nations! Do we want to live tranquil and prosperous lives in the place to which our God has brought us, in the shelter of our King Cyrus! If you force us to go back to

Judea, so as to be a light to the gentiles, you will only remove our people far from God and cause our brethren in the Exile wholly to embrace the cult of the gods of Babylon. They are already bowing to them, and what brought them to it? The false prophecies of this prophet. Your desire will never be established."

"Never be established!" A mighty and terrible roar broke out from the weak and feeble son of Nahum, Eliakim, the oldest of the disciples of Ezekiel. Everyone was greatly amazed that such a tremendous sound should have emanated from this emaciated sage. His eyes flamed, his skinny arm, thin as an arrow shaft, stretched forth and his bony finger was pointed like a lance towards the company of false prophets who surrounded their spokesman, Manasseh of the House of Shallum.

"Our fathers said this too. I see before me at this very moment my teacher and master, the crown of my head, our prophet Ezekiel, standing before the children of the Exile and rolling forth his message like the thunder:

"As I live, saith the Lord God,
    Surely with a mighty hand
    And an outstretched arm,
    And with fury poured out,
    Will I rule over you.
    And I will bring you out from the people,
    And I will gather you out of the countries wherein you are
        scattered
    With a mighty hand
    And an outstretched arm,
    And with fury poured out.
    And I will bring you into the wilderness of the people.
    And there will I plead with you face to face,
    Like as I pleaded with your fathers in the wilderness of the
        land of Egypt,
    So will I plead with you,
    Saith the Lord God.

251

"So spake Ezekiel to your fathers. Do you want to be like the nations of the world, like the families of the earth which worship wood and stone; do you speak thus unto us? The zeal for God does not speak from your throat as you lyingly tried to convince us. Yours is a zeal born out of narrow jealousy, a zeal conceived of a desire to live a life of tranquillity, a zeal inspired by those who hired you to spread hatred of Zion; that is what has gone out of your throats. And the righteous blood that you have shed, the blows that you smote the servant of God who brought us His consolation and salvation, cry out aloud from your hands for vengeance."

So spake the old prophet of the lying falsehood and hypocrisy that Manasseh, Eliezer, and all their band had uttered. His words were like the bitter drink administered as a test to the woman suspected of adultery.

"Indeed, the proof is now clear that they are traitorous and treacherous to the rock from which they were hewn and sought the evil of the prophet."

Eliakim approached the prophet, who was still standing alone facing his accusers, with only Neraiah, son of Seraiah, on guard a pace behind him. He embraced him and said:

"Come, take your rightful place among the sons of the prophets. For you are a brother to us. Jehovah of Hosts has appeared to you and made you His holy servant in order that you should bring the good tidings of the redemption to Israel. Happy art thou that it was your fate to give your back to the smiters and those that plucked your beard in the task on which God sent you. You are the equal of Isaiah, the son of Amoz; your stature is that of Ezekiel and Jeremiah. Your portion shall also be like theirs."

The elder of the disciples of the prophet Ezekiel led Isaiah and sat him down in a place of honor among the sons of the prophets.

The latter arose one after the other and said:

"You are our brother. We are ready to stand by your side and help you in your holy work for the sake of the God of Israel."

Great joy descended upon the sons of the prophets. They

252

exulted in the redemption which was now on the way. They seemed to see it actually becoming manifest. Greater than this was their joy to feel the Holy Spirit descending upon them, for every one of them felt a sacred delight and trembling investing his limbs and a fervor being poured over his eyes. They all saw visions and uttered prophecies.

Haggai, pale and emaciated, raised himself up. He was still very young, and he spoke in the name of his master.

"Listen to me, my brethren, the sons of the prophets! You all know that the crown of our heads has been taken away. Our father, Daniel, has been taken from us. Before he departed to go to the hidden and secret places of heaven, he called unto us and he said: 'I am going from you to my Father which is in heaven; but you stay here at the side of this prophet despised and rejected of men. He is troubled and confounded by the visions that he sees, and so say you unto him—'Long is the way that yet you have to tread. God has fenced it round with bounds. The end of the road is hidden but it leads to the end of days and Israel is treading along it. She wanders from one side to the other, sometimes goes astray and rebels but keeps on going. There are paths that lead wrongly and paths that lead back, but Israel goes on. Let your heart be strong and your spirit firm, for Israel will surely reach the goal which God has ordained.' Thus our teacher spoke to us in his testament. Our father and teacher willed it and so we have come to thee, O prophet, to stand at thy right hand."

Haggai concluded and Zechariah opened up his parable. He was a very young man and not yet able to achieve mastery over the thronging press of his imaginings. This is the vision he related:

"And it came to pass during the night when our candle was extinguished that I beheld a vision. I was standing at the uttermost end of a dark forest. The thing happened just as dawn was breaking and behold, the corners of heaven began to pale and the dew was still heavy upon the grass and the trees. In the place where I was standing was an abundance of green rushes which was still lush with the mists of the morning. The sun came up to warm and dry the trees and the earth. I was still standing and looking this way and that, when I beheld a white city sparkle at the corner of heaven and a tender hart went forth from the trees of the black forest. It had a burning Menorah between its horns. It stalked along at a stately pace. Then it entered the white highway which God opened up before it and it parted the green rushes all dappled with white flowers. So the hart was going gently and safely on towards the white city shining far off. And as it went the Menorah shone upon its head."

Then the prophet knew that it was Israel that was going forth from the dark night free from the talons of the ravening beasts which had held her captive and safe from their gaping jaws. She was going to Jerusalem rebuilt, which God had established for her once again under the bright sun.

The prophet was at ease again. He had found his consolation.

# CHAPTER FIVE

HIS wounds still unhealed, the prophet came back to the congregations, the market places, and the shut-away courtyards, wherever exiles were to be found. He aroused them, charged them, reminded them who they were.

He had forgotten his pain and suffering as though they had never existed. The spittle that had been flung in his face was like reviving showers; the blows that had rained down on his flesh were like a spur to rejoicing, a shout of triumph to the God of Zion.

Fire burned in his blood, zealousness for the God of Hosts, the Only Creator, the Omnipotent, the Ruler over all existent things.

They said that the abomination, Bel Merodach, had cloven out the heaven and the earth when he went to fight against his parent, Tiamat, who had conspired to bring back the world to primal chaos. Who was this Bel Merodach that aspired to be likened to the Creator of all? Bel Merodach was an inert mass. At one time they poured him of molten gold; another, they hewed him out of stone; but he always represented the fabricator of flesh and blood who made him. The Maker of the works of creation was neither matter, nor body, nor the likeness of a body as the Babylonians believed; certainly not as so many of the exiles were at that time repeating and stammering after them. The Creator of the world was One at the beginning. He made everything in it—He was the God of Israel.

The God of Israel did not go forth with a spear and a net to capture his mother, Rahab the serpent. The God of Israel did not need to make war on anyone; for all was His, both good and evil alike. He needed no beginning, for before Him there was nothing. Creation had never existed a moment without the presence and the authority of God and only continued by His grace. The spirit of God hovered over the face of the primal chaos, the emptiness and formlessness, the darkness, the water; for besides Him there was naught.

It seemed as though God had opened a small crevice through which he could see the closed secret of the work of creation from end to end. From one end of eternity to another in the depths of the sea of darkness, a peal like thunder rolled, proclaiming, "Let there be light!" The sound was heard and he became aware of bright pools shining and spreading in the sea of darkness. The sea of darkness was now all overlaid with blue wings from the coverlet of heaven. From these, layers of light were radiating out and penetrating everywhere. The clouds massed in billowing waves, lifted up on wings and floating over the face of the firmament. As they moved they sent forth from among them the stars, suns, and moons, strewing them across the expanse of the sky. The stars, suns, and moons were disseminated by their own flight over the broad pure waters. Light came and the brightness of day irradiated the sea of darkness which was held cupped in God's hand.

Only now did he discern the fearful winds which raged across the sea of darkness while terrible storms surged and soared there. Everything boiled in the sea like a witch's brew. Pillars of mist rose upward like mighty towers; some took the likeness of Rahab and some of the great dragon, monstrous images thrown up as though the dark sea had been the habitation of all the dwellers in Sheol. The emptiness and formlessness that had been held captive within it broke out with raging fury, struggling to be free. Then the voice of God was heard once again rolling with a sound of empyrean thunder, rending and tearing the firmament like an elemental sword, breaking down the walls of time and rending Rahab, the dragon, and the other monsters: "Let there be a firmament in the midst of the waters and let it divide the waters from the waters." He saw the heads of the monsters droop down like smitten dogs and sink into the abyss. Part of the sea sank down to the depths below and part rose up into the air, mounting higher and higher, and as it rose becoming increasingly light and mingling with the curtains of the heights of heaven that shrouded eternity from above.

The prophet brought his vision before the sons of the prophets and the elders. He did not mention the idol Bel Merodach nor allude to it with even the slightest hint. But those who heard his words knew quite well to what he referred. Had not so many of the exiles gone a-whoring after Bel Merodach, believing that he was the creator of the world? After he had explained to the sons of the prophets his vision of the work of creation, he lifted up his hands to heaven and prayed to the God of Israel, to Jehovah, the Creator of all things. His prayer was made up of polished verses, for he had written it down and worked over it, so that the words chosen might be a fit medium for the vision that was to be enshrined in them: a casket of gold embellished with precious stones.

"Awake, awake,
  Put on thy strength,
  O arm of Jehovah,
  Awake, as in the ancient days,
  In the generations of old.
  Art thou not it that hath cut Rahab
  And wounded the dragon?
  Art thou not it which hath dried the sea
  And the waters of the great deep
  And hath made the depths of the sea
  A way for the ransomed to pass over.
  Therefore, the redeemed of Jehovah shall return
  And come with singing unto Zion,
  And everlasting joy shall be upon their heads.
  They shall obtain gladness and joy;
  And sorrow and mourning shall flee away."

257

When he left them, the prophet went about again from synagogue to synagogue, from neighborhood to neighborhood. He visited every place where the exiles were to be found, where they dwelt or where they worked, at their anvils or their stores or their stands in the market places. And wherever he came, he encouraged, charged, and reminded them. He paid no attention to their curses; he heeded not their insults; he was not dismayed by their threatening, raised fists. The murmuring and disillusion were still great among the exiles. They were also presently obsessed with the great fear that they would be expelled from Babylon because they refused as a whole community to accept the divinity of Bel Merodach after the new rulers had publicly proclaimed that he was the god of the empire and all who dwelt therein. They were afraid of the things the prophet did. They shook like driven leaves lest he impinge upon the honor of the god that was mighty in Babylon, as was his wont to do, and so bring calamity upon them. Whenever he appeared they begged of him to leave them alone.

"You will bring down disaster upon us. Our near neighbors already know that you despise Bel Merodach and that we Jews are the only people in the whole empire who reject his lordship. Get you gone, lest you involve us in disaster."

"We are despised and made light of by all the people who dwell in Babylon. Our neighbors mock us and treat us as idiots."

"They call us aliens. They say Babylon is not our rightful place because we do not worship their god. They drive us away from the markets and expel us from the fairs."

"They steal the morsel of bread from our mouths. Soon they will drive us out of our houses. We will have to sleep under the open sky and we shall have nothing to give our wives and little ones."

"What have you done to us? Your own eyes can see that God has forsaken us and has left us to the mercy of wild beasts with ravening jaws. Why do you incite them against us? Why do you bring their fury against us?"

"Choke his mouth with dust! Drive him out of here! Anyone can see that he is the cause of all our troubles."

258

The prophet saw confused and terrified faces before him, hands trembling with fear, Jews imploring him with broken timid voices, craven spirits, and mumbling lips to have mercy on them, their wives, and their little ones.

So he stood up among the crestfallen, troubled exiles and the bereft of counsel. His eyes flared with the burning indignation that their spinelessness and lack of spirit kindled in him, but his fury was quenched at the same time by tears of compassion that welled up in him for them. The state of apprehension and fear they were in was not just the result of the incitement by the messengers of the House of Murashu but also of the contempt and belittlement that were their daily lot from their Babylonian neighbors. After their gods, and especially Bel Merodach, had been so exalted by the new rulers, the Babylonians had suddenly become conscious that the Judeans were the only element in the whole empire that held out and did not bow the knee to the reigning deities. They were the only people obstinately to maintain the worship of a foreign god that their ancestors had brought from the land whence they came into exile. If this was indeed so then it stood to reason that they were strangers in Babylon.

Against all this the Judeans could not detect the slightest sign that Cyrus would fulfill any of the promises to which the prophet had testified. Cyrus had not even come to Babylon, and his son Cambyses, who wore the regalia of kingship, was silent. But not so the Babylonians. They mocked them and quarreled with them, told them that their God had forsaken them, and jeered that the god of Babylon did not want them. Babylon was not their home. They were aliens there. This was not their place. The Babylonian officials slowly but steadily whittled away the special privileges which previous rulers had conferred upon them. The officers oppressed them, the judges dealt with them very severely, the unruly mobs attacked them and drove them away from their stalls in the markets. Wherever they turned, they heard the mocking and sneering laughter, as though they were the scum of the earth, abandoned by God and by man.

They imagined that all this came about because of the prophet. The blows they had smitten him had not helped. The plucking out of the hair of his beard had not made him desist, nor had the spitting in his face. They drove him away in vain. Whatever they did was of no effect, for he was afraid of nothing. And latterly, since the elders had proclaimed that he was a prophet of truth, he had gained many friends among the sons of the prophets and they stood beside him ready and prepared to help him.

How long? How long would they be suspended over an abyss of nothingness? They were being rooted out of Babylon, torn up like foul weeds, and yet were not being returned to their own land. They were persecuted, insulted, and despised.

And the prophet would not leave them alone. They smote him again, but it was as though he had not been touched. He stood before them, his arms outstretched, and entreated them as a father entreats his son. He spoke to them with bowels of compassion as a father consoles an unhappy child:

"Thus saith Jehovah:
I, even I, am he that comforteth you.
Who art thou, that thou shouldst be afraid of a man that
    shall die,
And of the son of man which shall be made as of grass?
And forgettest Jehovah thy maker,
That has stretched forth the heavens,
And laid the foundations of the earth,
And has feared continually every day
Because of the fury of the oppressor,
And I have put my words in thy mouth.
And I have covered thee in the shadow of mine hands,
And laid the foundations of the earth,
And say unto Zion,
Thou art my people."

"Where does he get such confidence? Where? Where?" Everyone was asking himself and his neighbor as the slender young prophet went among them with unflagging energy, impassioned as though he were being consumed with fire. Exalted and ecstatic with the power of the vision that burned in him, he did not cease at any time to sing the songs of hope and consolation. He had been disappointed by the failure of his hopes; he had been mocked in his expectations and yet his spirit was that of a bridegroom among mourners. He sang a song of life in a house of death. The people gradually became accustomed to him; to this young man who wandered about, always accompanied by Neraiah, son of Seraiah, who tended him as a father does an ailing child. And indeed the prophet was a sick child, for a fever had entered into him. It may have been a good or a bad spirit, but it continually groaned and cried out with his voice. They smote him no longer; no more did they tear his beard. They let him chatter as he would and no one paid any attention to him. He no longer spoke of the god of Babylon; no more did he mention the name of Cyrus. He only expressed the visions he saw. Sometimes he spoke to himself as though he held converse with spirits which none but he could see.

He stood among the company of exiles in the courtyard of the Bethlehemites, who still flocked to hear him. When he spoke they felt the charm and melody of the songs of degrees that the Levites had sung in the holy Temple. No prophet that had arisen had spoken words to them as warm, as heartening, and as sweet as this Isaiah. He clothed his thoughts in melodious phrases that entered the heart and took possession of it. They soothed the bones as with cool dew; they allayed sorrow and turned sadness to sweetness. As though with a sorcerer's rod, the prophet's words transported them to green pastures beside still waters about which David, son of Jesse, the king who came from their own city, had so sweetly sung.

Now the exiles who dwelt in Babylon were connoisseurs of language. Many of them still reflected with delight on the visions that Ezekiel had spread out before them with his prophetic enchantment. Because of this they referred to him as the "preacher and the maker of parables." What difference could it make to the situation if the words of the prophet were to be fulfilled or not; if God himself had indeed put words into his mouth as he claimed, or if a familiar spirit, a ghost, which had chosen his body as a habitation, was crying out of his throat.

It did not much matter. It was pleasant to abandon oneself to the flow of gentle eloquence which came from the prophet. Here in Babylon, the speech of their children was becoming increasingly corrupted by the vernacular, and so there arose among the parents, most of whose own fathers had come from Judea, longings for the sharp purity and clarity of prophetic speech. It was very precious to them. They derived an exquisite pleasure out of weaving it into their prayers and the psalms that were composed in Babylon. The words of the prophet aroused longings in them for Jerusalem, irrespective of whether they wished to return there or not. The longings were very pleasant in themselves.

Unto them, in their street, by the benches where they worked at their crafts for a strange people in a strange city, the prophet brought the vision of Jerusalem which had visited him in the latter days. Jerusalem bound with bonds, Jerusalem ashamed, forsaken by God and her inhabitants, abandoned to dust and ashes, to ruins upon which she sat in her mourning. Jerusalem, his mother and theirs, the chosen one of God, who had drunk the cup of God's fury to the dregs. This Jerusalem, drunken not with wine but with bitterness, standing with difficulty upon her feet and worthy of consolations. God himself would wipe away her tears and comfort her as He had consoled Rachel, the mother of Israel. Jerusalem had drunk and quaffed the cup of trembling for all Israel. For the sins of Israel and Judea, God had abandoned her. The prophet saw her in her bereavement: bowed down, broken and alone, with the last survivors of her children crawling about her ruins like crazed folk, like people possessed of demons, faint and dying of hunger. Most of her children had gone away from her into exile, and, alas for her, they had forgotten her quickly and there was no one to take her hand at a time of calamity and downfall. Strangers plowed her fields and aliens lived in her houses. The people were scattered throughout the towns and cities of Babylon and did not even want to know her any more.

In a mighty voice, full of confidence and consolation, albeit tearful, the prophet sang before the Bethlehemites the song of his mother's gladness and her sorrow, the song of her fall to the dung-hill and her exaltation to the heights, the song of her shattering and recovery, in words that God alone could have put into his mouth:

"Awake, awake,
Stand up, O Jerusalem,
Which hast drunk at the hand of Jehovah the cup of his fury.
Thou hast drunken of the dregs of the cup of trembling, and
    wrung them out.
There is none to guide her among all the sons that she has
    brought forth;
Neither is there any to take her by the hand of all the sons
    that she hath brought up.
These two things are come unto thee,
Who shall be sorry for thee?
Thy sons have fainted,
They lie at the head of all the streets as a wild bull in a net;
They are full of the fury of Jehovah,
The rebuke of thy God."

His tone changed and became gentle as though he actually saw the mother Zion standing before him.

"Now therefore hear this: she is afflicted and drunken but not with wine."

His voice changed again and he roared with a tone of thunder which struck awe into all those roundabout who came forth from their houses to gaze upon him:

"Thus saith thy Lord, Jehovah,
And thy God that pleadeth the cause of His people.
Behold, I have taken out of thy hand the cup of trembling,
Even the dregs of the cup of my fury,
And thou shalt no more drink of it again.
But I will put it into the hand of those that afflict thee,
Which have said to thy soul,
Bow down that we may go over;
And thou hast laid thy body on the ground,
And as the street to them that went over."

They went forth to look at him as people go out to see a jester with enchantments in his mouth, to wonder over his beautiful phrases, at his conjuring tricks with words. They went forth to mock him, to despise him and revile him. But his words entered into them and were absorbed by their flesh. The hot passion of his speech burned out all the impurity, dross, and uncleanness that were gathered up within their hearts through the years of captivity and servility in the Babylonian exile. As with a white-hot iron, they were purged of the servile cringing of the lackey in front of his powerful master and of the fear they felt for their neighbors. Their fathers' blood once more streamed through their veins. The implicit obedience and action they had pledged at the assembly at Mount Sinai passed once again like a storm through their thoughts and lifted them up as on eagles' wings, bearing them high and carrying them to the land of their origin. Their eyes saw their mother, Jerusalem. She stood like a bride before them and lifted her hand to them in grace and love.

Tears of joy started in the corners of their weary eyes. In their nakedness, in the dragging burden of their work at the forges, in the face of their enemies and their oppressors, the Babylonians, they fell down with their faces to the earth, lifted their hands to heaven, and sang with indignant hearts flaming with a lust for vengeance:

"By the waters of Babylon, there sat we down...."

# CHAPTER SIX

FINALLY, in the month of Marheshvan, of the year in which he conquered Babylon, Cyrus entered the capital to be anointed emperor of Babylon and ruler of all the kingdom of the earth.

Never, in the whole of its history, had Babylon seen such a triumphal procession. No monarch that had before trod the streets of that metropolis had ever been surrounded by so many kings, by such a multitude of satraps, by governors from so many provinces; accompanied by so many bodyguards and courtiers of so many nations and peoples. Towering head and shoulders above all the retinue and the warriors who marched around him, his Persian garb gleaming beneath the golden robe of Babylonian royalty that flowed from his shoulders, a gold crown upon his head, Cyrus led his bodyguard from the gate of Ishtar in the Avenue of the Processions to the palace of Nebuchadnezzar.

The massed forces of Cyrus, the brilliance of their variegated uniforms, the camels, elephants and leopards, did not excite the Babylonians so much as the three troops of the king's personal bodyguard. They were a sign and a witness that the dominion of the three mighty powers which had, each in its turn for generations, held lands and peoples without number beneath their sway, was now united under one head. One will ruled over them; one king, terrible and fearful, whose power was limitless, now commanded them all. On his right marched the king's personal guards, the Persians clad in short tunics, quivers of arrows on their shoulders. The warriors, with their short beards, stepped out in the full vigor of their youthful strength, in perfect unison with their king. On his left was the Assyrian troop, in their dress of antique mode; their awe-inspiring, full, curled and plaited beards, their conical helmets high on their heads and their copper-covered lances in their hands—lances which had broken the heads of kings and despatched their peoples into slavery. They tramped along with a thunderous tread, in that ominous irresistible inevitability which had in former times struck terror and dread into the hearts of nations and brought them under subjection. Behind the king came his Babylonian bodyguard. These were all high-ranking officers, who had commanded troops that once served the king of Babylon and who had gone over with their men to the service of the victor monarch.

The triumphal processions of the rulers of Assyria and Babylon had always made a great feature of crushed captive kings and their generals, bound in chains and fetters. These three companies of personal bodyguards, composed of officers of the highest rank marching in formation, witnessed and announced more eloquently than any words could do that a great change had taken place in the world. An old era had died; a new era had been born.

Rameses II, king of kings, Tiglath Pileser, Sennacherib, Nebuchadnezzar—none of these mighty conquerors had ever sat so securely on their thrones as did Cyrus, the king of Persia and Media, on the seat of monarchy in the palace of the kings of Babylon with its hanging gardens, with its vast halls embellished with the graven tablets from which stood forth the scenes depicting the overwhelming and crushing triumphs of Nebuchadnezzar. The eternal celestial struggle between Tiamat and Bel Merodach was graven in ivory and embossed in gold upon the throne on which Cyrus now sat. He was arrayed in the Assyrian robe of majesty which Nebuchadnezzar had brought from Ninevah together with the throne as a spoil of war. There was another bas relief upon the throne. It depicted Bel Merodach investing Nebuchadnezzar with the crown and scepter of Babylon. It was this crown which now graced the high head of Cyrus, the Persian, while the scepter which symbolized dominion over the peoples of the earth was grasped firmly in his hand. Grouped around the king were the great ones and nobles of Assyria and Babylon, satraps and pashas, every one of them lord of a province in the dominions of Cyrus. Each was resplendent in his chain and ring and the golden badge of his authority. To the right and left of the throne stood the two rulers of the city of Babylon itself, Cambyses, the son and heir, and Gubaru, the lord of the governors of Babylon, who had by his craft and diplomacy brought over the priests of E-Sagila to the cause of the new monarch.

The same day, the great king summoned a deputation of the leaders of the Jews who dwelt in Babylon. It included Shaltiel, the senior prince of the House of David, his son, Zerubabel, Jehozedek, the son of the chief priest, Seraiah. There was Jeshu, son of Jehozedek, and notables of the fathers' houses of Babylon and the surrounding settlements of the exiles.

At a signal from the king, Gubaru, Pasha of Babylon, came forward with great ceremony to the rolling of drums and the flourish of herald's trumpets. Two scribes appeared before him and held up a clay tablet before his eyes. He read aloud:

*"Thus saith Cyrus, king of Persia, the Lord God of Heaven hath given me all the kingdoms of the earth, and He hath charged me to build Him an house at Jerusalem, which is in Judah.*

*"Who is there among you of all His people? His God be with him and let him go up to Jerusalem, which is in Judah, and build the House of the Lord God of Israel, He is the God which is in Jerusalem."*

While the deputation of the exiles were still staring open-mouthed, trembling, stirred to the depths, their hearts fearful and shaking, the king's voice was heard again.

"And these shall be your boundaries."

At a sign from the king, two scribes brought in a great clay tablet on which a plan of Jerusalem and its environs was engraved. The Pasha of Babylon pointed out the boundaries with his finger. They were cut out from the coastal plain to the seashore, excluding

Samaria, Schechem, and Galilee. Jerusalem was shown there and the hills roundabout it as far as Hebron.

Pallor spread over the faces of the exiles, but before they could recover themselves, the king spoke again.

"I am not restoring the kingship of the House of David. I am your monarch and you shall be under my protection and rule. I have extended my grace to you and appointed my own governor over you. His name is Sheshbazzar."

A tall man, dressed in Persian style, came forward and stood before the king.

"This is the governor I have set over you. His title shall be the 'Prince of Judah.' He will lead you back to Judah and I entrust you to his rule. Any prince of Judah who wishes to go with him to help in the building of Jehovah's house is free to do so. But I am not restoring the monarchy of the House of David."

He turned to the man who stood before him.

"Sheshbazzar, Prince of Judah."

The appointed governor fell with his face to the ground at the foot of the king.

"I am entrusting Judah to your care. Take the Judeans, those who wish to return to Jerusalem and help in rebuilding the sanctuary of their God. And whosoever remaineth in any place where he sojourneth, let the men of his place help him with silver and with gold, and with goods and with beasts, besides the freewill offering for the House of God that is in Jerusalem.

"Make my will in this matter known to return the Judeans to Judah in all the provinces of my empire."

There was a short silence and then Cyrus called:

"The treasurer of the empire of Babylon!"

Mithradates came forward and fell with his face to the ground before the throne.

"Mithradates, bring out the vessels of Jehovah's house, which Nebuchadnezzar took away from Jerusalem and gave to the temple of his own gods. Count them and hand them over to Sheshbazzar, the governor of Judah."

With this latter command, the audience ended, leaving the heads of the Exile both astounded and heartened.

Joy and fear mingled together in the hearts of the exiles. Confusion, jumbled ideas, and bewilderment were the marks of the attitude of the leaders and rulers when Cyrus's manifesto became generally known. By every stall and store in the great market, in all the alleys and courtyards, in the synagogues, in all the points of settlement in city and village; in the metropolis, in Tel Aviv and Tel Melach alike, groups of Jews gathered, weighing, arguing, hair-splitting, and disputing over the great event. Great arguments broke out in the palace of the House of David, among the sons of the prophets, among the elders and the priests. Great as was the joy, not less was the fear of the unknown that the news held.

"They have poured into our land from Sodom and Edom, like a sewer or cesspit that has overflowed, and have flooded the whole country. The Edomites who only yesterday paid servile tribute to us are today the lords of the country. They have come up from the Negev, the south country, from Transjordania. They have come down from the hills and occupied our parts of them and have taken for themselves everything of any value. The Samaritans, our blood cousins, have hurried down from the mountains of Ephraim and settled in Jerusalem. Where then shall we live, having been allocated the dried-up hills of Judah from around Jerusalem to Jericho and Hebron? Where shall we find a place to live? How can we be expected to exchange the fat fertile lands of Babylonia, which drink in water day and night and are nourished by the canals as a child is nourished by the full breasts of its mother, for the craggy hills of Judah whose slopes have been washed clean for years by the early and latter rains? Where shall we get our daily bread, pasture for our cattle and nourishment for our babies?"

To the bazaar came simple peasants who dwelt on the broad meadows near Tel Aviv and in other rural settlements on the network of canals that radiated from the Chebar canal.

"I shall bring those who return a rich gift. Two mules, a horse, and a silver bar I was saving to make a bracelet for my wife. I shall certainly not leave here. I might even go as far as a yoke of two fine oxen, and that is that. My lot is quite all right in Babylon."

So spoke Giddel, the wealthy landowner of Tel Aviv who had recently added a fine field to his estate after a poor peasant had defaulted on a debt to him. The same sort of story was heard from the workers and artisans in the market places and courtyards around the bazaars.

"To whom shall we sell our goods? To the leprous Ammonites who run about the ruins of Jerusalem with their tails sticking out of their torn cloaks? What do these barefoot beggars want with our fine dyed cloths? Maybe they will leap for joy over our women's embroidered sandals? Perhaps they will buy our beautiful girdles for their worn-out and raddled wives."

"Ha! Do you think they will grab for good money our spices and oils out of which half of us make our living, to get rid of the stink that clings about them?"

But more serious and weighty were the considerations pondered by the heads of the Exile and the chiefs of the House of David, the elders, the priests, the sons of the prophets. In those circles the debate went on quietly, without the raising of voices. They turned the matter over and examined it in all its aspects; they gathered all sorts of groups together for mutual consultations. They assembled the heads of houses, the more prominent priests.

"An alien prince shall rule over us, one of the king's satraps, with the title of 'Prince of Judah.' He is not of the Davidic stock. It seems as though Cyrus deliberately overlooked the princes of the Davidic house who dwell among us, who are rightly entitled to rule, and chose one of his own people whom no one knows."

So one of those assembled at the palace of the House of David expressed the universal doubts.

"In spite of all these considerations, I feel that the great king nevertheless sanctified Jehovah's name in the sight of everyone, in the presence of all his vassals, satraps, and commanders. In the sight of all the peoples who live in his dominions he called our God the God of Heaven who had given him dominion over all the earth. The position of the people of Israel has risen wonderfully in the eyes of the people of the world. Surely the words of the prophet have been fulfilled."

Thus Zerubabel tried to encourage the people.

"He also ordered the return of the Temple vessels from the royal treasury and their transfer to the keeping of the 'Prince of Judah'!" exclaimed Jeshu, the son of Jehozedek.

"To whom did he hand them over? To the chief priest? He gave them to an uncircumcised stranger. To one impure whose touch alone is sufficient to pollute them," a fanatical priest stormed.

"And as for talk of having sanctified God's name in the sight of all, let us reserve judgment. Cyrus has many gods and is not going to quarrel with any deity. He fights against peoples and states and as soon as he subdues one of them he accepts their god and looks upon him as a partner. Today he says that God handed him the kingdom of the earth. Tomorrow he will say this about the god of another people, about Bel Merodach or some other powerful demon. He does not find it hard to make such statements."

Nevertheless all eyes were lifted up to the young and wonderful prophet. Only yesterday he was banned and made a laughing stock. Today part of his prophecy had been fulfilled and so all hung expectantly on his utterance. Even though the whole redemption he had promised had not been fulfilled, it was patent to every eye that it was God's veritable truth that came out of his mouth. The whole prophecy might well be fulfilled in stages. Accordingly, Zerubabel, Jeshu, and some of the elders and sons of the prophets and priests came to him in his small hut. They wanted to know if he had any message from God to communicate to them. He knew they were perplexed. He saw the fear in their eyes and perceived how their joy was mingled with fear and anxiety. But it was still difficult for him to understand why they were so upset and apprehensive; why they were so utterly dependent upon Cyrus's utterance. Was Cyrus their saviour; did the redemption depend upon Cyrus? Who was Cyrus that they should so stand in awe of him? He said to them:

"When Sennacherib set his foot upon the neck of the children of Israel near Lachish he thought that he was the master of the world and would hold dominion for ever and ever, that all peoples were given into his hand for the rod or for lovingkindness. Nebuchadnezzar thought so in his day, too; at the judgment of Riblah when his chief executioner severed the heads of the princes of Judah, the sons of the royal house, and that of Seraiah the High Priest and counted them out before the king. At that moment, Nebuchadnezzar believed he had finally sealed the fate of the kingdom of Judah and that it was doomed to eternal destruction. Where are they today, these magnificent kings? So it is with Cyrus. He is an insect. Today he flies about, tomorrow he is no more. Was it Cyrus who expelled you from your land and took you into exile? Why then do you depend upon him and wait upon him so fearfully to redeem you? He did not sell you. For naught were you sold. No one took money from Cyrus to get possession of you and no one will have to pay Cyrus to redeem you. You will not be redeemed with money. It is not Cyrus that will determine your lot and set rulers over you. God will do this. If today Cyrus writes upon bricks and tablets, he is writing in sand. Tomorrow will bring the rain, and all his fine words will be washed away as though they had not been. Therefore, be not dismayed nor afraid. God and none other shall redeem you."

The prophet was waiting for a sign, for a vision, so that he could bring them a word of encouragement. And indeed one night a vision visited him. He summoned Neraiah and told him of it and asked him to commit it to writing. It was his answer to their fear and confusion. Then he brought the vision to the exiles, the elders, the priests, the fathers' houses, and the sons of the prophets, for they were all awaiting his word. On the following Sabbath, he spoke his consolation in Be Knishta, the great synagogue of the elders. And this is the answer God put in the mouth of the prophet:

"Awake, awake, put on thy strength, O Zion;
Put on thy beautiful garments, O Jerusalem, the holy city;
For henceforth there shall no more come into thee the
uncircumcised and the unclean.
Shake thyself from the dust; arise and sit down, O Jerusalem.
Loose thyself from the bands of thy neck, O captive daughter
of Zion.
For thus saith Jehovah:
Ye have sold yourselves for nought;
And ye shall be redeemed without money.
For thus saith Jehovah the Lord.
My people went down aforetime to Egypt to sojourn there;
And the Assyrian oppressed them without cause;
And now—
What have I here, saith Jehovah,
That my people is taken away for naught?
They that rule over them make them to howl, saith Jehovah;
And my name continually every day is blasphemed.
Therefore my people shall know my name;
Therefore they shall know in that day—
That I am He that doth speak:
Behold it is I."

It was the God of Israel that sent them into exile and it was He that would redeem them thence. He, and not a stranger. He, and not flesh and blood. No one on earth had the power to fix boundaries for them or appoint princelings over them. No! No uncircumcised nor stranger would have dominion over them; no satrap, but one of their own from among them.

A new spirit was stirred up among the exiles. The ancient blood of their forefathers seemed to stream through their veins once again.

The Temple vessels which Sheshbazzar had received from the royal treasurer, Mithradates, were laid in order on tables in the palace of the House of David. Priests attired in their white tunics stood by the tables so to prevent any layman touching the holy objects. The sons of the House of Shallum and the Sons of the Servants of Solomon stood on guard at the doors. Five thousand and four hundred was the number of the vessels upon the tables: bowls of silver, basins of gold, goblets, knives, kettles, censers, and other dishes; all pure gold and silver.

The people streamed through to feast their eyes upon the sight of the holy vessels. They had been restored; they seemed to live again. King Solomon who had endowed the Sanctuary with the vessels was not dead; it was Nebuchadnezzar, who had taken them away to destroy them, who was dead. He was no more and the vessels were alive. They had come back to life and the people were being revived along with them.

The first to respond to the proclamation of Cyrus, after it had been disseminated as decreed throughout the empire, were the priests. The king had not announced the restoration of the State but of the Temple and the renewal of its worship. It was thus natural that the priests should be the first to embrace the opportunity of the return to Zion. The Exile had raised their stature immensely in the eyes of the people. If the nation had thronged its courts and offices when the Temple stood in Jerusalem, in the exile it was the priests who went out among the people, visiting them wherever they were to be found and reading them extracts from the Pentateuch and the other Holy Books on Sabbaths and festivals in the synagogues. This scriptural reading had taken the place of the sacrificial service of the Temple. It was to the priests that the religious-minded among the exiles turned for counsel and spiritual direction in matters appertaining to the observance of the commandments. In the Jewish agricultural settlements, the

274

tillers of the ground still paid their tithes to the priests, more out of respect for tradition than because the law required it. The priests were looked to for guidance much more than the rulers and secular chiefs of Judah, even the members of the House of David. The standing of the latter had indeed declined gradually as the Davidic kingship sank into obsolescence. But in place of this maternal regime there was a rise in the importance of the priesthood as the repository of religious truth and the stronghold of the spiritual kingdom.

In those days the head of the priesthood was Jeshu, son of the aged Jehozedek. He contended with the chiefs of Judah in the palace of the House of David.

After Cyrus had issued his manifesto, Zerubabel and Jeshu had gone to the governor, Sheshbazzar, and acknowledged him by his new title of "Prince of Judah."

Despite the fact that Cyrus had not committed the leadership of the exodus from Babylon to a scion of the House of David, to whom it rightly belonged, but had given it to an alien, Zerubabel was still quite ready to serve the governor with goodwill and help him in his difficult task. He accorded him the honor due to his office of Prince of Judah and fulfilled his requests. He was constant in this obedience despite the opposition of his father, Shaltiel, who was legally entitled to the Davidic crown. The aged prince could not forgive Cyrus for discriminating against the House of David. The bitterness of the great merchants and heads of houses also determined Zerubabel to persist in his course of conduct. They had claimed that the redemption was not the real thing because it did not carry political independence with it. Zerubabel, on the other hand, accepted the view of the prophet that redemption did not in any case come from Cyrus but from God and that the monarch was only His tool whom He would cast aside as soon as he had performed the part of the Divine purpose assigned to him, in favor of another who would bring about the perfect redemption.

The priest Jeshu, son of Jehozedek, had the same belief and adopted the same course of conduct as Zerubabel.

The aged Jehozedek was the son of Seraiah, the last High Priest who officiated in the Temple at Jerusalem and who had been led in copper fetters with Zedekiah to the judgment of Nebuchadnezzar at Riblah. Here they were leading forth his father, the High Priest, in his ceremonial garments, his hands bound behind his back. The victim cast one last glance about him before his head was cut off and cast aside. Thereafter, he continued to stare at Jehozedek from the mound as if he wished to tell him something. The son knew what the father wanted to say. His slaughtered father wanted to charge him to keep himself pure and hallow his days so as to be ready for the redemption when God would return with His people to Zion and rebuild the Temple. He was to keep himself fit to officiate as a priest on the Sanctuary; to take his place as Chief Priest and serve in the office he, the father, had filled before Nebuchadnezzar had reft him away and extinguished the flame of his life.

But was this day the one which his father's dead eyes, staring out of his severed head, had charged him to await in holiness and purity? Was it really the day of vengeance and triumph, the day of recompense for all the agony and tribulation? This salvation which came from an alien hand, from a grasping palm which opened but a fraction to release without grace and with reluctance that which it held. The hand that gave back neither the kingship to the House of David, nor independent rule, but appointed a foreign governor who would reign as "Prince of Judah." Was this the redemption?

This was not the view his son, Jeshu, took. Let the nest but be rebuilt ... The Holy Temple was Israel's nest. Jerusalem was its place, the tree in which the nest belonged. Let the bird return to its nest, the fledglings were already trying their wings. Cyrus was the beginning of the redemption, the whole restoration could be expected at the end of days. From the beginning until the end of the redemption many waters would pass. The priest, Jeshu, was also ready to serve the governor, Sheshbazzar, faithfully and

276

obediently, and assist him in the task with which he had been entrusted.

Sheshbazzar was an Assyrian aristocrat by birth and breeding and had had a lifetime's experience in high offices of state. His whole mien testified to his ancient noble Assyrian lineage but, nevertheless, his attitude towards the Jews was such that he might have been one of them. He devoted himself utterly to the task with which he had been entrusted. He respected the finest susceptibilities of the exiles and understood their special apprehensions with regard to the sacred vessels, which he did not touch with his own hands nor allow his men to approach. He appointed the priests to take charge of the vessels in the palace of the chiefs of Judah.

All kinds of rumors spread through the Exile about the origin of Sheshbazzar. Some held that he stemmed from an ancient noble Jewish family that had assimilated long ago into the Assyrians and that he really came from an Israel royal house that had been taken captive by Sennacherib. Some of these had afterwards been brought to Babylon by Nebuchadnezzar. Sheshbazzar had been a page in the Babylonian court and in royal service all his life. When the priests of Bel Merodach made their compact with Cyrus, he, together with the rulers of Babylon, had gone over to him. Gubaru, the governor of Babylon, knew of the Israelite descent of Sheshbazzar and had confidence in his loyalty to the king of the Medes and Persians and so had recommended him to Cyrus for the office of "Prince of Judah." There was really no foundation for all these rumors that circulated among the people. Whether they were true or fabricated out of thin air, the fact was that Sheshbazzar kept his genealogy a secret. However, his attitude and inclinations towards the Judeans were as clear as day.

Emissaries went out from Babylon to the settlements of Judeans throughout the kingdom. They came to all the villages, cities, and heads of families and brought the good tidings of the restoration of Zion. The news was not universally received with joy and enthusiasm. In the older settlements, Tel Aviv among them, where the Judeans lived in prosperity and flourished and waxed rich from the fruitful produce of the soil, the news brought confusion rather than rejoicing. How could they be expected to leave their solid, well-built houses, their fat lands which yielded three or four rich harvests a year; the sleek herds of cattle and their fat sheep which grew so quickly; and go to a land they no longer knew and which they had heard of only by hearsay in grandfather's tales? They would give a very handsome donation and help the establishment of the Temple. But, let others go in the meantime, those who had not done so well and did not live on such good land. Let the poor, who lived a hard life in the cities, go.

That is how it fell out. In spite of their disappointment that Cyrus had failed to fulfill the prophecies of Isaiah, it was as if a new spirit had come over the people. Some of the Judeans who, with their fathers, had always been faithful to the prophets' words of instruction and consolation and the Law the priests had inculcated in their teaching in the synagogue Sabbath by Sabbath and festival by festival, responded to the call of King Cyrus. They inclined a sympathetic ear to the exhortations of Zerubabel and Jeshu, who came to speak to them in the name of Sheshbazzar, the Prince of Judah. The heads of houses appeared as one man at the great council which Sheshbazzar convened in Babylon for discussion of the procedure to be followed in the return to Jerusalem.

The families of the exiles very jealously treasured and preserved, even in Babylon, the purity of lineage of their fathers' houses. In this genealogical pride and solidarity they saw the best shield against that assimilation with the Babylonians which in the course of time had begun to threaten the oldest Jewish families. The authority of the head of the house was absolute, and anyone who belonged to it had to obey his dictates willingly and without complaint. The headship of the house was the cement which bound the whole family together, making it a compact group proud of its ancestry and traditions. The severe patriarchal discipline, which had proven a strong bar against assimilation while the exile lasted,

278

was now a prime factor when the people had to gird themselves for the return in bringing it to practical fruition.

Twelve representatives, corresponding to the twelve tribes of Israel, were chosen out of the heads of houses to help the Prince in preparing the exodus. The twelve transmitted decisions to the other heads of houses and these decided, without the possibility of any appeal, which families would have to go back to Judah. Those who had struck strong roots into Babylon, which could not be pulled up without destroying their possessions, and who were, therefore, bound to remain: merchants, tillers of the soil and craftsmen, were made subject to heavy imposts to finance the immigration.

The fathers' houses were called after their heads: the sons of Shephatiah, the sons of Arach, the sons of Pashhur, and the like. Some houses which originated in one city or neighborhood in Judah were similarly constituted in the Exile and they usually formed a single community named after their Judean city; for example, the Bethlehemites, the Anathothies, Kiyat Yearimites, and so forth. This relationship to a city or area in Judah aroused sweet memories in the minds of the group in question and longings for the redemption. The cities and forsaken villages in the home-land, "cities and mothers in Israel," were now calling their children home just as a human mother would.

The prophet could not stay for a moment in his hut beside the abode of Neraiah. The song which welled up in his heart bore him on its wings. In all the courtyards, markets, squares, workshops, eating houses, oil-presses, wherever Israelites were to be found in the vast city, to men of Judah of the seed of Abraham, cast about, weary, worn out in their search for a crust of bread, he brought the tidings of the redemption, the songs of consolation with which God was comforting them. And not in Babylon alone. He also went out to the villages and settlements and brought the message. One day Neraiah ferried him across the canal and on to banks of the Chebar beside which dwelt the great and prosperous settlement of Tel Aviv. In the synagogue called after Ezekiel, the prophet lifted up his voice to the people of that center.

"How can you have the heart to plough your fields in a strange land so long as your homeland fields are in alien hands, stolen and despoiled by the uncircumcized Moabites, men of Sodom, and the unclean Amalekites? When you lie on your beds in the stillness of the night, do you not hear your mother's weeping borne aloft on the wind over the wilderness? How can you so stop your ears as not to hear her calling to you, her children, to hasten to her aid? The jackal Moab crosses the border and refreshes herself on the remnants of the kid that the lion Babylon took as prey. The hyena Ammon leaves in the fields traces of her claws stained in blood. Zion has no one of the sons she raised who can come and drive out these ravening beasts from her inheritance."

Thus the prophet mourned in the hearing of the inhabitants of Tel Aviv.

When he came thither and saw the fat fields and the prosperity that had become the portion of the Judeans there, he felt a great jealousy for desolate Zion and wasted Judah. Wherever his eye turned, he saw a purple expanse of fields with golden barley ripening in the sun, aureate veils floating like waves in the wind. Hidden from sight in the forest of yellow sheaves, the wide network of canals spread out. Only the colored sails of the boats and barges, which seemed to float in the air, hinted at their existence. In the harvested fields, amid the stubble, flocks grazed, weighed down with heavy fleece, lambs, goats, and cows sleek with good feeding.

Mirroring the prosperity in the fields were the ruddy faces and sturdy bodies of the farmers gathered in the synagogue. To the prophet these broad backs, mighty thews and sinews, and the aura of sheer male strength that their sun-and-wind-tanned faces exuded, seemed very strange. As he looked upon them, his thoughts flashed back to Judah. He saw the desolate land, the hills whose fruitful soil had been washed away by the rains. He beheld the ruined houses, the neglected orchards, the broken walls. He beheld the remnant of the fugitives who had been left behind as slaves to Nebuchadnezzar, wandering to and fro in frenzy and terror, fleeing from every Moabite and Ammonite, tyrants and rulers over Israel in her own land, who had invaded their lands and had appropriated every good field and coveted everything of value they possessed. His eyes saw the mothers whose dried and flabby breasts drooped emptily as their skeleton-like babies groaned in their arms, while their other children, fevered and emaciated, crawled at their feet and cried out for a crust of bread. His eyes saw the mountain upon which the Temple had stood with pillars of smoke going up not from the holy sacrifices but from the high places of abomination. He knew what they signified. The uncircumcised had come there and worshipped idols on the mountain, passed their children through the fire to Moloch, polluted and corrupted themselves in the orgies and fornications of Ishtar worship. All these vile rites were practiced in the place that God had chosen for His dwelling place, the stone of foundation . . . the binding of Isaac, the prophet Isaiah . . . the ruins of God's Temple. On these ruins the gentiles did whatever seemed good in their eyes.

And the children of this shamed and desolate land were here in Babylon tilling alien soil and planting alien orchards.

Tears choked his throat. His voice sobbed and moaned like a dove as he came back in his thoughts to the congregation of peasants of Tel Aviv and told them of the vision he had seen and of mother Zion, a prisoner of grief:

> "There is none to guide her among all the sons she hath
>     brought forth,
> Neither is there any that taketh her by the hand of all the
>     sons that she hath brought up. . . .
> Thy sons have fainted,
> They lie at the heads of all the streets, as a wild bull in a net.
> They are full of the fury of Jehovah,
> The rebuke of thy God."

Though their hearts had waxed fat, though they had grown attached to the cooking cauldrons and taken pleasure in the roast meat, memories of ancient days began to stir in their hearts. The elderly among them still recollected what their own eyes had seen, the others knew it from hearsay: old vineyards on the slopes of the hills, sunrise and sunset, rams' horns sounding, calling from hill to hill. Whitewashed cabins, shaded by cypresses, hiding in the mountain hollows. Flocks of snowy sheep climbing up the hillsides, leaping over the valleys. Priests clad in white, staff in hand, leading pilgrims over the mountain trails. Now their feet were standing on a bare hilltop and a clear horizon broke into view before them. From its limits, a radiant light was shed upon the shimmering city, silvery with haze. The metropolis seemed to be leaping over the heights and going down into the valleys. Now it hid itself, now it was veiled in towering cypresses and thick-leaved olive trees. And far, far away, in a corner of the horizon, the pinnacles and domes of the Temple burned like flames of gold. The flourish of silver trumpets was heard announcing that the gates of mercy were open and ready to welcome the pilgrims into the House of God.

From eyes heavy with age tears flowed, and a mist covered the eyelids of the young. The longing glances of the people were absorbed and found answer in a throbbing chord in the prophet's heart. His eyes were shut tight and a radiance passed over his pallid face. His white brow shone like one of the golden blossoms of the High Priest and his aquiline nose quivered with emotion. He stood up and a heavenly enthusiasm burned in him, while every sense was a-tremble to gather in the voices that came to him from worlds unseen. Suddenly, with a convulsive shudder, he wrapped his gaunt body close in his white robe.

He beheld them with the eye of the spirit. He saw their feet, leaping over the mountains like harts, like does from peak to peak. God had sent his hosts of angels over the whole land. Over all the hills and valleys, over all the broad earth from end to end, over all nations under the sun, wherever they dwelt; over all rivers and streams which flowed from one end of the world to another. God sent them to come unto every isle and shore and there burst into the song of good tidings. He heard the music echoing from hill to valley and valley to hill. Not the voices of great waters, not the roaring of a lion, not the voice of lute and pipe. It was the sound of the morning star peeping through the fog of night, whispering through the quiet streams murmuring along their banks of dewy grass.

The prophet raised his right hand and sang his vision in tearful joy:

"How beautiful on the mountains
  Are the feet of him that bringeth good tidings;
  That publisheth peace;
  That bringeth good tidings of good;
  That publisheth salvation;
  That saith unto Zion:
  Thy God reigneth.
  Thy watchmen shall lift up the voice;
  With the voice together shall they sing;
  For they shall see eye to eye, when Jehovah shall bring
    again Zion."

With ineffable joy, an ecstasy that knew no bounds, that broke all bands that tied them as Mother Zion was tied, the prophet lifted up his song:

"Break into joy, sing together,
  Ye waste places of Jerusalem.
  For Jehovah hath comforted his people,
  He hath redeemed Jerusalem.
  The Jehovah hath made bare his holy arm
  In the eyes of all the nations;
  And all the ends of the earth
  Shall see the salvation of our God."

How he yearned to bring his people back to the pure Jerusalem, which God had saved with an everlasting salvation and in which the hands of her afflicters would trouble her no more. And he bent his fierce and inflexible will on all those about him, who were deep-rooted in the soil of Babylon:

"Depart ye, depart ye, go ye out from thence,
Touch no unclean thing!
Go ye out of the midst of her, be ye clean,
That bear the vessels of Jehovah."

Recognizing that they were worried in case they would have to leave behind all the property and possessions they had acquired in Babylon, he tried to reassure them. They must know that they would be given time to arrange their affairs without confusion or haste; to set everything in good order:

"For ye shall not go out with haste,
Nor go by flight;
For Jehovah will go before you,
And the Lord God of Israel will be your reward."

They surrounded him, their eyes flowing with tears of joy and remorse. They kissed his hand and his cheeks.

They were ready to cast everything aside, leave all that they possessed and go up to Judah. A new spirit stirred in them at the words of the prophet, a spirit of redemption, and they looked forward to salvation. This spirit began to move the whole people.

When the prophet returned to Babylon, he heard of the response the people had made to the proclamation of the Prince and the elders. Exiles with their wives and little ones were coming into the city from all corners of the empire. They brought their flocks and equipment for the journey. They had left their property behind them and were utterly content to rely upon the mercy of God and go on their way. The voice of the grumblers and opposition had been silenced. In all Babylon no one spoke a contrary word. The brothers of the House of Murashu and their servants sulked and skulked in their houses. Many of their most fervent followers joined the returning ones. The word of Jehovah was being fulfilled; the vision was taking on reality; God was returning His people to their inheritance.

This was an entirely different people of Israel. Isaiah saw them at this time in one clear and good light. They were purged of their sins; they had paid the full penalty for their transgressions. The bonds of their curse were loosened. They were freed as was their mother, Jerusalem, from their shackles, and they would be an ensign and a light to all peoples. The name of God would be exalted in all eyes after it was seen that He had saved His people after scores of years of servitude. And Israel, His people Israel, who had longed for her God and after all remained faithful to Him, who believed that He had chosen her from all peoples and had looked forward expectantly for her salvation—Israel was worthy that all peoples of the world should incline their heads to her. For she did not possess stone idols in the shape of oxen for gods; she had no armies to wage war for her. For years and years had she been humiliated, scorned, and cast aside because of her weakness and battering. Now she was exalted, given the stature of a giant, and walked upright through the land to the mission which was her destiny.

The prophet began to sing of the days that were coming to Israel, a song of triumph:

"Behold my servant shall deal prudently,
 He shall be exalted and extolled and be very high.
 As many were astonished at thee;
 His visage so marred unlike that of a man,
 And his form unlike that of the sons of man;

285

So shall he sprinkle many nations;
The kings shall shut their mouths at him;
For that which had not been told them shall they see;
And that which they had not heard shall they consider."

The awe of God descended on the people, and they asked one another in astonishment and fear:

"What shall we see and hear that we have not seen and that we have not heard?"

# CHAPTER SEVEN

S CARCELY had the seal of Cyrus hardened on the proclamation which began with the ceremonious words: "Thus saith Cyrus, king of Persia, the Lord God of Heaven hath given me all the kingdoms of the earth..." when that monarch went forth to bow down before Bel Merodach.

On a platform decked with floral wreaths, with oaken carvings, the golden image of Bel Merodach was set up in the Avenue of the Processions. The priests of E-Sagila had brought it out on their shoulders from the tower of Babylon with the most reverent ceremony. The High Priest, Sharezer Bel, stood at the right of the god and Gimil, wife of the deity, on its left as they received Cyrus, who approached in the company of his son and regent Cambyses, Gubaru, the governor of Babylon, and his retinue, which included the most noble of Babylon; the satraps and the commanders of the army. The king, in his gold embroidered royal robe, the crown upon his head and the scepter of majesty in his hand, bowed down and prostrated himself upon the high platform to the god, Bel Merodach.

As Cyrus rose to his feet, a flourish of silver trumpets was heard from heralds stationed at the four corners of the square who sounded a signal for silence. A hush fell upon everyone. Two scribes, bearing the great cylinder, drew near the king. The royal herald at once read out the writing to which regal approval was now to be given.

The manifesto was a lengthy one and was written on a cylinder of clay. People stood as though frozen to the spot trying to hear the words that rang through the empty air. The manifesto pro-

claimed ... "Merodach turned in every direction, seeking a righteous king after his own heart ... He chose Cyrus, king of Anzan,
and called him by name to rule the whole world ... The lord Merodach who protects his land saw his upright works and the grace
that dwells in his heart and rejoiced ... He commanded him to go
up to Babylon, his city; he marched at his right hand and helped
him like a friend and companion. His forces were innumerable
... as the sands of the sea ... They marched in full panoply of
war ... Without a battle, Merodach brought him in to his city of
Babylon and saved his city from every calamity ... King Nabonidus, who did not fear Merodach, was delivered into the hands of
Cyrus; and all the inhabitants of Babylon and their lords bowed
down before Cyrus and kissed his feet."

The king then went on to enumerate, in the manifesto, all the
kingdoms which he had reestablished, the peoples he had liberated
and whose gods he had returned to their cities, and concluded by
telling the Babylonians that they should pray every day to Bel
Merodach and Nebo to grant him a long life.

"Speak a word from the depths of your hearts on my account,
and pray to Bel Merodach, my lord and god, that he grant Cyrus,
the king who is his servant, and his son Cambyses, long life and
a peaceful reign."

Couriers and horsemen were standing ready with swift chariots.
They were instantly prepared to set off and repeat the proclamation in every far-off place, in the distant cities and the islands beyond the sea, telling how the king, in his manifesto, had acknowledged Bel Merodach as the creator and protector of all men, the
god of the world by whose will Cyrus had been graciously endowed
with the rule over Babylon. They would also publish the king's
prayer and desire that all peoples should bow to Bel Merodach, all
mouths should praise him and pray to him for long life for the
king and his son, and for peace over Babylon.

Once more the houses of the Babylonians were adorned with
flowers, colored draperies hung from all the windows, and
countless images of Bel Merodach appeared in all the streets sur-

rounded by oaks which were brought, with their roots and branches, from the groves so that in every place it would be possible to worship the god and rejoice in him.

The metropolis shone with a shower of lights which poured their radiance from the towers and the housetops, from torches and bonfires in the streets, from the flares on the prows of the ships which sailed in festive procession along the canals. Their red light glowed back in fiery reflection from the mirror-smooth surface of the water. The deep blue vault of heaven, with its bright congregations of stars, was, as always when Babylon was in festive mood, obscured by the thick clouds of rack and smoke, the pillars of vapor, and all kinds of sharp, acrid smells that emanated from the sacrifices that the people burnt to Bel Merodach—the savor of roast meat and parched corn, grease and frying, the odor of blood streaming on the flames from the severed necks of calves, of scent of frankincense and other spices.

Now it became clear and manifest beyond the possibility of misunderstanding, not just to the Babylonians but to the Judeans as well, that Cyrus would not bring the peoples whom he had conquered and brought under his suzerainty to the God of Israel, but to Bel Merodach, the god of all men who walked upon the earth. The situation was clear: just as Cyrus had sent back all the peoples who had been exiled in Babylon together with their godlings to their native cities, so he was sending the Judeans, with their Temple vessels, back to their own land. The incident had no special significance to Cyrus in relation to the people or the God of Israel. It was only the impudent Judeans who had put a special face upon affairs, had arrogantly persuaded themselves to the belief that all the recent events had taken place just for their sake and at the command of their God so that all peoples should come under the shadow of His dominion. Thus their prophet had spoken to them, an unknown man somewhat confused in mind who saw strange visions. They had been foolish enough to believe him.

Similar arguments to these of the Babylonians began to be heard among the Judeans. Especially so was this true of the section who lived prosperous and easy lives and had nevertheless only yesterday, after Cyrus's original proclamation to the Jews, believed that he would in truth further proclaim the God of Israel as the God of all the peoples, as the prophet had foretold. They had been momentarily swept away, had bent the knee to Him, and had forgotten their unrelenting opposition to the idea of a return to Zion. They were ready to look upon Cyrus not only as the saviour of the Jews, but as the redeemer of all nations. They had also been prepared to accept Isaiah as a true prophet, the harbinger of the redemption, the messenger whom God had sent to proclaim the momentous good tidings to them.

"Did Cyrus free only the Judeans?" many were heard to ask among the exiles. "He also liberated Assyria, Lydia, Aram, and the whole of Ethiopia, many, many cities beyond the Tigris, and sent all their gods back to their rightful homes. Nabonidus brought the strange gods to Babylon, to shelter beneath the kind heart of Bel Merodach; Cyrus came and returned them at the command of the same god of gods. Thus Cyrus proclaimed before the whole world. Thus likewise he does to the Judeans and the Temple vessels. Jehovah has nothing to do with all this. Jehovah has forgotten us. He hides in the fastnesses of His heavens and no longer wants to know us. He has thrust us away from His presence. If this indeed be the shape of things, why should we leave Babylon and return to a land from which He has hidden His face? Is it not better that we should remain where we are in Babylon and worship Bel Merodach before whom all peoples bow and to whom every tongue utters praises?"

"This is nothing but a major struggle between Merodach, the god of Babylon, and Jehovah, the God of Heaven, for dominion over all the peoples of the earth whom Cyrus had brought under his rule. Just as Bel Merodach prevailed over his mother Tiamat, goddess of chaos, so he has now vanquished Jehovah, the God of Heaven. He has succeeded in drawing Cyrus to him, has driven Jehovah away to His remotest heaven, and has assumed the lordship of the universe."

Thus spoke the enlightened among the Babylonians, and they were not a few of the enlightened among the Judeans who were prepared to follow this view.

Once more those who hated Zion raised their heads: the brothers of the House of Murashu and the false prophets who basked in their favor. There were Judeans who withdrew from all share and portion in Judah and Israel and publicly proclaimed that Bel Merodach, the god of Babylon, was their god. Many indeed were the notables, especially those who held important public offices, and the more powerful merchants and men of wealth, who participated fully with the Babylonians, the commanders of the army, the satraps and pashas, in the ceremony of swearing an oath of fealty to Cyrus, King of Babylon, and Merodach, her god. They offered incense on the altar before this image which had been brought out of the sanctuary and set up on a platform in the Avenue of the Processions.

But it was not just the wealthy and the important officials who abased themselves to the gods of Babylon and forsook the faith of their fathers. Doubts and confusions racked the common folk also. The adherence of the son Cambyses to Bel Merodach had not shaken them; but the open proclamation of Cyrus came as a staggering blow. They were afraid of what the future held for them. They were daunted by the rain of curses, insults, and mockery of their fellow citizens. They were sorely disappointed and deceived in their most sacred emotions. Upon whom should they vent the guilt for the obloquy which had become their lot, if not upon Jehovah who had been overcome by idolators, if so many of the gentiles and even their own brethren were to be believed? There was also the prophet who had brought before them his visions of the future and his dreams which had no fulfillment. He kept on regurgitating them and chewing them over as a cow chews the cud and still maintained that they were true prophecies. Surely it was he who was to blame!

His emaciated body once again became a focus for blows and beatings by the exiles. His face was the recipient of their spittle and his beard the target of their angry hands and nails. Once again the cries were heard:

"Get out of here, belly swollen by the east wind!"

In the secret recesses of his heart, the prophet had still believed that Cyrus, in spite of all his vacillations and despite his ignorance of the mission upon which he had been sent and the duty put upon him, would rise, in spite of everything, when the moment for redemption came, to the task that God had imposed upon him. He would fulfill it just as the prophet had foreseen in his vision. The One and Unique God of Israel would be proclaimed God of the whole earth, so that all might know as He had told the prophet:

"That from the rising of the sun to the going down thereof there is none beside Me, I am Jehovah, there is none else."

When Cyrus had declared before the leaders of the Jews that the Lord God of Heaven had given him all the kingdoms of the earth, he had fulfilled the prophecy that he, Isaiah, had uttered. In this proclamation the prophet saw the beginnings of fulfillment and expected that on the morrow or the next day, Cyrus would proclaim the sovereignty of the God of Israel, "from the rising of the sun to its going down," over all lands and over all peoples.

"Is God a man, that He should change His mind?" he queried, and answered himself: "Lift up your eyes to the heavens and look upon the earth beneath; for the heavens shall vanish away like smoke and the earth shall wax old like a garment, and they that dwell therein shall vanish in like manner; but salvation shall be for every one and my righteousness shall not be abolished."

The world was Jehovah's. Whatever He wished, He created in it. He did not form the world to become chaos. He had formed it so that it should be the place where His characteristics would reign—uprightness, lovingkindness, and mercy—between man and man and even between the beasts of the field. To Him every knee would bow and every tongue would be lifted up.

"Who can prevent him?" So spoke the voice in his heart. "And He shall make the wilderness as Eden and the dry place as the garden of the Lord. Joy and gladness will be found therein ...

Law shall go forth from Me and my judgment shall bring quiet to the nations." The voice which spoke to him had never ceased from that day to this and it still rang within him. "My justification is near, My victory hath gone forth, My arm shall judge the nations. The peoples of the isles hope for and await My arm."

Who then could forbid or impede His purposes? Was there any authority in the world beside His? Was there a corner, a hidden or remote place, a cave, a cleft, or crevice in the whole of space, a flash of an eyelid on the eternity of time, which was not under His governance? His glory covered the heavens like a garment and filled the whole world just as water covered the face of a bowl. Was there a breath emitted by the mouth of any living thing in any of the most secret worlds unless by His will?

"To whom should He be compared?" cried the prophet like a wounded lion from his lair as he lay in his hut beside the hovel of Neraiah. "Should he be likened to Bel Merodach? God does not wage war against Satan, who is under his sway. There is no power in the world either for good or for evil which He does not control. He created light and darkness. He makes peace and brings trouble on the world. 'I am Jehovah, there is no god beside me.'"

Once again the prophet saw the vision before his eyes. He heard the voice of God cleaving in twain Rabah, the monster that symbolized primal chaos and filled the whole abyss of night that prevailed over the world. The thunder of God rolled forth and engulfed the depths; it reverberated to the length and breadth of the world, from one end to the other, to known and unknown vastnesses, to the secret and innermost fastnesses of the most exalted inner chambers of the height of heights. The monster of chaos was rent in twain, half was lifted up to the skies as though borne upon the wings of angels and half sunk into the bottomless abyss. The vault of light and order was revealed between the firmaments and became filled with the works of God's hand. Satan was his servant; he had no will of his own. Jehovah used him as He willed just as He made use of hail, the storm at sea, or the whirlwind in the desert. And if the primal serpent sought to lift its fanged head to do evil, to rebel against the God Jehovah, then he was punished by Him as was any other creature that had sinned. He was reduced to crawling on his belly, to feed on dust. He was put beneath the heel of man who would crush his head. Only man, the crown of creation, had been endowed with a free will, for God had wished to exalt him, to make him a partner in His work since the six days of creation. Thus he would gain certain rights for himself so that he might come unto God of his own volition. Therefore, God had placed a thirst in man, a longing for Him, and man felt the urge to seek Him always. If he could not find Him, then he made idols for himself to slake his thirst for God until his eyes were opened and he beheld the God of Israel. Thus even the idols that man's own hand had made, ugly and repulsive though they were, were the work of God. Merodach was a puppet that God had made to be used by the gentiles as a godhead until the day dawned that they attained wisdom and knew the way to Jehovah.

How then could Bel Merodach, who was a molten idol without even so much of the breath of life in his nostrils as the lowest insect possessed, despite all the rights, powers, and achievements that the nations of the world ascribed to him, how then could Merodach be a stumbling block to the will and intentions of God?

He, the prophet, alone was to blame; he and no other. His eyes had deceived him, his ears had misled him. The hope of the redemption had dazzled him, had led him astray, fostered delusions in him, and made him utter words which God had not spoken. It was just as Daniel had warned him. He had seen a worm crawling upon one leaf of the cabbage and had imagined the leaf was the whole world and the worm the Messiah of God. If so, then he had come to Israel as a false prophet. He had set the image of the king of Persia before them like an idol of gold or silver. He had crowned him with the title of Messiah; he had robed him in the array of the redeemer and proclaimed him the servant of God, saying:

294

"These are thy gods, O Israel."

In that case, he was a seducer and an inciter, a stumbling block to the children of Israel; a prophet of false messiahs. If so, his punishment was death. The prophet stretched himself out on the floor, face upward, and prayed:

"Mine, mine is the guilt! I have sinned, I am guilty, I am to blame. I have led them astray. My eyes were plastered up so that I could not see; my lips were unclean and I passed words through them that my heart invented. Thy people are pure, clean of all transgression. It is I who led them astray. Bring me my punishment as an inciter and seducer, but have mercy and pity upon Thy people. Keep them and guard them. Make an end of me in the fury of Thine anger, but return, I pray thee, the people of Israel to their inheritance."

The prophet lay thus for a very long time on the floor of the hut, his face clasped in his hands. He neither ate nor drank and sought to die. . . .

Neraiah was standing over the prophet and bending his head down to him. In a voice full of compassion, breathing concern and love, he entreated him. His voice trembled with tears.

"Zerubabel and Jeshu the priest are waiting at the door. They have come to seek the word of God at your lips."

While he was still speaking, the two men burst into the hut.

"The mothers have come to the bearing-stool but have no strength to bring forth. How, at a time when the people need your consolation as never before, at a time when all long to see you and hear from you, can you hide your face?"

"The word of God is hidden from me. God has cast me away from his presence like a vessel for which he no longer has any use. Let Haggai and Zechariah stand up for you. They will go to Zion with you and strengthen your hands. God has thrust me away from His presence."

"What has happened to you, O prophet?" Zerubabel cried angrily. "Just because Cyrus proclaimed that his god is not the God of Israel but the gods of Babylon you speak thus. Did not

295

you, yourself, tell us time and time again, 'Who is Cyrus, that we should be concerned about him? He is a staff in God's hand, like Assyria and Babylon. He is here today and tomorrow is cut off and no more. He is a worm crawling upon the leaf of the cabbage and thinks confidently that the leaf is the whole world.' Can you turn your back upon the mission upon which God has sent you just because Cyrus has turned to a molten idol of gold? Today Cyrus worships Merodach, tomorrow he will worship Shamash, or Nebo, or a block of wood or a stone image or the like. But the God of Israel is living and enduring for all eternity."

"Cyrus after all has done according to God's command," added Jeshu. "Israel will return to her land and the tribes will once more be a people. Jerusalem will be rebuilt again and the Temple raised up on its ancient site. Our brethren come from all the settlements, with a song on their lips and rich gifts in their hands, and are ready to go up to Judah and build the House of God. And only you, the messenger of God, you, the prophet that brought the tidings of the redemption, you hide yourself!"

"God spoke to me through a voice in my innermost heart. 'Is it a light thing that thou shouldst be my servant to raise up the tribes of Jacob, and to restore the preserved of Israel? I will also give thee for a light to the gentiles that thou mayest be my salvation to the ends of the earth.' He did not return Israel to their own land for their own sake but that they should be a light to the gentiles. To bring His salvation to all men from one end of the world to the other does Israel return. Cyrus has performed his mission deceitfully. In his eyes the God of the universe is not Jehovah but the abomination, Bel Merodach. It was not Israel which was set aside to be the light to the nations, but Babylon. Ashamed and confounded Israel stands, and God's name is profaned. Cyrus performed his mission deceitfully, and my lips are unclean. How shall I carry God's word in my mouth?"

Zerubabel and Jeshu went away in utter confusion.

The prophet lay on the floor as he was before they came, torturing and chastising himself. A long, long time he remained there alone with his face to the ground. As he stretched out there, oblivious of time, he heard a voice speaking in his heart:

"I have not thrust you away from me. Your lips are not unclean but you are a rebellious slave, a priest who has abandoned his altar."

The prophet was not terrified nor fearful of the voice. He roused himself from his lethargy like a wounded lion and cried aloud:

"Thou didst open mine eyes and I heard. Thou didst sow Thy consolation and expectation in the heart of Israel and in my heart and I guarded the seed. Thou didst send me to them and I went. I spoke the word Thou didst put in my mouth. Thy word. Thy consolation it was I brought to them. Thou didst lift them up to the highest heights; Thou didst appoint them as a light to the nations. From the height of Zion Thou didst send forth Thy voice like thunder, saying: 'Thou art my servant Israel wherein I glory.' Thou didst gather them under Thy hand, clothe them in Thy garment which was their glory. They were called by Thy name. Now look about and behold how despicable Israel has become in the eyes of the nations. To guard Thy glory are they become the target of contempt and shame every day. Despised and rejected as a man who has no designation or honor, as one who has ceased to be a man and is no longer reckoned among men. So Israel has become in the sight of the gentiles. She is not a light to the nations. She is a blind servant harnessed to the commands of her Lord, as a serf to the millstone going round dumbly day by day.

"Look around and behold. It is not to Thee that every knee bends but to the abomination, the golden inert mass, Bel Merodach. Cyrus, whom Thou didst designate Thy servant, did not bring the nations to Thee but to an idol of wood and stone. It is not Thy law that is being spread to the isles and not Thy judgment that is enlightening the peoples, but that of the idol of Babylon. Thine honor is trodden under foot and Thy children upon whom Thy name rests are a laughing-stock, despised by all and robbed of the semblance of men. With their very flesh they guard the slightest shade of Thy glory so that the wicked should not

297

trample upon it. In their disgrace, Thou art disgraced, and in their profanation Thy name is profaned. When they are mocked, Thou art mocked. How long, O God? How long? Why should Jacob alone pay the full price for his transgressions? Give me a sign, a demonstration! Why does Israel suffer so? Why does evil befall the righteous while the wicked wantons in his transgressions? Look around and behold. Babylon exults and shouts in triumph. A filthy harlot, she flaunts and revels in her pride while Israel is a butt for scorn and laughter just because she puts her trust and faith in Thee. Didst Thou not speak through my mouth and did I not hear Thy voice in my heart? Didst Thou not open up mine eyes to see what Thou didst have to show me? Not for my sake, no! Not for my sake, but for Thy children to whom I brought Thy word and comfort! All their hopes are upon Thee; they have no one but Thee."

These agonies of soul sapped away his strength and he sank into a kind of drowsy half-consciousness, like the shadowy last moments of a dying man. However, all his senses were alert and in this waking coma he saw and heard God leading the tribes of Israel to their homeland.

Once again he was on the road to Zion. Once again he saw the vision reveal itself as on previous occasions. The children of Israel were passing through the wilderness as though borne aloft on angels' wings. They were soaring up and earth and heaven sang over against them. Before them, he saw shaping itself in the shadows once again the form of Abraham leading his son Isaac to the sacrificial altar.

Once more his heart was afflicted and saddened by what he saw about him and he besought God to interpret the vision for him. He suddenly realized that he was a man apart from the assembly. He was alone in an unknown place, neither wilderness nor habitation. All around was desolation. Neither man nor house was to be seen. A fearful silence hung in space and the light which illuminated it was neither day nor night. It was the light which God had stored away in his firmament. He was still thinking how fearful was the place, when he saw a twig suddenly breaking through the ground before his very eyes. It was a twisted and mystic root like that of an old olive tree. The twig ripened and grew in the time-space of a lightning flash. In a moment, it had taken human shape. It was that of a being so deformed, so smitten and tortured, so utterly devoid of any wholeness, that it almost lost the likeness of a man. His feet were so thin as to be only skin and bone. They were twisted and bowed and bent beneath the weight of the body which they tried to support. The arms were long and unnaturally thin, useless and withered limbs. His head was sunk in complete listlessness upon his chest. Although it was manifest that this was a man smitten unto death, he still stood upon his feet and his skeleton-like form cried aloud with the cry of the blood that poured from his wounds. He lifted up his head from his chest with strength from some secret source, and his eyes blazed forth with unconquered radiance. They were the eyes of a man who had found a way to accept and justify the judgment. The humility of which the eyes spoke gave to the tortured body and the bloody vesture of his wounds a sense of victory, making the whole broken frame a sacrifice, like a lamb that is dipped and rinsed and brought to the altar.

The prophet was still rooted to his place in the toils of the vision when a voice from on high came to him. He did not perceive the likeness of a woman but only heard a wailing female voice lifted up over the mountains in bitter lamentation.

"He is despised and rejected of men,
  A man of sorrows, and acquainted with grief;
  And he hid as it were our face from him;
  He was despised and we esteemed him not.
  Surely he hath borne our griefs,
  And carried our sorrows;
  Yet we did esteem him stricken,
  Smitten of God and afflicted."

The prophet looked around and saw that his feet stood upon the peak of the world. Hill and valley rose and fell away, all covered with tender hyssop, the virgin greenness of the time when creation was fresh. The hyssop carpeted the whole distance wherever he turned. This was an empty and unpopulated world such as the foot of man had never trodden. It was in its pristine state but appeared ready to accept its first inhabitants. Through rifts in the mist the horizon glowed with broad rays of sunlight illuminating the peaks of the mountains. Here were crags terrifying in their massed grotesqueness. Here were ranges covered by giant vegetation. From horizon to horizon, from every hill and valley, over the limitless distances, the voices of men came to him. They drew nearer and nearer and he heard them proclaim:

"But he was wounded for our transgressions,
He was bruised for our iniquities:
The chastisement of our peace was upon him;
And with his stripes we are healed."

Suddenly from the opposite horizon the voices were answered:

"All we like sheep have gone astray;
We have turned every one to his own way;
And Jehovah hath laid on him the iniquity of us all."

Silence came down upon the world; a silence of complete tranquillity. The voice of the woman was heard again:

"He was oppressed and he was afflicted;
Yet he opened not his mouth;
He was brought as a lamb to the slaughter,
And as a sheep before her shearers is dumb,
So he opened not his mouth."

300

The lamentation of the woman ceased and the single voice that echoed from hill to hill was heard again like the noise of a mighty cataract pouring down into the abyss. The voice was as near as that of a man who stands next to his fellow and drives his point home with his finger. But the prophet saw no man. He heard only the voice rolling down to the depths below:

"He was taken from prison and from judgment.
And who shall declare his generation?
For he was cut off out of the land of the living.
For the transgression of my people he was stricken."

The tear-racked voice of the woman was heard again:

"And he made his grave with the wicked;
And with the rich in his death;
Because he had done no violence,
Neither was any deceit in his mouth."

The voice reverberating from the height answered her:

"Yet it pleased Jehovah to bruise him,
And he hath put him to grief.
When thou shalt make his soul an offering for sin,
He shall see his seed,
He shall prolong his days,
And the pleasure of Jehovah shall prosper in his hand."

The voice of the woman:

"He shall see the travail of his soul and shall be satisfied."

Silence came down upon the world once again, a silence pregnant with fear and terror but, nevertheless, ending in tranquillity. The approaching voice was heard again, as though a man was standing and speaking close to him. It rolled down thunderously, shattering the space from horizon to horizon with its roar:

> "By his knowledge
> Shall my righteous servant justify many,
> For he shall bear their iniquities.
> Therefore, I shall divide him a portion with the great,
> And he shall divide the spoil with the strong,
> Because he hath poured out his soul unto death,
> And he was numbered with the transgressors,
> And he bare the sin of many
> And made intercession for the transgressors."

The prophet woke from his vision. He knew that this came to him by the grace of God. But what did it mean? He knew that God had shown him Israel in her affliction, persecuted to the point of death like a fledgling tortured by cruel and pitiless men, the gentiles, as God had said:

"Thus saith Jehovah, the Redeemer of Israel, and His holy One, to him whom man despiseth, to him whom the nation abhorreth, to be a servant of rulers. Kings shall see and arise, princes also shall worship, because of the Jehovah that is faithful, and the Holy One of Israel, and he shall choose thee."

But what Israel had God shown him? The Israel of yesterday, that had transgressed and had exacted full penalty from God? But perhaps, heaven forbid, this was the Israel of tomorrow, the delivered of Israel, whose sins God had pardoned and whom He had returned to the land from which she had been exiled. It could not be possible that this afflicted man whom he had seen should be the symbol of sinning Israel. His ears had heard clearly the voices proclaiming and witnessing that he was crushed for iniquities he had not done. In spite of the fact that his hands were clean of violence and his mouth of deceit, God had seen fit to crush him with illness, to see if his soul were worthy to be a sacrifice. God had

302

sanctified him to be a sacrifice in order that he might take upon himself the iniquities of others so that the desire of God should prosper through him.

What should be the interpretation of the vision? God was returning Israel to her own land so that she be a victim bound upon the altar, as she had been time and time again in his vision, and that not for her own iniquities. So that she might be a sacrifice of atonement for the iniquities of others which she took upon herself, was God returning her to Zion. But since when had God seen fit to punish a man for the sins of another? Had not He proclaimed by the mouth of His prophet that "the soul that sinneth it shall die, the son would not bear the iniquity of the father, nor the father that of the son, for the righteousness of the righteous would be upon him and the sin of the wicked upon him!" Was it to be understood from this that Israel would eternally suffer for the sins of others? Was this the reason for the afflictions that came upon Israel, and was this why the righteous were in travail?

He lifted up his eyes to heaven and cried in a voice of weeping:

"O my God, my God, let me not be brought to an end because of lack of knowledge; let me not perish for my defect of insight. Open mine eyes and let me see the way that Thou hast marked out for Israel. Open my heart to understand the meaning of these signs that Thou givest me. Let me bring Thy word of comfort and promise to Thy people who are confused like straying sheep."

In his heart he heard a voice which said:

"It is not for you to know or understand My way. Not for you nor any born of woman to know My mystery. I opened your eyes to see and your ears to hear. What you saw and heard, that bring unto your people to whom I sent you."

Crushed like a slave before his master, the prophet summoned Neraiah to his room and ordered him to write down what he had seen and the words he had heard. Because the meaning was not clear to him, he sang the vision of the suffering servant of God exactly as he had heard and seen it.

He notified Zerubabel, Jeshu, and the elders who had proclaimed the return to Zion, that he had seen this vision by the grace of God.

Great indeed was the passionate desire in all hearts to draw upon the consolation of God, as the prophet had promised them, and the words of comfort he had for them were vitally necessary.

With the last remnants of his strength, the prophet arose before the important assembly. In a weak voice, he read before them the vision, opening with the words:

"Who can believe our report, and to whom is the arm of the Lord revealed?"

A deep silence fell upon the gathering when he had finished telling of the suffering servant of Jehovah. A heavy grief held them all. Their heads nodded speechlessly and they looked at one another as though wishing to say:

"Can we believe our ears?"

At last one arose and asked the prophet:

"Why do you hint in your words? Do you want to tell us that Israel is returning to her land to be the sacrifice for the sins of others? Do you wish to tell us that God brings us back to Zion and Judah to suffer there and die and be buried with the wicked? If that is indeed what you claim, then they are right who say we should remain in Babylon."

"Alas and alack! He has not brought us words of comfort but of lamentation and mourning. Lamentation upon Israel!" others said.

One of the priests, expert in the Law, asked the prophet:

"Our lawgiver, Moses, told us that we should listen to the voice of God and keep His commandments so that our days and the days of our children should be long upon the earth which He has given us. And if we do not hearken to the voice of God and do not heed His commandments, all the plagues with which He smote the Egyptians would come upon us. And you preach exactly the opposite. God will smite the righteous for sins he did not commit, so that he should be an atonement for the sins of others. Since when has God

304

punished one soul for the sin of another? Did not the prophet who preceded you say, in the name of God, that a father would not bear the iniquity of the son nor the son the iniquity of the father?"

The priests and elders rose one after the other and asked the prophet wonderingly:

"Did not this man of sorrows so smitten by the hand of God suffer for sins that he himself committed? Since when did God smite a soul for the sins of another?"

"It is clear to us that God only punishes sinners. He preserves the righteous and brings blessings upon him."

"Surely an evil spirit possesses him!"

"The word of God has departed from him."

"He brings us neither salvation nor consolation, but curses and sorrow."

"We have had enough of him. Let him go his way. He is cast out by God. Do not listen to him."

The prophet did not seek to answer the accusations and complaints that the assembly heaped upon him. His lips were sealed. He bent his head and rested patiently like a dumb lamb, beneath the objurgations and curses that fell upon him.

Zerubabel hid his face in his cloak to conceal the tears that pressed to his eyes.

"Yesterday you said of Israel: 'His visage was marred more than any man, and his form more than the sons of man. So shall he sprinkle many nations, the kings shall shut their mouths at him.' Today you say: 'He is cut off as from the land of the living and he made his grave with the wicked.' Is this to be the end of Israel, the Israel that was to raise up many nations and for whom kings would shut their mouths when they saw what had not been told to them? You speak to us like one of the enemies of Israel!"

"Our ears are weary of hearing such talk!" shouted one.

"You are right; what ear can bear such words?" voices were heard crying.

Many were very angry and many more in despair.

In another moment the prophet would have been trampled down beneath the feet of the angry crowd, had not a mighty voice shouted:

"Let him be. Can't you see that he is mad?"

"True. It is obvious that his mind is deranged."

# CHAPTER EIGHT

NERAIAH took the prophet by the hand and led him to the hut on the branch of the canal. He laid him down in his bed and sat by his side to care for him in his weakness. His fine, tender skin was transparent and smitten with a milk-like pallor and was flaccid and limp on his face. His eyes were sunken deep in their sockets and haunted with pain. The prophet seemed to have all but left this world and it seemed that in but a brief moment the soul would leave the wasted and shrunken body and take flight into the region where his spirit already ranged.

Once again they had all abandoned him. The heads of the returning exiles no longer asked after him; no one came to hear his prophecies. They had all forsaken him; every one, save only Zerubabel.

The latter came and sat down beside his pallet of palm leaves. He took the prophet's hand in his own and tried to encourage him.

"The God of our fathers has breathed a new spirit into His people. There is no other explanation. Pay no attention to the scoffers of Babylon. Every day brings new groups of exiles who wish to return to Judah. They come from every place, from the remotest corners, with their wives, children, herds, and flocks. They come with joy and song. It is your words, prophet, that have driven deep roots into their hearts which still bring forth their fruit. All your predictions are being fulfilled. Lift up your eyes, O prophet, and behold they are all gathering and coming, coming to you, clad in fine raiment like a bride entering the bridal chamber."

The prophet listened with closed eyes and uttered not a word.

"That's how he has been. He eats no bread; he drinks no water;

he utters no sound," came the shocked voice of Neraiah from his corner.

"Do not your ears hear the song of redemption that bursts out around you? Rise, O prophet! Rouse yourself and bring the people your word of comfort and encouragement."

The prophet was silent.

"He must surely hear the song of the redemption. Each of his limbs, every pore of his skin, listens to the song. The shouting comes from far and near. The echo of multitudes of men flowing and streaming with the joyous beat of drum and cymbal and full-throated song, the sound of joy and gladness: 'When God brought back the captivity of Zion, we were as those who dream.' "

God had shut door and gate fast in his face. He had walled off from his eyes the worlds beyond the horizon, the regions where the visions he used to see were brought into being. The darkness of the narrow grave shrouded him about. Round the walls of the sepulcher, from outside, he could hear the joyful song of the redemption. He drank in the exultant shout of those going up to Zion but could not join in with them. At the beginning of the way leading into the wilderness he encountered the man of sorrows, and understood only too well that the path to redemption had to lead through the binding and sacrifice of Isaac as he had been so often shown in his vision. His jealousy for Israel burned and flamed in his heart as strongly as his zeal for God. The two passions seared and consumed him. Why should Israel be the sacrifice for the redemption of the peoples of the world? Why, like the goat sent to Azazel, should she bear the sins of the nations? God had opened a small crevice before his eyes through which he could perceive that Israel was led on the way of redemption like a lamb led to the slaughter. How could he sing the song of comfort and confidence that God had put in his mouth?

He would keep back and withhold the expressions of gladness and consolation that Jehovah had opened in his heart. Had he really become an obstinate ass whom God had thrust away? Had God in truth passed his spirit from him and endowed it upon others? He would continue in secret to bear the burden of Israel's sorrow and would not be weary until God had pity upon him and opened up for him a lattice through which he might behold the light treasured up for Israel at the end of the way. Then he might be able, with greater patience and fire, to sing the praises of Israel, to express the recompense that she would inherit at the end of days. Israel was the bearer of the hope of the world and if her chastisement had a purpose and an aim, then the whole of creation was purposeful and not aimless.

He stretched out with his face buried in his hands and prayed to God:

"O Thou who showed me the pains and chastisements Israel had undergone because Thou didst choose her to be Thy servant, open up mine eyes to see the reward that awaits her at the end of days. Not for my sake, O my God, but for Thine shouldst Thou do it, so that I may bring the hope of salvation to all Thy creatures, so that hope may overflow the chambers of my heart."

It suddenly appeared as though God had heard his supplications. A voice spoke in his heart:

"Thou who hast been sent to bring the good tidings of redemption to Israel, turn to thy father and ask him for the interpretation thereof for his spirit moves in thee."

With the despair of a drowning man who grasps at a straw, the prophet raised his voice and cried out:

"O eyes of Israel, incline your right hand; deliver me from the mire of trembling and confusion in which I have sunk up to the neck. The waters have come even unto my soul."

Deep sleep fell upon the prophet and he found himself with his feet upon the courtyard of the Temple. It was desolate, its halls broken down, and its stones scattered everywhere in heaps. Thin wisps of smoke were ascending skywards from the ruins of the broken Temple. The prophet knew whence these smoke clouds came. The gentiles, who had profaned the Temple, had erected altars or. its site and were offering sacrifices to their idols.

The prophet closed his eyes. In his dream he did not wish to hear or see. His heart wept. "Gentiles have come into thine inheritance. . . ." He ran to a forgotten corner within the courtyard boundaries, to a place hidden by the fallen ruins. How strange this nook appeared to him. It had neither altar nor man. It was the first time he had ever beheld this spot. He had not known that, within the precincts of the Temple, there existed a single square yard which was free from defilement, from these filthy abominations that befouled the sacred premises. Despite the fact that all the buildings that once stood there were now mouldering rubble, a spirit of quiet holiness and blessed piety reigned in this particular place, as though God himself had cleansed it and taken special care to keep it pure of taint. One last spot of His holy fane had God hidden for Himself; perhaps for some great and mighty purpose that would be enacted there. A tremble of holiness seized the prophet and he thought: "How wondrous is this place."

He was still standing rapt and in sacred mood at the stillness and purity, when he became aware of the presence of an aged man. He was old and white and sat solitary upon a stone in the midst of the ruins. The ancient held a finger to his lips to warn the prophet to allow no sound to escape him. The prophet looked at him and his heart quaked. He knew this old man. He had seen him more than once in his vision. He was much advanced in years. He was gaunt and tall and his height seemed to tower even as he sat. His white curled hair fell down upon his neck and covered his shoulders. His snowy beard lapped down on the silver blue cloak that covered his whole form. His feet were bare.

A holy radiance shone from his massive and pale countenance, just as it had done whenever the prophet had seen him in his dream. The prophet waited for the ancient to speak but the lips upon which a smile was dawning remained locked. The prophet could restrain himself no longer and asked quietly:

"Deal kindly with me and tell me what is this place upon which my feet tread."

310

"Cast your shoes from off your feet, for the ground upon which you stand is holy. Your feet stand upon the Temple mount, the hill which God will, at the end of days, exalt above the mountains and the valleys and to which the nations will flow."

"And who art thou?"

"I am the man to whom God revealed the end of days when all nations would flow to this mountain of Jehovah."

The prophet fell at the feet of the ancient and sobbed:

"Alas, O my father! I am called by your name and Jehovah has put your word in my mouth. God has sent you to show me my way. Put understanding in my heart to discern His way. I pray thee, teach me! Let mine eyes know the meaning of the signs I see and the interpretation of my visions which is hidden from me."

"Rise up, my son, and sit at my side. Your prophecies and mine are one prophecy."

"Teach me, O my father, to know when will the words you spoke in God's name be fulfilled. When will come the end of days that you foresaw?"

"This is not in my power to tell you. It is hidden in God's mind. I sit here and every moment and second expect that the root of the redemption will spring forth, that the prince of peace will appear, that nation will no longer lift up sword against nation, and the whole earth will be filled with the knowledge of God. It is not I alone who sit thus and wait. All the prayers for the redemption gather into this place. All the hot tears that are shed in agony for the redemption are gathered here, all the chastisements that the sons of men suffer on account of it are treasured here. All are counted and registered. Arise and sit beside me, but what you see and hear must be sealed away from the living within your heart until 'the day cometh.'"

As he spoke thus, the aged prophet stretched forth his hand, lifted up the young prophet from the ground, and sat him by his side.

At first, all the prophet heard was the breathing of the silence that seemed to lie in ambush like a lion in the clouds. Suddenly, a thunderclap sounded, rolling mightily over mountain and valley, echoing and reverberating, increasing in force until it reached the height.

"For you are a holy people to the Lord thy God. God has chosen you to be His peculiar people out of all the peoples on the face of the earth."

"The thunder was the voice of Moses," said the old prophet. "It is lifted up every day over all lands beneath heaven to remind the children of Israel of the yoke and obligation placed upon them."

Once more silence reigned: a twilight silence, the silence of the realm of neither-day-nor-night. A bright, golden halo coruscated on beams of twilight iridescence, a crown of rays shining with the light hidden away at creation. The shadowy form of a woman floating with a beat of wings appeared beyond the halo. A curtain seemed to rest in the air and hide her shape from sight as with a veil. And just as a bird falls plummeting when pierced by an arrow in flight, so the shade of the woman fell to the earth. The curtain parted. The shining halo seemed lit by the radiance of the Divine presence. A voice was heard on high; it was that of a moaning dove.

"Alas, God of Mercy! Unto Thee do I come, whose mercies are spread out over all created things. Unto Thee I come, who placed in the heart of every mother Thy grace of mercy which makes her feel compassion for her children. Unto Thee I come to seek mercy for my children. Other peoples are also the work of Thy hands and Thou endowest them with a life of plenty and tranquillity on the lands Thou hast given them. Only my children hast Thou forsaken. How long will Thy people be a target for the darts of the gentiles? When shalt Thou yield them rest for their tired feet? Have mercy and pity upon the children of Abraham who loved Thee and fulfill the promise which Thou didst make him in the covenant between the pieces. They are Thy inheritance. They call upon Thy name. The gates of mercy are closed before them. Let justice be done if not mercy."

The moving entreaty trembled through the whole of space with a sound of muted thunder. A voice was heard from the midst of the halo of fire over the woman's head:

"Refrain thy voice from weeping and thine eyes from tears, for there will be a reward to thy work, saith Jehovah, and return from the land of the enemy."

The voice was still; the shade of Rachel vanished and from another corner of the horizon another womanly shadow drew closer. She was also draped in black. Her head was bowed. Slowly she floated near, alone and solitary.

As Rachel had done, so she too fell prostrate upon the ground and lifted her hand to the ring of light that sent down its radiance from above; she called in a voice bitter with weeping:

"Alas, Father of all created things. Two sons there were who struggled within me and two nations were separated from my flesh. They suckled at one breast and in spite of this Thou didst sow eternal enmity between them. I also bore my share of their war. I loved Jacob and for his sake I deceived his firstborn brother. Esau is also my son, and if Thou didst drive him away from Thy presence, Thou didst drive me also with him. My blood streams in the veins of Esau as much as it does in those of Jacob. As Jacob is my flesh, so also is Esau. In their sufferings I suffer; and when they are in pain I, too, am in pain. I am both the sacrifice and the one who offers it. My compassion for Esau is as great as is my love for Jacob and between them both my heart is rent in twain. O God, I pray Thee, will the sword make bereavement for me forever? Who will bring healing to the wound of my torn heart; who will close up the rent in my heart? I pray Thee, Father of all creatures, I pray Thee who chose me to be the mother of them both, have mercy upon my son Esau. Open up his eyes so that he should see Thy light. Put understanding in his heart to know Thee and recognize Thy way. I beseech Thee, father him under the shade of Thy compassion. Receive him into Thy covenant just as You took his brother Jacob, for they were both born from one seed, that of Abraham who loved Thee. I pray Thee, O God, do it so that they

313

may both live as brothers in the spirit even as they are brothers in the flesh."

"That is Rebecca, offering up her prayer to the Lord of all. Every day she rises up from her grave and comes here to the gates of mercy, to pray for her son, Esau, just as Rachel prays for her son, the people of Israel," so whispered the old prophet into the young man's ear.

"I hear no voice answering her prayer, as Rachel's was answered."

"When the promise made to Rachel is fulfilled, then too shall Rebecca's prayer be answered. For both prayers are one, the supplication of a mother in Israel to the Holy One of Israel. God made a condition, the one shall not be redeemed without the other. Neither can have complete redemption by himself. It will come at the end of days, when the word of God, that came to me, shall be fulfilled: 'They shall not hurt nor destroy in all my holy mountain and the earth shall be full of the knowledge of the Lord as the waters cover the sea.'"

"God also opened my ears: 'I put my spirit upon him. Judgment shall He bring forth to the gentiles . . . He shall not fail nor be discouraged until He have set judgment in the earth; and the isles shall wait for His law . . . I, the Lord, have called thee in righteousness, and will hold thine hand, and will keep thee, and give thee for a covenant of the peoples . . . for a light of the gentiles . . . to open the blind eyes, to bring out the prisoners from the prison, and them that sit in darkness out of the prison house.'"

"Thy prophecy and mine are one."

"But tell me, until the end of days, until the last day, what then will be?"

"Small salvations will come from time to time. They will illumine the face of the earth for a moment like a flash and pass away. Then again the powers of the spirit will gather themselves and attempt to bring a new victory. These will be small salvations, but every one of them will be a rung in the ladder of the great

314

redemption. Every victory will demand its price and none will be purchased except through sorrow and chastisement."

"He has set up signposts on the long road to redemption, and at each He created an altar of binding. These are the bindings for the sacrifice mine eyes have seen as they went before the children of Israel on their way to Zion. What are they for? Tell me, O my father, I pray thee; for you are the eyes of Israel! Your eyes pierced through to the hidden secrets until you reached the end of days that waits for us when we go forth from the path of our former chastisements. The great victory, the complete redemption. Tell me, I beg of you, light up mine eyes so that I should know what is the meaning of the signs and the visions that torment my spirit and make dim my eyes. It is only by your power that I can find the meaning. God has closed up all the other avenues before me."

So the young prophet entreated the ancient, his hands uplifted towards him.

"What do you want to know, my son? What torments your spirit?"

"Enlighten mine eyes to know the reason for the chastisements by which the redemption must be purchased. And why should Israel alone bear the burden of the iniquities of the nations and atone for them with her blood? Why should Israel be the goat sent to Azazel for the transgressions of the gentiles? And why did God send me this vision in the form of the man of sorrows who stands and looks out by the gates of Jerusalem for the redemption which hastens to come? What is the meaning of the voices that I heard in this place where we are speaking? I have seen with mine own eyes the vision and heard the voices with my own ears, but the explanation of the vision is walled off from my understanding. Only by your strength alone, O my father the prophet, can my heart be made easy and my spirit be delivered from its sore distress."

"Even to us, the prophets, not all the chosen virtues are given nor are all doors open. The peculiar gift of understanding the reasons for God's acts are given by Him only to those upon whom His spirit rests, to him who will bring righteousness for all eternity. To us is given but an eye to see and an ear to hear, and what we receive we bring to those to whom God has sent us. We are the servants of the Omnipotent Creator. On us it is laid to perform our mission with closed eyes. Nevertheless, some part of the matter has been made manifest to me and what I know, you too shall know. For you are my spirit and he who carries my word further on. Therefore shall I answer all your questions in good order to the extent that I have been vouchsafed to understand and permission to answer.

"My son and my young prophet, let it be known to you that the chastisement of the scourge is sweet; and pleasant is the thrust of the sword on the mission of the God Jehovah and for the sake of His glory. Just as gold is melted by fire, so is the heart reduced and made obedient in the furnace of chastisement. All suffering and pain endured for the sake of God are but a step towards Him. He will wrap you around in the cloak of His grace and will heal you with the balm of His love. Only the chosen ones are selected to feel the burning pains of punishment, the light that shines from Him. This selfsame light will cure your pain, just as the tender love of a mother soothes the hurt of the child that takes refuge in her bosom. You have already tasted of the honey of the love of God which came with the bitterness of infliction. Your beard was plucked out and the skin of your cheeks seared, your face was covered with the spittle of filthy men. What taste did you taste then?"

"Every drop of spittle that touched me purified me as though I had bathed in the waters of the Paradise and every weal of chastisement clothed my flesh with a garment of honor and crowned my hair with the diadem of God's choice," answered the young prophet.

"So shall all be who are hurt for the glory of the Creator of all things. They put on the garment of glory and are crowned with the diadem of choice. I, also, tasted in my flesh the bittersweet pain of torture that burned my body. Three years as the servant of God did I walk barefoot and naked upon the stones of Jerusalem. In summer, the heat consumed me, and the frost in winter. When my time came to change over into the next world, Manasseh in his fury sawed through my flesh as he cut down the oak in the forest in which I had been hidden. He was enraged because I had spoken censure of him on account of the image he had brought into the Temple. God wove me a garment from the mists of the clouds; in the chastisements that I suffered I was purified and cured. God will still send more and more messengers after us to the sons of man and every one of them will have the same lot as ours. Thus man shall fight a great war for the sake of God; for the triumph of good over evil; for the victory of order over chaos. Come with me and see with your own eyes the great struggle that humanity shall wage for his maker's account until the end of days."

The prophet seized the young man's hand and led him to the wall in which was set a locked portal which towered up to heaven. It seemed to them both that they had reached the end of the world.

"My son, your feet are standing before the gate that shuts off the future from the eye of man. By the power of prophetic vision that has been bestowed upon you, you will pierce the door. Make a hole in the gate, look through, and see what you shall see."

The prophet's eye pierced the gate and his face darkened.

"What do you see, my son?"

"I see an abyss. It is full of smoke and swirling mist. One side of the deep is dark with the shadow of death and one is alight with the radiance pouring forth from the closed corner of heaven. The light is breaking through to cleave the darkness and gain dominion over it. But from the side of night, mists are rolling up in columns like the hands and fingers of angels of destruction and they are pressing back the light to the blind corner of heaven. Now I see sons of men ... they are embedded, swallowed up in the gullet of the deathly darkness and smoke whorls and are struggling to get free, to break out of the bands of night which

bind them . . . now the likeness of men shapes itself out of the curling clouds of smoke . . . I see their limbs; I discern their heads,
pushing forward out of the abyss of darkness . . . they are woven
into diverse shapes out of the smoke . . . their heads are those of
wild beasts, monsters that the world has never previously seen . . .
the monsters are swallowing up the shapes of men and dragging
them back again to the abyss of darkness . . . it appears, it appears
that the great battle is going on here between light and darkness . . .
it seems that this is the war between good and evil."

When the prophet had recovered from his deep emotion, he
repeated: "That is what I have seen in the gate of the future."

"You have seen well, my son," said the aged prophet. "Be it
known to you that you have looked into the maw of Rahab, who
holds captive the future. God clave Rahab and separated between
the waters above and the waters below, and between the two he
made his creatures dwell. The future is still embedded in the jaws
of Rahab and he dwells within us. Clouds of smoke whirl up
around our hearts and darken our eyes. But the world has endured
but a day and man's life is nothing but the blink of an eyelid. Man
is still plunged in the abyss of the jaws of Rahab. He is sunk in
confusion and a chaos of smoke and rack. He girds up his power
to be free. He desires to be quit of the pillars of confusion. God has
set stations for this and has made signposts on the man's long way
to perfection.

"God loved man with an abundant love, as was shown in
greatest measure when he elevated him over all his creatures,
giving him the power to choose between good and evil, so that he
became His partner in the imposition of order upon chaos. The
Creator of all endowed man with the merit to free heaven and
earth by his power from the grip of Rahab's jaws, just as He Himself freed this world and created His creation upon it. That is the
reason for the trials which the righteous bear. The righteous man
fights against Rahab, not just for his own sake, but for that of his
brother man. He pays in blood and trembling and sweat for every
inch of order that he wins from the jaws and claws of Rahab,

318

the symbol of chaos and formlessness. Every cubit of order won is a cubit further along the road to perfection, one more rung in the ladder leading up to the great redemption."

"O my father and teacher, you have opened my eyes so that I understand the sufferings of the righteous. Now I would further inquire: why has Israel been sentenced to endure nine measures of sorrow and chastisement that the Creator of all things has brought down upon the world? Why should Jacob by himself pay the full penalty for the iniquities of his brother Esau?"

"You have asked a weighty question. Be it known to you that Israel among the nations is like the righteous man among the peoples. It was of his own free will that Jacob took over the birth-right that Esau yielded him in return for a mess of pottage. Since he took over the birthright, Jacob also took over the privileges that were given to the patriarchs. Esau was left outside, and having lost his privileges did not even share in the covenant God made with Abraham. Since all the responsibilities and all the yoke of the statutes and judgments were placed upon Jacob's neck, so his redemption could come only when Esau had been brought into the covenant that had been made equal with Jacob and not before. Jacob would be chastised for Esau's iniquities until the redemption came. Despised, ashamed, and confounded among the peoples of the earth he might be; but if these peoples thought that Jacob would be in darkness forever and would never see light..." the prophet suddenly raised his voice and proclaimed... "the people that walked in darkness have seen a great light; upon them that walked in the shadow of death, a light hath shone."

"How will Israel be able to endure their sufferings? They are but flesh and blood!"

"Each and every one of Israel is but flesh and blood, but the whole of Israel is a spirit of the spirit of God. Jacob will die a hundred strange deaths, but from every one he will arise and live again. The people of Israel cannot pass away and disappear from the world. Whenever the nations think they have cut down the tree completely, there springs up from the last twigs a noble tree which strikes deep roots in divine soil. Its branches spread out and multiply and many nations gather in its shade and enjoy its fruits. The God Jehovah has lifted up His right arm and sworn that Israel will not be blotted out from the face of the earth. 'I shall chastise Israel in judgment but I shall never utterly make an end.' For the people of Israel is the root of the redemption which God has caused to spring forth so that there may be hope for the whole world."

"Be praised and exalted, O my master and teacher, for the words of consolation. They have given me heart and assuaged my pains. May I pray of you to tell me further what is the meaning of the man of sorrows whom I met at the going out into the wilderness before the gates of Zion? His shape was not that of a man, but of a twig cast upon the dungheap and despised by all creatures."

"Alas, my son, God has opened your eyes and shown you the twig that will bud from the root. You have seen the twig from the stock of Jesse."

"The man of sorrows, that had ceased almost to be a man, from whom all creatures turn away their eyes?"

"He is the suffering heart of Israel and the hope of the whole world. He it is that goes before them as they return to Zion."

"The man of sorrows?"

"He is the man of redemption. The price of the redemption. The sponge which absorbs within itself all the sufferings of Israel and the whole world."

"Who is he?"

"He is the man that you and I have brought as a consolation and recompense to Israel and salvation to the world."

"What is the reason for his affliction?"

"He is the heart of the righteous, for he is the heart of righteousness. He is the heart of all who wait patiently for the redemption, for he is the heart of the redemption. Just as all the veins in the human body reach to the heart and gather vitality from it, so all who suffer in this world, on account of righteousness and on account of the redemption, meet in this man of sorrows, and all their

320

pain and grief are gathered in by him. For know this well: not Israel alone will pay with affliction for the redemption. There are many other peoples who wait expectantly for redemption and must pay its price. All the sadness and sorrow of those who so wait passes through this man's veins and heart, and they will be afflicted in his flesh. Come, see and hear the weeping by which the world purchases redemption."

The aged prophet took the younger one by his hand and led him to a quiet river. The stream flowed gently and softly along amid avenues of weeping willows and was swallowed up in the distance in a burning forest which stood out against a horizon bathed in golden flame. The red coruscation of the flames of the forest was reflected by the mirror like waters of the stream.

"Hearken well to the quiet sob of the waters and tell me what your ears hear."

"I hear a groaning that breaks the chambers of my heart. It is like the moan of old men, sitting by banks of the river and sighing. I hear a bitter lamentation as of gasping mothers and a faint wailing comes to my ears as of children crying in sorrow."

"You have heard well, my son. Your feet are standing upon the banks of the river into which are poured all the tears of all who mourn over Zion, of all who are afflicted and weep for the redemption. These tears are of Israel and the nations of the world alike. All the tears of all the weary and sorrow-laden are gathered like pearls into this stream. All groans flow down to it. The river passes through the burning forest and winds around the feet of the Throne of Glory where the tears which Jehovah sheds over the sufferings of His holy ones are added to its volume. His tears are mingled with theirs and the sighs of the afflicted. It should be known to you, my son, that not only do men suffer and pay the price of redemption; for God suffers with them. He is with every righteous man in his tribulations. He tastes the bitter drop of sorrow and shares the pangs with which are purchased man's salvation.

"To me also God has revealed the suffering of Israel. These are His words to me: 'When thou passest through the waters, I will be with thee: and through the rivers, they shall not overflow thee: when thou walkest through the fire, thou shalt not be burned: neither shall the flame kindle upon thee. Thy prophesying and My prophesying are one.'

"Now pierce the depths of the river with your eyes and tell me what you see."

The prophet gazed into the waters. He snatched his eyes away immediately and hid his face in his cloak.

"My father, my father, my eyes cannot bear it," groaned the prophet, his face muffled in his garment.

"Look and gaze down right to the river bed. Force your gaze to penetrate to the very bottom of the stream of tears so that you will know to the uttermost the grave meaning of the words which God puts into your mouth. Do this if you wish to be a prophet in Israel." So the aged prophet commanded the younger in a voice of binding authority.

Once more the eyes of the prophet peered deep into the waters of the river. A cold sweat dripped from his face and his whole body trembled and shook with the fearful things he saw there. This time he did not snatch his eyes away in terror from the depths of the stream.

"What do your eyes see, my son?"

"I see a river of blood, crimson and boiling. I see blood streaming from tens of thousands of corpses and draining into the river. Blood spurting from the necks of babes and from tortured old men. Blood of mothers and their sucklings; blood flowing unto blood and mingling with it. I see multitudes of bodies without number. They are writhing and palpitating with the cruelties and agonies of torture and pain as they are punished with a thousand cruel deaths. I see impaled bodies twisting on stakes, their veins bursting from their suffering and their groans drowned in shouts of laughter. I see bodies fixed to wooden stakes in the midst of mounting flames while the voice of a fevered multitude makes

322

festival against the background of the crucified, screaming with delight as the flames envelop the beards and cloaks of the burning victims. I hear the prayers of those burnt alive, choked and silenced by the pious chants and hypocritical psalms of their lying persecutors. I see gigantic furnaces and thousands upon thousands entering their doors and being consumed to ashes. Myriads of people perishing and suffering by a thousand deaths to the sound of the screaming and laughter of the completely indifferent. This is a river of tears. This is a burning river of blood into which pour millions of wounds. The blood surges up and fills the stream and its banks overflow because of its abundance."

"This is the river of blood and tears that are poured out for the redemption. Every drop of blood and every smallest tear is gathered in by God. Immense as is the wickedness, so mighty also will be the redemption. As the transgression is great, so also is the sacrifice. All the veins of all the righteous pass through the heart of Israel, the suffering servant of God which you saw. Every sorrow and pain is felt in his body. Every transgression raises an abscess upon him. Every iniquity makes a bruise upon his flesh. For he is the heart of the redemption into which are gathered all sufferings and torment. He dies every day at the hands of the wicked and every day he rises up again and lives, for he is laid like Isaac upon the altar, ready for death. But God does not desire to slay him. It was this self-same Israel whom the God Jehovah showed Moses in the bush which burned and was not consumed. He is the eternity of Israel. God created him and watched over him and guards him until the eternal redemption."

"Alas, O prophet, when, oh, when will the end come to his afflictions? When will the fire cease to burn the bush?"

"When evil will pass away and wickedness will cease from the earth and the God Jehovah alone reigns over all the world and all men are brothers. In that time, the sufferings of Israel shall cease and be assuaged even as will those of all the righteous. As the God Jehovah said unto me: 'He will destroy death forever and the God Jehovah will wipe away tears from off all faces, and the reproach of His people shall He turn away from off all the earth, for Jehovah hath spoken it!'"

"I pray you, my father, you have shown me the path of blood to the redemption, show me one bright glimpse, one flash of the light that shines therein."

"Go along the length of the river as it flows. Turn your eyes to its channel and follow whither it leads."

The prophet walked along the river, and he saw the burning horizon where the river clave the fiery forest and was lost within it. His eye penetrated beyond the forest where the main stem of the river branched out among green pastures. He saw the waters gradually become clear and fresh until they took on a pure transparency. Beasts of the plains drew near to the banks of the stream and drank of the waters and were reflected there in their peace with each other. Then suddenly the prophet recognized the river. It was the selfsame stream which split the wilderness asunder. It was the river which God had shown him many times in his visions of the return to Zion. Along the banks of the river he now discerned many men traveling. They were the exiles returning from Babylon, but among them also were those who came from other dispersions. They were too numerous to count. Multitudes, multitudes, congregation by congregation, they streamed along both sides of the river. The stream lifted itself up and flowed to the celestial clouds. In a moment, the river and those who walked along it were exalted and carried over the tops of the mountains. They reached a bare height. Now he was standing on the pinnacle of the world; from this eminence he saw green meadows spreading out in the plain and myriads of people on the slopes of the mountain. They covered the face of the valleys and were climbing up to the pinnacle of the mountains. He was still gazing at them when suddenly his eyes beheld the heavens above the mountain and the Holy Temple raised up on pillars of fire. The Temple was open. It had no dome. The heavens burning with a white iridescent light were its covering. The whole earth was suspended below in empty space.

The prophet saw all the mountains and plains covered with

324

people. With a song, they were moving in from the horizon, from all corners to the top of the mountain, to the shining sanctuary, intoning and chanting:

> "Come ye, let us go up to the mountain of Jehovah,
> To the House of the God of Jacob
> And he will teach us of his ways,
> And we will walk in his paths.
> For out of Zion shall go forth the law,
> And the word of the Jehovah from Jerusalem."

The vision ceased in a flash. The curtains that had previously parted before him came together. Once again, the old Isaiah and his young disciple were standing beside the gate that shut off the world from the future.

"My father, it is your vision I have seen," cried the young prophet.

"It is also your vision, my son; for yours and mine are one vision. It is the vision of all those who mourn for Zion and wait in grief for the redemption and patiently expect the salvation. In every generation this vision will be seen. Generation will hand it down to generation until, in the end, the promise which the God Jehovah gave His people, Israel, shall be kept and hope will come to the world. Then shall all people beat their swords into ploughshares and their spears into pruning hooks; nation shall not lift up sword against nation, neither shall they learn war any more. They shall not destroy nor do hurt in all My holy mountain, for the earth shall be full of the knowledge of God as the waters cover the sea."

# CHAPTER NINE

IN spite of everything, as though a mighty hand had seized them by the locks of their hair and plucked them out of their settled homes, the Judeans came and streamed into Babylon from all the places whither they had been dispersed. They arrived with their wives and children, their manservants and maidservants, their herds and their flocks, at the palace of the House of David in the metropolis. It was from this place that exiles were preparing to go forth to Jerusalem with the Prince of Judah, Sheshbazzar, at their head, to return to their homeland. It worried them not at all that Cyrus had proclaimed that Bel Merodach and not Jehovah was the god that had summoned him to Babylon to proclaim freedom to all the peoples. Those who were now streaming into Babylon on the way to Zion completely ignored the manifesto of Cyrus relating to the divinity of Bel Merodach. They believed implicitly in the prophet's words that it was Jehovah who brought Cyrus to Babylon to free his people, Jehovah and no other. This was the truth and the thing that mattered.

The prophet's words, entering their hearts as a seed of consolation, had put forth stalk and bud and these had ripened into a flower of faith and confidence in the God of Israel. Firm in this covenant with their God, which broke through and cast up for them a way into a broad and prosperous future, they went forth to Babylon with song and joy. The Babylonians were smitten with wonder at the numerous caravans which came into the city every day, by every possible road and path. The returning exiles came up in ships, boats, and barges by means of the canals. The citizens saw them passing by with what they had kept of their possessions, their bundles of clothes, their vessels, their baskets and jugs laden on the backs of asses, mules, camels and even on their own shoulders. Some families brought maid- and manservants loaded like beasts of burden. Each of these caravans was composed in the main of Judeans drawn from one Judean city who had settled down together in the same settlement in Babylon. They now entered the gates of Babylon in ceremonial array to the chanting of choirs and the music of pipes. This mass invasion of Judeans who pitched their tents in the courtyards of the palace of the House of David, in the Avenue of the Processions, who overflowed in their thousands into the alleys, squares, and empty fields about the palace, aroused great curiosity among the Babylonians.

They had heard that the exiles going up to Zion had left well-founded estates in Babylon, fat fields and richly developed fruit-yielding orchards. Many of them had prospered in Babylon; this could be seen by the many slaves who went with them, their heavy loads of goods, their bales of multicolored textiles, their rolls of cloth, their bundles of wool, their many hampers packed with household effects, and their numerous asses carrying barrels of good oil. They were leaving behind townlets and villages, fine settlements rich with fertile ground and, relying only on the mercy and favor of their God, were going forth into a desert way.

The matter formed a heated topic in the wine cellars, in the market places, and all places where people congregated. They knew that in Judea a savage struggle awaited them with those who had encroached upon their borders and taken possession of their lands, those rocky tracts that brought forth rocks and boulders but gave no water. In spite of all this, they preferred their own weeds and thistles to Babylon's fat, well-watered lands. The Babylonians saw how wonderful was their joy in spite of all these disadvantages, how elated they were at the prospect before them. They observed how the Judeans trembled with joy as they carefully scrutinized their origins and their genealogies. For not everyone who came to Babylon and sought to join the return was permitted to do so. They were subjected to a rigid examination. It was the responsibility of the elders, priests, and heads of houses to investigate every family and every community to determine from which tribe they sprang and if they really belonged to the people of Jacob. Only those who could satisfy the test were allowed to join the convoy.

What driving force was this that steeled them for every kind of sacrifice, that rendered them oblivious of every obstacle that lay in wait for them along the road? What power was this that made them hold cheap the price they would be compelled to pay to be numbered among those who had the privilege of going up to Zion? This could only be on account of the prophet who had breathed his words into them, a new spirit which predisposed them to become the servants of Jehovah, ready and prepared to wear the yoke of His commandments, be it acceptable in itself or a grim necessity. The desire to be reckoned among the participants in the Divine purpose sprang from the passion for the redemption which would turn the wilderness they would have to traverse into a veritable paradise and their barren land into the mountain of Jehovah.

But the prophet, who had secretly treasured the vision of the redemption and had communicated it to the people in such beautiful phrases, remained outside all this activity. When he aroused himself from his sleep, he felt that he himself was that man of sorrows who subsequently found healing, that he had seen in his vision. Just as He had done for his father Isaiah, God had woven for him, too, a shining garment of the floating clouds and had wrapped his suffering body in it. But within the garment his body was rent in twain, sawn asunder. The fate of Israel and her mission, the desirable path that opened for her, had not yet given him surcease. He could not as yet become reconciled to the idea that Israel was returning to her native land to be offered up as a sacrifice.

At this time, Zerubabel, whose heart was always with the prophet, came to him and said:

"Come with me and feast your eyes on the glories that God has

328

showered on His people. Your words are being fulfilled. It is as though angels of light had come down from heaven and were taking them on their wings and gathering them in to return to the land of their fathers."

The prophet raised himself from his pallet and, trembling with weakness, clung to the arms of Zerubabel and Neraiah. Together they went slowly to the courtyard beside the palace of the House of David, where the people were encamped. The prophet lifted up his eyes and sought the sign that he had so often seen, the altar of the binding of Isaac, going before them. He saw it no longer, nor did he behold the other signs which foretold the pains that would meet them along their road. In the west corner, towards which the way to Judah wound, he discerned only the flames of the setting sun. The westering sky was covered over with a bright, amber light glow, and in the fiery sea swam the Temple. Its dome was ablaze with a brilliant amalgam of gold and silver radiance. This was the view which the ancient Isaiah had revealed to him. The seven-colored rainbow, the symbol of the waters of the flood in Noah's time, was arched over the Sanctuary which floated on high, the token of pardon and forgiveness. Joyful voices were heard raised in song from the midst of the amber sea which suffused the west with its effulgence, the song from the throats of the Judeans swelling like a roar of mighty waters. He was able to hear every word of their chant with perfect clearness.

As though a great hand had descended and removed by force the burden and restraint that had rested upon his spirit and his lips, the inspiration of prophecy rushed upon him. The prophet burst out into a shout of joy:

> "I see! At last, I see!
> Jehovah goeth before you;
> And the God of Israel is your reward."

The spirit moved in the prophet. His eyes were opened again. He could see once more.

329

Once more his feet stood before the gate of Jerusalem that opened on the wilderness, on the bare hill whence sprouted the twig from which sprang the man of sorrows. But this time the hill was not carpeted with hyssop, thorns, and bare patches like a skull from which the hair had been shorn. A plenteous shower moistened the face of the earth with dewy freshness and washed the surface of the rocks, the craggy hills, and all the surroundings. Carpets of tender grass covered the mountain and all the rocky barren expanse roundabout. The hills of Moab, which seemed to be in the corner of the world, were still lit up with the brilliant gold and silver glow as though they were the gates of heaven, but the soil at the base of the rocky hills was clothed in green verdure like a garment of grace and love. Freedom had been proclaimed to the world, and deliverance had come from the curse that weighed it down like the burden of a heavy transgression. The air throbbed with comfort as though God had wiped away tears from off all faces. The world was like a babe that had been disturbed and had found peace and delight in the touch of his mother's hand, like a newborn child, still overlaid with the dew of heaven. All around him breathed quiet, peace, and a deep tranquillity.

The pure green mountain stood ready to receive the lambs and the beasts of prey who would lie down on it to pasture together. The height had changed its character and become a holy mountain upon which none did evil or destroyed, for the earth had become full of the knowledge of God as the waters cover the sea. Just so had the prophet foreseen it in his vision. He stood upon the mountain and awaited the twig that was to spring forth from the stock of Jesse, the branch that would grow up from its roots. The mountain descended from heaven and crouched down at the gate of Jerusalem, which opened to the wilderness ready to welcome those who came up unto Zion. Now he saw them coming. From all corners of the world they flowed, like rivers of living water. They rose from the depths and ascended, community by community, like the waves of the sea. Those who came up were

330

not just the returning Babylonian exiles. All the generations yet to be born came with them, together with all the generations that would in future attach themselves to them. All those of the latter days, all the people of the world, accompanied them. A great song welled out of their mouths and, rising up to the splendor of heaven, re-echoed the good tidings over the whole earth. God had wiped away the tears from off all faces. God had comforted His people.

The heavens were one burning rainbow, flaming like a banner over the heads of those coming up.

The heart of the prophet was filled with a song of redemption as the pomegranate is filled with juice. He exulted in a prophecy of consolation:

"Sing, O barren, that didst not hear;
    Break forth thou into singing and cry aloud, that didst not
        travail with child;
    For more are the children of the desolate
    Than the children of the married wife,
    Saith Jehovah.
    Enlarge the place of thy tent,
    And let them stretch forth the curtain of thine habitations.
    Spare not,
    Lengthen thy cords,
    And strengthen thy stakes."

Like a man recovered from a mortal illness, like one tortured and persecuted to the verge of death who finds comfort and rescue, like one who knows the healing balm of a mother's tender hand and feels that he has been purified, that he is good, that he has been chosen especially, so the prophet felt the grace of consolation, healing and purifying not him alone but all created things. He saw the whole world as a pure and spotless home for man who was born anew. All hatred had faded away, all iniquity had been effaced, all arrogance had melted from the heart of man. Israel was born afresh. She was pure again as an innocent virgin, fit to be sanctified unto God as a bride is betrothed to her husband.

Israel walked among the nations of the world. She was a bride wearing the weeds of her widowhood, but beneath these somber garments could be seen shining the array of her eternal virginity which had never been soiled. Israel had passed through all the flames; she had been drowned in all the seas. God had laid bare to the prophet the paths of chastisement she would have to tread. Wild beasts lay in wait for her from all sides. They crawled and came forth from caves and lairs, their balefully wicked, green eyes glared at her, their claws were sunk in her living flesh like burning tongs. Jaws, like the open grave, gaped ready for her. They tore her flesh, they plucked out her hair, they rooted their claws deep within her. The whole body was wounded, marked and rent, pained and afflicted. But from all these hard trials, from all the torture chambers, from all the furnaces, Israel went forth, new, pure, and without blemish, like a bride who, though having fallen into the hands of oppressors who outraged her with every cruelty, yet kept her virgin chastity.

He saw once again the eternal symbol of Israel, the burning bush of Moses in the wilderness, and he met it now before the gate of Jerusalem. The bush burned with fire, and was not consumed, for evil could have no power over it.

In the Be Knishta, before the chiefs of the House of David, the priests, and the elders of Judah and Israel, the prophet brought his song of victory. He recounted his psalm of the redemption, the vision of the renewal eternal of Israel, the revelation of her eternity.

His strength was utterly consumed when his companion, Neraiah, brought him to Be Knishta. He was like a plant that has already given out all its flowers. He was eaten up by his visions and blasted by the fire that burned within him. So he came unto them, swaying on his feet.

His pale young face was lifted up, and as he stood before them he looked like a sacrificial victim. He brought out his words clearly, fresh as though they were filtered through living waters as they passed from his throat and came into his mouth:

"For a small moment have I forsaken thee,
But with great mercies will I gather thee,
In a little wrath I hid My face from thee for a moment,
But with everlasting kindness will I have mercy on thee,
Saith Jehovah, thy redeemer.
For the mountains shall depart,
And the hills be removed,
But My kindness shall not depart from thee,
Neither shall the covenant of My peace be removed,
Saith Jehovah that hath mercy upon thee.

"For fear shall shake thee, lest a power over which I have no power shall harm thee; lest you fall into the hands of arrogant nations, beasts of prey, and they shall pierce thee with their instruments of destruction and plant their claws in thy flesh and bite thee with their jaws. Be ye comforted; for this is My word unto thee, saith Jehovah. There is no power but Mine and no dominion besides Mine.

"Behold, I have created the smith that bloweth the coals in the fire,
And that bringeth forth an instrument for his work,
And I have created the waster to destroy.
No weapon that is formed against thee shall prosper,
And every tongue that shall arise against thee in judgment thou shall condemn,
This is the heritage of the servants of Jehovah,
And their righteousness is of Me,
Saith Jehovah."

# CHAPTER TEN

WHEN he saw the people gathering together into Babylon from the whole of the empire on the first stage of their way back to Zion, the prophet had asked to dwell among them. Consequently, Neraiah had carried him in a padded litter to the court of the Bethlehemites. There in an attic chamber Neraiah carefully tended the prophet, keeping constant watch at his bedside. There was little left of him but a bundle of bones clothed in a white skin and wrapped in a white cloak.

On the straw pallet shaded by palm branches he lay still and silent, like a man in whom there was no longer a breath of life. The pale face was upturned to the sky that could be seen through the palms. His eyes were shut and only the matted hair of his beard and chest stirred slightly as he breathed. Apart from this, there was no sign that he was still alive.

His writing materials were laid on a bench by his bed: stylus, pens, clay tablets, and ink. Neraiah sat beside him devotedly. He was almost afraid to move. He was ever ready and alert to serve him and to note down any words he might utter. But the prophet was silent. His lips were sealed like his eyes. Then later, his heart-beats grew loud, his nostrils were distended as he panted to draw in a breath of air. The rise and fall of his chest, and the nervous distention of his nostrils, told Neraiah that the thoughts of the prophet were lifted up on the wings of vision. So he sat silent, holding his breath, concentrating with all his power not to disturb the prophet from seeing the visions which held him in thrall and kept him captive as his soul prepared to depart from him.

In his vision, he was standing on the Mount of Olives and looking at Mount Moriah opposite. He saw the returned of Zion over against him. They were purifying the site of all its pollution, smashing down the high places of the abominations and laying the foundations of the Sanctuary anew. At their head stood Zerubabel and the priest Jeshu. There was great activitiy on the mountain. People were carrying stones, planing wood, and dragging along cedar beams. The priests were attending to the cleansing of the Temple vessels, pressing out and refining oil and preparing the hangings. He saw how God was indeed healing the hurt of Zion. God had once again made the sun to shine over Jerusalem. He had returned her light unto her, the radiance of the six days of creation. The light flooded the ruins of Jerusalem with beams dropping down grace. The whole appearance of the desolate city had been altered by the amber effulgence. The ruins became fortresses and citadels now; rays of light wove them into halls of molten splendor. Every one of the stones of Jerusalem again took on its original shape and face, was transformed into an ornamental block, shining, sparkling, and coruscating.

The Kidron River separated him from the new Temple which he could not approach. The Kidron fell into the Valley of the Son of Hinnom which wound around Mount Zion. This valley had been appointed as a place for retribution from the most ancient times. All impurity of Jerusalem flowed into it. The fragments of the idols that had been shattered on the Temple mount were thrown there. There also were cast the remnants of the broken altars which the kings of Judah and Israel had once erected to foreign abominations and idols in order to worship them, fragments of Moloch, Ashtoreth, Baal. In the heap of refuse, too, were mingled the bones of their forsworn priests. In his vision the prophet saw the Valley of the Son of Hinnom filled to overflowing, like a river in springtime, with skeletons of idols and men and mighty heaps of refuse and ashes. But nevertheless, the seven-colored rainbow, God's sign to Noah, was suspended over the valley.

Suddenly he heard a song going up from the Valley of the Son of Hinnom and mingled with the chant of those who were going down from the hills of Jerusalem, a song of praise and glorification of God. From its dust and rubble, even the Valley of the Son of Hinnom was singing praise of God. This was surely the great day of forgiveness and pardon. God in His glory was Himself purifying the unclean and exalting it unto Him. He was making an end of arrogance while allowing the arrogant to remain in life. He was wiping away tears from all faces. He was removing all boundaries. He was making the crooked straight. He was smoothing all the rough places. He was bringing the righteous and the wicked alike under the shelter of the wings of His grace. To all who were thirsty He was giving pure water to drink, without price and without demanding any return.

Out of his great faintness, the prophet cried in a voice brimming over with joy:

> "Ho, every one that thirsteth,
> Come ye to the waters!
> And he that hath no money,
> Come, buy ye and eat!

"Come ye, every one that is hungry, and eat the bread of God, for this is the day of forgiveness and pardon. The table of Jehovah lies open and laid ready for everyone."

He suddenly beheld a crown of fire lifted up over the Mountain of Moriah. It was exalted upon wings to the heights. The crown, like a moon surrounded by stars, soared upward higher and higher to the empyrean till it reached the celestial sea of brilliant amber radiance. There it was immersed and hidden from view.

"This can only be the crown of David that God has taken up to heaven."

The prophet awoke from his vision.

With the last of his strength, he summoned Neraiah to take the writing materials and put down the message that he was leaving as a testament for the exiles going up to Judah. His last words would restore their hearts, would uphold them and give them comfort and strength for all time to come, in all the flames through which they would have to pass. It would help them to meet all the stumbling blocks and stones that would lie in their path which now began and would lead on to the end of days.

God had taken the crown of David from the earth unto Himself. There it would be guarded and stored for him that would come at the end of days. The kingdom of the House of David was no longer an earthly kingdom; it was henceforth a kingdom of Heaven. God had made an everlasting covenant with Israel through the hand of David, through the grace He had vouchsafed to him, through the Messiah that would come out of David.

The prophet dictated his last testament to the people of Israel:

"Incline your ear and come unto me,
Hear and your soul shall live;
And I will make an everlasting covenant with you,
Even the sure mercies of David.

"Nor do I make this eternal covenant for you alone by means of My grace and the sure mercies of David:

"Behold I have given him for a witness to the people,
A leader and commander to the people.
Behold thou shalt call a nation that thou knowest not,
And nations that knew not thee shall run unto thee,
Because of Jehovah, the God,
And the Holy One of Israel for he hath glorified thee."

It was this longing for the Messiah with which the prophet wished to endow Israel. This would be the goal of Israel, her purpose and her mission, and for this she was going back to her land.

God was near to every man, and whosoever sought Him would find Him. Even the wicked, if he would only forsake his evil way. If only the transgressor would shake himself free from his arrogant imaginings and return to God, then He would surely have mercy upon him, for He was the eternal and inexhaustible fountain of grace and forgiveness.

> "For my thoughts are not your thoughts,
>     Neither are my ways your ways,
>     Saith Jehovah.
>     For as the rain cometh down and the snow from heaven
>     And returneth not thither,
>     But watereth the earth
>     And maketh it bring forth the bud,
>     That it may give seed to the sower
>     And bread to the eater,
>     So shall my word be that goeth forth out of my mouth.
>     It shall not return unto me void.
>     But it shall accomplish that which I please,
>     And it shall prosper in the thing wherein I sent it.
>     For ye shall go out with joy,
>     And be led forth with peace.
>     The mountains and hills shall break forth before you into
>         singing
>     And all the trees of the field shall clap their hands.
>     Instead of the thorn shall come up the fir tree,
>     Instead of the brier shall come up the myrtle,
>     And it shall be to Jehovah for a name,
>     For an everlasting sign that shall not be cut off."

When, with the last of his strength, the prophet had ended communicating to Neraiah in writing the words of his final consolation to those going back to Zion, he commanded him to bring Zerubabel to him to his attic chamber. He must come before he departed for Zion with the returning exiles, for it was laid upon the prophet to make known the word of Jehovah concerning him.

Neraiah found Zerubabel near the Camp of Judah, which was the name now given to the place where those who were preparing to go had congregated. He and Jeshu the priest were busily and heavily engaged in the vast labors of final preparation before the expedition set out. But when Neraiah told him that the prophet had sent for him, he left everything and came at once.

Zerubabel bent down over the failing prophet. He looked into his eyes and said to him:

"O eyes of Israel, rise up and come with us. Behold, O prophet, and see that the Camp of Judah stands ready to depart from Babylon. In a day or two we shall be starting. Your prophecy has been fulfilled. Do not forsake us now. Come with us and be our guide along the road to Zion even as you were our guide in the Exile."

The prophet shook his head feebly.

"I shall not be your guide any longer, for the Lord of all the earth has turned aside my path. He has set a bound about me and I can now go only unto Him. Others will come in my place and will be the guides for Israel."

"Tell me, who shall they be?"

"You yourself!" cried the prophet and summoned up his strength to look straight into Zerubabel's eyes.

"I? You know full well that an alien is Prince of Judah."

"No. A stranger shall not be the prince of Judah. You shall be the prince and Jeshu the priest shall stand at your right hand and Haggai the prophet at your left and they will support you when you come to build the House of God."

Zerubabel turned pale. The prophet closed his eyes. He panted heavily as he struggled to draw some breath into his lungs. With his eyes shut, he fumbled blindly, seeking the hand of Zerubabel. When he found it, he grasped it tight with his fingers and said:

"Blessed be this hand that shall build the House of Jehovah,

339

but from this selfsame hand shall the kingdom of David be withheld."

"Only from my own hand," cried our Zerubabel with deep emotion.

"From your hand and that of all that come after you," the prophet pronounced, laboring out every word. "From the hand of all the generations until..."

"Will the House of David then be utterly and finally cut off from the earth?" asked Zerubabel, and there was a fearful confusion on his face and in his voice.

"Heaven forbid! The God Jehovah has made an eternal covenant with the House of David because of the lovingkindness and sure mercies of David. At the same time that God showed me your pure hands building anew the House of His sanctuary, He also revealed to me the crown of David borne by wings high above the earth unto heaven... so also He told me that the kingdom of David would pass from the earth and be treasured up by Him in heaven for His sake, to await him that would come at the end of days. Because of this, He told me concerning him; 'Behold, I have given him for a witness to the people, and leader and commander to the people.'"

"Who is he?"

"His name was with God in heaven before He created the world. God created the redemption even before He decreed servitude. He prepared forgiveness and pardon before the snares of sin and iniquity. He created peace before He brought war upon the world. The spirit of God moved upon the face of the chaos and formlessness before He breathed order upon them. For His sake are you returning to Judah. For His sake shall you build the Holy Temple so that you may prepare the world to become pure and so that Israel may become purified in order to be a sign for the nations."

"Alas, O my father, the luminary of Israel, open for me just a crevice into the hidden future worlds that are revealed to you. Let me see it. Let me behold him that will come with the crown of David on his head."

"It is not in my power to do this. But there will come to you at some time a moment of Divine grace and lovingkindness. One day the spirit will rest upon you and you will know and understand why the God Jehovah delivered His people from the furnace of Babylon and brought them back to His holy mountain. Since you will know this, you will also see him. And when you behold him, you will understand why Israel suffered chastisement and great afflictions for being the chosen and peculiar people."

"I pray you have pity upon me and tell me, when shall he come, he that shall bring an end to our sufferings? When shall he come that shall free man and the world from the fetters of evil and arrogance and bring eternal peace between man and man, between beast and beast, as you foresaw and also as Isaiah the son of Amoz foresaw before you, just as you both depicted in your visions?"

"This, too, I cannot reveal to you. It is a mystery hidden from all those born of woman. We were given only the longing and expectation of the redemption. We were also given faith, and this is what binds us to the God Jehovah. This faith is the ladder whereby we mount to the Master of the Universe in Heaven. Let this ladder of faith be removed and once more we fall into Sheol. Go, O Zerubabel, and lead the remnant of Israel to Jerusalem. Take with you on the way the faith in the Master of the Universe and the passion for the redemption. These will uphold you. These will turn the wilderness into a paradise before you and remove every stumbling stone that lies in your path to the redemption. Hearken and give good ear: God has entrusted the remnant of his flock to your hand. Hearken and hear: I have chosen you to store up my last message in your heart. These are the latest words that God has spoken to me for the exiles who are now leaving Babylon to go up unto Zion:

"For ye shall go out with joy,
And be led forth with peace;
The mountains and hills shall break before you into singing,
And all the trees of the field shall clap their hands."

341

The prophet was silent and motionless for a long time. A brooding quiet reigned in the chamber. Then at last Isaiah spoke in a whisper:

"Not for your sake alone do you return to Judah. You go back to Judah for the sake of the salvation of all the nations."

With these words he took his leave of Zerubabel and of the Exile.

The sound of singing and joy of those going up to Zion penetrated to the attic room in the courtyard of the Bethlehemites. It seemed as though the shining stars were beaming on them alone; the heavenly flocks which were bathing themselves in the pure cloud streams in the sky above Bethlehem, moistening them with the splendor of a rising, majestic song. Never for a moment did the joyous chant cease:

"When Jehovah turned again the captivity of Zion
We were like them that dream."

Beside the prophet, on the floor, sat his constant, beloved friend and faithful protector, Neraiah. He looked upon him and saw the prophet utterly consumed by the fire that burned within him, like a branch of a bush that had been scorched and parched by the east wind and the sun of the wilderness and now lay on the hot sand. But the appearance of this branch was that of a man. This face was that of a child in spite of the matted beard and sidelocks, so full it was of innocence, so suffused with a childish unawareness of all sin and passion. A faint shadow from the deep and heavy eyebrows fell over the glazing eyes sunk deep in their sockets. A smile of joy hovered upon his closed lips. It seemed to Neraiah that they reflected a vision, that the closed eyes saw into hidden worlds in which the soul of the prophet already wandered. The countenance of the prophet was a mighty psalm of comfort, a song of deep tranquillity.

Neraiah bent his ear down close to the mouth of the prophet and heard the last words he breathed as his soul left his body:

"I will also give thee for a light of the nations that my salvation may be unto the ends of the earth."